THE B

"Snappy writing, a page-turning story, and fresh world-building make *Dying Bites* a satisfying meal of a book."
—Kelley Armstrong,
New York Times bestselling author of
Men of the Otherworld and *The Awakening*

"*Dying Bites* is wacky, unpredictable, fresh, and amazing. I would kill to write as well as DD Barant. Seriously." —Nancy Holder, author of *Pretty Little Devils*

"This engrossing debut adds another captivating protagonist to the urban fantasy ranks...Barant's well-developed world offers intriguing enhancements to mythology and history. Jace is remarkable, strong-willed, and smart, and she sets an unstoppable pace. Look for the Bloodhound Files to go far."
—*Publishers Weekly* (starred review)

"A heroine with plenty of guts, moxie, and a sense of the absurd. [A] fresh and original take on urban fantasy...Huge kudos to Barant for spicing things up with a story that expertly integrates detective work, kick-butt action, and a wacky sense of humor. Make sure you get in early on the outstanding new Bloodhound Files series." —*Romantic Times*

"DD Barant builds a strong world and fills it with fascinating characters that will delight and entertain. *Dying Bites* is a well-written urban fantasy with a gripping plot and a heroine who is quite believable with her very
MORE...

human flaws. I'm looking forward to seeing more in this captivating world."   —*Darque Reviews* (starred read)

"Five stars. An exciting new series. It has humor, mystery, and adventure. A great book!"   —*Affair de Coeur*

"Barant does an excellent job introducing a whole new world where vampires make up the majority of the population...quick and engrossing...a great new series."
—*Romance Reader*

DEATH BLOWS

BOOK TWO OF
THE BLOODHOUND FILES

DD Barant

St. Martin's Paperbacks

This is a work of fiction. All of the characters, organizations, and events portrayed in this novel are either products of the author's imagination or are used fictitiously.

DEATH BLOWS

Copyright © 2010 by DD Barant.
Excerpt from *Killing Rocks* copyright © 2010 by DD Barant.

For information address St. Martin's Press, 175 Fifth Avenue, New York, NY 10010.

ISBN: 978-0-312-94259-5

Printed in the United States of America

St. Martin's Paperbacks edition / April 2010

St. Martin's Paperbacks are published by St. Martin's Press, 175 Fifth Avenue, New York, NY 10010.

10 9 8 7 6 5 4 3 2 1

On the day I write this, my dear friend Jeanne Robinson goes to her first session of chemotherapy. A few days ago her friends and family threw a benefit to help defray costs of treatment, and the item I donated to the auction was the choice to either appear as a character in this book or the right to dedicate it to whomever you chose. Stevie McDowell won the bid, and her dedication appears below.

For Jeanne Robinson, someone who I am proud to call my friend. Jeanne has managed to touch so many people during her years as a dancer, choreographer, Soto Zen monk, author, wife, mother, sister, daughter, and friend. A lifelong artist and whirling vortex of organizational energy known as Wired Buddha, Jeanne is a fearless and fierce champion to her friends and family as well as all others who are lucky enough to enter her sphere. Jeanne Robinson is one of those old souls that make the rest of us poor mortals better for having known her. Thank you, Jeanne, for being a true heroine and keeping so many of us safe from the things that go bump in the night.

ONE

All I can see through the night-vision goggles are the eyes of the vampire I'm pressed against; the rest of his face is kind of obscured by the large-caliber handgun I have jammed up his nose. It makes his voice sound extremely nasal.

"I dode know why I shouldund just rip your priddy liddle throde oud," he says. "I really dode."

"Well, then, let me explain it to you. My name is Special Agent Jace Valchek and I work for the National Security Agency of the Unnatural States of America. I am a bona fide, one hundred percent real human woman, I'm not from around here, and the shiny piece of metal currently deviating your undead septum is a Ruger Super Redhawk Alaskan .454 chambered with silver-tipped, teakwood bullets. I know that last piece of information doesn't mean a whole lot to you since guns never really caught on in this particular reality, but you saw what it did to your two friends from twenty feet away. I'm a whole lot closer. So unless you're ready to pay the Grim Reaper the time-debt you owe his bony ass, I'd suggest you think of my weapon as a glorified crossbow that shoots very tiny arrows very, very fast."

He thinks about it. He stinks of fermented blood and Cloven, the pire equivalent of meth—actually methamphetamine cut with just enough garlic to let it affect his metabolism. His breath, which technically he shouldn't have, is terrible. I'm going to have to disinfect the gun later just to get the smell off it.

"Whad do you wad?"

"Aristotle Stoker," I hiss.

"Nebber heard ub hib."

"Sure you have. AKA the Impaler? Leader of the Free Human Resistance? Same guy that released that video on the net that turned a few million hemovores and lycanthropes into living mummies for a while? *That* Aristotle Stoker."

I'm getting real tired of Gus's bloodsucker-with-a-head-cold routine—plus, my trigger finger's a bit too close to his fangs—so I ease up, just a little. He takes this as a sign that I was kidding about blowing his head off, and grins. He's short, pudgy, and balding, and no casting director in my world would ever have hired him to play a vampire. Here, he's just one more neckbiter on a planet full of the living-challenged.

"Hey, take it easy. I got no reason to stand up for that guy—why would I want to get in the middle of some human thing? I mean, I don't know much, but you don't have to go all Lugosi on me."

"Stoker. Where is he?"

"If I knew, I'd tell you. But I only saw him for like ten minutes, okay? And that was over a week ago. He picked up a few things he had on order, then took off. No idea where he went."

Gus is a black-market dealer in various esoteric items—charms, weapons, the occasional shipment of Cloven or Bane. Right now, we're in a shipping container buried in the middle of a bunch of other shipping containers in a storage lot just outside Seattle. A real rat-in-a-woodpile kind of office, but pires didn't need things like light, air, or heat. The only way to get in or out is a tunnel that connects to a sewer outflow pipe, and he keeps guards posted on that. Luckily, I haven't come alone.

"What did he pick up?"

"Couple of books and an amulet. Amulet was kind of pricey considering that it doesn't even work, but he paid the bill without haggling."

"Yeah? What's it supposed to do?"

"Detect rockheads. Uh, no offense."

I can hear my partner clear his throat behind me, a noise a bit like gravel in a coffee grinder. "None taken," he grunts. Charlie Aleph's a golem, three hundred or so pounds of black volcanic sand poured into a human-shaped, thick-skinned plastic bag and animated by the spiritual essence of a prehistoric tyrannosaur. Not offending him is a good thing. I know people who've made whole careers out of it.

"And the books?"

"The Ahasuerus Codex and the *Aenigma Veneficium*. Don't ask me why he wanted 'em, 'cause I don't know."

Neither do I, but my background in arcane textbooks is limited to what I pick up through osmosis; I'll have to ask Eisfanger what significance those two titles have when I get back to the office—

Gus tries to bite my hand. Yeah, his mouth is right there, and most pires make a hungry cheetah look slow, but it's still a loser move—I mean, all I have to do is twitch.

Unluckily for Gus, I'm in a twitchy mood.

His skull slows the bullet down just enough that the slug only ricochets four or five times off the walls—after all, we're in a big metal box. By the time Gus's body hits the ground it's mostly bones; looks like his time-debt was a few decades at least.

"Damn it," I say. No matter how tough I act, I don't take ending a life lightly. I never used to, anyway. "I am *sick* of people not taking me seriously."

"Tell that to the two other guys you shot," Charlie says. "The ones lying outside and moaning. Pretty sure they're reevaluating their estimation of you right now."

"Sure, *after* I shoot someone they show me some respect. As long as they don't collapse in a pile of decomposing calcium, that is."

"Maybe you should switch to a different weapon."

"Maybe I should get a more supportive partner."

"Yeah, I hear there's a long waiting list for that."

I give him the finger, which seems to be universal no matter which universe you're from. He ignores it, which is also standard.

We go back outside—it's the middle of the night—and call an ambulance for the two muscleheads I shot. One's a pire, the other's a thrope; he's still in half-were form, a large wolf-headed guy dressed in cargo shorts and a Hawaiian shirt. Thropes can't talk when they're in were form—their mouths aren't shaped right for it—but he's giving off this continual high-pitched whine that's really getting on my nerves.

"I believe this is yours," Charlie says. He holds up what's left of a deformed silver slug between thumb and forefinger.

"Where'd you find that?"

"About two inches into the hole it made in my chest. And my shirt. And my lapel." Charlie dresses like a private eye from a Raymond Chandler novel, right down to the fedora, but his suits are always immaculately tailored. He appreciates getting holes in them about as much as staining his alligator-skin shoes with raw sewage—which is how we'd started the evening.

"Yeah, ricochets can be a bitch. Sorry. Want some gum to patch it up?"

"And smell like Juicy Fruit for the rest of the night? No thanks. I think I prefer the raw sewage."

"That's not sewage. That's the smell this case is starting to give off."

"We'll find him, Jace."

"Yeah. Sure." Catching Aristotle Stoker is the only way my employers will give me a ticket back to my own universe, a nice comforting place of global warming, war in the Middle East, nuclear weapons—and no vampires, werewolves, or golems. The only magic I ever want to see again involves a top hat, a rabbit, and maybe a two-drink minimum.

But I've been chasing his trail for the last three months, and it's getting colder and colder. What makes things even worse is that the number of cases I'm being asked to consult on is steadily rising—the consequences of Stoker disseminating a viral video with nasty long-term consequences. Yours truly managed to reverse the immediate mummification effect, but many of the thropes and pires who were exposed are showing varying degrees of mental instability. Until now, the supernatural races of this world have been immune to insanity—as a result, they have very little experience in dealing with it. As a criminal profiler for the FBI, I have lots . . . more, in fact, than anyone on the planet.

So I'm currently in high demand, even if I'm not exactly popular. The other agents in the NSA office I work out of call me the Bloodhound, which I prefer to see as a testament to my tracking abilities as opposed to any reference to a female canine—or the fact that my boss is a pire with a reputation for liking human women. Scarlet Fever, they call it.

Of course, nobody says that to my boss's face. David Cassius might look like an eighteen-year old blond surfer, but he's so old his time-debt might actually cause him to fossilize if anyone manages to stake him. Not that I expect that to ever happen—he's hasn't stayed undead as long as he has through luck.

The ambulance finally arrives, along with some local law enforcement. The cops aren't too happy about two wounded thugs and a dead pire, but I don't much care. I flash my NSA badge and tell them to take it up with my boss if they have a problem.

We climb into our own car, a bulky Crown Vic, and head back for the office. Charlie's driving while I stare out the window and brood. I'm really more of a snapper than a brooder, so I say, "My Latin isn't too good, but the Ahasuerus Codex rings a bell."

"It should. Ahasuerus is supposedly the father of all golems, the guy who created the spell that animates us."

"And the amulet Stoker bought is supposed to be a lem detector, but it doesn't work. Not that you guys are real hard to find."

"Yeah. We're ubiquitous."

I shake my head. "That werewitch who tried to kill me—Selkie? She claimed Ahasuerus was still alive." That wasn't the only thing she claimed, but I didn't want to go into that at the moment.

"That's just an urban legend—like the one about the albino bats that live in subway tunnels and eat people's eyes."

"Maybe the amulet Stoker bought isn't supposed to detect golems. Maybe it's supposed to detect golem *makers*."

"Don't need an amulet for that. Nearest factory is in Renton."

My cell jangles. It's Cassius. "Yeah?" I'm not real big on formality.

"Jace. I need you at a crime scene."

"Just had one, thanks. Couldn't eat another bite."

"This is different. It's Gretchen."

That gets my attention. Gretchen Petra is a pire and NSA intelligence analyst, as well as being my closest female friend—in this reality, anyway. She's been acting kind of odd lately, preoccupied and secretive, but since that's kind of a given in her line of work I haven't paid much attention to it.

"What's wrong? Is she all right?"

"Just get over here." He gives me an address, then hangs up before I can ask any more questions.

"Okay," I say. "This is new."

The crime scene is a penthouse in a high-rise overlooking the bay. From the heavily smoked windows I deduce the occupant is a pire; from the furnishings, an extremely wealthy one.

The body's draped over a treadmill in the middle of the room. The vic's dressed in a head-to-toe red outfit with yellow boots, the kind of thing pires wear during the day to shield themselves from sunlight. No goggles, though, and the face mask doesn't cover the mouth. So far, it doesn't rank that high on my weirdness scale.

All that's left of the body is a skeleton, not unusual for a pire. But this guy's skeleton is *green*—and giving off what seem to be little arcs of electricity, sparks flickering in the empty eye sockets of his skull, glinting off the polished emerald of his teeth. Just to make sure we get the point, there's a lightning bolt emblazoned on the chest of the suit and little lightning designs around the wrists and waist.

And then I recognize him. Of course.

Cassius is standing next to the body, dressed in his usual black business suit. He nods at Charlie and me as we come in, but doesn't say anything. Damon Eisfanger is examining the body without touching it, but he looks up and waves when he sees me. "Hey, Jace." Damon's a thrope with both arctic wolf and pit bull in his lineage, so he's as pale as an albino and square as a linebacker, with ice-blue eyes and short, bristly white hair. He's about as geeky as forensics shamans usually are, which is to say a lot. "Pretty bizarre, huh? Know why the skeleton's green? I think all the calcium in it has been changed into copper. Good conductor, though gold would have been better."

"Maybe the killer was on a budget. And all the sparks?"

"Lightning. I mean, I've only done some preliminary readings, but this is not house current we're talking about here. This is actual lightning, magically directed. It wants to leave, but there's nowhere for it to go; the treadmill isn't grounded."

"Gretchen was the one that found the body," Cassius says. "She's in the bedroom, composing herself."

"I'll talk to her in a minute," I say. "Okay, Eisfanger—even I recognize that costume, and you're about seventeen levels above me when it comes to geekdom, so go ahead and spit out whatever clever pun you've been holding in for the last twenty minutes before you explode."

Eisfanger looks a little taken aback. "I'm afraid I don't, uh, have anything to say. I mean, I guess I could say something about this being shocking, but that seems really obvious—"

"That's all you got? You've got a dead superhero named the Flash on your hands and you can't come up with a single punch line?"

"A what?" Now he just looks confused.

"The Flash. Guy in a red leotard, runs really really fast. I think he had a TV show, too. Come *on* . . . he's been Flash-fried. I'll be back in a Flash, but he won't. My camera doesn't work 'cause the Flash is dead. You're really disappointing me here."

"A superhero? What is that, a really big sandwich?"

I frown at him. "*Really* disappointing."

The expression on Eisfanger's face has gone from confused to bewildered, and he turns to Cassius to see if he gets the joke. Cassius frowns, too, but at me.

"Jace. Neither Damon nor I have any idea what you're talking about."

I stare at them and blink. Something punches me, very softly, in the pit of my stomach. When I first got here—this world, I mean, not this room—that punch would have been a lot more solid. It landed every time I'd been lulled into a sense of normalcy about this world and something abruptly leapt out at me and screamed that I was very, very far from home. You know, like reading the ingredients on a bottle of soda pop and learning it was full of gerbil's blood, or seeing a commercial for a water bed that lets you literally sleep underwater—handy for those who neither breathe nor prune.

"Comic books," I say. "You don't have—wait. I *know* this world has comic books; Dr. Pete showed me his collection once."

Eisfanger's eyes go wide. Cassius doesn't look surprised, but then he almost never does.

"*Comic* books?" Eisfanger repeats. He says it with more or less the same intonation you'd use for the phrase, *Eat my own liver?*

Cassius sighs. "I was afraid of that. The books Dr. Adams showed you were all pre-1956, correct?"

"Uh—I guess so. Why?"

"Because they've been illegal since then. Did this Flash exist prior to '56?"

"I'm not sure. I don't think so."

"Then we're dealing with cross-universe contamination." Cassius studies me with cool, calculating eyes. "The killer may be from your world, Jace."

He lets that hang in the air a moment, knowing the impact it'll make on me. "Go talk to Gretchen," he says. "She could use a friend right now. Second bedroom on the left."

I'm thinking furiously as I leave. Does a killer from

my world mean a possible way back for me? Why the hell would comic books be illegal? And what was Gretchen doing here in the first place?

I knock on the door to the bedroom tentatively. "Gretch? It's Jace."

"Come in."

I open the door. Gretchen sits on the edge of a massive canopy bed, her knees together, a box of tissues in her lap. Gretchen's a pire, apparent age in her mid-thirties, attractive in an intense kind of way. She always wears her blond hair in a tight little bun, her makeup is immaculate, she speaks in an elegant British accent, and her wit is sharp enough to give a suit of armor paper cuts. I've compared her, more than once, to a predatory Mary Poppins.

Right now her hair is a straggly mess. Tears have streaked her mascara. Despite that, her voice is strong, her smile firm. "Hello, Jace. I do hope you're going to lend us a hand."

I sit down next to her. "Yeah, of course. What *happened*, Gretch?"

"I—was paying a call on Mr. Aquitaine. He—"

"Aquitaine? Is that—"

"Yes. Saladin Aquitaine. He and I were to go out for dinner. There was no answer when I rang up, so I let myself in. I have a key. I discovered him just as you saw. I called David immediately."

I hadn't even known Gretchen was seeing someone. "So you and he were . . . involved."

"We had an intimate relationship, yes. We've known each other for years, but only recently have we decided to . . . explore further options."

"Friends with benefits?"

"Not exactly." She turns to look at me, and a little of the grief she's feeling forces its way to the surface. It doesn't get far; she shoves it back under with a brittle smile.

"I do apologize for not mentioning him, Jace. I've been doing intelligence work for so long I compartmentalize everything. Yes, Saladin and I were lovers, but that's never been anything but casual for decades. About three months ago I came to a decision, and approached him with an offer. He agreed."

Her face stays calm and composed, but a single tear tracks its way through her ruined eyeliner and down her cheek. "I'm pregnant, Jace."

Pregnant. That's a heavy word at any time, but for pires even more so. The old-school neckbiting method was made illegal long ago, which is good since the current human population is less than 1 percent of the global total. The way pires procreate on this world is through magic; basically, both parents donate six months of their life for every year their child ages. At some point the spell that made the whole thing possible is canceled, and all three go back to being immortal—only the parents are now a decade or so older, while the kid is twenty-one.

I have no idea what happens when one of the parents dies before the baby is born.

I put my arm around her. "Gretchen, I'm—I don't know what to say. I'm stuck somewhere between 'I'm sorry' and 'Congratulations.' "

"Stuck. I suppose that's what I am, as well."

"What happens now?"

"I assume the full time-debt for the child. A normal pire pregnancy is nine months, but the mother ages only four and a half; many couples accelerate the progress of the fetus to match. That's what we did. But now that he's dead . . . I don't know, Jace. I just don't know." Her voice remains steady, but a second tear has joined the first. If I were to touch it, it would be as cold as a melted snowflake.

"What did he do, Gretch? For a living, I mean."

She plucks a tissue from the box and dabs her face. "He was a geomancer. His specialty was talking to dormant volcanoes, locating kimberlite pipes for diamond speculators. Geological features operate on a very different time frame, so he would have conversations that would last for years. Sometimes they were fruitful, sometimes not."

I glance around the room. "Looks to me like he hit at least one jackpot."

"Yes, he was quite wealthy. He was a very patient man; I thought he would make a wonderful father."

"Who would do this to him, Gretch? Did he have any enemies?"

"You should speak to Cassius about that." Her tone is abruptly cool, and I think I've offended her before I realize she's simply being professional. Whatever Saladin Aquitaine was into, Cassius knows more about it than Gretchen does—which means this case is getting more complicated by the minute.

"I'll do that. Hang in there, Gretch." I give her shoulder a squeeze and then stand up.

I stride back to the other room, where Eisfanger's taking pictures of the vic. Charlie's in exactly the same position he was when I left, hands clasped in front of him, feet slightly spread. He's very good at being immobile. "Okay, what are we looking at here?" I ask Cassius directly. "There's no local cops, so I assume this is off the books."

"Yes. This is going to be a closed investigation, Jace, and I want you to handle it."

"We'll see. First of all, are we sure this is Saladin Aquitaine?"

Eisfanger lowers his camera. "No fingerprints or DNA, but the remains still have a psychic residue. I'll check it against our animist files."

"Okay. Second, who was Saladin Aquitaine and why would someone kill him?"

"He was a successful geological surveyor, a geomancer. He made sizable donations to a number of political parties and organizations. He was fairly active socially. I don't know why anyone would want him dead—which is why I called you." There's something he isn't telling me, but with Cassius that was almost always the case. I'll have to dig for it.

"You think this is the work of someone mentally unbalanced," I say.

"Don't you? I admit I don't have your level of expertise, but this hardly looks like the work of either a professional assassin or a burglary gone wrong."

I shrug. "No? I'll tell you what I see. Two shamans, some professional jealousy, and a magical pissing match that got out of hand. The other guy tossed a spell intended to be used on landscape instead of flesh-and-blood, and this is the result—Mr. Coppertop. Don't tell Gretchen I said that."

As a theory it was full of holes, but I wanted Cassius to point them out—one of the best ways to get information is to make your source prove how smart he is.

"Uh, there's one big problem with that," Eisfanger interjects. He's waving a device that looks a bit like a cell phone with a dual antennae in slow circles over the corpse's head. "This guy wasn't killed by the lightning—or by having his bones transformed. Those were both done postmortem."

I frown at him. "Wait. So the whole scene was staged? The treadmill, the costume, the electric skeleton?"

"I don't know about the treadmill—"

"Pires don't exercise, genius. So what did kill him?"

"Sharp silver object through the heart. See?" Eisfanger points to a small notch on the underside of one rib. "Chipped a piece off going in—wooden stake wouldn't have done that. I'll take a closer look once I've drained the voltage, but I'm betting I find traces of silver."

Cassius shakes his head. "Someone went to a great deal of trouble to do this. Someone either from your world, or with access to its knowledge. Anyone that goes to this much trouble to send a message—and I think we can both agree that this is supposed to be a message—tends to want that message understood."

I sigh. "Unless they're speaking their own private language that only the voices in their head understand."

"Oh, I don't know about that," Cassius says. "I think there's at least one person in this room who might be able to translate."

"It's not me, is it?" asks Eisfanger. "I mean, I'm still working on that sandwich thing . . ."

"Look, I'd love to help out," I say. "But I just got a lead on Stoker, and that is who I'm here to catch. I have a contract that spells it all out, no pun intended."

"I've been meaning to talk to you about that," Cassius says. "There's a problem."

My stomach drops to somewhere around my knees. The contract I signed states that once I catch Stoker, I get to go home—but if my employers don't want to honor it, what exactly are my options? Hire a good lawyer and hope I don't die of old age while the case makes it way through the courts?

Cassius sees the expression on my face—and looks away. "Cross-dimensional travel is difficult. In order to put you back where and when we removed you, conditions must be just right. The shaman we used to bring you here is now . . . unavailable."

"So? Use another one!"

"We can do that. Unfortunately, it means that the passage of time becomes an issue. The original shaman can return you to your world within minutes of you having left it; a new one couldn't. In fact, the opposite would be true—years would have passed since you left. Decades, most likely."

And now my sunken stomach is turning into a clenched, icy fist. "Like being in a coma, I guess. At least I'll still have my youth—"

"No. The spell would age you, as well. I'm sorry."

Right. They said they'd return me, but they didn't specify the condition. "You know, my incentive to do my job is sort of going down the tubes here."

"Then let me rectify that. Aquitaine was well connected. There are certain favors I could call in if you were to locate his killer—favors that would eliminate the problem I just mentioned."

"The shaman would stop being unavailable, is what you're saying."

Cassius at least has the grace to look uncomfortable. "This isn't blackmail, Jace. The situation is what it is. Help me, and you help yourself. I promise I'll do everything in my power—"

"Save it. I'm on board." I haul my gut back into place with one deep breath, and let the anger already simmering there thaw it out.

So now I've got three people to find. A superhero-obsessed killer, a rogue human terrorist . . . and the son-of-a-bitch who dragged me to this world in the first place. Unavailable? I need to have a little talk with him about the meaning of that word.

Or the world that I go back to won't be mine anymore.

TWO

First things first.

I go through all the procedures that start every investigation: I talk to his neighbors, get in touch with his last few clients, ask the standard questions: Was there anyone who would want him dead, was he involved in illegal activities, did he have a gambling or drug problem? No to all of the above—though I do get a sense of what sort of person he was.

"The thing about Sal Aquitaine," a geologist named Gary Wyndham tells me over the phone, "is that he had this certain way of looking at the world. Some people thought he was a snob, but that wasn't it. He didn't just talk to mountains, he *identified* with them. He was the calmest guy I've ever met in my life; just sort of let events flow around him without taking any of it personally."

"So he was passive?"

"I wouldn't say that. Hey, a mountain can kill you just as easily as a forest fire—it just does it with a lot less drama. One second you're standing on a cliff, the next you're a big red stain at the bottom. Sal was quiet, but he could drop a boulder on your head without blinking."

"Yeah? He drop boulders on the heads of anyone in particular?"

"It was just a figure of speech. If he had any enemies, I didn't know about them—or friends, for that matter. Sal would go off for months or even years, spend the whole time camping in a mountain range in the middle of nowhere. You spend that much time talking to geological features, it has an effect; I got the feeling Sal didn't feel that connected to the world. Not the parts inhabited by people, anyway."

I think about that after I hang up. What would it be like, being cut off from your own kind for years, nothing but ageless rock to talk to . . . and then I remember who my partner is. If mountains had the same kind of deadpan sense of humor Charlie did, you'd either find it entertaining or commit suicide sometime in the six months between a setup and the punch line.

I wonder how would it feel to come home. A welcome return to civilization? Or simply a burst of frantic noise between long periods of stillness?

He hadn't completely abandoned the company of his own kind—his relationship with Gretchen showed that. Maybe having a child was his attempt to reconnect with the rest of the race, to put down roots that weren't made of bedrock.

Maybe he was just scared of coming back one day and finding out nobody remembered who he was.

Or cared.

I take a look at Sal's computer, but his e-mail is encrypted with some sort of voodoo that Eisfanger tells me he can't break in my lifetime, so no leads there. Security footage from the lobby of his building reveals no lurking maniacs carting around treadmills—I don't know how it wound up in Aquitaine's living room, but it didn't come in through the front door. A once-over of his apartment turns up nothing more interesting than a collection of Moroccan recipe books and a freezer full of lamb chops.

None of which surprises me, though I was hoping to get lucky. The first-timers usually start with someone they know or have some passing connection with—but this doesn't feel like that. This feels like someone with a big old pot of crazy that's been simmering a long, long time and finally boiled over. He or she put a lot of time and thought into it, and isn't going to be tripped up by something as elementary as killing an old lover or getting caught on camera.

But really, I'm just dotting the *i*'s and crossing the *t*'s until I get what I'm really after.

An invitation.

The entrance to the Four Color Club is not exactly what I expect. Cassius had warned me that the comic book subculture in this world was vastly different from mine; he'd said they were secretive and dangerous, black-market magicians and rogue shamans playing with types of sorcery the government had outlawed decades ago. They bore about as much resemblance to the *Simpson's* Comic Book Guy as Hello Kitty does to a hungry lion.

But some of them apparently still live in their parents' basement.

By "parents" I mean the city of Seattle, and by "basement" I mean beneath the Fremont Street bridge. That's where I'm standing right now, looking up at an eighteen-foot-high stone statue of a troll rising from the earth. Only his upper body is exposed, so I guess he'd be close to forty feet tall if he ever climbed out of his hole. He's got a crushed VW Bug in one massive paw, and he glares at me with an eye made from an old hubcap.

Vehicles rumble by overhead. I wish Charlie was with me, but the only invitation Cassius was able to wangle was for one. I take a deep breath and let it out with a single word: "Kimota."

The troll's mouth opens, revealing a stone staircase spiraling down. I enter.

There are no lights, and once I'm around the first few turns the light above vanishes completely. From what Cassius told me, their clubhouse isn't actually in the bowels of a stone troll; this is just one of the spots they've temporarily anchored a mystical gateway to. Come back tomorrow, and you can scream "Kimota!" until your head explodes and nothing will happen. The true location of their secret headquarters is, well, secret.

I round the final bend in the staircase. There's a small antechamber here, with a door at the end of it. The door is outlined by a strip of glowing purplish-red light, with an illuminated yellow line running down the center and a thin belt of glowing blue across the middle. The lines divide the rectangle of the door into panels, all of them black, and there's a doorknob shaped like a little white word balloon. I grab it and turn.

On the other side is an immense cave. The ceiling must be fifty feet above me, with stalactites half that length hanging overhead like a battalion of Damoclean swords. The floor is an intricate mosaic of comic book panels under transparent tiles, and the rock of the cave has been surfaced with white walls that reach to a height of around twelve feet. Small spotlights mounted on their tops angle downward to illuminate the framed artwork hung on them, and there are numerous white leather armchairs scattered around. The only other door is a large, oak affair at the far end, and the only person in the room other than me is a man wearing a black leather jacket, jeans, and sunglasses. He looks to be in his twenties, with tousled, mid-length black hair and a friendly smile on his face. He's clearly expecting me—he gets to his feet and walks forward as soon as I come in.

"Hello," he says. His accent is British, but more relaxed

than Gretchen's. He offers me his hand and I shake it; the coolness of his grip tells me he's a pire. "I'm Neil."

"Jace Valcheck. Thank you for agreeing to talk with me, Mr. . . . ?"

He smiles, revealing incisors definitely meant more for puncturing jugulars than rending meat. "Just Neil will do. Is it all right if I call you Jace, or do you prefer Special Agent Valchek?"

"Jace is fine." I glance around me. "This is an impressive place."

"Oh, this is just the foyer. Some nice pieces in here, but the specialty galleries are really something to see—though I'm afraid I can't show them to you." His smile becomes apologetic. "But I will try to answer any of your questions."

"Fair enough. I guess I should start by saying that the 'Special' in 'Special Agent' means I'm from an alternate reality, one without thropes or pires. I didn't know a whole lot about comic books there—except that Hollywood seemed to like turning them into popcorn movies—and I know even less about them here."

"Well then, you're in luck. I happen to know quite a bit about comics—both in this world and in yours." He chuckles at the look on my face. "It's not that odd, really. Comics in this reality are a conduit for powerful magics, including those that facilitate contact with other universes. And comics from your world have always concerned themselves with multiple realities—since the late 1950s, anyway."

"The 1950s. My boss said something about that being when comic books were declared illegal here?"

Neil nods. "Oh, yes. The *Seduction of the Innocent* murders. Terrible business . . . but also responsible for all this." He indicates the whole room with a sweep of his leather-clad arm. "This was built by comic book magic. You understand how most magic works here?"

"Yeah. It's all based on animism—the principle that all things, living or unliving, have a spirit inside them."

"Correct. There are different schools, but the two main ones are based on African sorcery and Japanese Shinto. In your world, Shinto is mostly a religion based on ancestor worship; here, it became an active magical system. On both worlds the Japanese call the spirits that live in everything Kami. And a magical book encoded with illustrations of spells—"

"—is a Kamic book. Got it. But why illustrations instead of just words?"

"It's the nature of animism. A picture is a more literal representation of an object than a word, which is an abstract symbol. And animism is largely the magic of objects." He walks over to the right-hand wall and points. "Take a look at this."

I get closer and study what he's talking about. It's a black-and-white page from an old comic book, dealing with a junkie trying to shake down a young woman—his dealer, apparently—for drugs. When she doesn't produce them quickly enough, he threatens to stab her in the eye with a hypodermic.

"*True Crime* Number Two," Neil says. "May 1947. The story was called 'Murder, Morphine and Me,' written and drawn by Jack Cole. Published in both your world and mine—though here the morphine was cut with garlic— but with very different social consequences."

"How so?"

"A man named Fredric Wertham recognized the inherent power in such images. On your world he was a doctor, a psychiatrist, who campaigned against the influence of comics; here he was a low-level shaman who saw mystical possibilities in the form that had never been explored before. He tried to get a job at *True Crime,* but was unsuccessful. Eventually he got himself hired by EC

Comics, which primarily published fantasy and science fiction at that time. Wertham convinced them to launch a much darker imprint."

Neil pauses. "I can't show you any examples of *Seduction of the Innocent,* unfortunately; they were all destroyed. Only three issues were produced, but they were truly . . . *outstanding* works. Horrifying, of course, but that was their point."

"So they were horror comics?"

"I suppose that's as good a definition as any. They dealt with murders, murders of the most inventive and disturbing kind. The thing was—though no one knew it at the time—they weren't fiction." Neil smiles at me again, a gentle smile that makes the room a little colder, and I'm suddenly very glad I have my gun with me. "Wertham was taking the blood of his victims—lycanthropes, mainly—and adding it to the ink of the printing presses. When the comics were read, they completed a sort of mystical circuit, one that he was able to draw a great deal of power from. It was very clever."

"Yeah, they always think they're clever. How'd he get caught?"

"That's the truly fascinating part." Neil takes a few steps forward and stops in front of another framed piece of art. This one is a full-color cover, depicting a group of brightly costumed superheroes battling a bunch of guys in hooded cloaks. The banner across the top reads THE BRAVO BRIGADE and it's dated October 1956.

"Only a single issue of this came out, despite the fact that more copies of it were printed than any other previous comic. It was sold for a penny less than other comparable titles, though I'm sure they would have given it away if they could. But paying for something gives it power; magic is one of the original transactions."

I study the cover. "This is the Bravo Brigade fighting Wertham?"

"Wertham and his cult, yes."

"Tell me about them—the Brigade, I mean."

"Six members." Neil pointed at each of them in turn. "The female lycanthropic pirate is the Sword of Midnight; the glowing Roman gladiator is the Solar Centurion; the pire in the cloak covered with arcane symbols is Doctor Transe; the black woman in the tribal outfit riding the flying Zulu shield is the African Queen; the golem monk is Brother Stone; and the brass golem in the cowboy outfit is the Quicksilver Kid."

"Interesting bunch."

"The authorities fought fire with fire—sympathetic magic with sympathetic magic. In the comic, the heroes defeat Wertham and destroy his cult. In reality—this one, anyway—Wertham simply vanished. But there's more to the story than that."

"How so?"

"Even before the murders, there were people doing research along similar lines. The government came to us for help in stopping him—some of the founders of this club consulted on *The Bravo Brigade*—then decided we were too dangerous to be allowed to continue unchecked. We're tolerated, as long as we keep to our own little community, but comics are no longer published on any sort of large scale. We have to make do with what we can glean from other realities—which is rather lucky for you, isn't it?"

I frown. Neil is charming and likable, but his sunglasses are very, very dark—I can't see even the outline of his eyes. It's a little disconcerting.

"Hang on," I say. "If the government used the same kind of magic to fight Wertham, does that mean the Bravo Brigade actually existed?"

"That would seem to follow, wouldn't it . . . the supernatural races have their myths and archetypal heroes, Jace, just like yours does, but ours are more secretive; they live in the shadows of the past rather than the glare of history. But whether the Bravos were legends personified or simply imitating them, they were more than images inked on paper. They were actual people, with real power—though their true identities remain hidden."

"Saladin Aquitaine. Does that name mean anything to you?"

"I'm afraid not. Who is he?"

"The victim in the case I'm here about." I describe the body and how it was found. "I recognized the outfit from a comic book character in my own world, but I have no idea what the green skeleton or the electricity means."

Neil nods, his expression thoughtful. "The Flash. Interesting. Several versions of the character have appeared over the years, but this particular iteration sounds like Barry Allen. His first appearance—in October 1956—marks what most comic historians consider the start of the Silver Age."

"That's the same month the *Bravo Brigade* comic came out."

"So it is. As to the electrified skeleton, I believe it's referencing the origin of the character—Barry Allen supposedly gained his abilities when a lightning bolt hit a shelf of chemicals that then spilled all over him."

Green skeleton equals chemical reaction? I'd have to see if Eisfanger pulled any chemical traces from the bones. "Okay, how about parallels to this world—was there a *Flash* comic here? Are there any members of your club that have a fascination with the character?"

"The original Flash was named Jay Garrick. His character had more or less faded from the public eye by the time Barry Allen was introduced; if any of the other club members have a heightened interest in either of them, I'm not aware of it." His voice is just a touch cool; I suppose I can't really expect him to inform on his friends.

I try another approach. "You said comic—uh, Kamic book magic was used to contact other universes. Does that include travel between them?"

He hesitates. "In theory. It's rarely done, and requires a great deal of power."

"Like the kind of power Wertham had?"

"Yes. The actual process is called a crossover spell. But it requires a powerful focus—something like the Cosmic Treadmill." He smiles.

"A treadmill? The body was found draped over a treadmill."

"Oh? I was joking, actually—the Cosmic Treadmill was a plot device frequently used in the *Flash* comics. When powered by someone running at super-speed, it allowed time travel—and crossing over to alternate worlds. There was even a well-known comics editor named Julius Schwartz who wound up meeting some of the very characters he oversaw."

"Wait, I'm confused. An editor from my world met characters from a comic book universe?"

Neil moves on to the next piece of art, examining it like he's never seen it before. "Perhaps . . . that's the thing about comics, you see. They deal with so many different levels of reality, all of them intersecting on the printed page. Parallel worlds, Asgardian gods, shapeshifting aliens; angels and demons and robots from the future. Somewhere in that kaleidoscopic mix, the line between what really happened and what was merely imagined becomes blurred . . . and magic can sometimes erase it altogether. Maybe what happened to Mr. Schwartz was just a story—and maybe it wasn't."

The gentle cadence of his voice is hypnotic. Okay, the concept of using a treadmill to jump from one universe to another is absurd, but for just a second I have visions of *running* back home. I'll have to make sure Eisfanger goes over that treadmill with every forensic tool he has, magic and otherwise.

"The fact that the victim was skeletonized is intriguing as well," Neil says. "One of the major themes of the Silver Age was transformation. The enemies of the Flash—and there were many—changed him into all sorts of things: a wooden marionette, a living mirror, even a human lightning bolt. But I can't recall one of them turning him into a skeleton."

He glances down at his watch. "You'll have to leave now. One of our other members is on his way, and he wouldn't be pleased if he knew I was talking to you."

He pulls a small, dark blue candle from the pocket of his leather jacket. "Here. I'm afraid you can't come back here, but if you have more questions and you need to get in touch with me, simply light this just before you go to sleep."

I take the candle. "What is this, a mystic version of the Bat-Signal?"

"Something like that. It'll let us communicate on another plane of existence—much more secure than a cell phone, and with a great deal more bandwidth than e-mail."

"So it's like telepathy?"

"Not exactly—it's a type of magic called oneiromancy. You'd best hurry—Warren can get *extremely* cranky."

I'm halfway up the stairs before I can remember where I've heard that term before. *Oneiromancy*.

Dream magic.

I half expect the exit to dump me out in a completely different place, but I'm still under the Fremont Street bridge. No sign of Warren, but he's probably using a completely different entrance to get to the same place.

Charlie's waiting for me in the car, a standard-issue

dark blue sedan that the Agency thinks is inconspicuous. "How'd it go?" he asks as I get in. "Any leads?"

"Maybe. Let's head back to the Aquitaine place."

"Why? Forensics guys have already picked it clean."

"It's not the crime scene I'm interested in."

There are still cops posted at the door, but the body, the treadmill, and anything else of significance has been taken down to Eisfanger's lab. I turn on every light in the apartment and prowl around, Charlie dogging my heels.

"You take the living room, I'll take the bedroom. We're going to search it again, this time from top to bottom."

"What are we looking for?"

"Well, a Batpole would be nice, but I'll settle for a pair of long underwear and a cape."

That gets me a blank look. Of course, Charlie doesn't have to work real hard to accomplish that; impassive is his middle name. "You'll know it when you see it, okay? And it'll probably be well hidden."

We get to work. Searching a pire's home is like trying to read a book with every third word blacked out; there are certain things they just don't do, certain things they never use. For instance, male pires rarely own underwear. No boxers, no briefs—commando all the way. Why bother with an extra layer when you don't sweat or excrete? Hell, some pires actually get by with nothing but a coat of paint, like a car.

I find it, believe it or not, in the closet. Just casually hanging there, between a nice cashmere sweater and a tweed jacket—I probably looked right at it last time and thought it was a bathrobe. I pull it out and yell, "Charlie! C'mere!"

He's there in an instant, moving as quickly and quietly as a tiger. He eyes what I'm holding up and shakes his head. "Don't take this the wrong way, but you're really not much of a summer dress kind of woman."

"This isn't a dress, it's a robe." I trace one of the mystic sigils embroidered on it with a finger. "Saladin Aquitaine was more than just a geologist with a talent for finding diamonds—he was one of the Bravo Brigade."

"It's just a treadmill," Eisfanger says.

I glare at him from the other side of a worktable littered with parts. "I can *see* that. What I want to know is, does this particular treadmill have any particular *mystic* significance?"

Eisfanger looks trapped halfway between confused and wary. "You think this is a . . . *magic* treadmill?"

"Sure," says Charlie. "And get a move on, will you? We've got Satan's Conveyor Belt waiting to be processed."

I give my partner a look that could blister skin. Too bad his is made of plastic. "Don't use that tone with me," I say to Eisfanger. "You've got all *kinds* of weird-ass magic thingies here—why not a treadmill?"

"Well, it's esoteric enough," he admits. "I mean, I've never even seen one outside of a lab."

"Where I come from they're a substitute for running outdoors."

"But—"

"Don't make me explain it, all right?"

He shrugs. "In any case, I've gone over every component, and none of them is mystically charged in any way. They were all a little bored, actually; the machine used to belong to an NFL franchise, was used for testing. It's been dormant for at least six weeks." He picks up a gear and examines it critically. "I've already contacted the team. They say they got rid of some old equipment a few months ago—I think our killer got it from the dump."

"No prints?"

"No. And according to the machine itself, the last person to actually use it was Tyrone Bates—starting quarterback for the Memphis Lunar Knights."

"I hear he's got a hell of an arm," Charlie says. "But I doubt if he's much on calling up lightning bolts."

"How about the skeleton?" I ask.

"Postmortem just came back." Eisfanger picks up a beige file folder and hands it to me.

I open it and scan the first page. "You were right about the calcium being replaced by copper . . . and they found traces of silver just where you thought they might."

Eisfanger nods, allowing himself the smallest amount of smugness.

I read more, and frown. "Lightning strike confirmed, origin pending. No other chemicals found." The only other thing in the report that seems unusual is Aquitaine's date of birth: 1152.

"He was eight and a half centuries old," I say. "Even among pires, that's pretty impressive, right?"

"Sure," says Charlie. "But these old-timer cases can be a real pain. Pires that ancient have enemies older than the country they're living in. And the older the pire—"

"The craftier and meaner, I know. So you think the killer's another pire?"

Charlie shrugs. "Maybe yes, maybe no. Packs have been known to keep blood grudges going for generations, and thropes live about three hundred years anyway."

"Terrific." Even if I caught the killer, it would be like a fruit fly trying to convict a redwood. Come dance on my great-great-granddaughter's grave when you get out.

"How about the robe?" I say.

"Ah. Now *that's* much more interesting." Eisfanger beams and leads us over to another table where the robe is spread out. There are no crescent moons or stars among the symbols woven into it, but there's no doubt the runes are arcane; they almost seem to pulse with power.

"At first I thought this was just a really good replica of

a Doctor Transe costume," Eisfanger says. "That was before I started running tests. I—I think this is the real thing." He sounds embarrassed. "I mean, I think Saladin Aquitaine *was* Doctor Transe."

"You know about the Bravo Brigade?"

He scratches the bristly white stubble of his hair. "Well, sure—but they were called 'mystery men' back then, not 'superheroes.' Everybody had a copy of that comic when I was a kid. Not for long, though—the government recalled them, said there was some kind of health problem with the ink. Silver contamination, I think. They bought them back for twice the cover price."

That more or less dovetailed with what Neil had told me, though he hadn't mentioned the cover story—I guess he assumed I'd already heard it. "So tell me about Doctor Transe."

"He was their sorcerer. Large-scale animist stuff—he could talk to thunderstorms, mountains, oceans."

"Can't other animists do that?"

"Sure, but not like Transe. He could condense time, for one thing—a conversation with a geological feature that would normally take years, he could do in minutes."

Which would explain his success as a surveyor. "How about oceans or weather patterns?"

"The problem there isn't time—it's scale and complexity. Like an ant trying to talk to an elephant in a hundred different languages simultaneously."

I nod. "So he was some sort of genius?"

"Maybe, but he also had help. He carried a mystic gem known as the Balancer, supposedly able to juggle and even merge magical energies. In the comic, he uses it to transfer all the power Wertham has stored into a volcano."

"So why do you think Aquitaine was Transe?"

"I talked to the robe. You wouldn't believe some of the things it told me . . ." He shakes his head, grinning. "Incredible stuff. Just scraps, traces left over the years, but whoever wore this has been places and seen things I never even knew existed. Other dimensions, other planets, other times."

It sounded eerily like Neil's description of comic books. "We didn't find any gem, though," I say.

"Neither did my team," says Eisfanger. "I went back after you found the robe. Scanned the whole place with more sensitive equipment. Nothing."

"I wouldn't say that. I think we've just uncovered a motive—a damn strong one, too."

"Sure," says Charlie. "Blame the rock. You got a perfectly good suspect in the treadmill, but as soon as a mineral enters the picture you're ready to lock it up and throw away the key."

"We'll have to find it first," I say. "But at least now I have a list of suspects—though they're not going to be easy to track down."

"Who?" Eisfanger asks.

"The rest of the Bravo Brigade. Plus any surviving members of the Kamic cult—oh, and possibly Fredric Wertham himself."

I sigh. "This is *great*. Y'know, dealing with magic, vampires, and werewolves on a daily basis was getting kind of stale—but now I've got a homicidal superpowered *lunatic* to catch. Happy, happy me . . ."

THREE

The first person I talk to is Gretchen. I find her in her own office—one considerably bigger than mine—and close the door before I sit down. There's no easy way to broach the subject, so I just dive right in. "Gretch, were you aware that Saladin was also Doctor Transe?"

I think it's the first time I've ever actually seen her show surprise. "I beg your pardon?"

"Doctor Transe. The sorcerer from the *Bravo Brigade* comic book."

She frowns and thinks hard about it for all of a second, which is how long it takes her to completely revise an entire set of assumptions and replace them with new data. Gretchen's brain scares me a little. "Ah. That would explain certain things. No, I never knew—never even suspected." The look on her face now is more fond reminiscence than betrayal. "He was an extraordinary man. I don't suppose I should be that surprised."

"You're not angry he kept it from you?"

She sighs. "Considering what I do for a living, it would be like the pot calling the kettle black, wouldn't it? I suspect I kept many more things from him than he did from me—though, as secrets go, this is impressive. Do you think it's why he was killed?"

"Too early to say—but that's the direction I'm headed in."

She nods. "You'll keep me apprised?"

"Of course."

The next person I visit is Dr. Pete.

Dr. Pete was my physician when I first got here. He helped me deal with RDT—Reality Dislocation Trauma—and even got my heart restarted once while I was kind of busy saving the world. My heart's had some nasty things done to it, but Dr. Pete's the only one who's actually stabbed it with something large and pointy. I don't hold it against him.

It's kind of hard to hold anything against Dr. Pete—he's just a plain nice guy. Well, nice thrope, actually, but so's his whole family. He took me to visit them once, and while we were there he showed something else: his comic book collection. I figure he might actually have a copy of that *Bravo Brigade* issue, and if so I want another look at it.

I go to his office, but he isn't there. His receptionist—a female thrope with short blond hair and overlong eyelashes—tells me he's at the clinic.

"The government clinic?" That was where the NSA had put me when I first arrived.

She blinks once, slowly. I feel a gentle breeze wash over me. "He doesn't do any work for the government," she says. Blink. It's like being fanned by tiny palm leaves. "He's at the anthrocanine clinic on Pike Street. It's more of a shelter, really, but Dr. Adams provides free medical aid twice a week."

I get directions, thank her, and leave. I wonder if she's as dumb as she seems, and doubt it. Or maybe Dr. Pete just hired her to save on air-conditioning.

The clinic's in a rough part of town, just close enough to the touristy section to make the authorities nervous and ensure a continuous patrol of the membrane between them. On one side are lots of trendy restaurants, kitschy souvenir shops, and an open-air produce market; on the other, decaying waterfront buildings, weedy empty lots, and boarded-up storefronts. It's funny how many cities I've seen that pattern in—it's like some kind of Skid Row tourism virus, sprouting postcard stands and T-shirt shops in the tracks of winos and shopping carts.

The clinic itself is in an old logging warehouse, a freshly painted sign tacked over a scratched and dented metal door. I park, hope my car is still there when I get back, and walk up to the entrance. A few thropes loitering in were form at the corner sniff in my direction, their yellow eyes glowing with hostility, but I'm wearing some artificial wolf pheromone Cassius supplied me with; it tells them I'm an alpha female, not to be messed with. Which is true, but it's a lot less stressful to spray some AWP on than have to constantly prove it.

The noise—and smell—when I open the door is impressive. Barking and howling and whining and oh my God, the stink. Wet dog and doggy-do and dog that's rolled in something dead. With just a hint of skunk for added impact.

I can't see any actual dogs, just a wire-mesh door set into the far wall, but I recognize the teenager at the counter that blocks access. It's Alexandra, Dr. Pete's niece. She and I have become Internet friends—we share similar tastes in music—but I rarely get to see her in person.

Of course, seeing Alexandra can sometimes be disturbing. She's into a fad called corpsing, which uses a charm to temporarily let parts of your body decompose; the first time we met, I could see her brain. She seems to currently be intact, studying a textbook on the counter, and looks up when I come in.

"Hey, Jace!" she says, smiling. "What are you doing here?"

"Looking for your uncle. He here?"

"Yeah, he's in the back, getting ready for the change-over."

"I didn't know you volunteered here."

She grimaces. "Volunteer? More like *sentenced*. I got busted breaking curfew and this is my punishment." She shakes her head. "If any of my friends come in here, I am just gonna *die*."

Ah, the teenage werewolf. Vulnerable to silver, wolfs-bane, and embarrassment. "Not doing the rotting corpse thing anymore?"

She rolls her eyes. "Uncle Pete won't let me do it here—worried that one of the inmates is gonna eat one of my eyeballs or something. So what? I mean, it's not like it won't grow back."

Talking to Alexandra is always interesting. Any time I feel like I'm starting to adjust to this world, I can count on her to remind me there are depths of weirdness I haven't explored yet. Adolescence is another universe all by it-self.

And then the naked dwarf throws himself against the wire mesh.

The *happy* naked dwarf. His eyes are bright and merry, a huge smile on his face. "Yippee!" he shouts. "Yippee! Yippee!" He clutches the wire mesh in both hands, star-ing at Alexandra and me like we're his best friends in the world. "Yippee!"

"That's Bo," Alexandra says. "He's always the first to change—'cause he's so little, I guess."

The barking is dying down. Bo is still yelling "Yip-pee!," but now other voices are joining in: a deep bass call-ing out, "Hey! Hey! Hey!"; a woman shrieking, "Yeah!"

over and over; and a lot of different variations on "Food!," "Eat!," and "Hungry!"

Alexandra looks glum. "Sun's down. Don't listen to them—we fed them an hour ago. Changeover always makes them hungry, but it's not worth the mess they make to feed them again. You sure you want to go in there?"

The naked dwarf abruptly spins and runs away. "What the hell," I say. "I love making new friends."

I come around the counter and she hits a button, buzzing open the electric lock on the door. I make sure it shuts securely behind me.

There's a huge room on the other side, lined with pens and lit by overhead fluorescents. Dr. Pete is down at the far end. He and a tall, bulky man in a black T-shirt and sweatpants are trying to get Bo to put on a pair of boxers.

I walk the length of the room, glancing in the pens. Each of them contains a naked man or woman, of varying ages, sizes, and races. Some glare at me sullenly, some wave eagerly, some ignore me completely. By the time I get to Dr. Pete, I think I have a pretty good idea what's going on.

Bo runs up to me, finally wearing the boxers, and does his best to sniff my crotch. He doesn't seem to take it too hard when I push him away. "Hey, Doc. What's the deal with the reverse thropes?"

Dr. Pete runs a hand through his shaggy brown hair and gives me a rueful smile. I still think he looks a little like a young Harrison Ford, though today his eyes have the tired wisdom of a Humphrey Bogart. "Anthrocanines. Dogs who have the lycanthropy gene, usually passed on by an ancestor who was bitten by a thrope. Infected dogs pass on their genes in two ways—to people through bites or scratches, and to their own offspring. But dog weres don't transform into wolves—they change into humans. As long as the sun's down, anyway."

"How about during Moondays?" Moondays are festival held by thropes every month to celebrate the three days of the full moon—while it's up every thrope has to shift to were form, whether they want to or not. It's kind of like a hairy Mardi Gras.

"They actually get a little smarter then. Doesn't last long, but I've got some pire volunteers who try to teach them a few things when their IQ spikes." He glances at his assistant, the large man who's been studying me but hasn't said a word. I notice for the first time that he's also barefoot. "Like Galahad here."

Galahad's hair is a patchwork of brown and white, his skin a pale pink. His lips are big and rubbery, his eyes large and alert. When Dr. Pete says his name, he smiles and his body shakes—I realize that he's twitching his butt from side to side, ever so slightly. It's both cute and a little creepy.

"Maybe this is a dumb question, but—why are they in cages?"

Dr. Pete sighs and rummages in the pocket of his white lab coat. "Because—despite what they look like—they're animals, Jace. Homeless animals. They don't understand the rules and they don't care. They get hit by cars, they break into businesses and steal food, sometimes they even attack children—though pire and thrope kids can usually take care of themselves. The two kinds of people they're the biggest threat to are human beings and themselves."

"Like urban apes," I say, staring at one cage. The guy in it is over six feet tall, broad and muscular, with short, bristly brown hair covering his scalp and chin. He meets my eyes and makes a noise somewhere between a growl and a grunt.

"Yes. We look after them here, give them food and shelter and keep them out of trouble. Most of them are harmless, though there is the odd troublemaker. A few of them have even become addicted to alcohol—and when they're drunk they get completely out of control."

I'll bet. I had visions of a group of drunken, naked men and women gleefully rampaging through a liquor store, the Tarzan of the Grapes tribe. "So they don't have the supernatural immunities thropes have?"

"No. Their life span is only ten, twelve years. They get sick or injured, it takes them a long time to heal."

Bo has trotted into an open cage on his own and lay down on his stomach on the bed. Dr. Pete walks over and closes the door quietly. Galahad follows him, always staying exactly four feet behind.

"What are they, usually?" I ask. "Bo and Galahad, I mean."

"Bo's a pug. Galahad's a Saint Bernard with a little coyote in him. Gally, go keep Alexandra company, okay?"

Galahad says, "Okay," in a friendly baritone, then trots away, his bare feet slapping on the concrete.

"Let's go in the back, it's quieter." He leads me to a small office in the corner and shuts the door, which muffles the din somewhat.

The room isn't large, and it's mostly filled by a small desk with a laptop on it and a pile of plastic sacks of dog food that reaches to the roof. Dr. Pete perches on the edge of the desk and motions me to take the one chair.

"What's up, Jace? I haven't seen you in a while. RDT not back, I hope?"

"No, it seems to be gone for good. No more attacks. Felt a little jittery the first week you took me off the medication, but fine since then. The reason I came to see you was less medical and more personal."

He raises his eyebrows and smiles. I feel myself start to blush. Dr. Pete and I are just friends, but—well, there are friends, and then there are friends you sometimes imagine naked. Of course, as my physician, Dr. Pete doesn't have to use his imagination.

"Uh, I should have said *professional*," I add. "As in a case I'm working on. I was hoping you could give me some help on the subject of comic books."

"Comic books?"

I give him a brief rundown. Despite what his receptionist told me, Dr. Pete works for the National Security Agency—part-time, anyway—and can be trusted. I don't mention Gretchen's pregnancy, though—she deserves her privacy.

"Yes, I actually do own a copy of *The Bravo Brigade*," he says. "It's a collector's item, worth a fair bit of money. When do you need it?"

"The sooner the better."

"I'll drop it by the NSA office first thing tomorrow, all right?"

"Yeah, that'll be fine. How's your new assistant working out?"

"Alexandra?" He laughs. "She's fine. I think the main reason she doesn't want her friends knowing she works here is she doesn't want them seeing how much she enjoys it."

"Shortening her ironic distance, huh? No wonder she's upset."

"What about you? Doing more than just working, I hope."

"Uh . . . been kind of busy."

He frowns at me. "Jace. I told you, the best cure for RDT is putting down some roots. That means more than just hunting for Stoker."

"I catch Stoker, I don't have to worry about roots."

"Your RDT comes back, you don't have to worry about anything."

I sigh. "Except who gives my eulogy, right? Okay,

okay, I promise I'll get out more. Alexandra and I have a date to hit some flea markets this weekend."

"That reminds me." He opens the drawer in the desk and pulls out a battered cassette tape. "Got this from a friend of mine. Thought you might like it."

I take it warily. The faded printing on the plastic reads SIGUE SIGUE SPUTNIK, a name I actually recognize. "I don't believe it. You don't have Elvis, but a one-hit-wonder New Wave band from the 1980s pops up on both our worlds."

"You're welcome. And I thought you weren't fussy when it came to your collection."

"I'm not." Finding music here that's the same as in my world has become my hobby, and the cultural divide is vast enough that I can't afford to be choosy. Country, jazz, rock, folk, TV jingles—I'll take anything I can get. "Thanks, really. I appreciate it." I frown. "But how did you know?"

"I have my sources," he says with a smile. I was a little hesitant to tell him about my hobby at first—I thought he might disapprove of an attempt to hang on to my past as opposed to adapting to the present. He didn't, though; he said it was actually a healthy approach, one that would help ground me to my current reality. I think he's just glad I'm doing something other than chasing a psychopath.

"Looks like this place keeps you busy. You enjoy it?"

He grins. "It can get a little intense at times, but it's rewarding. Dogs and thropes don't always get along, but I like them. And they've gotten more than their fair share of bad breaks on this world."

I know what he means. During World War II, dogs in the Axis countries here were rounded up and gassed as part of Hitler's lycanthropic purity program; it gave a whole new meaning to the phrase *mongrel races*.

Dr. Pete glances over at his laptop, then frowns and taps a key. "Not you again," he murmurs.

"Problem?"

"There's this thrope that's been hanging around the back door for the last week. Always gone when I go out there."

He turns the laptop around, shows me a security feed from a camera. I can see the outline of a thrope in half were form in the shadows, yellow eyes gleaming. Looks like he's wearing a trench coat.

"Hanging around a were dog shelter? Maybe he's just looking for a handout. I'm kind of surprised you even have this level of security—I mean, what are you guarding, your supply of Kibbles and Bits?"

He gives me a sad look. "Jace, the residents here have the instincts of animals and the intelligence of children. And about forty percent are female."

That gives me a sick feeling in the pit of my stomach. Technically, dogs and wolves are the same species, but what Dr. Pete's describing would be like taking advantage of the mentally handicapped. "Right," I say tightly. "Excuse me."

I'm out the door before he has a chance to say a word. "Hey!" he calls after me. "Hold on!"

I stalk down the line of pens, exciting all kinds of shouts from their occupants. I notice for the first time that it's more than just single words: Some of them can form short sentences. A bright-eyed girl with long blond hair falling over her eyes peers at me from her bunk, where she's perched on all fours. "Play with me?" she asks, trying to wag a nonexistent tail. "Play with me?"

I've built up a pretty good head of steam by the time I reach the wire-mesh door. Dr. Pete steps in front of me. "Jace, take it easy. That guy hasn't actually done anything wrong—"

"And neither have I," I say. "I'm just going to have a little conversation with him." My voice is eminently reasonable.

He sighs and lets me past. Galahad leaps up from the chair he was sitting in, eager to be included in whatever is going on, but I march right past him. Alexandra says, "So, we still on for this weekend?"

"Absolutely," I toss over my shoulder. "Thanks for the help, Doc."

I'm deeply grateful to Dr. Pete for all the help he's given me, but I'd be doing this even if I hated his guts. Certain kinds of predators shouldn't be tolerated.

I stop at my car and get a little something from the trunk. They slide into the special reinforced pockets I had added to the lining of my jacket, where I can get to them quickly. The Ruger's a more efficient weapon, but nobody here's afraid of it. When I'm going for intimidation, something else is required.

I walk around the corner, past the mercury sodium glare of the streetlight and into the darkness of the alley. I can smell ripe garbage and the acrid stink of thrope urine. No sign of the thrope I'm looking for, but I can see the red telltale of the security cam mounted over the back door. There's a large metal Dumpster just past it, though; plenty of room for a thrope to crouch down beside it, out of view.

If he's there, he can probably smell me already. "Hey, pal," I call out. "Police. Step out where I can see you. Now."

Nothing. I reach inside my jacket with both hands, right hand to the left, left hand to the right. I pull both weapons out smoothly, eighteen-inch-long ironwood shafts, each tipped with a conical silver head. I hit the release studs with my thumbs, snapping both foot-long silver blades out and locking them at a forty-five-degree angle, turning stakes into scythes. Razor-sharp silver over a steel core, with an embedded ironwood strip running down the center of each blade. Good for impaling or decapitation, against thropes or pires.

I edge around the Dumpster, scythes ready. There's nobody there. I put my foot against the Dumpster, give it a little shove. It rolls easily, obviously empty. Looks like Dr. Pete's stalker has slipped away again.

I snap one of the scythes shut, holster it, and pull out a flashlight. No obvious tracks, but that doesn't say much in a paved alley. No smoldering cigarette butts or handy discarded match packs with an address scrawled on the back.

But there is something. Something freshly scratched in the paint of the Dumpster, little red curls of paint dangling from shiny grooves in the metal. It's a *kanji,* a Japanese symbol that looks oddly familiar.

When I first got to this world, I was under a lot of pressure, which led to some bad decisions—one of them was a Japanese thrope named Tanaka. We only spent one night together, and that night is kind of blurry. Tanaka wanted to continue the relationship; I didn't. Despite things that happened later, I always thought of Tanaka as a basically decent person.

But he'd done this once before, showing up on my doorstep unexpectedly. Dr. Pete had been there then, too. I'd managed to defuse the situation, but Tanaka was clearly not the kind of person to give up easily.

That's only one possibility, though. I'd made more dangerous enemies in Japan than a jilted lover; specifically, a Yakuza *oyabun* named Isamu. Charlie and I—well, mainly Charlie—had turned his number one assassin into a pile of dust, and Isamu didn't strike me as exactly the forgiving type.

But the Yakuza is a pire organization; using outside help for a vendetta this personal seems out of character. I pull out my phone, take a few pictures of the symbol, then head back inside to assure Dr. Pete and Alexandra that the lurker is gone. Galahad isn't smiling anymore; he keeps staring at the door with a frown on his face. He knows something isn't right.

Smart dog.

When I get home I do some research. The *kanji* isn't a Yak symbol. It isn't a reference to unrequited love or doomed romance or ninja revenge. Its meaning is, literally, "great difference."

Great difference. Between what? My world and this one? The human and canine forms of the were dogs? Life and death? It could mean almost anything.

I call Gretchen at the NSA office. "Gretch? Need a favor."

"Go ahead." She sounds fine, as sharp and focused as she always is. I hope it's not just an act.

"I need to know if my old friend Tanaka is still in Japan. Definitive proof. And if he is, I guess I need to know what Isamu's up to."

"Ah. Eat some bad sushi and looking for someone to blame?"

I smile. Attagirl. "Just letting my paranoia out for a quick run. Call me back, okay?"

"I'll ring you within the hour."

I fish out the cassette Dr. Pete gave me. It's a dead medium, but I've salvaged devices of varying vintages from yard sales and junk shops in the last few months. I dig out an old tape deck and slide the tape in.

I'm nodding my head to "Love Missile F1-11" when Gretchen calls back. "Jace? Your former paramour is currently drinking single-malt in a whiskey bar in Tokyo. The report on Isamu is more extensive, but essentially he's very busy defending his territory from two different rivals at the moment. Do you need the details now, or would you like to view them at the office?"

"I'll look at them when I come in, Gretch. Thanks."

After I hang up, I try to figure out if Isamu would waste resources on an enemy an ocean away during a turf war. I doubt it; he's more the trapdoor spider type, willing to wait until just the right moment to strike. One of the advantages of being immortal. But if it isn't him and it isn't Tanaka, then who?

I sit and listen to the musical advice of a couple of guys with three-foot rainbow Mohawks; they want me to "shoot it up," but they're not too clear on who I should be aiming at.

I do some more research before heading in to the office. It's about 11:00 PM, but these days I don't get to bed until three or four in the morning; too much going on at night in a world where half the population is allergic to sunlight. Gretchen's forwarded some files on the case to me, and there's a fair bit about the Bravo Brigade online. After an hour or so, it becomes clear where the next step in the investigation lies.

I'm going to prison.

FOUR

The place is called the Stanhope Federal Penitentiary. It's in central Washington, just outside of Spokane, and houses some of the worst offenders in the state: rapists, murderers, gangbangers, and racketeers. It's the place they held Al Capone after his tax evasion conviction, and I'm told the prison guards hold a raffle to see which con gets the honor of staying in his cell. Nice to know Al is still contributing to society long after someone beat him to death with a sack full of silver nickels.

That's on this world. I can't recall exactly how Capone bought it back home, but I'm pretty sure it had nothing to do with spare change and a vampire mobster. No silver coins in circulation now, of course. Even in Al's day they were a rarity—he was actually killed with his own collection. Apparently he used to make thropes he wasn't happy with swallow them.

From the outside the prison looks like any other correctional facility: high walls of gray concrete, watchtowers at the four corners flooding the surrounding area with light. The front gate is a massive, iron-barred portcullis that looks like it could withstand a bulldozer. Silver razor wire glints on the tops of the walls like predatory tinsel.

The guards, like the inmates, are a mix of thrope and

pire. The two who escort me from the front gate to the intake area are both pires, a short Hispanic man named Olmerez and a tall, skinny one named Bicks. Bicks's skin is so pale it's almost translucent, blue veins clearly visible on his neck and the backs of his hands.

They take me down a concrete corridor, barred electric gates buzzing us deeper into the complex. They hand me off without a word to an impassive black woman behind a Plexiglas-screened counter, who checks my ID. She directs me to another room, where I have to pass through a metal detector and then be okayed by a staff shaman who makes me stand in a circle of salt and state that I am not in possession of any fetishes, charms, or cursed objects. Finally, I'm put in an interview room to wait for my subject.

She shows up in the company of a guard about fifteen minutes later. Her name is Cali Edison, she's a thrope serving a four-hundred-year sentence—and she's the only incarcerated member of the Kamic cult I've been able to find.

Cali's a tiny, wiry woman with ferociously orange hair cut short. She looks like she's in her 40s, but her file says she's closer to a 120. She's dressed in a jumpsuit almost exactly the same shade as her hair, and wears a pair of manacles that look strong enough to hold an elephant. The guard, a massive, black-furred thrope in half-were form, motions for her to sit down, then locks her cuffs to an eyebolt jutting out of the table. He catches my eye, signs *be careful* so that Cali doesn't see it. I don't know what they expect her to do, but they're not taking any chances.

"Hi," I say. I'm sitting at the other end of the table, her file in front of me. "I'm Special Agent Jace Valchek. I'd like to ask you some questions about the Kamic cult."

"I'm Cali Edison," she says, just a trace of a drawl in

her voice. "I'd like to screw the president of the United States and then eat his tongue."

"Good for you. Everybody needs a dream."

"I can't smoke while I'm in these cuffs."

"Or without a cigarette."

"Ain't that the truth. Got one?"

"I've got a whole tobacco patch growing out of my ass. Talk to me and I'll bring in the harvest early."

She grins with small, sharp teeth. "Ain't been nobody to see me in years. Ask away."

"Tell me about the *Seduction of the Innocent* murders."

"That was a long time ago."

"How's your memory?"

"Gets better when I'm smoking."

I fish a pack out of my pocket. I don't smoke and most thropes I know don't care for the smell, but Charlie tells me it's still a pretty common vice for inmates—they're immune to cancer and don't have anything better to do.

I light one myself, then lean forward and stick it in her mouth. She takes a long drag and blows the smoke out her nose. "Ah, I think it's coming back to me," she says. "Not that there's much to tell. Wertham was a real smooth talker, you know? Convinced me and a bunch of others we could grab us a whole lot of power without anyone even noticing. 'Like embezzling from the dead,' was the way he put it. 'Course, a fair number of folks had to wind up dead in the first place, but that part never bothered me much."

Her eyes are flat and hard, the eyes of a predator looking for weakness. Being in prison for half a century has whittled her down to a core of cold stone, more lem than thrope.

"What happened to the rest of the cult?"

"Dead. The Brigade, they weren't interested in arresting us. They did their damn best to wipe us out—not that I blame 'em. We weren't exactly holding back, neither."

"So how'd you survive?"

She pulls on the cigarette with her lips, sucks in air from the side of her mouth to inhale with the smoke. "Someone had to."

"Wertham didn't." I don't know if that's true or not, and I'm interested in seeing her reaction.

"No, they stuck him in a coffin and nailed it shut. But as the leader, he was always the one that had to die. It was somebody like me they had to keep alive."

I frown. "I'm not following."

She snorts smoke out her nose. "But I was. And that's the kind of survivor they needed, somebody not too high up. Somebody who was there, who knew the story but wouldn't be a threat."

She leans forward in her chair, the cigarette dangling from her lips. "That's how Kamic books work, honey. The power isn't just in the object, it's in the tale. And a tale don't exist unless someone's there to tell it."

I'm starting to see. Wertham created his own chronicles of murder and mayhem, but they didn't give him any power until they'd been read. The Bravo Brigade countered that by creating a narrative of their own, one also read by the masses—but they kept a witness around as well, someone for whom the story was more real and immediate than anything in print. A sort of sacrifice in reverse, kept alive to help keep the story a living thing.

"What about the Brigade themselves? Wouldn't they be enough?"

"The Brigade never did like the spotlight. They cut me a deal—I'd talk to reporters, tell everyone what happened, and they'd let me live. Brigade disappears, government denies they ever existed. Makes 'em real and unreal, all at once. Power in that, too."

"Tell me about them. The Brigade."

"What for? You've read the comic, you know all you need to." She leans back and rattles off a list in a bored voice. "Doctor Transe, the Solar Centurion, the Sword of Midnight, Brother Stone, the African Queen. And the Quicksilver Kid, of course. Can't forget *him*." She sounds contemptuous, bitter, and I see an opportunity.

"The Quicksilver Kid. He the one that took *you* down?"

Anger flashes in her eyes. "Yeah, that's right. But it didn't happen the way the comic said it did. It was written like some big showdown, with the Kid using those damn silver knives of his to pin me to a wall. You wannna know what really happened? He stabbed me in the back. Literally. Transe hadn't patched me up afterward, I'd be as dead as the rest of them."

"Guess you owe him, then."

She spits the butt of the cigarette onto the table. "Yeah, I got him to thank for the last fifty years in here. I'm real grateful."

"Transe is dead." I watch her reaction carefully.

She laughs once, a hard, angry bark of pleasure. "Yeah? One down, then. How'd he get it?"

"Can't tell you that. But I will say I'm looking into the other members of the Brigade."

Her eyes narrow. "Yeah? Which ones you talk to?"

"None of them, yet. Thought I'd come to you first."

She gives me a slow, nasty smile. "Sure. You got no idea how to find any of 'em, do you?"

"No," I admit. I let her savor her victory, her moment of power. After fifty years, it's not much to let her have. "They haven't been seen or heard of since you were put away. But I can tell you that Doctor Transe's real name was Saladin Aquitaine."

If the name means anything to her, she doesn't show it. "He was probably the most powerful one—and you wouldn't be here if it was anything but murder."

I shrug, not giving her anything, letting her figure it out on her own.

"Guess I'd be first on your list of suspects, except my alibi is pretty much made of concrete and steel. And now that you know the rest of the cult didn't survive, you figure the killer must be one of the Bravos."

"Unless you're lying."

"Me? Oh, I'm as honest as a silver dollar. Burn you just as quick, too." She grins. "But I don't know what you expect to get from me. I got no love for the Brigade, but I made a deal with 'em. I go back on that, they might decide to break their contract, too. And it ain't like I got anywhere to run."

"I'm not asking you to break anything. You agreed to tell their story, remember? All I'm asking is for you to tell me a little more than you told everybody else."

She considers this. "Let's say I did. How's my situation gonna improve as opposed to staying the same or gettin' worse?"

"Don't know that it is. But I'm giving you a chance at revenge; after fifty years in here, I'm betting that'll taste a whole lot sweeter than just about anything else I could offer." I smile at her for the first time. "Besides—this might be the only chance you get. If one of the Bravos has gone bad, he or she might decide to pay you a little visit, clean up some loose ends."

Her grin fades to a grimace. "Yeah, that's what I figured you'd say. Still, can't blame me for trying . . . so. Transe bit the dust and you think one of the others did him in." She stares at me flatly for a second, then smiles. "Got to be one of the lems. They always was kind of uppity—Transe, he was kind of a snob, didn't much care for working with them in the first place. Brother Stone put up with it—the whole 'turn the other cheek' thing—but it bothered him more than he'd let on. And the Kid? He's always had a temper. What I heard, he and Transe got into it more than once."

"Yeah? And how exactly did you hear all this, when you were working for the other side?"

Her smile turns cold. "Oh, you hear all kinds of things when they're sticking you full of tubes in the back of an ambulance and already figure you're a goner."

I know there's more to it than that, but calling her a liar isn't going to get me any more information. "Okay. So both Brother Stone and the Quicksilver Kid didn't get along with Transe. Any idea where either of them is?"

"I heard a rumor the Quicksilver Kid was working as a bounty hunter, tracking down bail jumpers in the Midwest. Figured it had to be him, 'cause he's still throwing knives instead of those little silver balls enforcement lems like so much these days."

Not much of a lead, but considering how much Edison no doubt hates the Kid, it's probably genuine. "Anything else?"

"One thing. Think I can get another smoke before you go?"

"Yeah, sure."

I take out another cigarette. Lighting the first one left my mouth tasting like an ashtray, so I reach out with the cigarette in one hand and pick up the lighter with the other—

Never seen a thrope transform that fast.

Thinking back on it later, I realize it was only her mouth that changed, her skull lengthening into a fanged muzzle so quickly it's like a switchblade popping open. Her jaws snap shut no more than an inch from my fingers, clipping the cigarette in half as neatly as a pair of scissors.

She changes back just as fast, managing to hold on to the shortened cigarette with her lips. She grins at me lazily. "Prefer 'em without the filter, anyways . . ."

I stare at her, trying to get my breathing under control. I forget sometimes I'm no more than one bite away from losing my humanity forever—not that she knows that. She'd probably just find it funny that I'd have to grow a few new fingers—

"Almost lost your endangered status, didn't you?" she says. "Pretty quick for a human. Too bad—nothing I like better than a few ladyfingers for a snack."

"How'd you know?"

"That gunk you're wearing might fool Joe Thrope on the street, but you're still pumping out all kinds of human stinks underneath. Living in a cage, you get kind of sensitive to anything new—and I haven't smelled a genuine OR in a long, long time." *OR* stands for "Original Recipe"—it's what thropes and pires call us "unenhanced" humans when they're being insulting.

I stand up and pocket the lighter. "Thanks for your help. Good luck getting that lit."

She smiles and inhales deeply through her nose. "Oh, I wouldn't want it lit now. Burning tobacco I can smell anytime—but it's been a few decades since I last had a hit of good old human fear . . ."

I can still hear her chuckling as I leave.

I leaf through the comic book Dr. Pete dropped off until I come to a panel depicting the Quicksilver Kid in action. He's the one who looks like a robot wearing a cowboy hat, though in fact he's a golem made largely out of brass. In my world he'd be shown blazing away with a pair of six-guns, but his weapons of choice are a bandolier of gleaming silver throwing knives. Most of the knives designed for throwing that I'm familiar with have a leaf-shaped blade, weighted toward the head to ensure it strikes point-first; in the comic, the artist has drawn them more like a traditional, bowie-style hunting knife.

The Kid himself supposedly has a brass outer shell, filled with mercury—hence the *Quicksilver* name. I always thought the reasons lems were filled with sand or made from clay had to do with malleability, but apparently a fluid and metallic medium is necessary even in a body where the joints are hinged and soldered. The Kid is said to be animated by the spirit of a "hundred rattlesnakes," which I guess makes him not only fast but mean. And probably noisy.

Charlie walks into my office without knocking. It's not much of an office, just a windowless room with a door, a desk, and two chairs, but it was one of the things I demanded from Cassius when it turned out my stay here was going to be a little longer than I'd expected. I don't care whether Charlie knocks or not; I'm more concerned about whether or not he breaks the furniture by sitting on it. Fortunately, Charlie seems just as happy standing as he does sitting—which is to say, not very.

"How was prison?" he asks.

"Vaguely informative and mostly made from rock. Kinda like you."

"How vague?"

"We're chasing a lem from the Old West. Supposedly a bounty hunter now."

Charlie nods. He's wearing a midnight-black fedora today, which makes his already black features virtually disappear. "The Quicksilver Kid, right?"

"Yeah. You know about this guy?"

"Sure. Even lems have legends."

"So what's his story?"

Charlie shrugs. "Built by a mad shaman type to be sheriff of some small town in the late 1800s. Town was razed by a pack of thrope *banditos,* and the Kid spent the next few years hunting every one of them down. No one was faster or more accurate than he was with a throwing knife, and he packed a bandolier full of them: enchanted silver blades called the Seven Teeth of the Moon. People said he could pin a firefly to a toothpick at a hundred feet with one of them."

"What happened to him?"

"Disappeared after he killed the last bandit. Wasn't seen again until that comic you're holding came out."

"How about since?"

Charlie hesitates, which is something he almost never does. "I don't know. You hear stories, but . . ."

"But what?"

"Like I said, we have our legends. Doesn't mean we believe they're true—just means we enjoy a good story as much as the next guy."

"Stop worrying about looking stupid and tell me the damn story, already."

"Some lems say he walled himself up in a cave and just let himself rust. Others say he learned how to disguise himself and is still out there today, working as a mercenary or a cop or a spy. Half the war stories you hear have the punch line 'and it turns out Captain Feldspar was really the Quicksilver Kid!' But they're just stories—though one company making lems did produce a 'Quicksilver' model for a while in the 1960s. Didn't last." He shakes his head. "Faulty joints. And of course they were actually filled with sand, not mercury—that just doesn't work."

"Except in comic books." I toss the issue down on my

desk. "Well, I got a tip he may be hauling in bail jumpers somewhere in the Midwest. Could be a dead end, but it's what we have to go on at the moment."

"I know some people in Kansas City. I'll ask around."

"Yeah, all right."

After Charlie leaves I go for a walk. It's raining out, which isn't surprising—this is Seattle, after all. That's okay, though; I do some of my best thinking while walking in the rain.

Dark, damp streets. Cars make that noise they only make on wet pavement. Neon shimmers off puddles on the tops of newspaper boxes. I jam my hands in the pockets of my trench coat and trudge into the night, questions percolating in my brain.

Question number one: Was the killer really crazy? The crime scene was certainly bizarre, but I was living in a bizarre world. The comic book references were strange, but they had a certain internal logic—after all, the victim himself had appeared in a comic book. I keep seeing that grinning green skull in the red mask, crackling with little arcs of electricity, and shiver. Dealing with organized psychopaths always gives me a very particular feeling, like I'm standing on top of a cliff; a cliff where the world makes sense right up to the edge, then drops away into a howling abyss of insanity. That cliff is where my quarry lives, close enough to normalcy to fool his friends and neighbors but one step away from sacrificing everyone he knows to the great Spider God that lives in his brain. And no matter how many times I've been on that cliff, I always get the same sickening little tingle in the pit of my stomach, the dizzying vertigo of madness.

That's what I feel right now.

That's what my intuition says. The facts are still open to interpretation: A valuable mystic item is missing, and the victim had powerful known enemies. This could still be a glorified robbery or a revenge killing I don't fully understand.

Question number two: What isn't Cassius telling me? Yes, Gretchen is one of his people and he protects his people like a pit bull does her pups, but the Bravo Brigade was a government team. Cassius knows more about them than he's letting on, and when I have enough information I'm going to have to confront him.

Question number three: How much does Gretch know? Was she aware of Aquitaine's other identity, or did he keep it a secret from her? Could Gretchen be a suspect—or even one of the Brigade?

The Brigade consisted of a pire, three thropes, and two lems. Two males, two females, two asexual beings. All sorts of possibilities for office romance, though I get the impression that pires and thropes don't hook up with each other too often—and the lems just don't go there at all.

Question number four: Is Wertham really dead? I haven't seen a body, and reports of his demise are kind of vague; in the comic, he's killed by an exploding volcano. Dramatic, but the kind of thing that makes exhuming a body difficult.

I sigh. A line of crows perched on the edge of a chain-link fence eye me suspiciously but make no move to leave, raindrops gleaming on their oily black feathers. The fence surrounds what used to be a gas station, now an empty square of patchy gravel; stunted weeds and white PVC out-gassing pipes stick up here and there like the periscopes of subterranean submarines.

I start to head back the way I came. I don't get very far, because there's a group of people up ahead blocking the sidewalk. I never noticed them approach, but there they are. They're standing facing me, not moving, in the shadows between two streetlights. Half a dozen, maybe.

The one in the center is obviously a thrope, his lupine silhouette a head taller than any of the others. His yellow eyes are only slits. He pads forward a few steps, the rest of his group staying where they are, and stops just at the edge of the pool of light I'm under. I still can't see his face, but his black-furred, claw-tipped hands are now clearly visible.

Thrope mouths aren't shaped for human speech, so they've evolved their own sign language. I've become fairly fluent, but even if I wasn't there's no way I can miss what he signs.

Hello, Jace.

FIVE

It's definitely not Tanaka.

The body language's all wrong, for one thing. Tanaka stood and moved with a grace that suggested a panther more than a wolf; this guy is more hunched over, less certain on two feet. He's big, though—must mass nearly as much as Charlie. Looks like he's wearing some kind of sleeveless vest and dark pants—no shoes, of course.

The rain is no more than a drizzle now, what native Seattlites don't even consider actual precipitation—they just say the air's a little damp. Little beads of moisture sparkle in his black-and-gray fur, making it look like someone sprinkled him with industrial-strength fairy dust.

I'm carrying the Ruger, but if they rush me I'm in trouble—pires and thropes are scary fast, and my gun has zero ability to instill fear in this world. If they attack, I'll have to kill each and every one of them before they reach me. Not good.

I sign back, *Who the hell are you?*

You can call me Tair. He signs each letter of his name, then punctuates it with a sign that encapsulates the whole thing.

What do you want?

To warn you.

About?

He chuckles. It's a sound that's more familiar than it is menacing, but I'll be damned if I can remember where I've heard it before. *A mutual acquaintance—Dr. Peter Adams.*

Why? Is he in danger?

Maybe. Maybe he is the danger.

That throws me. Dr. Pete is probably the most decent, ethical person I've met since I came to this world. *You've got to be kidding.*

He's not the person you think he is, Jace. What do you know about him, really?

Let's see. He's got a big family that loves him, he heals people for a living, he risked his own life to save mine—

That's not his family.

I don't have to bother signing *What?* The look on my face does it for me.

Do a little checking into the "Adams" family. You'll be surprised at what you come up with.

Why have you been hanging around the clinic?

Keeping an eye on the good doctor. Wouldn't want him to suddenly vanish without a trace.

"Threatening him is *really* not a good idea," I say, and suddenly the gun is in my hand. I know it won't impress any of them, but it makes me feel better.

Wasn't threatening him. Was threatening you. He growls to underline the remark, a deep rumble that practically makes my bones vibrate.

"Oh. That's different. Go right ahead, everyone else does."

Dr. Adams has a way of leaving town with unfinished business. That makes the people I work for very unhappy.

"Oh dear. Unhappy people, I *hate* those. They're *scary*."

He chuckles again. *You've got it wrong again. Being scary is my job.*

He motions with his muzzle, and his group glides forward. Not a pack, though—they're pires, not thropes. Interesting.

There are a lot of thrope gangs—the pack structure is a natural fit—but that doesn't mean there aren't any pires doing the same thing. The Bloods out of LA are all pires, and their leaders trace their roots all the way back to Egypt—which may explain their fetish for gold jewelry. Ankhs on thick yellow chains, rings with tiny gold pyramids instead of gemstones, bracelets embossed with hieroglyphs; more *Tomb Raider* than *LA Raiders*.

But the style doesn't stop at the bling. Pires who want to do their gangbanging during daylight hours have to cover up just like all the other blood drinkers—but instead of a nice face mask and hoodie from Abercrombie & Fitch, they wind strips of designer fabric around every exposed inch of flesh. Call themselves "wrappers."

Yeah, it's kind of ridiculous. But so are baggy pants that ride so low they show off your underwear, and the reason that trend started was purely practical, too—it made it easier to hide a gun. The wrappers, for all their Invisible Man/King Tut vibe, have more than style on their minds. Other pires don't go masked at night, but these guys do; wrapping is an excuse to hide—and sometimes swap—their identities whenever they want.

I won't bore you with a long description of every variation I see standing in front of me; let's just say it looks like someone set off a car bomb in the alleyway between a jewelry outlet and a bandage factory, and leave it at that.

They don't carry guns, of course. But they're large and mean and undead, and that's all they really need.

"Yeah, real frightening," I say. "You guys look like the remains of a bad ski trip. Don't you have a pyramid you should be guarding or something?"

"Bitch thinks she's tough," one of them says. "Must be tough, she sure ain't smart."

"Can't count, anyway," another says. "Must be that shiny thing she holdin' so tight. Got some major mojo goin' on."

"That what she want us to think, anyways."

I sigh. I've had special bullets made since I got here, but I had to provide the gunpowder from my one box of ammo; I don't have a proper recipe for the stuff, and I hate wasting it educating morons like this. "Yeah, yeah, it's my magical splatwand. I point it at you and you go *splat*. Wanna see?"

Tair spreads both his hands wide in an abrupt slicing motion. *Enough. Tell me, Jace, how do Dr. Adams and your enforcer get along?*

"Charlie? What's he got to do with this?"

He's a golem. I would have thought the doctor would show some . . . professional *interest.*

That makes no sense at all. Dr. Pete's specialty is human beings, not golems—not that lems *have* doctors, anyway. The closest thing they seem to have are repairmen.

Human beings are only the doctor's hobby, you know; his true interests lie in humanoid animism. And he wasn't always that particular where and how he got to practice.

My eyes narrow. I know what he's talking about now—the Gray Market, the underground trade in illegal lem manufacture. "Dr. Pete's not involved in anything like that."

Maybe not now. But he was—and the people he worked for aren't very happy with him. Sooner or later he's going to have settle accounts with them.

The biggest wrapper in the group, a guy almost as wide as he is tall, slams a fist into his open palm suggestively. It'd be more menacing if his thick fingers weren't bound in tartan fabric—it's like watching a Scottish mummy warm up for sumo. C'mon, then, y'wee fat man! I'll make ye squeal like the pipes at sunup!

What are you smiling at?

"Nothing," I mutter. Stupid brain.

Most of the pires are standing very still, but one of them seems a little twitchy. He's skinny—or maybe just seems that way because he's standing next to Mr. Sumo—and favors strips of powder-blue suede wrapped around his bony frame. I mentally christen him Anorexic Vampire Elvis Mummy, and notice that he's fingering a pire crucifix on a cord around his neck.

Crosses aren't much use against vampires in this world. Maybe it's because the supernatural races outnumber humans a hundred to one, maybe it's because the Catholic Church is now dominated by werewolves; whatever the reason, waving a cross in a pire's face won't do much more than annoy him.

They even have their own version, what they call the Blood Cross. It's a crucifix with two vertical bars instead of one, the bottom ends sharpened to points so they resemble a pair of fangs. They're about as common a symbol as a pentagram, so I'm not surprised to see it—I just wonder why he's wearing it on a cheap piece of string instead of a chain.

Until, of course, he rips it off and throws it at me.

People here are very fond of throwing things. Ball bearings, darts, *shuriken*, toasters—whatever comes to hand. It's partly because they don't have guns, and partly because they're strong enough to chuck a cat into orbit. Accuracy is usually another matter.

Unfortunately, in this case Anorexic Vampire Elvis Mummy seems to have been practicing. Either that, or he meant to kill me and screwed up.

The Blood Cross goes right through my wrist, the one just below the handgun. It hits so hard the only thing that stops it is the crossbar, and the impact jars the gun right out of my hand.

I stare in shock at the two silver spikes jutting from my arm. Jutting *through* my arm.

Then things get worse.

"Well, well," one of them says. Don't know which one, but he sounds delighted. "That cross one hundred percent solid silver. You ain't no bitch, after all—you nothin' but an OR."

Great. I go for my gun, they rip me apart. They know I'm human, so they might decide to drink me or turn me, just for fun. Or maybe they'll just sell me to a blood farm somewhere, and I can spend the rest of my existence being force-fed iron supplements and being bled once a day—

And then—in the middle of the night, on a dark, rainy Seattle street—the sun comes out.

Not out of the sky. No, the sun steps out from the shadows of a doorway, and it's shaped like a man.

A man dressed like a Roman soldier, to be exact: metal breastplate, leather skirt, sandals, tall crested helmet, metal greaves on his forearms and legs. Everything metal seems to be made of gold, and every inch of exposed skin shines with a brilliant white light, so bright it's hard to look at for more than an instant.

But an instant is more than enough. Pires wear smoked goggles or sunglasses during the day, but not at night; neither do the wrappers. A single glance at the newcomer is enough to provoke screams and six simultaneous See No Evil monkey responses; wisps of smoke from charred retinas seep between their fingers and curl into the damp air.

Tair's reaction is just as immediate. He leaps onto the hood of a parked truck, to the roof of a bus shelter, then onto the top of a two-story building, all within about two seconds. Then he's gone.

I'm holding on to my wounded arm with my other

hand, squeezing the wrist as tightly as I can to keep from bleeding to death.

I stare at the Solar Centurion. He stares back—or at least I think he does; I can't actually look him full in the face without going temporarily blind myself. My skin feels like I just stepped onto the beach in Tahiti.

And then, without a word, he turns ands walks away.

"Hey!" I call out, stumbling after him. "You can't just—"

The light radiating from his body abruptly flares.

When my vision clears, he's gone. I grab my gun and get out of there myself before the pires recover—though I suspect most of them will be blind for at least a day or two. I've already got two punctures, and don't really want to risk any more.

I get half a block away, hesitate, then go back and shoot the skinny one in the hand. It seems like the least I can do.

I go to the hospital. It's my first exposure to this world's brand of institutional medicine, and it's an eye-opener.

When I first got to this world, Dr. Pete took care of me in a little NSA clinic called the St. Francis Infirmary, and I've had checkups at his office since. I don't want to go to either place now, not until I've had a chance to investigate some of the claims Tair made.

The building's a lot smaller than most of the hospitals I've been to—pires and thropes rarely need medical attention. The waiting room is tiny, and there are only two other people in it: a middle-aged, balding pire who seems to have a cold and a thrope in half-were form with his detached right arm sitting in his lap. It twitches spasmodically from time to time.

They both study me curiously. "Why don't you just pull it out?" the pire asks, his voice stuffy.

"I don't want to bleed to death."

"It doesn't look that bad. Can't be silver."

"It *is* silver," I manage through gritted teeth. The thrope sniffs in my direction, then nods.

"Can't be," the pire says reasonably. "If it were, you wouldn't just be sitting there; the wound would be smoking and sizzling and incredibly painful—"

"Please. Shut. Up."

"Maybe it's painted wood. That can hurt just as bad as silver, but it doesn't smoke. Lucky for me, I guess." He sneezes explosively, leaving a fine mist of red in the air. "Sawdust," he explains. "Got a bunch in my lungs. Taking its time to work its way out, too. Wife says I should be more careful."

I know I shouldn't ask, but I can't resist. "How'd you manage to get sawdust in your lungs?"

"Oh, I was doing a little home renovation. They say you should use a mask, but I thought, *Hey, I don't breathe, what do I need a* mask *for?* Turns out pires *do* breathe, kind of. We use air when we talk. Guess I talk too much, huh?" He laughs at his own joke, which turns into a fit of coughing.

The thrope is over at the nurse's station, trying to get her attention. He can't sign with only one hand, so he's waving his detached limb around like he's trying to hail a cab. I guess having it sewn back on is faster than waiting to grow a new one.

I'm finally shown to an examination room, which looks pretty much like an examination room should. The tongue depressors are made of plastic. A pire doctor shows up, dressed in a suit as opposed to scrubs, and examines my arm carefully before grabbing the cross and yanking it out. I stifle a scream and the urge to punch him in the face. He seems surprised and a little fascinated by how much blood is pumping out, but he gets a tourniquet applied and then produces a suture kit. No anesthetic, just some amateur needlework—I wonder if this guy has ever stitched up anything he didn't wear afterward.

I ask him for some painkillers when he's done. He frowns, tells me he isn't sure they have anything "appropriate" in stock, then looks thoughtful and tells me he'll be right back.

I spend the next twenty minutes gritting my teeth and watching blood seep through my bandage. When he finally comes back, he has a small brown glass bottle in one hand. The label reads: LAUDANUM. FOR HUMAN USE. DO NOT EXCEED MORE THAN THREE DOSES PER DAY.

I grab the bottle and stuff it in my pocket, thank Dr. Jekyll, and head for home. On the way there, I pick up a bottle of extremely strong whiskey—partly for the pain, partly for disinfection. Some of the doc's instruments looked dusty.

I keep the Blood Cross. Never know when something like that might come in handy.

Alcohol on this world is usually laced with magic; necessary for beings normally immune to any kind of poison. The nonalchemical stuff is available to those who just want to enjoy the flavor, but in my exhausted and injured state I grabbed the wrong kind. I only had one drink after I got home, but it hit me hard—magicked-up booze isn't any stronger percentage-wise, but it always seems to get you drunk in some epic sort of way. You know, the call your high school boyfriend at 3:00 AM, pick a fight with the bouncer, tell your boss what you really think of him kind of way. Me, I just pass out in the bathtub fully clothed.

My cell phone wakes me up. I'm sore, I'm cold, my arm feels like it still has a piece of metal stuck in it, and my head hurts. "Hello?" I croak.

"Jace." It's my boss. Oh, joy. "Where are you? Charlie

says you left the office hours ago and he hasn't seen you since."

"Home. Had a minor problem to deal with."

"I need to talk to you. Get over here as soon as you can."

"Yeah. Sure. Be right there." He hangs up.

I clean myself up, change the dressing, put on some clothes that aren't covered in blood. Food can wait, but caffeine is a must; I put on a pot before my shower and slam back a mug on my way out the door. Ah, the glamorous life of a crimebuster.

Cassius is waiting for me in his office. He looks mildly perturbed, which could mean anything; Cassius is a master of projecting whatever emotion he thinks is useful in a given situation. Like they say in show business, the secret to success is sincerity—when you can fake that, you've got it made.

He's sitting behind his desk, and motions me to take a chair. "Jace. I need to know how the Aquitaine investigation is coming along."

"Slowly. When were you planning on telling me—"

"That Aquitaine was one of the Bravo Brigade? I wasn't—because I just found out myself." His voice is brisk. "The Bravo Brigade operation was highly compartmentalized. The operators we used—the Bravos themselves— were all powerful and secretive people. None of them was interested in becoming a public figure, and they only agreed to co-operate under the condition they be allowed to vanish afterward. Their actual identities were concealed at all times."

I nod. It makes my head ache. "You must have suspected something when you saw him in that costume, though—"

He shakes his head impatiently. "I had no idea. Comic books—there haven't *been* any since the *Seduction* murders, and apparently this Flash character doesn't exist in this reality even as fiction. All I was thinking of was

Gretchen's welfare, not the possibility that the victim was some long-forgotten crimefighter."

"How's she doing?"

"She acts as if nothing's wrong at all. Her spine could be used to shore up bridges."

"How about on the intelligence front? Information on the Brigade is pretty thin, and I really need to talk to these people."

"That's—not a good idea, Jace." He meets my eyes levelly. Pires don't actually have to blink—though most do as a simple reflex—and when Cassius wants to unnerve someone he deliberately stops himself from doing so. It's a good trick, but it's more effective when Anthony Hopkins does it as Hannibal Lecter—he at least looks like a psychopath, while Cassius bears a closer resemblance to a California surfer boy barely out of his teens. "For one thing, most of the files on the Brigade were destroyed—it was a precondition they insisted on. For another—well, let's just say that many of the arrangements the NSA works under rely on mutual cooperation and trust. We don't go back on our word, ever—it's a matter of credibility."

I understand. Cassius is saying that if he'd known the Bravo Brigade was involved, he'd never have asked me to investigate in the first place—there are too many skeletons rattling around in too many closets, and just because one of them has fallen out wearing scarlet spandex doesn't mean I should go around yanking open doors. All that would have been fine with me . . . except for Gretchen.

"So you're just going to leave her twisting in the wind?" I ask. "Too bad your baby's father is dead, government secrets involved, stiff upper lip?"

"No. I won't do that to Gretchen. I don't abandon my people."

"So you can't help me—but you don't want me to stop investigating."

"That's correct." He regards me calmly.

I rub my temples with my index fingers. "Sure. Yeah. No problem. Did I happen to mention I ran into the Solar Centurion yesterday?"

He raises his eyebrows. "I wondered if he was still alive. What did he say?"

"Nothing. Just showed up to spread a little sunshine in my life, I guess. Disappeared before I could talk to him."

Cassius nods. "Then it appears you're on the right track. Keep me apprised."

That seems to signal the conversation is over, so I pull myself to my feet and try not to look as if my arm's about to fall off.

"One more thing," Cassius says. "I have a charity event I'm supposed to attend on Wednesday and I'd rather not go alone—are you available?"

I frown. "Pretty sure my calendar is open. Do I have to dress up?"

"A dress would appropriate, yes. Bill it to the Agency if you don't have one."

Never say no to a government handout. "Yeah, sure. As long as the case doesn't catch fire."

"Good. See you then."

As I leave the office, my slightly befuddled brain asks me if I realize my boss just asked me out on a date. "Don't be ridiculous," I mutter to myself as I go in search of more coffee. Probably just did it to keep me off balance —bastard always has at least three strategies going at the same time.

Which leads me to wonder—considering the conversation we just had, exactly what does he want me off balance about?

SIX

"Think I got something for you," Charlie says, strolling up to me in the little kitchenette the office staff uses as a break room. "Parole officer in Topeka told me about a skip tracer named Silverado. Might just be the Quicksilver Kid."

"Topeka?"

"What, you don't have one in your world?"

"We do. That's why I sounded so enthusiastic."

"And here I thought it was my new suit." Charlie's wearing a charcoal-gray number, double-breasted, with matching hat and lizard-skin spats. He looks like he's on his way to a Mickey Spillane convention. "Anyway, Silverado isn't in Topeka. He's currently in our neck of the woods."

"Which neck, exactly?"

Charlie studies me for a second before replying. "Forget about necks. What's wrong with your arm?"

Damn. I'm wearing a long-sleeved jacket, but he must have noticed I'm favoring my wounded flipper; not much gets by Charlie. "Had a little accident with a sharp implement. Us clumsy humans, we're always damaging ourselves—"

He reaches over and grabs my wrist—not hard, just

firmly. I instinctively try to yank free, and even more instinctively yelp with pain as I put pressure on my stitches.
He lets go and frowns. "Let's see it, Valchek."

I surrender to the inevitable and roll up my sleeve. "It's
just a scratch."

"Peel back the bandage."

I do. He inspects the stitches with the practiced eye of
a battlefield veteran, which he is. "Hmmm. Kind of
sloppy. Do it yourself?"

"I don't do needlepoint."

"Neither does whoever sewed you up. What happened?"

"This." I pull the Blood Cross from my pocket and toss
it on the desk. "Got into a little disagreement with some
wrappers. He tossed this and I cleverly caught it with my
forearm."

Charlie picks up the cross, gives it a quick once-over,
then slips it into his pocket.

"Hey! Find your own damn war souvenir!"

"Don't worry, I'll take good care of it." His voice is as
hard and cold as a January sidewalk. "Right until I return
it to its owner."

The situations I encounter in my job can produce the
most eclectic combination of emotions, and Charlie's
statement is a prime example: I feel touched by his loyalty
but a little afraid of the controlled fury in his voice. I forget sometimes that Charlie is more than my partner; he's
my enforcer, a living weapon whose job is to protect me
and damage anyone who gets in my way. Having Charlie
around is like being shadowed by a hit man with a chip
on his shoulder and a crush on you.

"Easy, sandman. The pire in question won't be hurling
anything for a while, not unless he's ambidextrous."

"Details."

I give him the rundown on the confrontation and what

Tair told me about Dr. Pete, ending with the appearance of the Solar Centurion.

Charlie frowns. "He was following you."

"Unless those wrappers actually worship Ra the sun god, I'm inclined to agree. But he intervened on my behalf—not the actions of a guilty man trying to impede an investigation."

"Unless he's trying to mislead you."

"Could be. If and when he shows up again, I'll ask him. In the meantime we have a skip tracer to trace."

"Maybe we should look into Dr. Pete first."

I narrow my eyes. "No. We have an active case, and that's the priority. My accidental involvement with some half-assed gangsters spouting a wild story is not important. Now—where are we off to?"

Charlie's stubborn, but he knows better than to lock horns with me. "Granite Falls. It's about an hour away, in the foothills of the Cascades."

"Okay. Why is Silverado there—got a cabin in the woods or something?"

"He's working. On the trail of a guy named Helmut Wiebe, indicted for running a Cloven lab. Wiebe's from the area and is supposedly hiding out there."

"Got it. Let's go—I'll get Gretch to forward me the files while we're on the road." I slap my laptop closed, trying not to wince as I do so. Charlie watches me carefully, but doesn't say anything.

Granite Falls is a foothills town of about thirty thousand people. It's also the site of the Tsubaki Grand Shrine School, a major Shinto center where acolytes go to study. Like any college town, it has a drug problem, and since Shinto seems to attract pires that drug is Cloven, or Devil's Hoof: methamphetamine cut with garlic, just as nasty and addictive as good old regular meth is in my world. The difference between a hoofer and a crankhead is that a wired hemovore is just as likely to disembowel you to play with your intestines as he is to go into a laughing jag at the sight of his own.

Wiebe's file indicates he was a fairly major player in the area, cooking up high-quality product for the local market and even a little for export. He got into trouble when one of his rivals informed on him, shutting down his operation at a time he was financially overextended; he was forced to use a bail bondsman to get out of jail, then decided it was cheaper to forfeit the bond than risk going to prison.

Gretchen dug up plenty on Wiebe, but the pickings are extremely slim on Silverado. Licensed bail enforcement agent, but his license doesn't list his date of birth—or in a lem's case, date of activation. His home address is a post office box, his phone number a cell. Obviously, Mr. Silverado is a golem who appreciates his privacy; our best chance of tracking him down is to track down Wiebe first.

Which could be tricky. Wiebe is from Granite Falls, and his brother, Julian, is one of the priests at Tsubaki. If Julian is protecting his brother, we could be in for some major headaches, both political and supernatural. A Shinto priest is Gandalfian on the wizard scale.

Granite Falls lies at the beginning of the Mountain Loop Highway, a scenic route that winds through the Western Cascades and over the Barlow Pass to Darlington—too bad we're not going that way. We get on the I-5 to Everett and go east, taking Highway 2 then switching to the 204. The landscape is nice, lots of tall green pine and spruce lining the roads. After we pass through West Lake Stevens the countryside becomes a little more rural, cattle ranches or the occasional farm interrupting the tree line. A row of black Angus beef-on-the-hoof stare at me blankly as we drive past, chewing their cuds and thinking moody cow thoughts. I know how they feel.

At Frontier Village we head north on Highway 9, then onto the Granite Falls Highway. We turn off at Crooked Man Road, which leads to the massive red *tori,* the distinctive Japanese portal, of the school's entrance. We've timed our arrival to coincide with sunset—the school's alumni are mainly pires, and this is the beginning of their day.

The school is large and sprawling, the layout very organic and non-institutional. We find a parking lot almost completely hidden by trees and get out of the car.

"Where do you want to start?" Charlie asks me.

"Wiebe's brother is head of the Aikido Department. Let's go see if he's in."

I take a deep breath of air, enjoy the heady aroma of pine. I'm a city gal, but I can appreciate natural—or in this case, carefully tended—splendor as much as the next person. We stroll through a Japanese garden of elegant plants and night-blooming flowers, over an arched wooden bridge and past clusters of students hurrying to classes. Ages vary widely; I see women with 1940s hairdos and polka-dot skirts alongside men in kimonos and teenagers wearing jeans and sweatshirts. There are also more thropes than I expected, many of them in full were form, loping along with book bags strapped to their backs. I remark on this to Charlie.

"Not so surprising," he says. "Lot of hemovores are into Shinto, but the Northwest has more thropes than pires. Lot of thropes from the Midwest come here to study, too. Like the climate, I guess."

Makes sense. There are plenty of Asian faces, but lots of non-Asian ones, too—Shinto is a global belief system now, vying with African witchcraft for popularity.

We find the Aikido Studies building, a low-slung

structure with a pagoda roof. Inside, students in loose-fitting white clothing are paired off, practicing throws, holds, and strikes. Aikido is particularly well suited to pires; much of the art consists of techniques designed to protect the practitioner from cutting blows to the neck or thrusting attacks to the torso. It's popular in the Shinto movement because of its emphasis on the integration of spirit with nature, of inner harmony. It's also one of the most peaceful of all martial arts—the intent of most Aikido techniques is to redirect an opponent's force without harming him.

We stand at the back of the room and watch for a while. A bubble of unexpected sadness rises up in me; I haven't been to a dojo since I came to this world. The familiarity of the outfits, the atmosphere, makes me nostalgic—but only until I see an actual attack and counter. A black female pire who appears to be in her twenties faces off against an Asian woman of indeterminate age. The flurries of blows, feints, and blocks are so quick they're only a blur; it reinforces my sadness, making me feel like an ex-heavyweight being reminded of his glory days. Ridiculous, of course—pires' reaction times are simply better than a human being's.

All the more reason to get back to the gym. If I run into a pire—or a thrope, for that matter—with any martial arts training at all, I'm so far past toast even charcoal would consider me burnt. I promise myself I'll start looking for a dojo when we get back to Seattle.

The melancholy lingers, though. It makes me think of my sensei, a beat-up ex-marine named Duane Dunn; wide grin, thick white handlebar mustache, and more wrinkles than God. His gut makes him look like he spends more time on the couch than the gym, but he's in better shape than guys I know in their twenties who run marathons. Duane would probably do a lot better here than I am—he loves a challenge more than anything. "The only thing better than winning a fight," he used to say, "is getting the snot kicked out of you by someone better than you are."

"I think that's him," Charlie says. "The brother."

I look, but only catch a glimpse of someone in baggy black pants and a loose white top vanishing through a doorway. "Come on."

We hurry after him. "Did he see us?" I ask.

"Not sure."

The door leads to a hallway lined with offices. No sign of Julian, and with a pire's speed he could have reached the end of the hall and turned the corner by now. I curse under my breath and break into a trot. "Check the offices!" I call back over my shoulder.

Down the hall, around the bend, down another corridor. At the end, right or left? This place is a maze. I go right. More hallway, more offices. I should stop running, this is pointless, I must have lost him by now. Another branch, go right again. Keep going right in a maze and you'll always find your way out, but what if he isn't heading for the exit?

And then I see the fire door straight ahead me, just clicking shut.

Doesn't mean a thing, of course, but I slam into it at full tilt anyway, hitting the bar with my hip and flinging the door open with a bang.

Julian Wiebe glances at me in surprise. He's dressed in loose black trousers and a wraparound white jacket, his wispy blond hair ruffled by the evening breeze, and he's in the act of handing an envelope to his brother. Helmut, wearing black jeans just as baggy and a puffy jacket just as white, looks like he's making fun of his sibling's fashion sense. The look on his face, though, is closer to angry suspicion than mockery.

"You set me up!" he cries, and bolts down the path.

I give chase, which means running past Julian—except that he grabs me when I get within reach and does something very quick that leaves my arm locked behind my back. Damn it.

"I'm a federal agent," I snap. "Let me go, *now*."

I can't see Julian's face, but I can hear the conflict in his voice. "I—he's my *brother*—"

"Then don't make things *worse* for him—"

"Too late for that," a voice says.

Helmut marches back into view up the path. He's got one arm locked behind him, too, and a gleaming silver knife at his throat. His captor is a golem dressed in black jeans, a fringed brown rawhide jacket, and a battered straw cowboy hat with the brim curled up on the sides. His face is a pockmarked bronze, sculpted into a grim expression and hinged at the jaw.

"Let the lady go," Silverado says.

"Let my brother go."

"Don't think so."

I still have one arm free. I reach for my gun—and Julian puts just enough pressure on my arm to make me gasp and freeze.

"Looks like we have us a situation," Silverado says. "'Cept you ain't no killer, Mr. High Priest. And a broken arm don't mean much to a thrope."

True, but despite Silverado's best guess that's not what I am. Broken arms *do* heal, though . . . I wonder if I should go for my gun anyway. As long as I can ignore the blinding pain, I should be able to shoot him. Of course, I didn't really come here to turn one of the school's educators into a pile of smoking dust.

"You don't know who you're messing with," Helmut growls. "*Show* him, Jules."

"Let. Him. *Go,*" Julian says, and extends one hand, palm up and fingers spread, toward his brother.

The area we're standing in is a little wooded park, with two benches and a waterfall trickling over a boulder and into a rock-edged pool. At Julian's gesture, the waterfall's trickle becomes a gush, a cascade—and then the flow of water *bends* in midair, as if an invisible drainpipe has just been stuck under the flow. It surges toward Julian and Silverado, splashes at their feet, then winds around their legs like a watery anaconda.

"Lems don't need to breathe any more'n pires do," Silverado says calmly.

"Water can do more than drown," Julian answers.

He's right. The stream of water that's curling around them redirects itself so that it's only wrapped around Silverado's body. Then it condenses, looking more like a silvery blue tube than a torrent of liquid. I hear metal creak, and think of submarines at the bottom of the ocean. I have no doubt Julian has enough power to crush Silverado's metal shell like an egg.

"And silver can cut more than meat," the lem says. He slashes downward with the big, bowie-style knife at one of the aquatic loops coiled around him, and cuts it in two.

Julian bellows in pain as the snake bursts like a water balloon, releasing me as he collapses. Helmut, the knife no longer at his throat, breaks free and lunges forward. I try to stop him and get a quick lesson in pire versus human strength, as I go from being one Wiebe's captive to another. Julian is facedown on the path, knocked out by some kind of psychic backlash.

"I'm not as subtle as my brother," Helmut snarls. "Let me go or I'll just rip her head off." He's got me around the throat with one arm, his fingers hooked around my upper teeth with the other. I don't know if he's actually strong enough to do that, but I smell the acrid stink of Cloven on his fingers and know he's crazed enough to try.

Silverado holds the knife by the blade, handle up. I can

tell from his stance he's getting ready to throw, and I really don't think he can take Helmut out with me in the way.

"Don't do it," Charlie says.

Helmut whirls to the side, taking me with him. I can taste dirt and nicotine on his fingers. Charlie's just come through the fire door, and his own throwing arm is cocked. He's got one of the iron-cored, silver-coated ball bearings he favors in one hand, and I know from experience he can bull's-eye a beer can at a hundred feet.

The bounty hunter and my partner study each other, me stuck in the middle. *This* should be fun . . .

"Either of you moves," Helmut warns, "and she goes top-less." He's standing sideways, Charlie to the left, Silverado to the right.

Both of them ignore him. "Don't much care about the drug-runner," Charlie says.

"Don't much care about the lady," Silverado replies.

"She's my partner."

"He's my paycheck."

I pull out my gun and jam it in Helmut's ribs. "Lef me go, ooh muvvafugga," I manage. He glances down, but otherwise ignores me. Lovely.

"A shooter," Silverado says. "Interestin'. Prefer she didn't use it, though."

"Understandable. How about we do this so neither of them gets too banged up?"

"Works for me."

Silver flashes red in the last rays of twilight. Twin impacts sound, so close together they merge into one: half meaty *thunk,* half loud *crack.* Helmut screams, in a much higher pitch than his brother did, and both his arms go limp. Charlie's shattered the elbow on the arm that was around my throat, while Silverado's knife now juts from the meaty part of Helmut's other forearm. I dive forward, out of his grasp, and resist the urge to shoot him just for good measure.

"You still got legs," Silverado tells him. "You wanna keep on usin' em, I wouldn't run."

I spit, trying to get the taste of unwashed pire out of my mouth, and holster my pointless gun. "Jace Valcheck," I say to Silverado, and pull out my ID. "And this is Charlie Aleph. NSA."

"Silverado, bail enforcement agent. But that probably don't come as much of a surprise." He's already got Helmut in cuffs, and yanks his knife casually out of the pire's arm as he hauls him to his feet. He wipes the blood off on Helmet's jacket, then slides the knife into a leather bandolier across his chest that holds half a dozen more.

"We know who you are," Charlie says. He picks up the ball bearing from the ground, clicks it back into its spring-loaded holster up his sleeve.

I nudge Julian with my foot, but he's still out. "Nasty kick that knife of yours has."

Silverado regards me, expressionless—or rather, with the one expression he has. "Magic don't like silver much, Shinto or not."

"You don't disrupt an animist spell of that power by sticking it with a shiny piece of metal," I say. "Not even high-grade silver." Two months ago I wouldn't have known that, but I learn from my mistakes.

Charlie crosses his arms. "Not unless the blades have a little magic in them, too."

"Everything's got a *little* magic in it," Silverado says. "That's what magic's all about—that bit of spirit in each and every thing. Now, if you'll excuse me—"

"Or in your case," said Charlie, "seven things."

The bounty hunter pauses. "Uh-huh. I can see you folks want to talk. How about I secure my commission here and we do this somewhere civilized?"

"I'll go with you," Charlie says. "Wouldn't want you to get lost."

"And I'll deal with Mr. Wet N' Wild," I say. "I think he'll be a lot more reasonable when he comes to with a headache and his brother gone."

"I need a doctor!" Helmet abruptly wails. "I'm wounded!"

"Relax," Silverado says. "I got some first-aid supplies in my car—I ain't about to let you bleed all over my seats, anyway. And you're a pire, ain't you? Just pretend you dropped your tray at the buffet or somethin'."

He leads his prisoner away, Charlie following close behind. "I'll call you when we're squared away," Charlie says.

I nod, then kneel beside the comatose Shinto priest. I hope he's in a better mood when he wakes up.

He is—better being a relative term, of course. For instance, he's in a better mood than a mother grizzly who's watching you use one of her cubs as a soccer ball. He's even in a marginally better mood than he was when Silverado short-circuited his brain.

A *good* mood being in, he is not.

"Where is my *brother*?" he thunders at me. Literally; lightning bolts are dancing around his skull, arcing from eye to eye behind his head like an electric halo that was put on too loose and slipped down.

I stare at him coolly, my arms crossed. "On his way back to prison, where he belongs. You can join him, if you like—I don't think your little April showers routine will impress them much at Stanhope."

He glowers at me, but after a moment he takes a deep breath and then lets it out. The lightning fades. He looks more sad than angry now.

"Look," I say. "I understand you were only looking out for family. You weren't actually harboring him, and you attacked me before I'd clearly identified myself. All that is forgivable—*unless* I find out you and your brother were in business together."

Now he looks more shocked than shocking. "Absolutely not! I *begged* him to change his life—even got him accepted at the school! And then he was arrested for making that *poison . . .*" He looks away, ashamed.

I nod. "Okay. But if it turns out you're lying to me, and you and your brother wanted to turn this campus into your own private pharmaceutical outlet, my partner and I will be back. Count on it."

He doesn't reply, just hangs his head. Pretty convincing, but I'm the cynical sort. I'll have Gretch go over his history with a microscope, see if he holds up. "I'll be in touch," I say, and walk away down the path.

By the time I find the parking lot where we stashed the car, I've persuaded myself that Julian Wiebe is on the up-and-up. Not because I have any faith in the honesty of the religious establishment, but because magic's involved. Shinto is all about connecting to nature, and there's no way the introduction of an artificial element like Cloven into the environment could go unnoticed by the other high-level shamans running the place.

I've been waiting in the car for about five minutes when my cell rings. Charlie gives me directions to a diner on the outskirt of Granite Falls, where he and Silverado will meet me.

There are only three vehicles parked at the diner when I pull in: a white minivan with a car seat and a BABY ON BOARD sticker, a flashy two-door Honda sports car, and a dusty black '68 Mustang with a loud thumping noise coming from the trunk. Guess I know where Silverado stashed his paycheck.

The diner's one of those places with lots of fake log paneling and deer heads on the walls, rows of booths down either wall and skinny little tables for two people at a time in the middle. I spot Silverado and Charlie at a booth in the far corner, two cups of coffee cooling in front of them. Lems don't eat or drink; their server must have made them order something. I slide into the booth beside Charlie and grab his—no sense letting it go to waste.

Silverado watches me without saying a word. He's taken his straw hat off, revealing something I haven't seen before: a lem with hair. It's short and curly, made of copper wire fine enough that it's been used for his eyebrows, too. His eyes are silver, his bronze features molded into permanent sternness. From this close, I can see that not only is his jaw hinged, but his lips are made of painted rubber. The paint is peeling, making them look chapped.

"Nice little mobile hoosegow you got out there," I say.

"Gets the job done."

The waiter, a pale, tubby pire with a combover, shuffles over and asks me if I'd like to order.

"Already have, thanks. But you only had to bring one coffee." I push the other one over to him. "This one's a mistake. Take it back."

Tubby blinks and says, "These two ordered those."

"I think you're confused," I say pleasantly. "That makes no sense. *Here's* what makes sense: My two friends came in to wait. They ordered a coffee for me, because they're considerate and thoughtful. You brought two by mistake, but they were far too polite to mention that. Then I showed up."

I put that special little edge in my voice that every law enforcement professional knows. "But I am *not* a polite person. I'm a cop. And I'm telling you that only *one* coffee should appear on our bill, not two. You following me?"

"Uh, yeah." He swallows. "You—you want anything else?"

"No, thank you." He grabs the coffee and turns tail, scuttling back to the kitchen where he can regale the cook with tales of his horrifying experience and how *those people* shouldn't be allowed in here.

"Mr. Silverado," I say. "Thank you for agreeing to talk to us."

"Talk's cheap. So is coffee, for that matter." He sounds more amused than impressed by my little blow for golem rights, but I don't care—it makes me crazy when people don't treat Charlie like a person.

"Silver isn't. Especially not enchanted silver—like the Seven Teeth of the Moon."

"Uh-huh. Or Excalibur, I guess. Or maybe that big mallet Thor uses for croquet when he ain't whipping up hurricanes."

"The Seven Teeth aren't myths, Silverado. You've got them right there on that bandolier."

He hasn't moved anything other than his lips; even though I'm used to Charlie, the bounty hunter's complete stillness is a little unnerving.

"Let me save you some time," he says. "First off, the only magic these here blades have in 'em are what sharpness spells I can afford on a bounty hunter's wage. And second, they ain't for sale." He pauses. "Sentimental value."

"Right," Charlie says. "You seem like a real sentimental guy."

"I cry at the movies."

"Yeah," Charlie says levelly. "Me, too."

"We're not interested in your knives. We're here to talk about the Bravo Brigade."

"That so."

I resist the urge to say *yep*. "Doctor Transe is dead."

He doesn't say anything for a moment, but I have no idea what he's thinking. "That's a shame," he says at last. "What's it to do with me?"

"You fought alongside him. Don't you care?"

"I'm just an old lem trying to make a living. I don't know about—"

"Stop. You're the Quicksilver Kid and we both know it. Talk to me straight or I'll make sure no law enforcement agency ever works with you again."

Another pause. He turns his head slightly to look at Charlie. "She any good?"

"Best I've worked with," Charlie says.

"You're still young. Me, I've worked with legends. But then, I guess you two know that." He looks back at me. "And I'd kind of like to keep on working. So ask me what you're here to ask me."

I ask him where he was on the night of the murder; he tells me he was here, trying to pin down Helmut Wiebe. I ask him if he can prove it and he produces gas receipts from a battered leather wallet. Not conclusive, of course—he didn't stay in a motel, and Seattle's an hour's drive away.

"Transe was killed with something sharp and silver," I say. "Sound familiar?"

"You have a shaman study the body, I take it?"

"Of course."

"Then you know it wasn't one of my knives did the deed. They got an energy all their own, one as singular as a fingerprint. Your shaman find anything like that?"

"No."

"Doesn't mean much, though. Could have used another weapon, couldn't I?"

"Let's assume you didn't kill Transe. Who do you think did?"

"I'd put my money on John Dark, myself."

I frowned. "Who's that?"

"You don't know about John Dark? I guess you're not as far along the trail as I thought." He puts his elbows on the table and leans forward slightly. "John Dark was Wertham's second in command. He vanished at the same time Wertham did, but with one big difference: He's been seen alive since."

"Cali Edison told me she was the only survivor."

"Yeah? Well, you shouldn't take everything ol' Cali says at face value. She's got a nasty way of turning on you."

"I noticed." There's an odd smell coming off Silverado that I haven't been able to identify; I abruptly realize it's sewing machine oil, like the kind my grandmother used to use on her old Singer. "What makes you so sure that Dark survived and Wertham didn't?"

"Saw him die. Right in front of me, in fact."

"Yeah? Who killed him?"

"Don't see how that matters now. Wasn't me, if that's what you mean."

"Then who?"

"You got any other questions, or are we done?"

Interesting. I get the feeling that he'd own up to it in a second if it were him, but he's protecting someone. "Tell me about John Dark."

"John Dark was the real boss of the cult. Wertham had the ideas, but Dark had the clout. Still does, in fact."

"Yeah? You know where he is?"

"Funny you should bring that up. I been hunting Dark a long time . . . kind of a hobby of mine, you might say. I understand he's somewhere in Washington State, maybe even Seattle. And then you two show up."

"Dark didn't send us," Charlie says.

"That may or may not be so. But even if he did, you might not be aware of it. Just the thing to slow an old cowboy down . . ."

"You don't seem too slow to me," I say.

"Slow, no. But old? When I replace a part, I could sell the worn-out piece as an antique."

"You sure could," said Charlie. "Except your parts don't wear out, do they? You're factory original, right down to your refill plug."

"Not true. I've got more patches than an old tire."

"Maybe so," I say, "but when you leak, it's not sand that comes out. It's quicksilver—which is how you got your name. And somehow, I don't think your mind is any slower than your draw."

"So I'm not stupid. Thanks, I guess."

"I didn't say you were a genius. I just meant you think like a cop."

He turns his head ever so slightly to study me. "That I do," he says. "Some folks say I think like a rattler, all speed and venom, but that's not the truth. I was built to be a lawman, and that's what I am."

"Laws change," Charlie says.

"That they do. Me, I try to stick with what I know; they might call me something different now, but I'm still doing the same job. Tracking down bad men and bringing them back to face justice."

"Yeah," I say. "That's what we do. Takes a lot of patience, doesn't it? People don't get that—they think about cops, they think about bravery, alertness, determination. They don't understand how much of the job is just about *waiting*."

"That's true." He pauses, a pause that gets longer and longer. I don't say anything to break it—that would contradict what I just said.

"There was this one time," he says, "when I was set up watching an old barn. Young girl had been kidnapped, and I thought she might be inside. Problem was, I didn't know if the kidnapper was, and he had detection spells rigged to let him know if anyone came snooping around. I tripped one of those, I could scare him off and cost the girl her life.

"So I waited." A fly lands on his face, crawls to the corner of his lip. He ignores it completely. "It was a hot day. She'd been missing a few days already, and I wondered if she was on the main floor or up in the hayloft. Ever been in a hayloft on a summer day? Heat rises up, gets trapped against the rafters. Like a big oven.

"I waited all day. Waited all night. Waited until noon the next day. No sign of the kidnapper, no sound from inside. Didn't know if the kidnapper was going to come back at all—in fact, he never did. Finally had to leave without ever going in. Ran him down two weeks later, spending the ransom in a bar in Laredo; thought he was free and clear."

"And the girl?" I ask.

"Oh, she was in the barn all along. Knew it before I left."

"If you didn't go inside, how—"

"The smell."

Right.

It's a horrifying story, but I understand why he told it. Every cop has a story like that, usually more than one, and it's one of things that binds us together. I might not have done the same thing in the same situation, but I knew what it was like to face that kind of choice.

"And the perp?" I ask. "He get what he deserved?"

"Watched him hang a month later. So did the girl's parents, for what good it did."

"Yeah," I say. "Cold comfort."

"Sometimes that's all there is."

There's another pause, this one not as long, and when he continues it's in a matter-of-fact voice. "Dark's a pire, born in 1431 or thereabouts. Powerful shaman, likes the African stuff. Spent most of the last six hundred years or so behind the scenes—he's a mover and a shaker, but he doesn't like people seeing him pull the strings." He falls silent.

"That's it?" I ask. "Kind of thin."

"He's a thin man. That's how he likes it."

There's more, but Silverado isn't going to give it to me. I switch subjects. "Tell me about taking down the Kamic cult."

"You've read the comic, haven't you?"

"I'd like a more direct version."

I sense he'd shrug if he could, but he just isn't built for it. "They'd already killed a bunch of folks. Dark had them set up in this old mansion on the side of a mountain, and they were fixing to kill a bunch more. We busted in and stopped them. That's about all there was to it."

"What about the power Wertham had accumulated? The comic said Transe redirected it into a volcano, making it erupt."

"Sure. Mount Saint Helens. Wasn't much of a blowup, but enough lava oozed out to destroy the house. We were all gone by then."

"You still in touch with any of them?"

"Not for years. Shame about Transe, though—he seemed all right to me."

"How about the others? You have any problems with them?"

He leans back in the booth. "We weren't exactly a close-knit bunch. I never knew the real names of any of the others, and I didn't want to. We were there to do a job, and that's just what we did. And speakin' of jobs, I'd kinda like to get back to mine."

"One more question. If John Dark was the real force behind the Kamic cult, who led the Bravos?"

He picks up his straw hat from the seat, snugs it down over his copper curls. "That'd be the Solar Centurion. He was definitely the man in charge—and if anybody knew where the rest of the Bravos are, it'd be him."

He gets out of the booth, moving with a clockwork

kind of precision. He looks back and nods at Charlie. "Good arm you got there."

"You, too," Charlie says.

The Quicksilver Kid turns and strides out of the diner. A moment later I hear the roar of the Mustang's motor as he burns out of the parking lot.

"Think he was telling the truth?" I say.

"Not all of it," Charlie answers.

SEVEN

When we get back to Seattle, I ask Gretchen to meet me in the break room. She's taken a close look at Julian Wiebe and gives him the all-clear; if he's involved in anything shady she can't find a trace of it. I give her the lowdown on what we discovered about John Dark, and she tells me she'll do a little more digging.

I ask her how she's doing. She tells me she's fine, but she seems a little distracted, not her usual razor-sharp self. Now may not be the best time to ask her about this, but I can't just ignore what Tair told me.

"Gretch, how long have you known Dr. Pete?" I blow on my cup of coffee, trying to make the question sound more intimate than professional.

Gretchen raises her eyebrows and takes a sip of her own tea before answering. "He's been with the Agency for several years. I don't know much about him personally."

That would be a perfectly reasonable answer coming from anyone else—but it's Gretchen's job to know everything she can about people, and she's very good at it. Her saying she doesn't know much about someone is like a master chef being vague about the ingredients in a soufflé.

"Any idea what he did before that?" I keep my tone light. Gretchen studies me for a second before answering.

"Well, he was a doctor, of course. Exactly what are you getting at?"

"It's been brought to my attention that he may have been involved in a less-than-legal enterprise." My own voice sounds stiff and unnatural. God, I hate doing this; investigating people I know makes me feel like some kind of peeping Tom.

Gretchen shakes her head. "Well, he is an NSA operative. Many of our people have skeletons in their closets, and Agency policy dictates that is exactly where they should stay. Whatever he's done, it's in the past." Her voice is firm, and I realize I've crossed some kind of governmental spook line. Asking questions is what I do for a living—but apparently, I'm not supposed to ask those questions about the people I work with.

"Yeah, of course," I say. "He's entitled to his privacy. I'm just worried about him, that's all—I think someone from his past has popped up."

"I'll pass that along to Cassius. We take care of our own, Jace."

Sure. Choosing whether or not you want to *become* one of the gang isn't always an option, but once you're here we're all one big, loyal family. I wonder if Dr. Pete signed up of his own free will, or if he was dragooned the way I was. If I want to find out, I'll obviously have to do so from some source other than Gretchen.

"One last thing," I say. "I'd like to talk to the shaman who brought me over."

"Why?"

"Because the evidence suggests the killer may be from my world. If so, I need to talk to someone with expertise in these matters." If what Neil told me is true, the killer is actually more likely to be someone from here who's simply been spying on my world—but I don't mention that. I have my own reasons to talk to him.

"That could prove difficult." She glances away as she takes another sip of tea. "It takes a very high-level shaman to perform that sort of transfer, and, no offense, but I'm not sure you're cleared for that information. The Agency frowns on transfer subjects being in touch with the shaman that performed the procedure, in any case." She smiles apologetically.

She's lying.

Gretch is good, but her body language gives her away. In fact, she may be *so* good that she's doing it deliberately, sending me a message she hopes I'll pick up but no one else will—and if that sounds paranoid, you haven't spent much time around the intelligence community.

I meet her eyes and nod. "I understand. Thanks anyway."

She holds my gaze for just a second longer than she should. "Not at all. I'll see if I can find someone more appropriate for you to consult."

Her expression softens. "And Jace—I appreciate all you're doing."

"Just doing my job," I say.

I find Damon Eisfanger where he usually is, up in his lab. He's got Saladin Aquitaine's green skeleton on a stainless-steel table, and a small jar in one hand; he's moving the jar in slow circles over the rib cage, muttering something under his breath in a language I don't recognize as he does so.

He looks over as I come in. "Hey, Jace."

"Hey, Eisfanger. Find anything new?"

He shrugs. "Hard to say. Thought I'd try a different approach—I'm interrogating the lightning itself."

"The body's still electrified?"

"Oh no—I drained that all off into a battery." He holds up the small jar. "I needed a good medium to talk to it, though, so I transferred some to this."

A pickled frog regards me dolefully from inside the jar.

It's definitely not alive, but there seems to be a certain spar-kle in its eyes just the same. "You electrified a dead frog?"

"Sure. It's the animist equivalent of adding a reagent to a chemical solution. The flesh of the frog acts as both a conductor and a translator, giving the lightning a more organic expression. That's the problem with talking to pure energy—its experience is so far removed from our own it can be hard to understand the language."

"But zombie amphibian you're fluid in."

He grins at me. "Technically, it's the one in fluid . . . but yeah, I can understand what it's saying."

"Which is?"

"That the lightning was generated by a storm, not magic. It remembers arcing downward into some kind of metal rod, and then bouncing around until it was released into the body. Magic was used to direct it, but it was cre-ated in the sky."

"How would that be different from other magic-based methods?"

"Some animists would call a lightning bolt directly from a storm. Most would use house current if they wanted to store it for later—raw lightning is harder to work with. This is the work of an experienced animist with a great deal of control."

I nod. "I'll keep that in mind. How would you say this animist would compare—in terms of power and expertise—with the one that brought me over?"

He frowns. "I'm not sure. I mean, somebody doing an interdimensional transfer is definitely in the same league, but it's apples and oranges—the type of energy involved is very different. I'd have to know more about the indi-vidual capabilities of both animists—"

"So? He's on the payroll, isn't he? Take a look at his file."

"I can try, but I don't know if I have the clearance for that."

"Go ahead—I'll wait."

He uses a workstation in the corner, and I resist the urge to follow him and look over his shoulder. Any information Eisfanger gives me will depend on him thinking this is routine; I don't really expect it to work, but any data at all will help.

"Huh," he says. "This is odd."

"What is?" I move a little closer, trying not to seem eager.

"Well, I'm looking at our animist database, and you're not in it. I mean, it looks like the transfer wasn't done by one of our people at all."

So Cassius went to an outside resource. Interesting. He'd told me that the reason I was selected had more to do with chance than design, that I was simply in the right metaphysical time and place; now I wonder if that was true. "Damon, it's starting to look as if the guy that brought me over may actually be connected to the Aquitaine case. I need to find him."

He spins around on the chair to face me. "Well, I don't know if I can help you find him, but I might be able to help you ID him."

"How?"

He gets to his feet. "Basic animist forensics. The more powerful the magic, the better the chance it'll leave trace behind—some minute bit of energy from the process. A really powerful spell—like the kind that breaches dimensional barriers, for instance—will usually leave traces of the shaman's life force, as well."

"Like a mystical fingerprint."

"More or less—it's how I got a positive ID on Aquitaine. I took a sample from the lightning, too, but the caster isn't in our database. I can run some tests on you and see if your guy is, though."

The tests start with Eisfanger telling me to take all my clothes off and stand in a circle marked on the lab floor. I raise my eyebrows at this, but he's completely serious and not at all embarrassed—something I take as a sign of professionalism as opposed to someone setting me up for a prank. I highly doubt Eisfanger would try to pull something like that, anyway; I think he's actually a little scared of me.

Once in the circle, I pretend I'm being examined by a doctor. A doctor who's swinging an actual shrunken head in a circle by the hair with one hand and blowing a cloud of red dust at me from the palm of the other, but still a professional.

There's a stack of envelopes and a jar full of cotton swabs at my feet. He tells me to swab my forehead, my throat, my chest, my belly, my groin, and the small of my back, and to put the swabs in the marked envelopes. When I'm done, he says I can get dressed, grabs the envelopes, and takes them over to a table with an iron brazier on it. He turns on a hooded fan, then lights a small fire beneath the brazier.

I watch him burn the swabs one by one, checking data on a monitor as he does so. "Fume hood has a filter in it made of spiderwebs," he tells me as I pull on my boots. "Very sensitive to magic emanations. The rate the web vibrates at corresponds to readings in our files."

I finish dressing and come over to stand behind him. "And the powder?"

"Psychically magnetized. The dust that collected on your chakra points should be charged with any residual animist signature."

He studies the screen and frowns. "This can't be right."

"What?"

"The reading I'm getting. Not only is this guy not in our database, the flavor is all wrong. It's . . ." He shakes his head. "There must be something wrong with the equipment."

"Tell me what the problem is."

"The kind of magic used to yank you from your world

to ours is most likely some version of HPLC—High Power Level Craft. But these traces are very close to what you'd see from a low-level animist, the kind of guy that does mass-production at a lem activation plant."

"What are you saying? Are you trying to tell me I'm a golem?"

"No, no, no. I'm trying to tell you only a five-star general gets to play around with these kinds of forces, and I'm finding the signature of a buck private. Although . . ." He frowns at the screen and moves a little closer, as if he can make the data change through sheer force of will. "These readings aren't exactly normal for a lem maker, either. The pattern's close, but it's sort of primitive. I guess something this simple might be able to support higher levels of power, but I don't think anyone's used this kind of configuration in hundreds of years."

Great. Whoever brought me over is apparently unknown, ancient, and ignorant, as well as being unavailable. It's a wonder I didn't pop out at the bottom of the ocean or something. "Thanks, Eisfanger. I appreciate it."

"Sorry I couldn't be of more help."

"You did your best. Tell anyone you saw me naked and I'll decapitate you with a rusty chain saw. Bye."

He has the grace to simply swallow as opposed to saying anything as I leave.

As if I don't have enough to think about, tonight's my date with Cassius.

I go home and try to figure out what to wear. Nothing seems appropriate—I haven't bought a lot of clothes while I've been here, and everything I have is designed for either work or comfort. I decide I'll take Cassius up on his offer of a dress and go shopping.

I pick something that's elegant but not too sexy, that

shows a little leg but won't give him a heart attack. Well, that's not possible, but I don't want him to get the wrong idea.

Of course, I don't know what the right idea is, either. Cassius and I shared a moment while I was hunting Stoker, and I still haven't quite figured out what it means. I'm usually aware of when a man is interested, but it's a lot harder to do when that man is also a professional spook and who-knows-how-old vampire.

I decide not to get my hair done; instead I go home and dither about makeup, and finally refine the whole effect down to moderately attractive divorced-but-not-desperate soccer mom on a blind date. With a babysitter who has to be home by eleven.

Eleven AM, in this case. Cassius picks me up an hour after midnight, in a long black limo driven by someone behind smoked glass. No one gets out of the car to open the door for me, which is fine—but I realize I'm going to be doing this all night, evaluating every little signal or nonsignal for potential significance.

I slide into the backseat and give him a cool, appraising look. No tux, just a slightly sharper version of the suit he usually wears at the office. He smiles at me, but again, it's just a slightly less formal smile than I get first thing every day. "Hello, Jace. Thank you for coming."

"A free meal's a free meal." That sounds a little snarky, so I back off and give him a grudging smile. "Plus a free dress. Hope you like it."

He gives me a quick glance, more evaluating than admiring. "It's fine."

Fine. Well, that's what I was going for, so I guess I can't complain.

The charity event turns out to be a five-hundred-dollar-a-plate fund-raiser at the Space Needle, for a cause I endorse—or would, if I'd known it existed. "The Foundation for the Preservation of Human Art?" I say. "I thought it was the artists that were endangered."

"They are. But it's more convincing to point at a human-created masterpiece as evidence that human beings are worth saving. Easier to get people to cough up donations, too."

It's statements like this that make me realize why I find Cassius so intriguing. Cynical at first glance, but with a core of stubborn idealism beneath it. I think it's why he does what he does.

He's staring out the window as we drive, his mind apparently on something other than me. I find myself staring at him, at those blond curls, the fine line of his jaw, those blue eyes behind long lashes . . . how can something so ruthless be wrapped in such a pretty package?

He catches me looking. I smile, refusing to be embarrassed. He smiles back, a little warily.

"So," I say. "Why'd you invite me?"

Subtle as a battering ram, but I don't have the patience for the kind of games an immortal can get up to; I'll probably be applying for Social Security by the time he asks for a second date.

"The only other humans you've met since you've been here are criminals. I thought it might be nice to introduce you to some others."

"Ah. Some others of my own kind. How thoughtful." It's hard to keep the bitterness out of my voice, and I'm not even sure why it's there.

"I thought you'd be pleased."

"I am. It's just . . . never mind." I shake my head, irritated at my own irritation. "It's fine, really. Thank you."

We ride the rest of the way in silence.

I've never been to the Space Needle in my own world, but I've seen pictures; it's always reminded me of a flying

saucer landing on a water tower. This one features a revolving restaurant called the Eye of the Needle, a swanky
place reserved for the evening by the foundation. We ride
up in the elevator with two other couples, everyone dressed
better than we are. I feel a little like someone's going to
ask me to start serving drinks.

The restaurant itself is softly lit, white linen tablecloths
and flickering candles. Flat-screen TVs hang on the curv-
ing inside walls, slowly cycling through images of famous
paintings, sculptures, and architecture: van Gogh's *Sun-
flowers,* the ceiling of the Sistine Chapel, the Taj Mahal.
Mozart plays softly in the background. On my world the
place would have the ambience of an upscale but anony-
mous restaurant; here, it feels like I've wandered into a
memorial service. Everyone's dressed in black, mostly
tuxes and evening gowns, though I spot a few more conservative suits and dresses. Pires and thropes are milling
about, sipping alcoholized blood from wineglasses and
eating canapés made from raw meat.

There's a lectern set up, so I suppose there'll be
speeches. I hate speeches—but I find myself wondering
what exactly the speakers are going to say. Do they have a
catchy slogan? A mascot? Will they raffle off someone's
wooden leg?

Shut up, brain.

"Would you like a drink?" Cassius asks.

"Scotch, rocks. Unmagicked, if possible."

"I'm sure it is."

I glance around the room after he leaves, then get
closer to the windows for the view. The skyscrapers of
downtown Seattle glitter to the north, while the lights of
ships drift atop Elliott Bay to the west. If the sun were up,
I'd be able to see the Cascades, and even the snowy bulk
of Mount Rainier in the distance—but it isn't and I can't.
The entire room is revolving, so slowly as to be almost

subliminal; if I stare out at a fixed point, it's enough to produce a tiny surge of vertigo.

I go for a stroll, figuring Cassius will find me—the room's just a big loop, after all. I stop now and then to admire something shiny in the distance. I'm looking out at an alternating grid of yellow and white that must be a suburb when someone taps me on the shoulder.

"Long lineup at the—oh." It's not Cassius, it's a woman in a stunning cocktail dress that looks like it's made of rubies and held together by willpower. Her hair is so black I have a hard time seeing individual strands, her skin as pale as a bulimic on a Ferris wheel. You could use her stiletto heels to rotisserie a suckling pig, or maybe kill it in the first place.

"Hello, dear," she says, grinning at me with blood-stained teeth. "Are you *exhibiting* here tonight?"

"What? Uh, no."

"Oh, don't be shy," she purrs. She gestures with a wineglass, sloshing a little blood over the rim. "I *love* human artists. Your work is so—*poignant.* So suffused with loss and longing and fear of death."

"You seem a little suffused yourself," I say. "Excuse me."

She reaches out and grabs my arm, her grip gentle but very firm—like an adult restraining an unruly child. "No, you don't *understand,*" she says. "Human art—it *touches* me, it really does. Your lives are so *ephemeral,* but you compensate by, by packing it full of as many experiences as you *can.* That's so *sad.* I mean, it's brave and inspiring and intense, but it always seems to have this haunted, *doomed* quality—"

Much like this conversation. I didn't bring along my gun or my scythes, which is probably fortunate—right now I'd blow my own brains out to escape. Or, more likely, hers.

"—I'd be interested, *very* interested in anything you're producing. Whatever the medium—I don't care. I just think that investing, *supporting* human art is important."

"I see," I say. "May I have my arm back now?"

She glances at her own hand as if she's forgotten it was there, then lets me go. "Oh! I'm sorry—a little too much of the Baboon Beaujolais, you know?"

"That's perfectly all right. Look—" I lower my voice to a whisper. "—I *am* working on something—very new, very edgy—but I'm sort of incognito, okay? I don't want to be pestered by every collector here."

"Oh, of course, of *course*."

"I have some people I have to meet, but I'll drop by your table and give you a little sample before I leave, all right? If you promise not to tell anyone else."

Now she looks rapturous. "Yes, yes, I promise!"

I nod carefully at her. She nods back, then saunters away, trying to look casual.

"Well," says Cassius as he walks up. "I see you're making friends."

"Oh, absolutely. The only thing that would thrill my new friend more than buying up my art at discount prices would be for me to drop dead once the check cleared."

"Your art?"

"Sure. Can't you tell I'm one of those angsty creative types? Everyone else can." I grab my drink out of his hand and take a healthy swallow. Not bad for a blend. "Let's find our seats, shall we?"

The tables are set for four apiece; we're sharing with another couple, a man and woman in their sixties. They introduce themselves as Brian and Sherry Toban, and shake my hand; I realize that they're both human, though it's hard to say exactly what gives them away. Brian's glasses, maybe, or Sherry's pierced ears.

"A pleasure to meet you," Brian says. He's a tall, bulky man, with iron-gray hair. "New to Seattle?"

"How'd you know?"

"I haven't met you before. I try to keep track of all our people."

Makes sense. I don't know how many human beings actually live in Seattle, but it's not hard to believe they all know one another. "I'm something of a workaholic. I don't have much time for socializing."

"Which is why," Cassius says, "I dragged her out to-night."

"Good for you, David," Sherry says. She's a small, bird-like woman with bright eyes. "We're glad you're here, Jace. It's always interesting to see what David's up to these days." Her voice is a little too precise, with the careful enunciation of someone who's been drinking and is trying to compensate.

"Same as always," Cassius says.

"Not *quite* the same," Sherry says, and giggles.

"I'm off to the bar," Brian announces. "Anyone for another?" I realize he's more than a little drunk, too.

"What the hell," I say. "Scotch, rocks."

"Yes it does," Brian says, and lurches off with all the ponderous grace of a battleship.

Brian, it turns out, *is* an artist. A few of his pieces are even here, hanging beside the elevator. He introduces me to a few more of "the Clan," as he puts it, other humans in the local community. I meet an Asian couple who look very uncomfortable and barely speak English, an over-weight man in his fifties who tries to pick me up, and a nervous-looking woman who chain-smokes the entire time we're talking. Brian never stops drinking, but he never seems to get any drunker; I realize he must be a function-ing alcoholic, that his intake is as carefully regulated and habitual as a diabetic using insulin.

I find it hard to blame him. I'm only a tourist; he has to live here.

It's one of the strangest dates I've ever been on. With Brian and Sherry there, we can't talk shop, though there's no shortage of conversation; Brian is one of those affable guys with a million stories, and all you really have to do to hold up your side of the dialogue is smile and occasionally nod.

Sherry isn't quite as good at holding her liquor. From the thinly veiled glances and the remarks she keeps dropping, it seems she and Cassius were an item once. Cassius treats her more like a favorite aunt than an ex-lover, flirting with her in that toothless way attractive men use to flatter older women. It's affectionate and playful and makes me feel a little sick to my stomach.

I excuse myself and retreat to the bathroom. Running into an old flame on a date is never fun, but when she's old enough to be your mother . . . which is when she strolls in right behind me. From the sly look on her face, I can tell it's time for a little girl talk.

"So, Jace," she says, checking her makeup in the mirror. "Your first trip on the Night Train?"

"Excuse me?"

"Dating a pire. You're at that age—I was wondering if you're serious about David or just a tick-tocker."

"A what?"

She carefully reapplies her lipstick. "You haven't heard the term before? Someone who's thinking about quitting daylight. Locking in their current age before they get any more wrinkles. Or is it just a sex thing?"

"It's—I don't what kind of thing it is. I don't know if it's a thing at all."

"Ah. Well, it can be hard to tell with David. He plays his cards pretty close to his vest. I'm sure he's interested in you, though—you're his type."

"You're the second person to tell me that. What exactly is his type? Tall? Brunette? Or just breathing?"

She smiles at me. "He likes them scrappy, Jace. Underdogs that refuse to admit they're any such thing. That was me, once." She shakes her head, a little unsteady on her feet. "I could have done it, you know. Switched teams. But Brian changed my mind." She leans back against the tiled wall. "There's value to a life with an expiration date. Not that we know when it's coming, of course—just that it's on the way. Pires don't have that. They all have that teenage conviction that they'll never, ever die—and sometimes they're even right." She laughs, but it's not a happy sound. "But nobody lasts forever. Statistics catch up with everyone, that's what Brian says. Immortality is just a guarantee you'll die in some bizarre accident with a stupid look on your face."

"Cass—David seems to have avoided that."

"When the sun burns out, David will be the one hosting the Daylight Failing Times party. He's harder to kill than a rumor."

I probably shouldn't ask, but I can't resist. "So, you and David. What happened?"

Her smile fades. "Time, I suppose. Time and life and all those things that happen to us poor human beings. They didn't happen to him, not the same way—and I guess I just couldn't forgive him for that."

She pushes herself off the wall, pushing the past away at the same time and replacing it with a brisk smile. I see the kind of willpower that takes, and think I understand exactly what Cassius saw in this small, fierce woman.

"Enough of that," she says. "I'll ruin all the hard work I just put into my makeup. Come on—I'll buy you another drink."

"I think I've had enough for now, thanks."

"Suit yourself. I know I always do."

The food is reasonable—they serve me a meatless lasagna that Cassius must have ordered ahead of time. I stop drinking scotch and start drinking coffee, but regret it before too long; the speeches are boring and surreal at the same time, like some kind of performance art piece I don't quite get. Brian and Sherry don't stay until the end, and I don't blame them. Sherry gives me a wink as they leave.

"Well," I say. "Alone at last."

"I'm glad you came, Jace. There's something I want to talk to you about."

Uh-oh. "I'm listening."

"It's about Gretchen."

Not what I was expecting, but that's probably a good thing. "How's she doing?"

"Not very well, I'm afraid."

"Oh? The last time I talked to her she seemed fine."

"She's good at putting up a brave front. But this pregnancy . . ." He trails off. "I don't know if you understand just how enormous this is. Gretchen was turned when she was thirty-seven; she's been that way for over a century. Even if she cancels her time-debt to her child when he's eighteen, she'll have aged to a subjective fifty-five. And she'll have done it without a partner."

"Yeah, I get that. It's tough, but so is Gretch; if anybody can handle the single-mom thing, she can. And her job is secure, right?"

"Of course. But there's something else, something I don't think she's told you."

Now I'm starting to get a little worried. "Which is?"

"She and Aquitaine opted for a shorter pregnancy,

condensing it to four and a half months. With his death, the process has continued to accelerate."

"So how long?"

He shakes his head, looking grim. "Her doctor believes it could be as little as a few weeks, or even less. It's putting a tremendous strain on her body, but she refuses to take any time off from work. I was hoping maybe you could talk to her."

"I'll do what I can, but I doubt if I can change her mind. Gretch makes a mule look easygoing."

"I'd appreciate that."

We leave before the sun starts coming up, which I'm grateful for; I'd like to get in a few hours of sleep before heading back to the office. Plus, I'm feeling kind of depressed—there's nothing like an evening of charity to really drive home the fact that you're a member of an endangered species. Every time somebody tells you how much they "admire" you, what they're really saying is, *Congratulations on not being extinct yet!*

Which reminds me—there's something I have to take care of before I leave. I visit the restroom, then find the pire in the ruby dress that cornered me before. "Here," I say, slipping her a small plastic vial that contained antacids a minute ago. "Some of my latest work. Very new, very edgy—I'm using a *liquid* medium."

"Ooooh," she says. "It's warm. Are you using *blood*?"

"Not exactly," I say.

Hey, she pissed me off. I thought I'd return the favor.

Once Cassius and I are back in the limo, he says, "I'm sorry."

"What?"

"For dragging you out to this event. You look a little overwhelmed."

"No, just outnumbered. One to ninety-nine, remember?

And frankly, tonight's representative sample didn't give me a lot of hope for the survival of the species."

He blinks. It takes me a second to realize I've actually shocked him.

"Oh, I get it," I say. "Human beings are a little bit of a sacred cow. Once you've wiped out their population you have to elevate the cultural status of the survivors—we're Noble Savages now, right? Who knew vampires and werewolves had political correctness?"

He shakes his head, but he's smiling. "We can get a little sanctimonious, especially at events like this. At least our hearts are in the right place—even if they're not beating."

"I applaud the intent, okay? And I actually had a pretty good time. I like Brian and Sherry."

"Good. I was hoping you'd get along with them."

And then there's one of those pauses. You know, the loud kind where you can hear the question hanging in the air that neither of you is willing to actually spit out. If I were to do so, it would probably sound something like this: "So, Brian's a drunk and an artist—good for him, there's at least two things he excels at. Oh, and stealing women from powerful immortal pires with movie-star good looks—the pire, I mean, not Brian. He looks more like the kind of guy you'd find working the bar at a really good Irish pub and how the *hell* did you lose a woman like Sherry to him?"

Yeah, I said it out loud. What a surprise.

"He's human," Cassius says. "I'm not." His voice is carefully neutral—not sad, not angry, not anything.

I slide over on the seat. He turns to look at me. I put one hand on his chest, hesitantly. "No heartbeat," I say. "No pulse, no breath. You don't excrete sweat or used food. Your hair doesn't grow, and neither do your fingernails. You don't shed dead skin cells. Anything else?"

"Only a few centuries' worth."

"That's a lot of living. Which I think makes you more human, not less." I move my hand from his chest to his hand. "All the things you don't have are just biology. All that living you've done, that's what makes you human—that's what makes you a *person*. You didn't spend all that time sleeping in a coffin and hunting nubile villagers at three AM, did you?"

"Only on long weekends."

"Well, everyone needs to party now and then." I squeeze his hand. "Look, I wasn't sure what to expect from tonight— but I get the feeling you're deliberately putting some of your cards on the table. I can tell you genuinely care about the welfare of human beings, and it's more than just guilt over what you've done in the past. Sherry gave me a little glimpse of your past, and . . . and my possible future. Right?"

"I wasn't trying to manipulate you, Jace."

I take a deep breath. "No, you weren't. You knew I was smart enough to figure it out and once I did we'd have this conversation and now we're having it. Up to speed?"

"Yes."

"Good."

I can feel another one of those pauses building up in the air, but this time it's not about what to say next and I don't think I'm quite ready for that, so I say, "Tell me about Sherry." Maybe it's not the smartest thing to say, but I'm a cop; when in doubt, ask for more information.

"Sherry. We were together for eight years. I never quite got over thinking of her as a fling."

From any other guy, that would sound immature. But this is an immortal I'm talking to, and he's being honest; to him, eight years is a summer romance. "So it wasn't serious?"

"I wouldn't say that—it was fairly intense. But toward the end, she was starting to think about . . . joining me. I wasn't ready for that, and I don't think she was, either. I was the one who introduced her to Brian."

"Ah. Think you did the right thing?"

"I don't know. Ask me in fifty years, after she's dead."

There's anger in his voice. Not at me, though. "Why put yourself through this if it hurts so much?"

"Isn't it obvious? I'm an addict, Jace." He still sounds angry, but there's a trace of black amusement in there, too. "There's a great deal of power in firsts. The very first time I loved a human woman as a pire, it consumed me. We were together for seventy years. I think that at the end, I hated her as much for dying as I loved her. I swore I would never put myself through such a thing again. I lasted nearly a decade before I broke my word."

He's got that faraway look in his eyes, memories who-knows-how-old playing inside his head. "Love and death, Jace. The most powerful cocktail in the world, and the most dangerous. And it seems to have become my drink of choice."

For once, I don't have a wise-assed reply. I know what he means, actually; what he's describing happens to more than just vampires. It can affect doctors, soldiers, nurses, cops, EMTs, firefighters . . . anyone who deals with death and hormones on a daily basis. Nothing makes love stronger than the knowledge it could be taken away from you at any moment—that's what a pire in a relationship with a human has to deal with, and the longer-lived the pire, the more pressing that knowledge becomes.

"I'll make you a promise right now," I say. "You're never going to see me in a coffin. I'm either going to do my job and go home, or I'll outlive you. Deal?"

"And if you can't? If you wind up stuck here?"

"If that happens, I guess I'll join your little club and turn all bitey. Beats sprouting hair every month and going back to eating meat."

"I can't imagine you—"

"Deal?"

He hesitates, then smiles. "Deal."

"Okay, then. Now drop me off at home, will you? I've got work in the morning."

The limo drops me off at my front door. I should get some sleep, but I'm still wired from caffeine, the aftereffects of the booze, and what just happened—so I hit the Net and do some surfing instead. I want to learn a little more about the golem manufacturing process and the specific type of animist magic used; Dr. Pete and I need to talk, and I want to be prepared.

The spells themselves deal with transferring the life essence of animals to a malleable mineral receptacle—usually clay or sand, but with variations that range from peat to iron filings. I'm reading an entry on animating early clay golems when I run into a paragraph that stops me dead:

The enchantment that brings life to earth is a simple one. It has been endlessly refined since it was first cast, but the elegance of the original spell has never been surpassed. Its format has been adapted to many other uses in almost every area of magic, including energy enhancement, food production, and computation. Some theorists predict that it could even be adapted for such far-flung uses as dimensional travel—though most admit that would require a knowledge of the underpinnings of the spell that only the original caster would have. Of course, some people believe he's still alive . . .

I stare at the screen. It's telling me that the person who used golem-related magic to whisk me here can only be one man.

Ahasuerus.

EIGHT

My talk with Gretch will have to wait. Charlie calls me at 3:00 PM, waking me out of a sound sleep, and tells me he'll pick me up in fifteen minutes. Another Bravo has turned up dead.

By the time he arrives I'm more or less awake, dressed, and mobile. I climb into the passenger side of the car and say, "I don't care if we're on our way to look at the dismembered corpse of the pope, I want coffee."

Charlie hands me a paper bag. Inside are a large coffee and a lemon Danish. "You're welcome," he growls.

When I've got enough down my throat to feel human again, I ask him where we're going.

"Docks. Body was found in a boathouse. Cassius says this one makes the last one look normal."

"Great," I mutter. "Wonder if there's any point in eating the rest of this Danish."

"You better. I spent a buck eighty-five on it."

"Really? Guess I should start calling you Rockefeller."

"I buy you breakfast and that's how you repay me? Bad puns?"

"Thanks, Rockefeller."

"Next time you get decaf."

"Oh, that's a decision you'll regret."

It's a typical Seattle day, overcast with chances of increasing grayness. The boathouse is down in Shilshole Bay, an area that's mostly private marinas. We pull into the parking lot of one that seems more low-rent than the others, the slips crowded with live-aboards and older boats. The boathouse is at the far end, behind a dry-dock area fenced off with chainlink. Two thrope officers are guarding the gate, sipping coffee from paper cups and looking bored. We flash them our IDs and they let us past.

The boathouse is made from weathered gray wood, but the door is steel-cored and has an almost brand-new frame and hinges. It's ajar, so we can enter without touching anything.

Inside, the floor becomes a dock, ending about halfway down the building's length. The walls extend into the water another fifty feet or so, the structure opening at the far end into the bay. There's a wire-mesh gate on a track across the opening, currently closed.

Cassius is standing over the body, wearing the same suit he had on last night, with a London Fog overcoat on top of it. He looks up as we enter but doesn't say anything.

The vic is a woman. Her body is wrapped in bandages, like a mummy, up to her neckline. She's sitting upright in a wheelchair, her hands on the arms.

What skin is exposed is a gleaming metallic orange in color. In fact, it appears to be made of metal—bronze, I'd say. What tells me that this is a corpse and not simply a detailed sculpture is the head—the top of the skull has been neatly removed, and placed in her lap.

Above her forehead, her brain has been cross-sectioned, sliced both horizontally and vertically into little cubes that someone separated from one another by an inch or so by impaling them with thin wooden skewers, producing a three-dimensional grid—an exploded diagram of thought itself.

"Her name is Lucy Barbarossa," Cassius says. "Otherwise known as the Sword of Midnight."

I nod. "No sword, though."

"No. We're still searching her ship, but I think the killer took it."

I glance at the edge of the dock and notice for the first time that there's something riding very, very low in the water. "Ship?"

"Submersible. Barbarossa was a smuggler."

"Not surprising," Charlie says. "In the comic she was a pirate."

I take a closer look at the gridwork brain. "Sixty-four sections."

"Any idea what it means?" Cassius asks.

"The answer to *What is eight times eight?*" I shrug. "I'm more interested in the transformation of the body. First copper, now this. And the wheelchair is obviously significant, too."

"How about the bandages?"

I can't help thinking of the wrappers, though none of them would be so boring as to use plain strips of white gauze. Still, it's a little unsettling—and not something I'm ready to mention to Cassius yet. "No idea. Who found the body?"

"Marina employee. Found the door open and checked inside. Didn't touch anything, called the police."

"How do you know this is Barbarossa?"

"I just do."

He looks at me calmly, and I scowl back. Right. More government secrets. "Any chance this could be something else? Smuggling's a dangerous business."

"Black marketeers aren't known for their artistic

sensibilities." He gestures at the brain. "Or whatever this is supposed to represent."

There's all sorts of symbolism going on here, but I still don't speak the language. "What did she smuggle?"

"Weapons, drugs, whatever paid the bills. She wasn't choosy."

"And the NSA tolerated this?"

"We let her make a living. Criminals aren't the only ones with a use for a good smuggler."

"Tell me about her weapon."

"The Midnight Sword. Two blades with diamond-shaped tips, one shorter than the other, mounted one atop the other to mimic the appearance of two clock-hands pointing to twelve. Said to be able to cut through time itself, providing the wielder with the ability to move more quickly than normal or inflict wounds that vanish an hour later—even fatal ones."

"Handy," says Charlie. "A blade with an undo option."

"Wait. So if the Sword was used on her brain—"

"It wasn't—these cuts are surgically precise. But yes, if the Sword was used the brain could conceivably reintegrate—if the wielder knew what they were doing."

"How about cause of death?"

"We won't know until the autopsy. Eisfanger's on his way to process the scene."

I walk over to the edge of the dock. I can see the sleek shape of a craft just below the surface, painted a deep blue, a small deck jutting up with an open hatch in it. Submarine technology was on the verge of mass commercialization in my own world, and every law enforcement officer I know was dreading it. Homemade submersibles that skated along just under the surface were already widespread and hard to catch—a true sub that could go a few hundred feet down would be close to a ghost.

I turn around. "That door looks awfully strong, and it

doesn't seem to have been forced. It's possible she let her killer in. Or he could have come in via water—has that gate been checked?"

"Yes. It hasn't been tampered with, above or below the water line. You think she was killed here?"

"Hard to say. There's no blood, but the condition of the body might preclude that. If she was transformed first, she might not have bled at all."

Cassius nods. "It must have been an ambush. She would have fought, given the chance."

"It was someone she knew, then. Someone she trusted, or at least didn't fear."

"Not necessarily. They might have gained entry through subterfuge—disguised as someone else, perhaps."

"Who? FedEx? Someone delivering pizzas?" I shake my head. "She was a professional criminal, and I get the distinct impression she wasn't a novice. She would have taken precautions."

"That's true," Cassius says, though he seems reluctant to do so. "But that would seem to eliminate your prime suspect—John Dark."

It's the first time I've heard Cassius say his name. "Gretchen brought you up to speed on our visit to Silverado?"

"Yes." He looks slightly uncomfortable. "I didn't want to discuss it last night, in a crowded room."

Funny, I don't remember the limo being crowded at all. "Then let's discuss it now. First off—how sure are you that Wertham's actually dead?"

"Utterly. I helped dispose of the body."

That's three people who are convinced Wertham is a dead end. Of course, any of them could be lying. "What can you tell me about Dark?"

"He's . . . being looked into."

"So you knew he was out there."

"I can't tell you everything I know about, Jace."

"Including the existence of the guy I'm trying to catch?"

He stares down at the water and jams his hands deep into the pockets of his overcoat. "John Dark's situation is complicated. Until you talked to Silverado, I thought it impossible for him to be involved. Now . . . now I'm not sure."

"Tell me where he is. I'll *make* sure."

"I can't do that."

"Can't or won't?"

"Can't. He's disappeared."

I throw my hands up in frustration. "Terrific. Can you tell me where he was, so I can try to track him down? Or would you prefer I handle this case blindfolded? I have a nice selection of scarves at home."

He puts his own hands up, palms out. "I'd prefer you concentrate on the case itself. I'll take care of finding Dark."

"*Will* you? Great, that makes me feel *so* much better."

Pires aren't immune to sarcasm, but NSA directors are. "Good. Seeing as this is the second murder of a Bravo, I've been given clearance to contact and warn the others. Most of them have already heard."

"But you still won't let *me* talk to them."

He doesn't say anything, which is answer enough. I shake my head and stalk toward the door. Charlie follows me without a word.

"Where are you going?" Cassius asks. "Eisfanger hasn't even—"

"Eisfanger can send me his report. I'm going somewhere that I might actually find some answers, instead of more damn questions."

Back at the car I say, "I'm driving." Charlie surrenders the keys without an argument. I lay a little more rubber than is probably professional leaving the parking lot, but I'm frustrated and there's nothing handy to shoot.

"We have a destination?" Charlie asks. "Or you just want to ram a few cars and call it a day?"

"I don't know about you," I say, "but I'm going home. And going to bed."

I light the candle Neil gave me and crawl under the covers.

Despite how wound up I am, it isn't hard to fall asleep—I really didn't get enough rest last night. The candle smells like musty paper and fresh ink, with just a touch of really strong soap. It's oddly familiar, though I can't quite place it. It reminds me a little of the smell of the corner drugstore where I grew up, the one that had an old-fashioned spinner rack of comics. It's taller than I am, and the colors on the shiny covers are all sharp and exciting. I pull one out of the rack and look at it; muscular men and women in skintight costumes are fighting monsters, shooting beams from their eyes and swinging from lines that don't seem to be attached to anything. The title is printed in large, impressive script, but I can't read it—it's a mishmash of letters and symbols, some alien language I don't recognize.

"Reading is unreliable in dreams," Neil says. He's leaning back against the pharmacist's counter, still wearing his sunglasses but now in a long white coat. "Most people can't read the same line twice; some people can't read text at all. A few—usually people who read a great deal while awake—can read, but can't remember any of it when they wake up. They simply remember the *sensation* of reading. Like going to a party where you're sure you had a good time, but all the details are fuzzy in the morning."

"So I'm dreaming?" It's obvious I am, but somehow it seems important to ask the question.

Neil's reply is to glance behind me. A hippopotamus stares back, then smiles. It's wearing braces.

"Fair enough," I say. "I've got some questions to ask you."

"Let's go somewhere a little less distracting," Neil says. He opens a plain white door and beckons me to follow him through it.

On the other side is a small, comfortable room. Two large leather armchairs face a fire burning merrily in a stone hearth. The walls are lined with filing cabinets made of polished oak with brass handles, reaching all the way up to the ceiling.

Neil sits down, now wearing a maroon velvet smoking jacket. I sit down in the other chair, and notice I'm dressed in a suit of armor. It's oddly comfortable.

"How can I help you?" Neil asks pleasantly.

"There's been another murder." I fill him in on the details.

"Mmm," he says when I've finished. "Yes, I understand what he's referencing. The Doom Patrol."

"Never heard of them."

"They're not as mainstream as some, though they have a long and rich history. The wheelchair is a reference to their leader, the Chief, who was disabled. The bandages signify Negative Man, who could release a mysterious being made of black energy from his body, and the metal body itself—bronze-colored, you say?—is no doubt meant to represent Robotman, a race-car driver who had his brain transplanted into a mechanical body following a crash."

"Yeah? Was it chopped up into a neat little grid first?"

"No. But that's where this gets interesting." Neil clasps his hands together under his chin. "The Doom Patrol has been around since 1963, but they had a major relaunch in the 1980s. A writer named Grant Morrison came on board and took the book in a much darker, surreal direction. One of the characters he added was named Crazy Jane, after a character in one of Byron's poems. She had multiple personalities as a result of child abuse—sixty-four of them, in fact."

I nod, staring into the fire. There are faces there, shifting in and out of focus as the flames dance. "Byron. So this Morrison was more literate than most comic book writers."

Neil frowns at me disapprovingly. "Many writers of the form are literate—it was the form *itself* that was juvenile, or at least it was perceived that way in America in the mid-twentieth century. Morrison and other writers like him were part of what was called the Modern Age—their concepts and writing took comics to new heights of maturity and complexity."

The first murder was with a silver weapon, the body dressed as the character who ushered in the Silver Age. "Was this Doom Patrol the first superpowered team of the Modern Age?"

"No. They were significant, but not the first—some would say that would be the X-Men. Of course, some people also claim that the X-Men were in fact merely a copy of the Doom Patrol in the first place." He shakes his head. "But the most influential team book of the time was undoubtedly *Watchmen*. It's widely cited as the most influential comic book ever printed."

"Why's that?"

"Many reasons: depth, structure, metaphysical concepts, layered characterization . . . but more than anything, it captured the zeitgeist of the time. I'm surprised your killer didn't reference it, instead—but it dealt largely with the fear of nuclear Armageddon, a problem we don't face here."

No, you just have rogue Elder Gods to worry about . . . "So why would the killer pick this group over the others?"

"The common theme I see is transformation. The Doom Patrol were regarded as freaks, victims that decided to turn their handicaps into advantages. Just as the Silver Age Flash was frequently transformed by his enemies, the Doom Patrol were transformed by fate. Initially, anyway."

The flames were beginning to take on a more definite shape. Something humanoid . . . "Initially?"

"Yes. Are you familiar with the term *retroactive continuity*?"

"Can't say that I am."

"It's a term that gained popularity during the Modern Age. It refers to changing a character's history—altering a hero's origin, for instance then stating that it's always been that way."

"Fictional revisionism."

"In essence. Comic books never used to worry about things like historical accuracy, but as the medium aged, the idea of a shared, consistent universe took hold. Characters that met each other were supposed to remember it when they met again. A worldwide disaster was expected to affect everyone, not just the stars of one book. This worked well at first, but many of these heroes were depicted as living in the 'real' world, and being affected by events in it. And unlike pires, human beings age. In order to remain consistent, the writers had to come up with an explanation for why someone who fought Nazis in World War Two was beating up muggers in 1983. Their solution was to create *staggered* universes, with the older versions of the characters in one world, and the newer versions in another. This, of course, led to a proliferation of alternate worlds and timelines, compounded by the number of different writers who each contributed his or her own vision; mix well for dozens of issues every month times several decades, and you wind up with a convoluted, contradictory history no one can make sense of. What began as an attempt to build a linear structure grew into a tangle of multiple Earths, multiple versions of characters, and multiple timelines. In an attempt to impose order, DC Comics published a series called *Crisis on Infinite Earths,* where they essentially rewrote that history. The multiple

Earths were merged into one, characters' backgrounds were revised to make coherent sense, and some characters were rewritten altogether."

The shape in the flames is getting clearer. It's nude, male, and—

Cassius.

I look away quickly. "What's this got to do with the Doom Patrol?"

"Morrison revised their origin. He revealed that their leader, the Chief, was in fact responsible for the horrific accidents that created them in the first place."

Betrayal. A common enough motive for murder—but who was betrayed, and who were the betrayers? Was the entire Brigade being blamed, or just Transe and the Sword?

I risk a quick glance at the fire. Cassius grins at me and gives me a little finger-wave. I look away again.

"There's something else you should know about Morrison," Neil continues. "His work frequently references meta-reality—the idea that fictional worlds are as real as our own, and that what we perceive as real is fiction to someone else. He's quite famous for a sequence where one of his characters slowly turns around, stares out at the reader and states, 'I can see you!' "

The nude flame-figure of Cassius is getting bigger. "And I see *you*," I mutter. "Okay, so this writer likes to play around with metaphysics. Does he have any connections to the character from the first crime scene?"

"The Flash, you mean? Well, Morrison has written him, but that doesn't necessarily mean anything; he's a popular writer and has handled most of DC's major characters at one time or another. But there's something else about Morrison that's much more pertinent to your investigation."

"Which is?"

"He's a practicing magician."

The flame-figure of Cassius abruptly dissolves, to my relief. "You're not talking about sleight of hand, right?"

"No. And he's not the only one. Alan Moore, the writer of *Watchmen,* is also a practitioner."

I frown. "Wait a minute. I thought magic didn't exist on my world."

Neil smiles. "Magic is universal, Jace. It simply manifests in different ways on different planes."

Two comic book writers. Two universes. Two sorcerers, and two dead heroes. "Is either of them powerful enough to travel from there to here?"

"I couldn't say. I would think it unlikely, but if they had access to some item of power, or an ally in this world, it's certainly possible."

An item like a gem that could shift mystic energy around? An ally like a member of a disgraced, once powerful cult?

"Ahem." It's not Neil talking; the voice comes from behind me. I turn in my chair to look.

Dr. Pete is standing there. He's also completely naked, and dripping wet. "A towel would be nice," he says.

"Uh—sorry. I don't have one."

Neil produces a large white bath towel from nowhere and hands it to him.

"Thanks." He starts drying his hair.

I give Neil an accusing look, but he just shrugs. "It's your dream, Jace. I'm just visiting."

I glare at Dr. Pete and will him to go away. He dissolves into a puddle of water on the floor. "Okay, then. I think we're done, unless you have anything else you think I should know."

"Oh, there are all sorts of things you should know, Jace. But that doesn't mean I know what they are." He gets up from his chair, walks over to the wall of drawers, and pulls one at chest level open. He rummages inside and pulls out—what else—a comic book.

He hands it to me. "Take a look at this. You may find it useful."

I study the cover. It's the Sword of Midnight, in a heroic pose at the prow of a ship. She's in half-were form, a snarling she-beast dressed in a pirate's brocaded coat and tricorn hat, with her distinctive blade held above her head. She's backlit by a horizon-level, blood-red sun.

"Moore's *Watchmen* also featured a pirate story line," Neil's voice says. "But that was mainly there as thematic counterpoint. The main plot concerns a group of heroes that are being targeted, one by one . . ."

When I look up, he's gone.

I open the cover and begin to read.

Neil was right: Reading in a dream *is* unreliable. In fact, I only get through the first panel—a full-page spread of a sea battle between a pirate ship and a freighter, with buccaneer lems chucking cannonballs between vessels— when it all turns into a live-action movie happening around me. I'm just a disembodied point of view, able to hear and see but not touch anything, and I seem to currently be perched in the crow's nest looking down.

Right into Lucy Barbarossa's cleavage, which is impressive but furry. She's directing the battle, her sword in one hand, dressed in those short pirate pants and a puffy-sleeved shirt. No eye patch or parrot, but she does have a jaunty tricorn hat perched on her hairy skull.

Another handy thing about dreams is that they make the impossible possible; in this case, for a thrope to speak while in were form. She's exhorting her crew to give no quarter, and it's working; in a matter of moments, the other ship has run up a white flag of surrender.

My POV zooms downward, making my nonexistent stomach surge into my noncorporeal throat, as Lucy Barbarossa abruptly leaves the deck, ducking inside a hatch and down a wooden ladder. I follow her as she heads into the bowels of the ship, to a heavy wooden door she unlocks with a brass key.

Inside, there's a man chained to the wall. He's wearing only a pair of trousers, and has the kind of muscular, smooth body usually found on underwear models or Hollywood actors. I can't see his face, though; some trick of the light keeps it in deep shadow.

The pirate queen uses another key to unlock his manacles, transforming back to a human female at the same time. As soon as he's free, the prisoner takes a step away from her, his face still hidden.

"We've taken her," she says. "The *Countess Bathory* is ours. Soon you'll be free."

"Will I?" he says. "I fear your crew will not give up such a rich prize so easily."

"My crew does not question my orders. Any who do will hang from the end of a silver rope."

The man rubs one of his wrists; clearly he's been doing some hanging of his own. "And you? I've been as good as your possession, these many months; it's not in your nature to surrender ownership of anything—"

And then she steps forward and throws herself into his arms, and the kiss that follows is . . . well, I'm just surprised the cabin doesn't burst into flames.

When they finally break apart, they stare at each other tenderly for a moment before speaking. "Ah, Lucy," the man says. "Perhaps belonging to you isn't quite as bad as I thought."

"Don't joke," she says. "I hate having you down here in chains. Stealing visits whenever I can, hiding this from everyone."

"You know we have no choice. We are bound by chains older and stronger than mere iron. Be thankful for the time that we've had."

"I am," she whispers. "I am . . . and I damn to Hell all those who seek to keep us apart."

"Then you damn us both, for this is as much my doing as yours. Take your plunder from the *Countess Bathory* and leave me there in its stead; your crew, eyes filled with pearls and gold, will soon forget the ransom I would have brought."

"But I will not," she says. "I will never forget what I have lost."

"Nor I, Lucy. Nor I . . ."

Their voices echo in my ears as I slowly drift into consciousness. I lie in bed, not moving, thinking about what I just experienced. Not just the comic book part, but my fireside conversation with Neil.

All in all, there seemed to be a pretty high ratio of naked men to clothed females . . . Cassius as fire, Dr. Pete as water? Wonder what that's about—if anything, I'd compare Cassius to ice. And Dr. Pete to . . . hmm. I don't know, actually. He's a little too clean-cut to be earthy, a little too safe to be fire, a little too reliable to be air. Maybe water is the best metaphor for him—water, after all, is usually a symbol of life.

And fluidity. And change.

I don't know what the pirate ship scene was all about, but it seems important. Lucy Barbarossa—her fictional version, anyway—seemed to be having some sort of illicit affair. But with whom, exactly? And was that the literal truth, or just some kind of metaphor?

The candle I lit before going to bed has burned exactly one-third of the way down before extinguishing itself—guess that means I can contact Neil two more times. I've only slept for about an hour, but my stomach is telling me it's time for dinner. I rummage in the fridge for some left-over pasta, then call Charlie. "Hey, sandman. Where are you?"

"Shooting some stick. There's a pool hall just around the corner from your place."

"Yeah? Good to know. Can you pick me up?"

"Be there in ten."

I meet him downstairs. The car's still parked in front of my building, and he comes strolling up the sidewalk, moving in that precise, elegant way he has. It's very different from the way Silverado moved—that was like watching a finely tuned machine, whereas Charlie is more like a big cat. Relaxed power, restrained violence.

"How'd the snooze-fest go?" he asks.

"Learned a lot. Not sure how much of it is useful."

We get in the car, Charlie in the driver's seat, and I fill him in as we head for Dr. Pete's.

"Huh," he says when I finish. "These writers—Morrison and Moore. They have counterparts on this world?"

I stare at Charlie and suppress the urge to punch him in the shoulder—it would only hurt my hand. "Damn it! I can't believe I didn't ask him such an obvious question!"

"Don't be too hard on yourself. You were asleep at the time."

"Didn't seem to affect Neil much."

"Neil's an oneiromage. It's his turf." There's a hard edge to Charlie's voice.

"Sounds like you don't trust him."

"I don't. I don't trust anyone who gives away convenient information, especially not when it sounds like they're betraying their own organization."

He has a point. "You think Neil's manipulating us?"

"I don't know. I just hate him being in your head."

I forgot how protective Charlie can be—the idea of me being on the astral plane solo no doubt bothers him more than he cares to admit.

"He's the best source of information we have at the moment," I point out. "About all we can do is follow the path he points us down."

"Yeah. And hope it doesn't go off the edge of a cliff."

I know I promised Cassius I'd talk to Gretchen, but I can't put off a conversation with Dr. Pete any longer. I need to know what, if any, connection the Solar Centurion has to Tair, and if any of Tair's accusations are true—because if they are, then Dr. Pete is or was connected to the black-market lem trade. I'm not sure where that particular trail will lead, but it might just go all the way to Ahasuerus, creator of the golem race—as well as the animist who brought me to this world and the only one who can get me safely home.

I call Dr. Pete's cell. "Hi, this is Jace—"

"Jace? Look, can I call you back? I'm a little busy."

"I really need to talk to you, Doc. Are you at your office?"

"I am, but this isn't really a good time—"

I'm used to people not wanting to talk to me. It still stings a little, but I've learned to ignore it. "I'm on my way. See you in a few minutes."

"But—"

I hang up. He doesn't call back, which I interpret as meaning he doesn't *really* mind if I show up. Interpretation is a wonderful skill.

I wonder if he'll use his receptionist as a buffer. I doubt it—that's the kind of weasely move you can only get away with pulling on strangers—but I'm perfectly happy with taking her on. Destroying underlings is one of the few perks you get with my job; I have fond memories of the time I made a clerk at the IRS break down and cry. But he really, really deserved it.

Alas, I'm denied the satisfaction of a decent battle—she's not behind the front counter. In fact, no one is.

"Hello? Dr. Pete?"

No answer. I hear something, though—a scratching, scrabbling noise. Claws on wood?

I draw my gun. Charlie's still down in the car—I wanted to talk to the Doc in private. I can get Charlie up here in a flash, but I don't want to overreact.

I move slowly and quietly out of the waiting room and down a short hall. Open doors on either side—examination rooms, both empty. The door at the end of the hall is closed, and that's where the noise is coming from.

"Dr. Pete?" I call out. "Is that you?"

The scrabbling intensifies, and now I hear something else—a whine.

I open the door.

A brown-and-white shape lunges at me, knocking me over. A pair of slavering jaws hover over my face, and I jam the barrel of the Ruger underneath them.

And then he starts licking my face.

I shove the dog off my chest, and ease the safety back on the Ruger. "*Bad* dog," I say. The St. Bernard looks at me and cocks his head, tail wagging furiously. He doesn't look ashamed at all.

"You look familiar," I say. "Did we meet at the shelter?" More wagging, and not a small amount of drool. St. Bernards have practically cornered the market on canine saliva—a few bulldogs are still holding out, but the writing's on the wall.

I glance around Dr. Pete's office. He's not there, but there's a large yellow legal pad with a note scrawled on it:

JACE—SORRY, BUT I HAD TO RUN. WILL EXPLAIN LATER. CAN YOU LOOK AFTER GALAHAD FOR A NIGHT OR TWO? HE'S IN QUARANTINE FROM THE OTHER DOGS (NOT CONTAGIOUS TO HUMANS). LEASH, FOOD, AND PANTS UNDER FRONT COUNTER.
    DR. PETE

I look over at Galahad. "Oh, you've *got* to be kidding."

Galahad gives me a big, doggy grin. I try to remember what my lease says about pets.

And wonder what the hell has happened to Dr. Pete.

NINE

The food goes in the trunk, Galahad in the backseat. When I get in the passenger side, Charlie and Galahad are sizing each other up in a cautious but nonconfrontational way.

"Just drive," I say.

"Sure. Dog park, pet store, or the zoo?"

"My place."

Galahad apparently decides that Charlie is all right, but his fedora needs further investigation. Charlie deals with the wet snuffling that follows by pulling out in traffic and lowering the rear window a few inches. Galahad succumbs to the lure of the open road and jams his head as far out as it can go.

"We're stealing Dr. Pete's dog?" Charlie asks.

"More like caretaking. The Doc's taken off and left me holding the doggie bag."

"Sure. Because of your copious spare time and carefree nature."

"You forgot my tendency toward nurturing."

"Sorry. Don't shoot me, okay?"

"Not in front of the dog, anyway."

It'll be dark soon. I'm in the middle of two ongoing murder investigations, Dr. Pete has vanished under mysterious circumstances, and now I have to take care of a large, hairy, and no doubt curious beast who'll shortly be transforming into a large, less hairy one with opposable thumbs. God, I hope he doesn't like to drink out of the toilet. Or the liquor cabinet.

I'm not sure how I feel about Dr. Pete disappearing. Worry and frustration are neck and neck. I don't know if he abandoned Galahad because he's genuinely in trouble, or if it's just a way to slow me down. Neither one seems like Dr. Pete's style.

But then, neither does working for a black-market lem factory.

"Charlie—what do you know about the illegal lem trade?"

"Too much. You get a lead on that amulet Stoker bought?"

Stoker. The guy I'm supposed to be chasing, the guy who's my one guaranteed ticket home—and apparently the guy I'm now too busy to hunt. Of course, if I don't find Ahasuerus, too, I'll be going home in a walker to a world that's forgotten all about me. Frustration puts on a burst of speed and pulls ahead of worry. "No. But it might be pertinent to one of the other cases." Not exactly a lie, though the Dr. Pete situation isn't an *official* case.

"Ugly business," Charlie says. "Lem activation is regulated internationally to prevent anyone abusing the system for cheap labor or soldiers. Countries that don't abide get hit with sanctions, but there's always someone willing to look the other way."

"So this happens primarily in other countries?"

"Who said I was talking about other countries?" Charlie looks even grimmer than usual. "Plenty of illegals get used in the U.S. Drug labs, mostly—if the lab gets busted, it's easier to just destroy the whole workforce and start over."

"Mass murder? That's extreme, even for drug cartels."

"Maybe where you come from. Here, it's just seen as the cost of doing business—besides, nobody really cares about a bunch of lems who have only been around for a few weeks. Most of them can barely talk." Charlie's voice is getting colder and colder, as if he has to distance himself from the subject to talk about it at all.

"So someone illegally activating lems would essentially be creating disposable slaves," I say. "That about it?"

"That's about it."

I wonder where Dr. Pete's gone.

And where he's been.

Galahad seems more than happy to explore my apartment. While he does, Charlie and I discuss what to do next.

"Can you stay here and watch him for a while?" I ask.

"So you can search for new and exciting ways to get yourself killed? Not going to happen."

"I can't leave him here alone."

"Obviously."

"Then we take him with us."

Right about then Galahad finds something that fills him with either joy, surprise, or anger—it's kind of hard to tell. But his reaction is heavy on the bass, repetitious, and *loud*.

"*That's* gonna go over well on a stakeout," Charlie says.

"Maybe he'll be less vocal in human form."

"Maybe he'll be just as loud, but with a broader vocabulary. *What's that? Look at me! Hey, are you a bad guy?*"

I groan and slump backward on the couch. "So we can't take him with us. You won't dog-sit. He can't go to the shelter. Which means I have to look after him?"

"Until you can get someone else to do it, yeah."

I'm already running through a list in my head. Pregnant pire probably not a good idea, Cassius out of the question—

"Hold on," I say, and dig out my phone.

And stuff it back in my pocket a minute later, dejected. I was sure Eisfanger would be available, but he surprised me—he's out on a date. Which leaves only one option I can think of.

"Hi, Alexandra?" Galahad comes bounding into the room with a quizzical look on his face, apparently looking for her, then starts barking enthusiastically to make her leap out of her hiding place.

"I can't look after Galahad for you," Alexandra says.

"That's—how—"

"Uncle Pete told me he had to go away for a few days. He tried to get me to do it first. No way."

Teenagers sometimes respond to threats. "Please, please, *please,*" I threaten. "I'll buy you a pony."

"Ew. I don't even *like* horse meat."

"Look, it's just for a day or two. I can't haul him around with me, and I can't just sit in my apartment looking after him."

"Oh, you'll be doing more than sitting. Galahad needs to be walked at least twice a day. Then there's the bending and the scooping."

I sigh. "Name your price."

"Hmmm. I'll call you back." She hangs up.

"Sounds like that went well," Charlie says.

"Shut up."

Galahad trots into the living room with a grease-stained paper bag from a fast-food joint in his mouth. He lies down at my feet and begins to patiently tear it apart.

"Hope you haven't spilled any food on your furniture lately," Charlie says. "Or your clothes. Or your rug—"

The phone rings. "Hello?"

"You have to call me Xandra."

"Excuse me?"

"That's my first condition. I want to be called Xandra instead of Alexandra, but my parents refuse to do it unless I can get three adults to agree to it first. You're number two."

"Fine."

"Condition Number Two: You pay me. Same rate as the shelter does, which isn't much. But I think that's fair."

"Sure, no problem."

"Condition Three—"

"Should I be writing these down, or will you e-mail me the entire thing?"

"Calm down, this is the last one. I can't start until tomorrow night."

I take a deep breath. "Deal. Can you be here before sundown?"

"Yeah, easy. I'm gone at sunup, okay?"

"Done. Thanks, Al . . . uh, Xandra."

"See you tomorrow. We're still on for the flea market on Saturday, right?"

The way things are going I really don't know, but I hate to bail on a friend—especially one that's just agreed to do me a favor. "Absolutely."

After I hang up, I turn to Charlie and say, "Looks like I'm in for the night. You don't have to hang around if you don't want."

"I don't mind. You get cable, right?"

"Rrrable," Galahad says.

I stare at him. "Oh, no. My life is *already* one step away from being a Scooby-Doo cartoon . . . Charlie, if you tell me you're thinking about buying a van and growing a goatee I will shoot you both and throw your bodies off a bridge."

"Sun's down," Charlie says.

So it is. And over the next thirty seconds or so, I watch Galahad go from being a bulky, brown-and-white dog to a bulky, naked man. When the transformation is finished, he gets to his knees and smiles at me uncertainly.

"Pants," I say. "Pants!"

A word that Galahad apparently knows, because he immediately starts looking around for the item in question. I dig out the large pair of jeans that were packed with the food and hand them over. Galahad slips into them with only a little clumsiness—I have to help him get them buttoned.

"Pete?" he asks me. He has the weirdest accent I've ever heard, kind of like a Swede who learned English in the Deep South.

"Pete's not here," I tell him. I point at myself. "Jace. Understand? Jace."

"Jayuss," he says. "Jayoos?"

Better than *Race Ralchek,* I guess. I point at Charlie. "Charlie."

"Charrrlay."

"I can see we're in for a stimulating evening of intellectual discourse," Charlie says. "Maybe I should go home, get my dictionary."

"Home?" Galahad says. He sounds hopeful.

"Not yet, big guy," I say. "You hungry?"

"Yeah! Yeah! Yeah!"

"Let's see what we can find for a growing, middle-aged man in my kitchen."

I make him a couple of ham sandwiches, which he eats with a great deal less mess than I thought he would. He does have the habit of taking enormous bites, but very little goes on the floor. He licks his fingers clean when he's finished and looks at me hopefully. "More?"

"Maybe later," I say. I pat his protruding, hairy gut. "You're not exactly starving."

I find an oversize T-shirt I sometimes sleep in and convince him to put it on. It's pink and has a big yellow flower on the front, but it's still an improvement. He doesn't seem to mind.

Charlie's already found an old black-and-white movie on TV. I show Galahad where the bathroom is and hope he knows how to use it—if not, the evening is going to go downhill fast.

Galahad wanders into my room, lies down on the bed, and curls up with his knees bent. He goes to sleep almost immediately—if I'm lucky, he'll stay that way.

I return to the living room. "What are you watching?"

"*Over the Moon,* with Danny Kaye. It's about a thrope who wants to be a song-and-dance star, but he keeps transforming when he's nervous and then he can't sing."

"Sounds hilarious."

"Hey, you haven't seen a pratfall until you've seen Kaye fall down the steps of the Statue of Liberty."

"All of 'em?"

"Yup. They did three takes, too."

"Guess the occupation 'stuntman' never really caught on here."

We watch Kaye clown his way through an audition and a job as a singing waiter. I've always thought he was funny, but watching what seems to be late-twentieth-century transformation effects in black-and-white—to comedic music, no less—makes me feel more like I'm watching the Twilight Zone than a comedy. And I don't mean watching an episode—I mean staring at a little window into the Zone itself. While a plastic-skinned golem animated by the life force of a *T. rex* chortles beside me on the couch.

Then things get weird.

Okay, so I have my vices. One of them happens to be chocolate, the darker the better—and I keep a stash in the drawer beside my bed. I guess I should feel lucky Galahad didn't get into the *other* drawer, but a disaster is a disaster. Even I know dogs aren't supposed to eat chocolate.

I catch him sitting on the edge of the bed, what's left of my 93% Pure Cocoa Indulgence Bar smeared across his jowly face. His look of bliss becomes one of guilt immediately.

"Oh, crap," I say.

The first thing I do is hit the Internet. It tells me that the ingredient in chocolate that dogs find toxic is called theobromine, and the darker the chocolate, the higher the dose. Uh-oh. On the other hand, Galahad masses more as a man than as a dog, and according to the chart I find he hasn't eaten enough to kill him—not in his present form, anyway.

But theobromine has a half-life of over seventeen hours, and the sun will have come up long before then.

Of course, we're also dealing with magic. Could be that were dogs in human form are immune to chocolate poisoning, or maybe they are while dogs. It takes me ten tortuous minutes of searching before I find a site that tells me it varies from breed to breed, but large breeds are more susceptible. Symptoms include hyper-excitability, hyper-irritability, vomiting, diarrhea and increased urination.

Oh, joy. This would explain why Galahad has decided to turn my small apartment into a racetrack. He races from room to room, bounding over and slamming into furniture at a breakneck speed, yelling "Bark! Bark! Bark!" at the top of his lungs. Not barking, you understand, just yelling the word over and over. My neighbors probably think I'm some kind of tree pervert.

Charlie finally tackles him and we lash him to a kitchen chair with some bedsheets. He doesn't really seem to mind this, but as soon as we have him restrained he changes his chorus to a more whiny "Pee! Pee! Pee!"

We untie him. He runs for the bathroom, where he demonstrates a surprisingly developed understanding of modern plumbing, and a complete lack of aim.

I'm not going to talk about the diarrhea.

It's a long and hectic night. By the time the sun comes up, I feel like I've been wrangling the Son of Kong in a live-action remake of *Monsters Run Amuck*.

Strangely enough, despite all the mayhem, I can't find it in myself to hate Galahad. He's really a sweet dog—it's my fault I left that chocolate where he could get to it. I'm sure he's nowhere near as frenzied as this usually, and despite "irritability" being one of the listed symptoms, he never gets angry with Charlie or me. Well, maybe a little annoyed when we have to hose him down in the shower. Mostly he seems pathetically eager to please, loves any attention we show him, and really just wants our approval. You could do worse in a pet.

When the sun comes up, we both heave a sigh of relief. I haven't stopped worrying, though—the theobromine is still in Galahad's system, and now is actually the most dangerous time. I keep a close eye on him, but when he seems fine after an hour I'm pretty sure he's going to be okay.

We've already decided on a plan for the day: We're going to leave Galahad locked in my bedroom, with food and water and some newspapers. Anything I think he might chew on I've moved to the living room.

I kneel beside the St. Bernard and scratch behind his ears. "Okay, Gally. I'm going out for the day, but I'll be back to check on you. You be good, all right? No barking."

He barks, once. I don't know if that's good or bad, but I don't have a lot of choice either way. I shut him up in the bedroom and we leave.

My work hours are kind of wonky, but I generally put in time during both the night and day shifts—I'll check in at the office and see if there are any new developments, then follow up whatever I'm working on. I usually get some Zs in somewhere between 4:00 PM and midnight—unless circumstances dictate otherwise. I think my record for going without sleep is somewhere close to a hundred hours.

We never make it to the office, though. Cassius calls and tells me to meet him at a storage facility in Renton. He sounds strange, more terse than usual, and hangs up without giving me any more information.

"Yeah, nice talking to you, too," I say. I give Charlie the address.

"What's the deal?" he asks.

"Beats me. Mr. Cheerful didn't say, just wants us to get there pronto."

"Huh," Charlie says.

Renton is a suburb of Seattle, thirteen miles southeast of the city. It's got a lot of heavy industry—several Boeing plants are located here, as well as a big lem facility. The address Cassius gave me is at the end of a cul-de-sac, a sprawling storage-locker place flanked by an auto-parts warehouse and a trucking firm. I don't see anything that looks like an Agency vehicle, but I guess Cassius could have parked farther away.

There's a pire waiting for us at the loading dock, standing just inside the raised rolling steel door out of direct sunlight. He's in full daywear, a loose-fitting hood over a black face mask with smoked goggles. Long gray trench coat, black gloves. His body language is tensed and expectant.

Cassius always wears the same daywear when he goes out. This isn't it.

We pull up and get out of the car. The pire motions us inside. I stroll right up to him and say, "Hey, Caligula. Not your usual duds."

"Discretion is vital," Cassius says. His voice is as stressed as his body language—but it's still a language I recognize. "Follow me."

He leads us into a maze of corridors, wire-mesh units stacked with furniture, cardboard boxes, old appliances; people's lives, crated up and caged like bad memories of the past. We stop at one that's been broken into, the wire-mesh door torn right off its hinges. The interior is empty save for a single steamer trunk, the lid open. There's nothing inside, but a faint smell still hangs in the air, something that reminds me of summertime. After a second I get it: canvas, warmed by the sun. We used to have an old army tent that would get that smell on hot July days, when we had it set up in the backyard for shade.

Cassius strips off his mask and hood. He doesn't look agitated, but his eyes are restless; they flicker from my face to the trunk to the fluorescent-lit corridors that stretch away on either side of us.

"What I'm about to tell you is something only a few people on the planet are aware of," Cassius says. "I would prefer not to—and you may share that view before long—but events have forced my hand."

"I'm guessing something's been stolen," I say.

Cassius raises one black-gloved hand. "Jace, please. I have a lot to tell you. Hear me out before you ask any questions."

"Go ahead."

"There's an organization known as the Hexagon. It's a very ancient, very powerful group of individuals who have influenced the course of civilization for many, many years. Their reach is global, their power immense. As with most long-lived organizations, they eventually suffered a schism in their ranks. A serious divide over their directions and methods."

Cassius takes a step into the storage unit and stares down at the empty trunk. "The split happened shortly after World War Two. The splinter faction was headed by a man named John Dark."

"The man I'm hunting."

"Yes. And even though Dark himself couldn't be responsible for this—not directly—I now believe he's the one behind the recent murders and thefts."

"What was taken?"

"The armor of the Solar Centurion."

I move closer to stand beside him, and peer into the trunk. There's something round and silver gleaming in the far corner. "How do you know? All I see is some empty luggage—up till now there's always been a body at these crime scenes."

"I know," Cassius says, "because I *am* the Solar Centurion."

TEN

"Nuh-*uh*," I say.

"I'm telling you the truth, Jace."

"But the Solar Centurion's armor generates sunlight! And you're a *pire*!"

"It emits solar radiation in one direction only, and every inch of my body is covered—even the parts that appear to be bare skin. It's a most effective weapon, especially against members of my own kind."

"And you kept it in a low-rent storage unit?"

He shakes his head. "It was protected by secrecy. The spells surrounding this trunk make it essentially invisible to anyone trying to find it."

"But someone did."

"Yes. The fact that they chose to steal it rather than kill me leads me to believe that the murders are being committed primarily to amass power."

"Or maybe," Charlie says, "the head of the National Security Agency is just too hard a target."

"Could be," Cassius admits.

"In which case," Charlie continues, "the natural time to stage an attack would be right about *now*."

I glance around. The fluorescents buzz like cheap hair

clippers. Nobody pounces on us from the shadows—which, granted, there aren't that many of.

"I think you'd better get out of here," I tell Cassius. "I'll call Eisfanger, get him down here to process the scene. And don't worry—I'll keep your name out of it."

Cassius nods. "I appreciate this. Come by the office when you're done and we'll talk further."

"Oh, you better believe it," I say.

"This is . . . unusual," Eisfanger says. He's walking the perimeter of the storage unit, holding what seems to be a dowsing rod, a Y-shaped stick with a small LED screen wired between the forks. "According to these readings, there's no magic here. None. And never has been, either."

"I was afraid of that." I shake my head. "This place has been—I don't know, *stealthed* against magic. Whoever stole the armor didn't locate it by mystical means, and the shielding is now effectively masking any magic traces the thief might have left behind."

"He might have left something more mundane, though," Eisfanger says. "The door looks like it was ripped off by brute strength. Good chance of some sort of transfer, maybe a grip impression." He puts the dowsing rod away and rummages in his kit.

I peer into the trunk again. "Come over and take a look at this. Over here, in the corner."

He does. "Yeah, I see it. Looks like mercury." He collects the silvery blob carefully into a small vial.

"Otherwise known as quicksilver," I murmur. "Keep an eye out for traces of regular silver, too, will you?"

I stand in the corridor with Charlie, letting Eisfanger work. "What do you think?" I say. "Silverado?"

"Seems a little too obvious. If there'd been a fight he

might have bled off a little, but this was a straight theft. Looks planted to me."

"Me, too. Somebody's trying to throw us off the trail."

"Which means we're getting close to something."

"No moss on you. Well, maybe a little on your north side."

"That's trees. If you're going to insult me, at least try for accuracy."

"Was I at least within a stone's throw?"

"Getting better."

So we were getting a little too near the truth for the killer's liking. There's only one thing I can think of that might have triggered that—my dream conversation with Neil. That suggests that the connection the killer is most afraid I'll make has something to do with comic books, and leads me to my next move.

"Charlie and I have to go," I tell Eisfanger. "Get the trunk to the lab and see if you can, I don't know, de-stealth it. Call me if you find anything interesting."

"Yeah, sure."

"Where we headed?" Charlie asks as we get in the car.

"To talk to a man about a comic book."

I punch in Cassius's number and don't waste time with small talk. "I need to know something," I say when he answers.

"What?"

"Who created the *Bravo Brigade*?"

"I thought that was obvious. The Hexagon assembled the Brigade to deal with the Kamic cult—"

"Yeah, I got that. Not what I meant. I mean, who were the people who created the comic? The writer, the artists?"

He pauses. "We used one creator, who wrote and drew it. Easier to maintain security that way."

"I need a name."

Another pause, longer this time. "All right. His name is Sheldon Vincent. He's a member of the Four Color Club."

"I'm going to have to talk to him."

"I'll call you back with an address." He hangs up.

Charlie glances over from the driver's seat. We're driving the I-5, and it's going on noon. The sky looks like it's made from stained granite. "He wasn't too crazy about the idea, was he?"

"No, but he'll go along with it. We're his best option to get that suit back, and I get the feeling that losing it has rattled him."

Traffic slows, stops. A truck loaded with landscaping gear belches blue smoke as it idles in front of us. "Funny," I say. "Never thought of Cassius as the superhero type."

"You haven't known him that long."

"Oh? You're telling me you don't find the idea of him dressed in glowing Roman armor, blasting bolts of light at a bunch of bank robbers, ludicrous?"

"Bank robbers, yeah. But on a battlefield, sure. It's not so different from what I did in the Persian War."

Charlie never talks about his life as a soldier. "How so?"

The traffic starts up again, slowly. "That suit of armor turns the wearer into a weapon. That's what I am. Put either of us in combat, we'll do what we were made to do."

"Destroy the enemy."

He gives me a pained glance. "Destruction is counter-productive. You just want to hurt the other guy badly enough to convince him to quit—or hurt enough people around him that he spends all his energy trying to save them instead of advancing."

"Ah. How enlightened." I stare out the window at a minivan full of sleepy-looking kids, their mother driving while their father talks on a cell phone. "I don't know,

Charlie. I guess I think of superheroes and soldiers as different things. I can see Cassius as a soldier—it's the whole symbol thing that doesn't seem to fit."

"Maybe it doesn't. We only have his word that he's the Centurion."

I sigh. "Yeah, the thought occurred to me. But I don't think so—if he really wanted to misdirect us he could send us right out of the country. This seems genuine."

The phone rings and I answer. It's Cassius, who gives me an address. "He'll be expecting you."

"Thanks." My turn to hang up abruptly, which is petty but sort of satisfying.

Sheldon Vincent lives in Queen Anne, a ritzy neighborhood on a hill right next to downtown. The view alone is expensive, let alone the sprawling house; it must have a dozen bedrooms, easy. We pull into the turnaround driveway and park under a Douglas fir that looks like it's been around since man discovered fire. Four marble pillars hold up the porch, and the front door is a massive affair you could easily turn into a raft, or maybe a yacht. We ring the doorbell and are greeted by an honest-to-God butler—a lem in formal wear. His skin is the same thick plastic as Charlie's, but the material inside isn't black sand—it's blindingly white, with swirls of pearly opalescence through it.

"Good day," the butler says. His accent is cultured and very British. "Mr. Vincent is expecting you. Please come this way."

We follow him through the requisite grand foyer with its crystal chandelier, and into a room with wide floor-to-ceiling windows and a white baby grand piano in front of them. Another gleaming lem works in the garden outside.

Vincent himself is sitting on the couch, drinking coffee. He looks like he just got up and hasn't even shaved; he's dressed in a blue flannel robe over red silk pajamas. He's balding—unusual for a thrope, but not unheard of—and has long muttonchop whiskers, streaked with gray, down either side of his long, lean face.

"Good afternoon," I say. "I'm Special Agent Jace Valchek. This is Charlie Aleph. David Cassius sent us over to talk with you."

Vincent nods, takes a long drink of his coffee while studying us over the rim of the mug. He swallows, then says, "Sit, please."

I do, but Charlie stays on his feet. That's fine—I trust my partner's instincts. "Mr. Vincent, I understand you're an artist."

"I paint, yes."

"That's not the kind of art I'm talking about."

"No, I don't suppose you are. You want to know about *The Bravo Brigade*."

He pauses, and I wonder if he finds talking about the subject difficult, or even distasteful; it's hard to imagine a painter living in this sort of house doing comic books. When he speaks, though, he surprises me.

"*The Bravo Brigade*. My greatest accomplishment, and greatest shame. Probably the best-known comic book in the world, and the one that helped end the comic book as an art form. It's not even that good, you know. I've produced far superior work since then—not that any of it's been seen by more than a handful of people."

"The other members of the Four Color Club, you mean."

"Yes. They're my only audience, now—though hardly their only source."

"Oh? There are more people like you? Underground comics artists?"

He chuckles. "No, not really. My competition has more esoteric origins—though that source suffers from certain disadvantages, as well. Shipping costs are astronomical."

It takes me a second to understand what he's referring to. "You're talking about comics from other realities."

"Yes, Agent Valchek. Like yours."

Somehow, I'm not surprised that he knows. He's wealthy, well connected, and belongs to at least one high-powered secret society, if not two. "About that," I say. "Of all the reasons I can think of to spy on other realities, reading somebody else's comic books seems kind of trivial. Is that really all you do?"

He takes another sip of his coffee. "It's less trivial than you might imagine, Agent Valchek. But yes, that's what we do—and our reasons are practical as well as artistic. Comics, you see, occupy a particular niche in animist magic. They are both a visual and literary depiction of events, drawing on a generations-long shared history and a collaboration among artists, writers, editors, and the readers themselves. As such, they have an affinity for cross-universe travel; they almost beg to slip from one reality to another. The energy cost to bring a single issue across is admittedly large—but the bandwidth, if you'll forgive the analogy, is still minuscule compared with any other medium. Far less than trying to eavesdrop on another reality's television or even a phone call."

"So it's a rich man's hobby. Expensive but basically harmless."

"You make it sound like collecting stamps. It's far, far more than that." He leans forward intently. "The art form has progressed so much since my fumblings with *The Bravo Brigade*. Jack Kirby's work alone would be worth all our effort, and there's been dozens, *hundreds* of artists and writers since him. I'm not sure whether I envy you or pity you, Agent Valchek; you come from a world of unparalleled riches, and you're oblivious to all of them."

"I don't know about that," I said. "I used to get a laugh out of *Doonesbury* now and then."

He nods. "You're being facetious, but it's a fair comparison. There are comics being produced in your world today that are just as politically aware and literate, and considerably more subversive. Grant Morrison's *The Invisibles,* which ran in the late 1990s, is a good example. It deals with alternate universes, contemporary magic, secret societies, and revolutionary cabals."

"Sounds familiar."

"That's not all. Morrison claimed the entire series was, in fact, one long and intricate spell."

"Really? What was he trying to accomplish?"

"What all magicians are trying to accomplish, Agent Valchek. He wanted to change the world."

It's the second time Morrison's name has come up. "This Morrison—does he have a counterpart in this reality? Or a writer named Alan Moore?"

Vincent gives me a crooked little smile. "If only they did—but sadly, no. Why did you ask to speak to me, Agent Valchek?"

"You know about the murders?"

"I've been kept informed."

"Who do you think is committing them?"

He hesitates. "It could be any number of people. Old enemies of the Brigade, perhaps—"

"I was under the impression that the Brigade was formed to deal with one specific threat. The Kamic cult."

"True, but all the members had their own individual histories long before that. Their own enemies."

"Such as?"

He shrugs, settling back in his seat, and crosses his legs. "I'm really not familiar with that aspect. I was brought in to create the comic—to take legends and turn them into myths, essentially. You'd need a historian to track down their exploits—though, from what I understand, they tended to avoid publicity."

I try another tack. "How about John Dark?"

He raises his eyebrows. "Dark? I thought he was dead. If he isn't, he'd be a powerful enemy . . . and, yes, fully capable of hunting down and killing every member of the Brigade."

"Tell me about him."

"He was the power behind the cult. Wertham was the one who came up with the principle of using comic books as magical foci, but Dark was the leader."

"So I've heard. Why wasn't he in the comic?"

"I was instructed not to mention him."

"Because of his involvement with the Hexagon?"

"Yes."

"How about you? Are you a member, too?"

He frowns. "Let me be perfectly blunt about one thing, Agent Valchek: It was made very, very clear to me when I was brought in on this project, all those years ago, that I was not to talk about—that group. Not then, not ever. So I'm afraid I can't discuss such a question, even to deny it."

Hmmm. That's probably a yes—but a very, very, paranoid one. Maybe even enough to qualify as a no. "Then let me ask you something else. Are you more than just an artist? Did you help craft the counterspell the *Brigade* comic was created to generate?"

"Of course I did. And just as Wertham used blood from his victims in the ink, I used blood—or in one case, mercury—from the Bravos in the crafting of our spell."

"How is that different from everyday animism?"

He finishes his coffee and puts the mug down on an end table beside him. "It's a matter of concentration. You can talk to the spirit of a boulder, even manipulate it to do things a boulder might not normally do, but in the end you're still dealing with the essence of a large rock. This is about taking that essence and both distilling and amplifying it. The object you concentrate such power in becomes more *itself* than it's ever been, and does so in realms other than just the physical."

"I'm not sure I follow."

"You've heard of Excalibur?"

"Sure. Mystic sword, yanked out of a stone by King Arthur."

"Well, Excalibur is more than just a sword—it's the ultimate representation of one. It's the *idea* of a sword, brought to life. As such, it exists as more than just a sharp piece of metal—it exists as a concept, as a piece of history. When we created the *Bravo Brigade* comic, we were crafting something with the power of myth—but it was also a physical object you could hold, like Excalibur. A focus both physical and metaphysical, one that formed a mystic connection between the people who read it and the Brigade."

I nod. "Cutting-edge stuff, no doubt . . . One final question. What would happen if you used that kind of magic on objects that were already mystically enhanced?"

He frowns. "You could make them more powerful, I suppose. Though there would be an upper limit—no object can absorb infinite power."

"I see. Thank you for your time, Mr. Vincent."

"I'm sorry I couldn't be of more help." He gets up and shakes my hand. "Perhaps I can be later."

"I'll call you if I have further questions."

"That's not what I meant." He meets my eyes and holds on to my hand for a second longer than necessary. "I meant you should contact me in case you require alternate *travel* possibilities."

He drops my hand and motions to the butler, who's mysteriously arrived without being summoned. "Phibes will show you out. Good day, Agent Valchek. And good luck."

Charlie follows me out the door. He hasn't said a word

since we arrived, and he holds his silence until we're back in the car.

"Well?" I say.

"Nobody ends an interrogation with a bribe," Charlie says as he starts the car. "Unless they're guilty of something."

We check in on Galahad and discover he's actually been pretty well behaved. I take him for a quick walk, and he does exactly what a dog is supposed to on a walk—which includes barking madly at pigeons, trying to eat an old candy bar wrapper, and demonstrating a bladder capacity equivalent to a watercooler, emptied a thimbleful at a time. For someone new to the neighborhood, he sure left a lot of messages.

Then it's in to work, where I square my shoulders and march in to talk to Gretch.

And find out she's not there.

"She took the day off," Mahmoud tells me. He's a pire—I think—though he's the only one I've met who wears glasses. "Don't know why."

"Thanks," I mutter. Guess a pire calling in sick would kind of spill the beans.

The rest of the shift is spent trying to track down Silverado—but he's vanished, too. He's dropped off his prisoner, but no one's heard from him since. I don't know if that's just the bounty hunter being careful, or if we have another victim on our hands.

I try calling Gretch. No answer.

I look in on Eisfanger in his lab, hoping he'll have something for me. He doesn't. About all he can tell me is that whoever took the armor is a lot stronger than most pires or thropes, which could be the result of either drugs or magic. Wonderful.

I finally give up and call it a day. Charlie drops me off at my apartment and I take Galahad for another quick walk before crawling into bed at around 4:00 PM.

I wake from a deep sleep into a deep groggy. My door buzzer is buzzing in that insistent kind of way that lets me know there's a teenager who wants to be let in. I stagger to the door, mutter something into the speaker, and let them in. Then I throw on a robe and head for the kitchen to brew some coffee.

To find it's already been made—by the large, naked man in my kitchen.

"Coffee?" he says, in a voice that sounds more like he isn't sure it *is* coffee and is requesting confirmation.

"Coffee," I agree. My brain is refusing to properly process what's going on, so I pour myself some coffee and try it. It's strong enough to etch concrete, which is just about right.

"Good *boy,* Galahad," I say. "My God, I may just have to keep you."

He grins proudly and waggles his butt.

"But you're *still* going to have to wear pants."

He gives me that over-innocent look that dogs do so well, that *What? Huh? I don't know that word* look.

"Pants," I say firmly, and he hangs his head and slinks into the living room.

There's a knock at the door. My brain starts functioning again. I check the peephole and see that it's Xandra—I vaguely remember her identifying herself, back in the Precaffeinic Era. I let her in. She's doing her corpsing thing today, half her face rotted away and one eyeball dangling down onto her cheek. Her left hand is completely skeletonized, and she's wearing a peek-a-boo top that shows off her ribs—literally. Torn jeans and army boots finish off the outfit.

"Hey, Jace," she says. "Hi, Gally."

"Xandra! Xandra!"

I shake my head. "You've got *him* saying it already?"

"Sure. He was my test case. He's actually pretty smart."

"So I've discovered. He made coffee."

She grins—well, the half of her mouth that isn't already exposed does. "Yeah, Uncle Pete taught him that. He said it was all about teaching him manual dexterity and simple tasks, but I think he had ulterior motives."

"Have you heard from him?"

She throws herself down on the sofa, and Galahad promptly tries to sit on her lap—at least he's wearing pants now. She pushes him off good-naturedly. "No. It's kind of weird, but I guess he could have gone back to visit his old friends or something."

I frown, and drink more coffee. "His old friends? From where?"

"I don't know—wherever he came from. We're not supposed to ask him about it. I think there was some big family tragedy, though; pretty sure he's an orphan."

I blink. "Wait. He's not really your uncle?"

"Sure he is. Oh, you mean by *blood*. I guess not, but he's a member of our pack—that's the important thing."

So Dr. Pete has a past, after all. "How long has he been a member?"

"I don't know—as long as I can remember. You'd have to ask my parents—but I wouldn't."

"Why not?"

"You probably don't know this, but it's kinda rude to ask about someone's former pack. You could maybe get away with it because you're not a thrope, but they probably wouldn't tell you anything."

"Ah. Thanks for the tip."

"No problem." She gets up from the couch and heads for the kitchen. "How are you fixed for food? I'm *starving*."

One problem thropes and pires don't seem to have is an obsession with their weight—maybe because one only drinks blood and the other has a really fast metabolism. In any case, the only thing that consumes more calories than a thrope is a teenage thrope.

"Yuck!" she says, her head in my fridge. "You've got all these *vegetables* in here. Some of them I don't even *recognize*." She stalks back into the living room, holding something at arm's length. "I mean, what *is* this?"

"That's a zucchini. It's really good in stir-fries."

She makes a face. "It looks obscene. These things grow in *dirt,* you know."

I consider telling her about fertilizer and where it comes from, and decide against it. "I know. Look, I'm going to have to go out and get you some supplies, all right?"

"Sure. We can both go, take Gally with us."

Galahad is looking hard from Xandra to me and back again. He's not entirely sure what's going on, but he seems to know it has something to do with a walk.

"You sure? No way I'm putting a leash on him."

"Don't worry—he sticks pretty close. And he listens to me."

I tell her to give me a minute to get dressed. I haven't had enough sleep, but I'm wide awake—might as well do something useful.

We stroll down to a supermarket a few blocks away, one of those huge glass boxes that sell everything from lawn furniture to children's shoes. I'm a little nervous about taking Galahad in there, but he behaves himself—only once do I catch him trying to tear open a package of hamburger, and he drops it with an ashamed expression when I bust him.

I let Xandra load up on pretty much whatever she wants—which includes lamb chops, smoked oysters, a two-liter bottle of something carbonated called Beefy Fizz, and prime-rib-flavored potato chips.

We're in the checkout line when I glance down the nearest aisle and see him.

Dr. Pete.

It's only a glimpse, but I know it's him. He's unshaven, wearing a black peacoat over a black turtleneck and jeans. He ducks out of sight as soon as I spot him.

"Hey!" I say. I sprint down the aisle without thinking. Galahad joins me, doing his best to keep up on only two feet. I reach the end of the aisle and skid to a halt, looking around wildly. No Dr. Pete in sight.

Galahad narrowly avoids slamming into me a second later. He casts about with his head up, breathing heavily through his nose, and I realize he may actually be able to smell Dr. Pete.

"Where is he?" I ask. "Where's Dr. Pete?"

Galahad sprints for the produce section, me right behind him. There's a loud crash before we get there, cans hitting the floor and glass breaking. We round a corner and see pineapples and grapefruits all over the floor, amid spilled salad dressing and a variety of canned goods that have been jolted off a shelf.

Standing in the midst of the mess is Tair.

He looks different under the blank glare of fluorescents, but it's definitely him. There's a gray stripe down the center of his head I hadn't noticed before. He looks angry—ears flattened back, fangs bared. There's no sign of Dr. Pete.

Where is he? Tair signs. *I know he's here—I can smell him.*

Galahad stops by my side and makes a sound that's definitely a growl. "Easy, Gally. Lose something, Tair?"

He's afraid to face me. Maybe the doctor needs a little incentive.

The supermarket is relatively deserted, but there's a few shoppers standing around and gawking at the spectacle; Tair reaches out and casually grabs one, a skinny woman with straggly white hair and a flowered sundress. Before she can do much more than yelp, he's snapped his jaws around her throat.

In one quick yank, he's ripped it out.

I've seen my share of ugly violence, but there's usually some warning. The woman flails and tries to scream as blood splashes everywhere. She must be a thrope, but the suddenness of the attack and the loss of blood has her in a state of shock; silver hair begins to sprout on her face and arms as she instinctively tries to transform.

Tair shoves her away and gives me a wolfy smile, his teeth dripping red.

"Galahad," I say. "Go to Xandra. *Now.*"

He whines, but obeys. I study Tair carefully as the old woman writhes and sputters on the floor.

No Sunshine Man to save you now, bitch. Maybe your precious Dr. Pete will show up to stitch you back together instead.

He takes a step toward me, flexing his fingers with their inch-long black claws as he signs. He isn't moving slowly out of caution—he wants me to scream, to draw Dr. Pete out of hiding.

He obviously doesn't know me very well.

ELEVEN

I don't have my gun with me. That's too bad for Tair.

What I do have is my scythes, tucked into their specially sewn pockets in the lining of my coat on either side. I've practiced cross-drawing them and flicking the blades open, and I have more than enough time to do so as Tair approaches.

And stops.

My old sensei Duane Dunn was a big believer in psychological warfare. "Best fight is the one that never happens," he used to say. "Nothing wrong with running away, but if your opponent can run faster than you, you're still in trouble. Better to make *him* run."

The scythes' blades are around a foot long. Most pires or thropes will hesitate when facing that much razor-sharp silver, but I find it's even more effective with a little demonstration. And here I am in a produce department . . .

There's a pyramid of cantaloupes right next to me. I snap a strike at the topmost one and bisect it along the equator, cleanly enough that the top half doesn't slide off. I do it without my taking my eyes off Tair.

His claws dance in the air in front of me as he signs. *My, what big teeth you have, Grandma.*

"All the better to disembowel you with, asshole. Only one needing stitches is going to be you."

He glances at the old woman on the floor, who's managed to shift into half-were form and is twitching weakly while clutching her throat. *How about her?*

"She'll be fine." He's trying to distract me.

And your arm? How's that?

It's actually throbbing like a son-of-a-bitch at the moment, but not enough to make me lose focus. "Thanks for reminding me. Where are your bandage buddies, anyway? There a sale on down at the Yarn Barn?"

He takes a step backward. *I apologize for their impulsiveness. A general cannot always control his soldiers.*

"A general that can't might find himself losing his privates," I say, making a suggestive but not serious swipe at him. Unlike the last time we met, Tair's gone completely commando; he's not wearing anything but fur and fangs. The fur hides most of it, but not all. "Especially if he parades them around in public."

We don't really need to do this, Jace. I'm not your enemy.

"No? Funny, the Blood Cross I pulled out of my arm says otherwise. And then there was that bitch-needing-stitches remark someone made . . . oh, wait. That was you."

I was hoping to draw out Dr. Adams. Apparently he doesn't care about your welfare all that much.

"Or maybe he just knows I can take care of myself." Which sounds good but is pure crap—before he vanished, I would have bet anything Dr. Pete would risk his life to help me if I was in trouble. He's done it before.

But not now.

As I said before, my business is with Adams, not with you. Since he's obviously fled, so have my reasons for staying. And with that, he turns and bounds away.

I don't bother chasing him. I kneel down and ask the

old woman if she's okay. She growls at me, struggles out of her sundress, and runs off down the aisle on all fours. Guess she'll be all right.

I sheathe the scythes and return to the checkout, trailed by a small group of curious shoppers. Xandra, unfazed, waves me over impatiently. "Come on," she says. "You have to *pay* for all this stuff, remember?"

I notice she's listening to an iPod—she probably missed the whole thing. Galahad looks at me with a worried expression and whines. I reach up, pat him on the head and say, "Good dog. Let's get you home and off the streets, okay?"

The cashier is looking at me strangely as she rings up my items, but nobody tries to stop me from leaving the store—I wasn't the one that busted it up, after all.

"Hey, look at this," Xandra says as she helps bag our groceries. "This cantaloupe's already sliced."

I don't tell Xandra about what happened or seeing Dr. Pete. She'll have a million questions, and I have no answers. It's starting to look like Dr. Pete was mixed up with some very bad people, and I just don't know how to explain that—I don't have enough information, I don't know what is or isn't true. Dr. Pete is the one with the answers, and he's the one who'll have to decide how much to tell his niece. In the meantime, she'll have to settle for blissful ignorance.

I do tell her one thing: to watch out for a thrope with a gray stripe running down the middle of his head.

We go back to the apartment and I get ready to go in to work—looks like I'm working the sundown-to-sunup shift for a while. I decide not to call Charlie; I don't want to screw up his schedule just because he's stuck with being my partner. He'll either show up at the office or call me, anyway.

There's a message waiting for me when I get in. Eisfanger wants me to see him in the lab. I head up there, wondering why he didn't just call my cell.

The lab is its usual combination of stainless steel and industrial tile, brightly lit by halogen spots that every now and then illuminate something that doesn't seem to belong: a broom that looks like it was put together in the 1700s, or an African tribal mask made from aluminum and high-impact plastic. Eisfanger's there, but no other techs are around—odd for this time of night. He's pacing when I arrive.

"Jace," he says, managing to look both relieved and worried at the same time. "Good, good. I have to talk to you."

"So I gathered. What's up?"

"I've managed to locate some—uh, *resources* for you," he says carefully. "In relation to that case I was helping you on."

"Which one?"

"The unofficial one."

Ah. Now I get it. "Okay. What do you have?"

He actually glances furtively around, as if espionage agents are lurking beneath his workstation. "Comics," he whispers.

"All right. Which ones?"

He hands me a bulky manila envelope, sealed with several layers of tape and a metal tab. "Here. Don't ask me how I got them, don't read them while there's a full moon, and get them back to me within twenty-four hours."

I take the envelope and frown. "Come on. Are they really that dangerous? Dr. Pete had a bunch in his basement."

"Not like this. These are from the *Seduction of the Innocent* murders. They're the only copies left in existence, and I'm not cleared to even be in the same room with them."

"Wait. You said this was pertinent to the *unofficial* investigation—"

"It is. The storage unit itself was completely devoid of mystical activity, but I did a wide sweep of the area around the building hoping that maybe the thief left something behind when they arrived or left. I found this." He pulls a glass vial out of his pocket that at first glance seems empty. Then I see it holds a minuscule, jagged-edged black rock. "This was stuck in a crack at the loading dock. I wouldn't have spotted it at all, except the energy it was giving off was so powerful. I ran a Specter-graphic analysis on it and came up with a match."

I study the black mineral. "What is it?"

"Volcanic rock," he says. "Produced by an eruption in 1956."

I close and lock the door to my office, and then I open the envelope.

There are five comics inside: the three issues of *Seduction of the Innocent,* and two others. I slip on a pair of surgical gloves, then look at the *SOTI* comics first.

The cover of the first depicts a man holding a severed wolf's head in one hand, and a bloody silver ax in the other. The eyes of the head are staring down at its own decapitated half-were body.

The second cover shows a blindfolded child with a smile on her face being led into a darkened room by a shadowy figure. The floor is covered with spring-loaded bear traps, the kind with big jagged metal teeth that lock shut on a leg when stepped on. For some reason, the drain set into the floor is the detail that disturbs me the most.

The last one depicts a thrope in full wolf form in a cage. The cage is suspended over a blazing bonfire, and is being lowered by a figure in a hooded robe.

I'm surprised by how much the images bother me. The

subject matter is grisly, but it's only ink on paper; I've seen far worse in person. It's more than that, and it takes me a second to place my reaction. It's smell—I'm having the same kind of visceral, slightly nauseous sensation produced by a really horrifying odor, like the smell left in a car that someone's died in. But there *isn't* any smell— just the sensation.

The paper has a slightly greasy feel to it, too, even through the gloves, and it's just as illusory—my fingers don't slide any easier against the paper when I try rubbing it. It's as if my mind knows that the comics are coated with some sort of foul, slippery substance that my senses can't detect.

The other two comics, though, don't produce that reaction. The first one is a copy of *The Bravo Brigade,* but the cover is different from the one Dr. Pete lent me: This one has no date or price listed, and the art depicts the Bravos facing off against a single man in a robe with his hood thrown back. I don't recognize him—he has a high widow's peak of jet-black hair, a hawk-like face with a sharp goatee and thin mustache. The banner beneath the art reads AGAINST THE DARK!

The fifth book is titled *Western Wonders.* The cover shows a very familiar-looking lem battling what seem to be Apache thropes—five lie dead or dying at his feet, the hilt of a knife sticking out of chest or throat, while another in half-were form leaps at him, tomahawk in hand; the lem's already got his arm cocked for another throw. The banner just below the title reads, THE LAST STAND OF THE QUICKSILVER KID!

I wonder why it's there. None of the other Bravos seem to have their own comic—there's no Sword of Midnight or Doctor Transe title. I leaf through it, but it's a pretty standard tale of cowboys versus Indians, with the Indians getting the short end of the coup stick.

I go back to the Brigade comic. Turns out it isn't a comic at all—it's a mock-up of one, twenty-two pages of rough panel layouts and scrawled notes in the margins. I pull out Dr. Pete's copy and compare them side by side; they're very similar except for one thing.

John Dark has been completely excised from the version that was released to the public.

I realize I'm actually avoiding reading the *Seduction* issues. It's not a full moon, so it should be safe—but I place them flat on my desk and use a pencil to turn the pages anyway.

I don't learn anything new. The stories are all stand-alone plots, usually dealing with some sort of betrayal or evil deed that winds up backfiring on the perpetrator. A question occurs to me, and the best person to ask is probably Cassius—he and I are overdue for a conversation anyway.

I walk down to his office and knock. There's no answer at first, and I wonder if he's disappeared, too—at this rate, I'm going to have to get a bicycle lock for Charlie. I knock again, and this time he tells me to come in.

He's at his usual spot behind his desk, but the room is much darker than usual; the only light comes from his computer screen. Whatever he's looking at, it has a lot of green in it.

"We need to talk," I say.

"The words every man loves to hear," he says. He taps a key and the lights come up, just enough to make the room feel more like a study instead of a dungeon. "You should know, Jace, that I can't tell you much about the Hexagon."

"I didn't think you would. My question is about the *Seduction of the Innocent* murders—specifically, the comics that were produced as a result. Which of the scenes depicted were duplicated in real life—the original crimes, or the consequence that always follows?"

He studies me for an instant before replying. "The consequential ones."

"That's what I thought." Those were the more horrifying of the two, of course—the initial murder scenes were bad, but the retribution that resulted was always worse.

"The spell generated a type of emotional dissonance," Cassius says. "Reading the comic generates horror, but it's tempered with a certain moral satisfaction that the antagonist gets what he or she deserves. Reversing the crime and punishing an innocent is a corruptive act—especially when subjecting an innocent audience to it. By approving of what befalls the villain in the comic, they're unwittingly giving metaphysical support to the actual murder."

"Essentially making them silent partners in the cult itself. Not exactly believers—more like endorsers."

"Exactly. Thus the title of the series—the ones being seduced were innocent of what was occurring."

"But John Dark knew exactly what he was doing."

Cassius doesn't respond.

I sigh. "You told me you now believe Dark is behind the murders, but you won't give me anything else? Not even the reason you changed your mind?"

"We had him under surveillance, which is why I know he didn't commit the murders personally. But the killings now seem secondary to the acquisition of the Brigade's weaponry—and that's very much Dark's methodology. I simply don't know who his agent is, or how they're communicating."

"Well, whoever they are, they now have the Sword, the Balancer gem, and the Solar armor. That's a powerful combination."

"If they can wield them. Mystic artifacts aren't like your gun—you can't simply point one and pull a trigger. All the Brigade's weapons were warded and keyed to their user—those wards can be broken, but it will take time."

"So why wait until they do? If you were surveilling Dark, you know where he is—can't we just bring him in, try to sweat him?"

He laughs without any amusement in it. "Oh, absolutely. Then maybe we can put the president in an interrogation room and get him to confess all the bad things he did in college."

I look at him skeptically. "You're saying he's out of our reach?"

"Not at all. I'm saying that any move we make directly against him better be as immaculate as the Virgin Mary and as solid as the Rock of Gibraltar, or the consequences will destroy us both."

"Ah. There goes my plan of locking him up until he needs to go to the bathroom."

"In any case, it doesn't matter. He's gone—vanished right from under our surveillance. Don't ask me how, because I don't know."

"Damn it! Is every person associated with this case going to vanish into thin air? First Dr. Pete, then Silverado, now John Dark—I can't even get hold of Gretchen."

He blinks. A shadow of an emotion flickers across his face, so quickly I almost miss it—what analysts call a micro-expression. I'm trained to spot them, and I identify this one immediately: guilt.

"What?" I demand. "What *about* Gretchen?"

"She's fine."

"Okay. Where is she *doing* this being fine?"

"A safe house. She's there with Dr. Pete."

I stare at him in disbelief. "But you asked me to talk to her."

"I know. I meant to tell you, but the theft of the suit was preying on my mind, and I—" He shrugs. "I forgot."

I glare at him. "No. You didn't. You told me you'd look into whoever was stalking Dr. Pete, and then he disappeared. You were worried about Gretchen, so you hid her in the same place. But you didn't want me following up on Dr. Pete, did you? So you decided that both their whereabouts should probably stay a mystery for now—which will hopefully keep me focused on the murder investigation and not sticking my nose into Dr. Pete's past. How am I doing?"

"Admirably."

"Yeah? Well, someone from Dr. Pete's past threatened to turn me into Hamburger Helper a few hours ago, I was starting to think one of my only friends here might be the latest victim of a serial killer, and I just found out my prime suspect is in the wind because my employer thought it more important to protect his privacy than help my investigation. *Now* how am I doing?"

"I realize this is a difficult situation—"

"You don't realize a damn thing. You knew all along and used that knowledge to manipulate me. So here's something you don't know: *I quit.*"

"What?" He actually looks startled.

"You heard me. Screw this case, screw the Hexagon, and screw *you.* I'm going to hunt down Stoker *and* the shaman that brought me here, and when I find them I expect you to honor your end of the bargain and let me blow this entire goddamn planet a good-bye kiss."

I close the door gently but firmly on my way out.

"You're kidding," Xandra says. "You really quit?"

"Not exactly."

We're walking through the Pike Place Flea Market on Saturday morning. It's a series of tents and booths set up down by the waterfront, selling everything from fresh fish to antiques. I think it's a little more run-down than the version in my world, but I can't say for sure because I've never been. All I know is that here, you can buy pretty much anything.

"I'm still working for the Agency," I say. "I'm just re-focusing my priorities."

Xandra's looking at some jewelry. No silver, of course—mostly gold and copper. "Trying to catch that Stoker guy, right?"

"Yeah."

"And you're sure Uncle Pete is all right?"

"I haven't talked to him, but Cassius says he's safe."

She picks up a Blood Cross made of wood on a leather thong and holds it under her throat. "What do you think?"

I try not to wince. "I think it reminds me of things I'd rather not think about."

She throws it back on the table. "Not really my style, anyway."

We've got Galahad on a leash, and he's doing his best to inhale the universe through his nose. I feel a twinge of affection, for him and Xandra both; I'm going to miss them when I finally go home. For now, though, I'm just going to enjoy strolling through the market, looking through piles of merchandise and assorted junk, marveling at the detritus of a culture very different from my own.

In twenty minutes of browsing, I see: a tattered cook-book on how to prepare field mice; a Kabuki face mask made entirely of smoked glass; an antique tooth file; a voodoo perm kit that claims to let curls survive up to thirty transformations; a videotape of a movie called *The Ter-minator* starring Bela Lugosi; a stack of magazines from the 1960s called *Fur and Fang Today*; and a pup tent made from heavy black plastic that seals hermetically. Guess even pires like to go camping.

I also uncover some music, in various formats. Among my finds are an old forty-five of Dean Martin singing

"Everybody Loves Somebody Sometime," an eight-track tape of the Beach Boys—okay, I'm pretty sure Brian Wilson and the guys never did a song called "Hairy Mary," but it's got a bunch of others I recognize and I'm kind of curious to hear what werewolf harmonies sound like—and an honest-to-God CD of Colin James and his Little Big Band. Swing dance music, which I love.

I do my best to ignore the creeping sense of guilt I feel for shopping when I should be working. Not only did I promise Xandra, but this little outing is also helping me refocus—buying music that reminds me of home keeps me connected to my goal, which is definitely *not* getting enmeshed in the politics of a secret society full of supernatural beings.

One of which might be able to get me home a lot sooner. Of course, the very fact that Sheldon Vincent dangled that in front of me suggests he has something to hide and would prefer I relocate to another universe before I discover what it is.

Not that he's the only one hiding something. The Quicksilver Kid didn't tell us the whole truth, Cassius is spending as much time hiding information as he is providing it, and John Dark—so far, the biggest puzzle in the entire case—is pretty much only a face on the cover of an old comic book.

A face that's right in front of me.

"Hello," John Dark says. "I understand you want to talk to me."

The first thing I do is look around for Xandra. She's a few stalls over, sorting through some clothes.

The second thing I do is check for Dark's security. Nobody obvious, which either means they're very good or he doesn't think he needs them. I choose the conceited but paranoid approach, which is good for both my ego and my safety. "Hello, John. Or would you prefer Mr. Dark?"

"John is fine." He looks more or less exactly like he was drawn: high widow's peak of black hair, thin mustache, triangular goatee. Sharp eyes above a small nose. He's wearing a long black jacket over a three-piece suit, both of which look expensive, and highly polished leather shoes.

"Would you like to sit down?" he asks. "There's an adequate coffee shop across the street."

"Let's go for a walk, instead," I say. "I could use some sea air."

"Very well."

I pull out my phone as we leave the market and hit the boardwalk. I call Xandra and say, "Stay where you are, okay? I'll be there in a few minutes."

It's a nice day, the sun peeking through a gauzy haze of cloud over the water. Seagulls swoop and hover, fighting over scraps of fish thrown away by vendors.

We stroll along like ex-lovers, the atmosphere strained and cautious; I almost expect him to say, *I've been thinking about you lately.*

"I've been thinking," he says, "about having you killed."

"You always were sentimental," I say. "What brought this on? I forget to send you a Christmas card?"

He makes a small sound, more like a snort than a sigh. "I hate talking in clichés. This conversation is going to force me to do so, and I resent you for that. However, it's not enough to get you killed. Yet."

"Haven't heard a cliché yet, either."

"Stop poking your nose where it doesn't belong."

"Ouch! You weren't kidding."

"You don't know who you're dealing with, you're out of your depth *and* your league, dead women tell no tales so don't make me tell you twice. Okay?"

"I think I get the idea. Do I have to talk like that, or can you understand regular speech?"

"You're a bright woman, Jace. Tell me why I'm here."

"Well, you've decided to let me live, at least for now. If you just wanted to warn me off, you'd do something horrific and violent. So you actually have questions for *me* . . . which you know you won't get to ask unless you agree to answer a few of mine. Also, I'm going to reward my brilliant deduction by going first. Who's killing the Bravos?"

He smiles. "I don't know. But I'll give you my best guess—the Quicksilver Kid."

"Why?"

"Sorry, my turn to ask a question. Who's backing Cassius?"

It takes me a second to figure out what he means. "I don't mean to be uncooperative, but if that question concerns the Hexagon, I have no idea. Cassius doesn't share anything with me he doesn't have to, and I've only met one other person who might even possibly *be* a member."

"Who?"

That's technically another question, but I give it to him. "Sheldon Vincent."

He nods but betrays no emotion. "Fair enough. To answer your question, the Kid was never treated as an equal in the team. Lems in those days weren't considered people—they were more like glorified servants, barely more than slaves. If any of the Bravos were to go rogue, I'd put my money on him."

"Okay. I guess you have another question coming."

He stops and faces the bay, his hands on the gray metal of the railing. "What do you know about me?"

"I know you were the real leader of the Kamic cult, and a member of the Hexagon. I know something happened that caused an internal split in the late 1940s. And

I know you still have enough clout that when the cult
failed, you cut a deal that kept you alive, out of prison,
and out of the spotlight. What I don't know is what caused
that split, or if it has anything to do with the murders that
are being committed now."

He glances at me, no expression on his face. "That's
not exactly a question, Jace. Which is just as well . . .
because what I have for you isn't exactly an answer." He
pauses, then says, "Ask Cassius about the future. And
how it's shaped by the past."

"Okay. Do I have to say 'knock, knock' first, or is it
already sufficiently riddle-like?"

He laughs. "I'm glad I met you, Jace. I hope we'll meet
again."

And then he turns and walks away down the boardwalk. I don't bother trying to follow him; I know an exit
line when I hear one.

TWELVE

I go back and find Xandra, who's wandered off despite what I told her. Galahad acts like I've been gone for a million years, licking my hand and looking up at me with that adoration dogs seem to have trademarked. I tell her I'm ready to go and offer to buy her lunch.

Charlie's waiting at the curb, leaning up against his car with his arms crossed and his fedora tipped back on his head. "Hey. I hear I'm unemployed."

"You're not. We're still hunting Stoker."

"We? This your new enforcer?" He nods at Xandra, who rolls her eyes. "Because I went to work yesterday and my partner wasn't there. Seems she showed up early, threw a hissy fit, and then quit."

"I told you, I didn't quit. I went home early and got some much-needed sleep."

"You're all rested up, then. Good. Get in."

I sigh, and hand my bag of music to Xandra. "Take Galahad back to my place, will you? He should be okay there for the rest of the day."

"What about lunch?" Xandra says. Teenagers have their priorities.

"Raid my fridge. I think there's still some stuff left from the other night."

She shrugs and says, "Okay, whatever. See you later."

Once we're rolling I say, "Where we going?"

"It's a surprise. Like you not calling me after blowing up."

"I needed some time away from work. To think."

"About what?"

"Work."

"I see."

We drive for a while and neither of us says anything. The best kind of partner knows when to push you and knows when to back off; Charlie's that kind. Somehow, he always knows when to shut up.

"I don't know," I say at last. "This case is impossible. Everybody knows way more than I do, and nobody's willing to talk. And those are the ones supposedly on my side."

"True."

I shake my head. "But I keep thinking about Gretchen. She deserves justice, and so does her kid. Plus, I've got the whole possibly-going-back-to-my-old-life-as-a-senior-citizen thing hanging over my head."

"Uh-huh."

I glare at him. "Is this you being supportive? 'Cause you kinda suck at it."

"I'm just waiting."

"For what?"

"You to rationalize the fact that you can't give up on this case. Well, *any* case, really, but this case in particular. It's entertaining—kind of like watching a cat chase its own tail. You know two things from the very start: that the whole process doesn't really make sense, and that the cat's eventually going to catch it."

"If I were the type to sputter, I'd be sputtering right now."

"With righteous indignation?"

"Yeah, that."

We fall silent again. It feels good.

Eventually I say, "John Dark approached me at the flea market."

"Did he threaten you?"

"No. He wanted to know who was on Cassius's side. I get the feeling that he's still a player in Hexagon politics."

"Makes sense. This whole thing could be an internal power struggle."

"Maybe. Why try to win over supporters when you can kill them and take their weapons?"

"While making it look like the work of a nutjab?"

"Nut*job*, Charlie."

"Really? Nutjab sounds crazier."

"How would you know? You don't have any."

"I have the objective perspective of an outsider."

Which reminds me of something else. "Dark also claimed the Quicksilver Kid was the most likely to turn on his friends. Said that lems weren't real well treated back then."

"If by well treated, you mean occasionally thrown down a well, then yes. But I have my doubts about him as a suspect."

"Why?"

"Golems are known for their loyalty. It's part of who we are, part of the spell that animates us. That's why we're used as soldiers, as cops. We may not be incorruptible, but it's awfully damn hard to make us turn on our own."

"Okay. But the Kid's not your average lem, is he? Mystic knives, mercury in his veins—and he works as a bounty hunter, a pretty solitary occupation. If he were mistreated by the other Bravos, he might want some payback."

"After all this time? What could have triggered it?"

I frown. "Maybe not what. Maybe *who*."

We pull up in front of a nondescript house in Tukwila, a Seattle 'burb. And I really do mean nondescript; Charlie warned me about the effect before we stopped, but it's still kind of disturbing. Except that it's *not,* because that's part of the enchantment at work. Much like the spell that doesn't let anyone in this world take the idea of firearms seriously, the spell wrapped around the house doesn't let anyone think about it too closely. Kind of a standing "these aren't the droids you're looking for" kind of deal, only it's a house and nobody ever remembers that they didn't notice it. Same thing with the firearm spell; not only do people fail to see the possible uses of any sort of gun, they fail to see that they fail to see.

In any case, there's a house there, and we go in. I'm pretty sure about that.

The first person I see is Gretchen. She's sitting on a leather recliner in the living room, sipping from a cup of tea and reading a newspaper with a bold headline in Cyrillic. She looks up when I enter and says, "Jace. How nice to see you."

I glance back at Charlie. "You found the safe house."

"In a manner of speaking."

Gretchen puts aside her newspaper—and my eyes widen when I see how large her belly is. The last time I talked to her was only days ago, and she was hardly showing; now it looks like she's about to pop.

"Gretch, are you okay?" I say.

"I'm fine, Jace." She puts her teacup down on a table beside the recliner, and shifts the chair into an upright position. "Just a little larger than I was. Well, quite a *bit* larger, actually."

"How far along are you?"

"Chronologically, about three months. Biologically, very close to term. The spell Saladin used has accelerated the process a great deal more than we expected." Gretchen always looks precise and ready, but she seems closer to exhausted now. Her usually immaculate suits have been swapped for stretchy pants and an oversize sweatshirt; despite all that, her cheeks are rosy and her smile wide. She looks truly happy.

"She's doing well," a voice says, and Dr. Pete walks into the room from the adjoining kitchen. He seems a little nervous, even though I haven't even drawn my gun. Yet.

"Hello, Jace. I'm sorry I haven't contacted you, but—"

"Agency protocol. I understand." I can't quite freeze the air around him, but I'm pretty sure I see icicles forming on his earlobes. "Galahad's fine, by the way."

"Uh, good, good. I really couldn't take him with me—"

"I understand."

"I wanted to call, but—"

"I *understand*."

"You can stop now," Cassius says, walking in behind Dr. Pete. "Dr. Adams was following my instructions. If you want to blame anyone, blame me."

"Oh, I do. I'm just so pissed I had extra left over."

Cassius nods, but doesn't rise to the bait. "I have answers for you, if you still want them."

I'd really like to make him sweat a little, but that's just not going to happen—you could put Cassius in a sauna in Death Valley at high noon and it wouldn't melt the ice in his drink. Guess I'll have to settle for yanking his chain. "Yeah? This because you realized I'm indispensable, or because of the chat I had with John Dark?"

Bull's-eye. He looks mildly startled, which for Cassius is like screaming, *WHAT?* I try to enjoy it for the millisecond it lasts. "You had a conversation with Dark?"

"Sure. About football, mainly. He's a big Seahawks fan."

"We can't talk here. Follow me." He strides through the living room and down a short hallway. I meet Dr. Pete's eyes and say, "Don't go anywhere." He nods.

Cassius unlocks a door at the end of the hall and heads down a flight of stairs. I go after him, but Charlie stays where he is. The stairs are metal and lead down to a secondary door, this one made of thick metal with a keypad lock. A safe room inside a safe house, compartments within compartments.

Cassius punches in the code and the door opens. Inside, a room with security feeds from all over the house, a small bathroom, two cots, and an office chair. I have no doubt the stainless-steel fridge holds the pire and thrope equivalent of emergency rations—probably beef jerky and powdered blood. Cassius waits until I'm inside and then shuts and locks the door.

"Afraid we're being spied on?" I say. "Or do you just not trust your own people?" It's a cheap shot, but I'm still feeling vindictive.

"I protect my people, Jace. That means not exposing them to information that could get them killed—or would you prefer I just let them in on everything I know? Maybe tattoo a big target on their foreheads, too?"

"What, and clash with mine? Oh no. Besides, once everyone starts doing it, it's no longer cool."

"I'm sorry you feel singled out."

"Getting used to it, actually. Sometimes it even makes me feel *special*."

He leans up against the steel counter that runs beneath the mounted security screens. "Let's stop this, all right? I need you. Gretchen needs you."

"Oh? Is catching the killer of her child's father going to accomplish some kind of postmortem paternal voodoo

I don't know about? Will it give her some of her life back?"

He looks down and to the side, at the monitor showing the living room. Gretchen is carefully getting out of the recliner, with help from Dr. Pete. "No. All we can offer her is justice."

"Can we? I mean, *justice* is a very ill-defined word, especially in our line of work. And it seems to get thrown out the window pretty damn quick when it conflicts with justice for someone else higher up the food chain. You want me to investigate, but you don't want me to rock the boat—once someone in the Hexagon is involved, suddenly all the rules change. One of them gets murdered, and suddenly the shaman that can send me home is 'unavailable'? How stupid do you think I—"

"Jace." His voice is hard, cold, and suddenly so is his face. He doesn't look like an affable eighteen-year-old surfer any more; he looks like a very old, very ruthless demon who's skinned the face from an eighteen-year-old surfer and stapled it to his own skull. *"I protect my people."*

"I get that. I just don't know who your people *are*."

"Then it's time for a demonstration."

That sounds ominous. And here I am in a sealed room with one of the most dangerous men I know . . . one who swore allegience to a powerful and very secretive organization long before my great-grandfather took his first breath.

"It's time to go, Jace," he says.

Uh-oh.

"You know," I say, "this reminds me of the very first time we met."

"Yes. You pointed a gun in my face then, too."

I'm as far away from him as I can get, but it's not a big room. "Actually, I shot you, remember?"

"Yes. In the chest."

"*And* the face."

"Fortunately, you were only using steel-jacketed bullets."

"Not anymore. Carved teak, tipped with silver."

"I know. I hear they're quite effective."

"You don't seem worried."

He sighs, and crosses his arms. "I'm not. I have three questions for you, though."

"Go ahead."

"If I wanted to get rid of you, would I do it myself?"

"Uh—" Suddenly I feel less threatened and more embarrassed. "Probably not."

"Second, would I do it while Charlie was around?"

Now I feel stupid *and* disloyal. I let the gun drop. "Never. Too dangerous."

"And third—would you like to meet the rest of the Bravos?"

I holster my gun. "Yes, please," I say meekly.

He laughs. "That is the worst attempt at contrition I've ever seen."

"That's because it's entirely insincere. I'm still mad at you. But I'm going to go upstairs and take most of my anger out on Dr. Pete, so you won't have to suffer through my horrible acting for long."

"Don't take too much time. We have a fairly lengthy drive ahead of us." He unlocks the door and heads back up the stairs.

"Where to?"

"Mount Saint Helens."

We rejoin the others. Gretchen is lying down in one of the bedrooms, Charlie is talking to Dr. Pete in the kitchen.

"Hey," Dr. Pete says when we walk in. "Charlie says I'm in trouble, but he won't say why."

"Not my call," Charlie says. "But I will tell you one thing."

He takes his hand out of the pocket of his coat and flicks it, almost casually, in Dr. Pete's direction. Something flashes through the air almost too quick to be seen, and then a silver Blood Cross is sticking out of the wall about three inches away from Dr. Pete's right ear.

"You better make it right," Charlie says, his voice soft. He turns his back on Dr. Pete and joins Cassius in the living room.

"What—what's this all about, Jace?" Dr. Pete says. He reaches out to touch the Blood Cross, then thinks better of it.

"It's about your past, Doc. You might have thought it was dead and buried, but someone's disinterred the corpse. A thrope by the name of Tair."

If he recognizes the name, he hides it well. "Tair? I don't know any thrope named Tair."

"He sure as hell knows you. He's the guy who's been hanging around the anthrocanine shelter—but it's not the were dogs he's interested in. It's you."

Dr. Pete shakes his head. "I don't—"

"He says he represents your former employers. The ones who dealt in black-market lems."

This time he does know what I'm talking about, and he doesn't try to hide it. "Oh, no."

"So it's true."

His voice is both sad and ashamed. "Yes. It's true."

"Care to explain?"

He takes a deep breath and lets it out. "I'm—God, I don't even know what to say that won't sound self-serving. I did bad things, Jace. I was young and stupid and broke, and none of that excuses my actions. I've tried to make up for it. Maybe I never can, but—"

"Whoa. How about telling me what you did before asking my forgiveness?"

He stops himself. "I—I can't."

"Why not?"

He looks miserable. "I signed documents, Jace. Other people were involved. I can't tell you any of the details, or I'll go to prison."

Great. More secrets. "Then I'll tell you what's been happening to me, okay? This thrope you claim not to know runs with a gang of wrappers—one of which put that Blood Cross in my forearm as deep as it would go. Then this Tair shows up while I'm chasing you and nearly decapitates a little old lady just to get your attention. Didn't work, though—guess you'd already hightailed it out of there. Next time he might come after Galahad, or even Xandra."

Now Dr. Pete looks sick. "I didn't know. And I swear I don't know who he is."

"Well, he seems to know you pretty well. And while you were hiding in this safe house, he was targeting the people you presumably care about to draw you out."

I yank the Blood Cross out of the wall and slip it into my pocket. "I want to help you, Doc, I really do. But going up against this guy without knowing his deal is liable to get me and who-knows-who-else killed. So give that some thought—*then* we'll talk."

I walk out of the kitchen. "Let's go," I say.

"Mount Saint Helens erupted in your world on May 18, 1980," Cassius says. We're in his car, all the glass heavily tinted, him driving and Charlie in the backseat. "Here, that event occurred on November 18, 1956, and was far less catastrophic—at least for the local population. For the members of the Kamic cult, *apocalyptic* would be a more apt description."

We're on the highway, heading south. The smoked glass cuts out so much of the light it's almost like driving at night, except none of the other cars on the road has its headlights on—they're all just dark, dim shapes hurtling past.

"We knew they were preparing for another ritual murder," he continues. "A young female thrope and her daughter. Our plan was for our two stealthiest members to slip into the house and try to locate the hostages first."

"The Sword of Midnight and the African Queen?" I guess.

"Yes. The Sword was not only a pirate but also one of the best thieves in the world. The Queen is a hunter, able to stalk the most elusive game without ever betraying her presence. They entered through an upper window, found the hostages on the third floor, and got them out.

"My job was essentially air support. The armor doesn't let me fly, but the Queen's sky-shield could support both of us easily. We rose to a hundred feet and turned the night into day."

"How about Transe?" I ask. "He was a pire, too."

"Transe was prepared, wearing a daysuit he'd made tearproof with magic. He was our big gun; we held him back until we needed him. The Quicksilver Kid and Brother Stone were our first wave."

"Foot soldiers," Charlie says.

"They were the best tactical choice. Both were close to indestructible, plus the Kid's knives could take down most threats before they even got close. And Stone insisted on going in first."

"Tell me about Brother Stone," I say.

"He's a monk, from a very esoteric and secretive sect. It's not that unusual to see lems in the priesthood today, but back then it was almost unheard of. Like the Quicksilver Kid, he's a singular creature; according to legend, he was a granite statue brought to life by prayer."

"Doesn't sound so different from other lems," I say.

Charlie grunts. "Except for the granite part. Granite

ain't exactly what you'd call a fluid medium—except in the good Brother's case. Not only could he walk and talk, he could also reshape his body into any form he wanted."

"Statue and sculptor, all in one?"

"Yes," Cassius says. "And he was a formidable fighter, as well—his strength was incredible. Between him and the Kid, the cult's members took heavy initial losses. Any pires who panicked and ran outside were incinerated. When we thought we'd softened them up enough, we sent in Transe, with the Sword protecting his back. Which is when things stopped going as planned."

He pauses. Cassius's car is some late-model sedan I don't recognize, with no obvious trademarks anywhere, and the engine is as whisper-quiet as a library at midnight. The silence and the dimness begin to make me feel less like I'm in something with four wheels and more like a passenger in a submarine.

"Wertham was in the basement, overseeing preparations for the ritual with John Dark. When they realized they were under attack, Dark sent Wertham to confront us.

"They'd conducted three previous rituals, and had amassed a great deal of power by doing so. Wertham was a genuine threat. He declined to take the stairs and burst from the floor into the central foyer of the mansion. And then—"

He shakes his head. "I couldn't see at first. But Stone and the Kid were both thrown through the wall and the battle was suddenly outside.

"It's difficult to describe the chaos that followed. Wertham, for all his power, was unskilled. He simply amplified the natural energy of every spirit within range, and told it to assault us. Trees, insects, furniture, rock—things grew to sudden, monstrous size and attacked. His inexperience made the energy driving them unstable, causing some things to merge into unholy combinations: I remember battling mass of thorny vines that had sprouted moth wings and taken to the sky . . ."

His voice is distant, his mind far away. I try to imagine what it would have been like, to have everything around you transform into a walking monsterscape that wanted your blood, and found it far too easy to do so. I've interviewed a lot of schizophrenics in my time, and this sounds all too familiar—the difference being, of course, that this is history as opposed to fantasy.

"Though the official version describes Doctor Transe defeating Wertham, it omitted an important detail. Transe wouldn't have been able to get near Wertham if Brother Stone hadn't done something he swore he'd never do."

Cassius's voice becomes quieter. "He took a life."

"Whose?"

"Wertham himself. Stone shaped his hand into an ax blade, his forearm into a lengthy handle. Granite doesn't hold much of an edge, but when driven by the kind of strength Stone had . . . it took Wertham's head right off."

"Hold on," I say. "I thought Transe was the one who beat him?"

"Transe dealt with the aftermath. He used the Balancer gem to divert the energy Wertham was channeling into the earth—if he hadn't, it would have killed all of us. Unfortunately, we were fighting on the slopes of an active volcano. We barely had enough time to get away before it erupted."

I nod. "So Wertham really is dead?"

"I thought so. Dark managed to escape, but he always had a contingency plan."

"I've seen the original designs for the comic," I say. "Dark is in it, but it doesn't mention Stone killing Wertham."

"Stone wouldn't allow it. Even though he knew it was

necessary, it troubled him deeply. He's never been the same."

"Where is he now?"

"You're about to see for yourself."

We turn off the highway and onto a narrow, winding dirt road. It snakes up through forest that's only an indistinct shadowy wall on either side of the car. A sign goes by that I can barely read: something about a temple, either twelve or seventy-two miles ahead.

"He founded this place at the foot of the lava flow," Cassius says. "It's dedicated to the thirteen people that lost their lives in the eruption, but it's really a monument to something else."

"Guilt," I say.

The temple is a blocky stone building jutting out of the cooled lava flow itself. There's no sign out front, no parking lot; it seems more like some kind of industrial outbuilding you'd find behind a hydroelectric plant than a religious retreat.

We park in front and get out. The sun's sunk low enough and the trees are dense enough that Cassius doesn't bother putting on a mask or gloves.

"He doesn't have cell coverage out here, or a landline," Cassius says. "So he isn't expecting us."

"We hope," I say.

The steps are carved out of the bare rock—actually, the more I look at it, the more I realize the whole structure is carved out of the lava flow. "This isn't a building—it's a sculpture."

"No," Charlie says. "It's a tombstone."

Yeah. I guess you could call it a mausoleum, but most mausoleums aren't cut from a single piece of rock—and try as I might, I can't find signs of a join anywhere. The entrance opens into a foyer, with benches against the wall and a frieze etched around an archway that leads into the building proper. I have to stop and study it before going any farther.

The only light is natural light, but there's enough coming through the doorway behind me to see just fine. Above the arch, the frieze depicts the volcano erupting, the lava and ash pouring down on either side. The faces of the victims can be seen through the swirling ash, mouths open in screams of horror.

"This must have taken a long time to do," I say.

"Decades," says Cassius. "And he's not finished yet."

We go through the archway. The room on the other side is much larger, the ceiling twelve or so feet high. It's laid out like a church, rows of pews divided by a central aisle, a pulpit on a raised dais at the end. There's no stained glass, though, just empty squares cut into the walls to let in light. The room is cold, and a breeze blows a few stray leaves in through one of the windows.

There are people sitting in the pews as well, but none of them turns to look as we enter. A few couples sit together and there's one cluster of four that's clearly a family, but most of the people are solitary and scattered, as if they can't bear to be close to another human being.

As we walk down the aisle, I realize the truth. They aren't human themselves; they're all statues.

There's a cross-shaped hole cut into the ceiling above the pulpit. This late in the day it's not letting in that much light, but it must be impressive at high noon—or during a full moon, for that matter.

"Brother Stone?" Cassius calls out. His voice echoes off the chilly rock. "We need to speak with you."

"Then speak," a soft voice says. It comes from a seated figure in the first row, a statue of a man in monk's robes—but of course, this one's not really a statue at all.

Brother Stone gets to his feet. He's just as Cassius

described him, a lem made of gray granite. There's something eerie about the way he moves, like those old stop-motion monsters in Ray Harryhausen films. His head is smooth, his features finer than I expected; he stands a little under six feet, the loose folds of his clothing concealing his build. He keeps his hands tucked inside the opposite sleeves of his robe.

"Do you know who I am?" Cassius asks.

"I do. Why are you here, Centurion?"

"Someone's killing the Bravos, Brother."

Stone nods. "Are we finally being punished for our sins, then?"

"We weren't the sinners, Brother. We put an end to those who were. Murderers who were preying on the innocent."

"And yet, we took innocent lives ourselves."

"It was an accident."

"It was a choice. And we must live with the consequences of our choices."

"I can't argue with that. But I can't condone someone picking us off, one by one, either. Doctor Transe and the Sword of Midnight are already dead."

Brother Stone looks troubled, but it's hard to tell if he's feeling sorrow or fear. "I am truly sorry. Despite what he did, Transe meant well. I invited him here many times to pray with me, to ask God for forgiveness, but he never came. Even so, I know the deaths that resulted from the eruption weighed heavily on his conscience."

"But not as heavily as yours," I say.

"This is Special Agent Jace Valchek," Cassius says. "And Charlie Aleph, her enforcer."

Stone glances from me to Charlie. "I see. Are you investigating these crimes, Agent Valchek?"

"I am. Would you mind if I asked you a few questions?"

Stone looks back at Cassius, who nods. "I suppose not."

"Good. Cassius, go wait in the car."

"Excuse me?"

"This is my investigation, and I don't want you vetting every single question I have. You either leave the Brother and I alone or drive me back to Seattle now. Your choice."

If there's one thing Cassius hates, it's not being in charge. I watch his face as he considers the situation, comes to a conclusion, then spins and walks out the door without a word.

Charlie gives me a look. "Better enjoy that one while you can," he says. "'Cause you'll be paying for it later."

"Hey, I've been running a tab for a while now."

"What about your . . . enforcer?" Brother Stone asks. His voice is curious, not condescending.

"He's not my enforcer, he's my partner. He can hear whatever I can hear."

"Really. I hadn't realized the NSA had become so enlightened. Things were very different in my day . . ."

"Yeah, I guess they were. For one thing, you had cults using comic books as a way to accumulate power."

"Yes. Wertham's group. They were evil men, evil women. They had to be stopped."

I glance around. "No offense, but this place seems to be saying otherwise."

"This place is my atonement, Agent Valchek. My attempt to right the wrong that we perpetrated."

"By commemorating the victims of the eruption. I understand that, but—"

"No," he interrupts gently. "I do not seek to memorialize. I seek to *save*."

"Are you talking about their souls?"

"No. I am talking about their lives—or more precisely, the lives of their other selves. Are you familiar with the theory of alternate universes?"

A chill goes through me, and I tell myself it's just the cold breath of the wind. "I know a little something about it."

"I belong to the order of Saint Moorcock. He postulated that though many versions of us may exist in many worlds, we have but one soul. Through prayer and meditation, we can influence those other parts of our self, give them advice, lend them strength or solace when they need it most. Guide them to being better people, and therefore make a better world—even though that world may be very different from our own."

"Self-evangelization? Physicians, heal thyselves?"

"In a manner of speaking."

"Interesting idea. How many members do you have?"

"I am the only one—on this plane of existence, anyway. But though I have only one soul, I have many bodies, many hands to do my work, spread throughout the multiverse."

"Okay—but it's a little late to save *these* people, isn't it?" I motion to the carved statues on the stone pews. "That's who these are, right? The victims of the eruption?"

"I've done my best to re-create each one." Stone takes a step forward and lets his hand fall lightly on the shoulder of one of them, a middle-aged woman wearing a hat and clutching her purse in her lap. "I worked from photos, mostly. And no, I don't think it's too late to save these people, Agent Valchek. I *know* there are multiple worlds, multiple realities, and I know that time does not always move the same in all of them. That is why I spend most of my time in meditation, trying to reach my Brothers on those worlds where it is still 1956, where the battle yet rages, where that fateful surge of energy has not been released. If Doctor Transe had only directed it skyward, these people might still be alive."

"What would have happened if he had? There must have been a reason he didn't."

"I believe it would have turned into a storm—a ferocious one, one that might have even taken lives of its own. But I do not believe it would have killed as many as the eruption."

"Hard to say, I suppose. The Northwest doesn't really get hurricanes, but a storm can still be deadly. With that much energy being tossed around, it's a pretty good bet someone would probably have been struck by lightning."

He meets my eyes, doesn't say anything for a second. "Yes," he says at last. "Someone probably would have."

THIRTEEN

The rest of the interview is less than illuminating. Stone has no alibi for either murder; he's spent all his time working on his bizarre mausoleum or meditating. He gets few visitors, and had none in the last week.

Charlie doesn't say a word while I talk to Stone, which I find a little strange. He usually hangs back and lets me take the reins, but I thought when another lem was involved he'd at least open his mouth. I ask him about it on the way back to the car.

"Busy keeping an eye on the monk," he says. "Something off about him."

"You mean the fact that he belongs to a secret order with an unknown number of members? Or that every member is him?"

"Neither. It's something about the way he moves."

"He's not like you, remember? Granite, not sand. I don't know how he moves at all."

Cassius is waiting outside the car, leaning against the hood with his arms crossed. He doesn't look angry, though—he's too professional for that. "Find out anything worthwhile?"

"Oh, definitely. I know where to get a great deal on chisels in Bellingham."

We all get in the car. There's still a little light left in the sky, and I roll down my window; it makes it feel a bit less like I'm traveling in a coffin on wheels.

"I did get this," I say, holding out my hand. It's a pebble I picked up outside the front door. "I'm pretty sure it'll prove to be a match to the one Eisfanger found outside the storage unit."

"Which only proves someone was both here and there."

"Yeah. Pretty easy frame to hang, too—Stone's isolation doesn't give him much shot at an alibi. But at least he's a suspect and not a corpse."

"For now," Charlie says. "We gonna just leave him out here alone?"

"His place has been under surveillance since the first murder," Cassius says. "But that doesn't tell us much. He rarely even goes outside, spends hours or days immobile while he's meditating. All we know for sure is that no one's been to visit him in the past few days."

I nod. "How about the Sword? Were you watching her, too?"

"Nobody found Barbarossa unless she wanted to be found—I still don't know how the killer did it. I wasn't even aware she was on the continent."

"How about the Quicksilver Kid?"

"He's easier to locate, but he still spends most of his time off the grid. We don't know where he was during the murders—you actually found him before we did."

"And lost him, too. Unless you know where he's gone?"

"Afraid not. He disappeared shortly after taking in Helmut Wiebe—we don't know where he is now."

"Which leaves one more Bravo—the African Queen." The fresh air coming in through the window is refreshing but cold; I roll it up reluctantly. "I really hope you're not going to tell me she's in—oh, say—Africa?"

"Not at all. She works in a game park in Oregon—we should be there in a few hours."

Charlie takes off his fedora, places it in his lap. "Tell me when we get there—I'm going to grab some shuteye."

"Okay." I turn back to Cassius. "That'll give us plenty of time to talk about all the things you *didn't* tell me before. You know, when you were lying to my face and pretending not to know anything."

"A few hours won't be enough. Choose your questions wisely."

"What's the deal with you and John Dark?"

"We had a disagreement over policy, which I can't go into. Next question."

"Tell me about the Sword of Midnight. I didn't have the chance to ask you any follow-up questions at the crime scene."

"Actually, you stormed off."

"Well, I was angry. And you didn't seem inclined to give me any useful information."

He hesitates. "All right. Barbarossa is—was—more than just a smuggler. She was actually the leader of a gang of international criminals, who dabble in everything from kidnapping to piracy. They have chapters in many countries, not always large but well respected—it's a sign of prestige to be asked to join, a sort of criminal elite. They're known as the Crooked Shadows."

"How about assassination?"

He considers that before answering. "Doubtful. The Shadows reserve killing for self-defense or revenge— they believe in stealing as an art form, one that's above murder. That being said, they've been known to go to extreme lengths to punish anyone who hurts one of their members—there's a story about a Mafia captain that robbed and killed one of them. The robbery they didn't mind, but they felt the killing was unjust. They imposed what they call the Beggar's Curse."

I've run into a lot of variations on magic since I've been here, but not actual curses. "How does that work?"

"It's not a curse per se—it's a condition. The victim has everything stolen from him, and I mean *everything*. His family and friends are driven away, everything he owns is stolen, he's made to lose his home and his job— and then, when he's broke and on the street, they take his sight, his mobility, his speech . . . you get the idea. They leave only his hearing."

"Why?"

"So that he can still hear music." He doesn't elaborate, and he doesn't have to; music is one of the most powerful touchstones we have for memories, and the victim of the Beggar's Curse would have only his memories left— memories of everything he had lost. It's one of the grimmest fates I can think of.

"If the Crooked Shadows are professional thieves, wouldn't they find the Brigade's weaponry an irresistible target?" I drum my fingers on the dashboard, thinking. "And if they're the artists you say they are, maybe this is all part of an elaborate scam. Maybe the Sword of Midnight isn't as dead as we thought."

Cassius shakes his head. "I thought of that. DNA tests on the brain material confirm it's her, and forensic animism shows that the only magic used was whatever changed her body into bronze."

"That's another thing. Transe's bones were turned into copper, presumably to better hold the electrical charge. What kind of magic is that?"

"Alchemy—the transmutation of one substance into another."

"No one's ever mentioned that one to me before."

"That's because it doesn't exist. You can't really change one thing into another—its basic nature will resist. All you can do is introduce a new element and persuade it to become dominant for a while; that's the basic principle behind lycanthropy."

"So the victims' bodies were infected with metalthropy?"

"Essentially. Like most transformations, it's temporary; Eisfanger tells me that the remains will revert, probably in a few days' time. He's going to do another autopsy then, see if we learn anything new."

I think back to the dream meeting I'd had with Neil, and the Sword of Midnight comic I'd read. Something rises up in my brain, dancing around like a drunken butterfly I can't quite catch; all I can pin down is a sense of doomed romance. "What do you know about Barbarossa's love life?"

"That depends."

It's not the answer I expect; I thought he'd either make a joke or deny any knowledge, not hand me an immediate equivocation. "On what?"

"On what you mean by love. Barbarossa was notorious for rarely having an empty bed, but she refused to get serious about any of them."

"I suppose the life of an international thief doesn't leave a lot of room for a husband or kids."

"No."

There's something he isn't telling me. "Cassius, were you and Barbarossa involved?"

He laughs and shakes his head. "No, absolutely not. She wasn't interested in pires, and I wasn't interested in her. I had the feeling she was involved with someone while she was with the Bravos, but I never found out who."

Lems were sexless, and the only other thrope on the

team was female. "Any possibility her and the African Queen had something going?"

"Unlikely. They didn't particularly get along, and in any case both seemed to prefer men of their own species."

"How about betrayal? Could this be a plot on part of someone close to the Sword—another member of her gang, maybe?"

"I just don't know, Jace." He sounds frustrated, an emotion I rarely see from Cassius. "Despite what you may think, I don't have all the answers—and the ones I *do* have I'm not withholding out of spite. I'm telling you everything I can, all right? If I *can't* tell you something, I'll tell you *that*."

"You'll be honest about your dishonesty?"

He gives me a rueful smile. "I'll avoid telling outright lies. Can you work with that?"

"Guess I'll have to."

"Good enough." He pauses, then says, "The Shadows have a code of absolute loyalty to their members. Even if one of them did break it and kill Barbarossa, she would never have betrayed the Bravos—and the killer clearly knows our secrets. Considering the Shadows' commitment to retribution, I find it hard to believe she was targeted at all, let alone by one of their own."

So now we have a gang of über-criminals out for blood to compete with, too. "Well, it does lend credence to the *mentally unbalanced* theory. The killer either thinks he's invincible, or he's working toward some goal so important to him that consequences have become irrelevant or secondary."

"Any idea what that might be?"

"When you're dealing with someone living in their own reality, the possibilities can be literally infinite—but I think I can narrow it down a little."

I lean back in my seat, close my eyes, and concentrate.

"We'll refer to him as *he* simply because most serial murderers are male. He's not killing for sexual gratification, but to accumulate power. That's not all that uncommon, even on my world; many killers believe that each murder makes them stronger in some mystical way. It's just that here, it's actually true . . .

"He's organized. He stages elaborate scenes and leaves few traces behind. The killings appear almost dispassionate, with little evidence of frenzy or anger—Transe was killed by a single well-placed thrust. The staging of the scenes is important to him, but Eisfanger hasn't been able to find any trace of magic energy that would suggest this is part of some elaborate spell. The comic book references point to a number of different concepts: alternate universes, transformation, the interface between the imaginary and the real."

My voice is steady, the words coming almost without conscious thought. This is my own ritual, my way of connecting to the case when my brain is crammed full of facts and frustration. Some part of me already knows the answer; I just have to let it find its voice. "He's intelligent. Driven. The crime scenes are messages in a language only he speaks, full of symbols he thinks are deeply relevant."

"What's the point to that? A message that can't be understood?"

I open my eyes, annoyed, the spell broken. "He *wants* to be understood—but on his own terms, in his own world. I've seen this before; the killer believes that if he can just make us view the universe the way he does, we'll agree with him. In his eyes, he's completely justified— we're the ones who aren't sane."

"And he thinks he can do that with cryptic messages?"

"Our language shapes how we think. The position of a verb relative to a noun, the way we use pronouns or assign gender to some words and not to others. He may be the only one who speaks his language, but understand it and you understand how he thinks. The problem is that he's clearly immersed himself in a subculture I have virtually no access to."

"The Four Color Club contact didn't work out?"

"Sure, if I want to spend all my time asleep—and it's all secondary information, anyway. I need to dig through this stuff on my own, do hands-on research where I can physically connect with the material."

"Sounds very old-fashioned."

"Well, I'd settle for a cross-universe high-speed broadband portal with full archival access to every comic book database in existence, but nobody's offered me one."

"Sorry. Cross-universe magic tends to be highly specific, very dangerous, and extremely limited. Not exactly what you need."

I sigh. "No. I guess I'll have to settle for whatever information I can collect on this side. Tell me about the African Queen."

"She's an actual queen, and she's from Africa."

"Great, thanks for filling me in."

"I thought I should start with the essentials. Her name is Catharine Shaka, and she's Zulu royalty—in fact, some would argue her bloodline places her on the throne itself. Politics in her country tend to be bloodthirsty, a mix of warring thrope tribes and shamanistic intrigues. She herself was the victim of an assassination attempt at an early age, which led to her being raised in secret by a powerful witch doctor."

"Which doctor?"

He gives me a look. "Anyway, the shaman taught her how to be a powerful warrior and gave her the sky-shield, a magical artifact that lets her fly and protects anyone using it from all harm. She's one of the best archers in the world, and a master of the thrope martial art *isilwane ukulwa*."

"If she's African royalty, what's she doing here?"

"Living in exile. The current faction in power is not exactly friendly to her family or her politics—which is why she keeps her true identity a secret."

"What are her politics?"

"She's a revolutionary. She'd like to raise an army, overthrow the ruling military junta, and establish a democracy."

"And how does the NSA feel about that?"

"Ambivalent. The White House would like to see a democracy in place, but they're not willing to commit significant military or political resources."

"Maybe she's decided to gather a few of her own."

"A possibility," he admits. "Though my sources haven't heard anything about preparations for a military action."

"The Brigade's weapons might be all the preparation she needs."

I think about it as we drive into the darkening twilight. A one-woman coup—a single warrior taking on an entire country. Is it possible? Not in my world, but here it just might be. Even if the idea is crazy, that doesn't eliminate Shaka as a suspect.

In fact, it makes her a more viable one.

The place Shaka is using as her retreat is called the Serengeti Safari Reserve. It's a game park for thropes, where they can experience the firsthand thrill of pulling down an antelope, gazelle, or zebra, either solo or as part of a group. Cassius tells me it's popular as a corporate team-building exercise.

There's a double-gated entryway through a high razor-wire-topped chain link fence. Once we're in, there are no signs warning us to stay inside the vehicle or not to roll down our windows; we're the predators here. I let in some of the night air, and to my surprise it smells dry, dusty, and much warmer than I expected for Oregon at this time of year.

"Magic," Cassius tells me. "They use animism to convince the entire area and everything in it—plants, earth, insects, air—that they're on another continent. Adds to the realism."

"Must be expensive."

Charlie's voice from the backseat makes me jump a little. He's so still at times it's easy to forget he's even there. "The people who come here don't care much about money. They're after something else."

"True," Cassius says. "They want to experience life as it used to be—or at least how they think it used to be. The thrill of the hunt."

"Commercialized and romanticized," Charlie growls. "I tried it once. Didn't do much for me." I sometimes forget that the life force that animates Charlie is that of a seven-ton carnivore that last walked the Earth sixty-five million years ago; when I do, he does something to remind me.

"Commercialized is right," I mutter as we get to the parking lot. It looks more like Disneyland in high season than a nature park—there are hundreds of vehicles here and a steady stream of people coming and going, mostly groups of young men but some families and couples, too. We park, get out, and join the lineup. Everything's lit by torches—gas or propane, though something's been added to make it smell like wood smoke—and the atmosphere's both quieter and more charged than I expected. It takes me a second to recognize the feeling—it's like lining up for a haunted-house ride on Halloween, that same combination of nervous excitement and morbid celebration, candy coating over a heart of darkness. Grinning in the face of death, and realizing he's grinning right back.

Even with Cassius and Charlie beside me, I don't feel at

ease here. I don't even eat meat—well, the occasional piece of sushi—and this place more or less worships the practice of killing and eating animals. Not that I have a moral leg to stand on, of course; thropes are carnivores, pure and simple, and I can no more condemn them for that than I can pires for drinking blood. As long as it's not my own.

But I still feel like a cashew in a room full of squirrels, and hope I remembered to apply enough fake wolf phero-mone this morning. I have visions of being taken down by an overenthusiastic family from Des Moines who didn't read the brochure. "Look, Martha! They got free-range humans here!"

I expect Cassius to flash his NSA credentials and by-pass the line, but that doesn't happen—I guess he wants to keep as low a profile as possible. Instead, he pays for a deluxe package for all three of us, and specifies the guide he wants.

"I'm sorry, sir," the woman at the wicket says. "Cath's booked solid right now, she won't be available for at least a week. If you'd like to try one of our other guides—"

"Tell her it's Ray Burnwell," Cassius says. "I have a standing reservation."

The woman frowns, but checks her computer. Her ex-pression changes immediately. "Ah, Mr. Burnwell. I'm *so* sorry about the mixup. I'll have her meet you in the Hunt-er's Lodge right away—she's out in the field, but can be back here in about, say, twenty minutes?"

"That'll be fine."

The Hunter's Lodge is one of those thatched-roof long-house affairs, with more torch lighting, a bamboo and rattan bar, and lots of wicker seating for lounging around on and fanning yourself with your pith helmet. We get a couple of beers from the bar and sit down, Charlie pick-ing a very solid-looking wingback chair made from oak.

I glance around the room. Almost exclusively thropes,

most already in half-were form and gesturing excitedly to one another in sign language, but there are a few pires here, too—I'm getting better and better at spotting the difference at first sight. It's a combination of things: subliminal cues like posture or gestures, more overt signals like paleness of skin or thickness of hair. And of course, the size of incisors versus canines.

There are even a pair of lems present, both the obsidian color that identifies enforcers. They study us from across the room with flat, evaluating stares, but don't approach us. Just as well—we don't need any extra attention. I wonder who they are, though; a couple of cops from the big city, maybe, trying to fuel the needs of the Kodiak engine growling deep inside the black sand of their bodies? Plastic-skinned army men on leave, trying to scratch an itch that push-button warfare doesn't satisfy, feeding a ghost hunger haunting a belly packed with dirt?

"Snipers," Charlie says, noticing who I'm looking at. "They work for the reserve. Their job is to throw a slug into any 'uncooperative' animal's brain."

I frown and take a swig of my beer. It tastes coppery, and I quickly spit it back into my glass. Really should know better by now than to sample anything without checking the ingredients first. "I thought the whole idea was to give the customers a firsthand experience."

Charlie grunts. "Yeah, well, that's what they *think* they want. Up close and personal, sometimes they have a change of heart. In that case, someone has to take care of the pissed-off twelve-hundred-pound Cape buffalo with claw marks on its ass."

"Isn't that what the guide is for?"

"In most cases. Sometimes they need backup—they hunt some pretty big game here."

I have a sudden flash of a group of thropes lugging a step-ladder while chasing a giraffe. "Shut up, brain," I mutter.

"Excuse me?" Cassius says.

"Nothing."

We sit and pretend to enjoy our overpriced drinks, though I don't actually consume any of mine. After half an hour or so, a tall, regal-looking black woman marches into the bar, a less-than-happy look on her face. She spots us and strides over, and I take the few seconds before she arrives to give her a quick once-over: Her skin is lighter than I expected, her hair cropped short over a wide but attractive face. She's dressed in tan cargo shorts and a matching shirt tied in a knot at her chest, her feet bare.

She stops and glares down at Cassius. "Mr. Burnwell, hmm? You're here to either tell me I'm finally going to get the backing I need, or deport me. Which is it?" Her English is elegant, shaded with a touch of Dutch Afrikaans.

"Neither. Have you heard about the Brigade?"

It turns out she hasn't. She sits down and joins us, and Cassius fills her in.

"Good Lord," she murmurs when he's done. "Saladin *and* Lucy? It's hard to believe."

"I thought I'd come down and warn you myself," Cassius says. "I understand you're not exactly in the loop these days."

She glances at him sharply. "Not in favor, you mean. I know how I'm regarded in Washington. And a phone call would have done just as well, David—except you can't actually see what I'm up to that way, can you?"

"No. And you're right—I *am* checking up on you. So far, all the evidence points to the killer being someone that knows our secrets."

"In that case, I should think *you're* the prime suspect." She turns and addresses me for the first time. "And who are you? It's not like David to bring his human playmates into the field."

I'm not surprised the pheromone didn't fool her. "I'm

Special Agent Jace Valchek, Cath—or do you prefer Your Highness?"

"I prefer to be left alone while I'm working, Ms. Valchek. While I do appreciate the heads-up, I was in the middle of tracking an injured wildebeest when you interrupted my night, and I'd really like to finish it off before it suffers any further." She gets to her feet. Even without shoes, she must stand six-four.

"I've got a few questions for you first," I say. "And royalty or not, you're going to answer them."

"I see. And if I decline?"

"Then you can find another country to be exiled to. You're a guest here, Ms. Shaka; play nice and so will we."

By the look on her face, she's more amused than offended. "Your kitten has claws," she tells Cassius. "All right, then—what do you wish to know?"

I question her about her whereabouts during the two murders, and she provides me with answers: She was here, working. There are hidden security cameras all over the reserve, so it should be fairly easy to confirm her alibi. She agrees to take me to the monitoring station to check the recordings for the last few days—they keep everything indefinitely, using the data to help track the movements and behaviors of the animals.

Cassius tells me he'll wait for me in the lodge. I shouldn't be surprised; he's simply adapted his strategy to how he thinks I'm going to act ahead of time. I tell Charlie to stay put, too, just to keep Cassius honest.

We walk along a wood-chip-strewn path lit by flickering torches, foliage rustling softly on either side. It's hard to believe I'm still in North America—guess their shamans know what they're doing. From the number of guests, I'd say they can afford the best.

"So," Shaka says. "Is this the part where just we girls talk?"

"Huh? Ah, actually, I've never been very good at the whole girl-talk thing. Not my style."

"Nor mine. I sense something different about you—other than that scent you wear to mask your humanity."

"I'm not from around here. 'Here' being reality as you know it."

"Ah. A crossover. Cassius always was willing to go to extraordinary lengths to get what he wanted."

I'm getting a little tired of the whole *ooh, you're Cassius's latest blood babe* thing. "What he wanted in this case was a specialist. I hunt maniacs—you know, that condition that thropes and pires don't suffer from? Oh, wait—that's not true anymore, is it?"

She ignores the jab. "A hunter of the mad. Interesting. I've had to put down animals that have been infected with rabies—I've even encountered a mystical strain that infects lycanthropes, though it's rare. I can't imagine how you could track an intelligent being afflicted with such a condition—wouldn't its actions be almost entirely random?"

"Only in the most severe cases. I deal largely with those with some ability to conceal their disease."

She smiles. "The half-mad, then. Does their madness make them easier or harder to catch?"

I find myself starting to like this woman—she asks good questions. "Both. They tend to have a very distorted worldview, which can make their logic hard to follow—but if you can manage it, it sometimes leads you right to them."

"That's the secret of successfully tracking any prey—learn to think like them. Know what drives them and you can arrive at their destination before they do."

"Thinking like a psychopath I can manage; where I come from, there are plenty of examples to study. Vampires, werewolves, and golems, though—not so much."

"This place must seem very alien to you."

"Yes and no. Mostly, it's very similar—cars drive down streets, people walk down sidewalks, shopping malls throttle suburbs. It's the little things that throw me off—the toothbrushes with multiple attachments, the candy bars with flavors like mutton."

"The loss of the familiar is a price all exiles must pay," she says. "I remember when I first came to this country thinking how strange everything smelled. But as time goes on, it's what I *don't* smell that I miss. The sweetness of the flowers that grew on the riverbank near my village; the rich, spicy stew my mother used to make. Sometimes I think I would give up everything I've worked for, everything I care about, just to have those scents fill my nostrils again."

I sigh. "Butterscotch pudding."

She smiles. "A childhood treat?"

"An adult vice. I'm not even sure where butterscotch comes from—about all I know is it doesn't seem to have anything to do with actual butter or scotch. And you don't seem to have it here."

She chuckles, and manages to make it sound sad. "I hope one day you will get your butterscotch pudding, Jace Valchek. If I ever hear of such a thing, I will be sure to let you know."

We reach another building with a thatched roof, though the door seems a lot sturdier than the lounge's. "This is the security center," she says. "Though the door shouldn't be ajar—I must have a word with T'Kwele—"

Her voice is casual, but she puts one hand on my chest and stops me dead. She makes eye contact, flicks a glance at the door and puts a finger to her lips.

And then she dives into a nearby bush and is gone.

I blink. If I hadn't been watching her, I wouldn't have known where she went—she made almost no noise at all.

What's going on here? Is she going to teach this T'Kwele a lesson about lax security? Am I supposed to walk in, or just stand here until something happens?

No. The look in her eyes was serious. She's operating on instinct, and that instinct told her something was wrong. And I'll bet her instincts are very, very sharp . . .

I draw my scythes as quietly as I can. Though I can hear distant voices and laughter, there's no one in this part of the compound. Not that I can see, anyway.

That doesn't last. The door to the security building opens and half a dozen pires spill out. In this case, identifying them as hemovores isn't difficult; each of them has oversize fangs, a high widow's peak of slicked-back dark hair, and a face white with makeup. They're all dressed identically, in knee-length black dusters with high collars lined in red satin.

Great. Now I have to deal with Lugosis . . .

FOURTEEN

Let me tell you a little about Bela Lugosi.

Lugosi was a Hungarian actor born near the end of the nineteenth century. He came to America in the 1920s and worked in both films and theater, starring in a Broadway play called *Dracula* that became a big hit; the movie that followed made him a star. That much is true in my world and this one, but that's about it.

See, in this world *Dracula* was a very different thing. It was still a work of fiction, but in a world of vampires and werewolves, it was more of a murder mystery than a horror novel. Dracula himself comes across more like a criminal mastermind out for world conquest than a bogeyman—still a monster, but one easier to identify with. For the pire readers, anyway.

The book wasn't nearly as successful, either—not until Bram Stoker stalked and murdered several pire hookers in London's Whitechapel district. Being a writer, he couldn't resist bragging about his deeds in print, sending letters to the local press—unfortunately for him, someone recognized his prose style and he was arrested. And hanged.

The fact that the murders had been committed by a human set off riots, with over two hundred human deaths before it was over. The novel catapulted to instant fame, and the serial-killer thriller genre was born.

The Bela of this world's portrayal of the old neckbiter was memorable for two reasons: first, the sheer physicality he brought to the role—he played him as a combination of Errol Flynn and Jimmy Cagney, with a little Bogart thrown in.

Second, Bela himself started off human. He became a pire in order to get the part.

I shouldn't be shocked at that. The list of things a hungry actor will do for even a small part, let alone a starring role, is long and humiliating. And all the obvious jokes about Hollywood bloodsuckers, immortality and the lack of anything like a soul are there, too. But I still find it horrifying—to give up your humanity, to change the basic nature of what you are, in return for success? I can't imagine doing that, despite the joke I made to Cassius.

But Bela could, and did. And though his career had its ups and downs—particularly during the 1940s and 1950s when musicals were big—he never acquired the painkiller habit that sidelined him in my world. Vampires don't get sciatica.

Still, his star had faded by the time the 1960s rolled around, and he spent most of the next two decades playing forgettable mob bosses in crime pictures. Until 1981, and a little film called *Raiders of the Lost Ark*.

I won't go into the differences between that film and the one I know—the important thing is that it relaunched Bela's career, and made him the go-to guy for cynical, flawed heroes who preferred to solve their problems with a slug to the jaw and a fast getaway vehicle. Over the years he's played parts that in my reality went to Clint Eastwood, Arnold Schwarzenegger, or Bruce Willis—he's terrific in the first few *Die Hard* movies. There's even a series of updated *Dracula* films where he plays the count as a kind of superpowered antihero, and it's these films that his most hardcore fans adore. They dress like him, wear the same kind of fang extensions he does, even try to talk like him; Bela never did lose that Hungarian accent.

And now I'm staring down a group of these wannabes. This is a lot more dangerous than it sounds. Lugosis tend to be Eastern Europeans who have survived genocidal wars, and their attitude toward anyone who isn't one of them ranges from contemptuous to predatory. They've been known to kill people as the punch line to a joke—the same sort of deadpan one-liners that Lugosi utters after setting someone on fire and throwing them off a building.

"Vell, vell, vell," the leader says. He's virtually indistinguishable from the rest of them, other than the fact that the medal hanging off the red ribbon around his neck is a little bigger than the others. "Vere's your friend, little thrope?"

"You tell me," I say. "All those little TVs in the room you just came out of? That's not cable."

He chuckles in a raspy kind of way. "Your friend seems somevhat camera-shy. But you know vhere she's going, *don't* you?"

"I'm guessing to get help. Sure you want to be here when she comes back?"

"She'll find dere's no one to get," the Lugosi says. "Ve have neutralized any possible resistance. But perhaps she vill come back if you scream loudly enough . . ."

That's the second time somebody's tried to use me as bait, and I'm starting to feel a little insulted. "You first," I say.

He lunges. He thinks I'm a thrope, so he's hoping to nail me before I transform and get bigger, faster, and stronger. I use a trick I learned from a biker with a pit bull: block with your forearm, giving the dog a handy target to sink his teeth into instead of your neck. It might seem like a somewhat drastic solution—especially when you consider how strong a pit bull's jaws are—but as the biker pointed out, it's a lot easier to sew a hollow section of metal pipe into the lining of your sleeve than a scarf. And I have a pipe with a coating of silver paint.

Both of Mr. Bitey's fangs snap with a noise like breaking chalk. I ram the silver spike of my baton into his forehead hard enough to dent his skull, and his eyes roll up in his head before he slides off my arm and drops to the ground.

"Now serving customer number two," I say.

For film fans, they're not that appreciative of my wit. In fact, rather than following the time-honored movie cliché of attacking one at a time, they decide to swarm me instead.

Which means I'm dead. Or lunch.

Pires are fast. I've been forced to compensate in a number of ways, one of which is my gun. I wish I'd drawn it now; there's no way I can take these guys down all at once with the scythes. I barely have time to snap the blades out before they're on me—

And arrows start sprouting from their eyes.

A wooden arrow through the brain won't always kill a pire, but wood penetrating any major organ can potentially be lethal. Two of them clatter to the ground in a pile of bones, and another screams and sinks to his knees while clawing at his face. I nail the one leaping at me with a backhand swipe; his head spins past me while the body crumples into a pile of rotting meat.

I face off against the last two. Neither of them is paying attention to me; they're looking around wildly for wherever the arrows are coming from.

"Get down on the ground and put your hands behind your head," I snap. "You don't have to—"

Two more arrows. Both heart shots.

"—die," I say softly. Nobody seems to be listening, anyway.

The African Queen steps out of the undergrowth. She's in half-were form, her fur dyed in a striking black-and-white-striped tribal pattern. She's got a compound bow in her hands, a quiver of black arrows clipped to it. She already has another shaft notched and the bowstring pulled taut.

"Hi," I say. "Can we talk now, or are you not done killing all my suspects?"

She tenses her legs and leaps, landing in the open door of the security outpost. She ducks inside.

I wait. She reappears a few seconds later, her bow lowered.

"Kind of hard to talk with your hands full," I point out. She hesitates, clearly uncomfortable with the idea of letting her guard down, so I hold up the scythes and say, "I've got your back, all right?"

She nods. A few moments later I'm looking at Catharine Shaka once more. "You have interesting enemies," she says.

"Not me. These guys were here looking for you."

She frowns. "I don't know them. They must be foot soldiers—assassins rarely travel in packs. But why send such ill-prepared thugs against—"

Her eyes open wide. "No!" She sprints past me, back into the bush, and this time I do my best to follow. I manage not to lose her, but only because she doesn't go far and makes no attempt to be quiet. I find her in a clearing, at the base of a massive banyan tree, on her knees. There's a large hole in the ground, as if something had erupted from the earth.

"Gone," she says, her voice as hard as flint. "It was a feint, meant to occupy me while their master stole the sky-shield."

"Or to draw you into the open so that he could take it from your body."

"That would not have happened—the shield protects the wielder from any harm. I thought it was safe here; it was hidden not only from sight but by powerful magicks."

"Same thing happened to the Centurion. Whoever this guy is, he knows how to find you."

"Whoever he is, he has made a mistake," she says calmly. "The *isihlangu* was given to my father's father's father, by the Sky God Umvelinqangi. It is a sacred artifact, meant to protect all of my countrymen, and I will *not* suffer it to fall into the hands of another." Anger sparks in her eyes, but her voice is cold and steady. "I will find this thief, and I will *end* him."

I believe her.

"Let's go update Cassius and Charlie. We'll get your shield back."

She nods sharply, gets to her feet and strides back the way we came.

We get back to the security hut, and I notice our body count is a little low—in fact, we're short one Count. I remember the one Shaka shot in the eye—looks like he was in better shape than I thought.

But not quite good enough to manage an effective escape. Cassius and Charlie come strolling down the path, Charlie frog-marching the Lugosi with one arm twisted up behind his back. The arrow still juts from the pire's left eye.

"Lose something?" Charlie says. "We found the pincushion staggering past the bar, spouting gibberish and blood."

The Lugosi doesn't seem to be all there. His other eye won't focus, and he's muttering what sounds like nonsense under his breath. Pires aren't normally affected by mental illness—or weren't, until recently—but brain damage by wood or silver is another matter. Ordinary humans have survived having all kinds of things rammed in or through their brains—a railway spike in one famous case—so why shouldn't a pire? He may be not be firing on all cylinders, but at least he's alive.

"We have to get him to a hospital," I say. "Cassius, you drive. Charlie and I—"

"No," Shaka says coldly. "He will not die. Not until he has answered my questions." She steps forward and grabs the arrow in one hand.

I expect her to yank it out, but she doesn't. She uses it like a handle to turn his face toward hers, slowly but firmly. He gapes at her, his remaining eye twitching and his mouth hanging open. "Calibration," he blurts. "Calipers. Contiguous. Con*tig*uous."

"Charlie, don't move," I say. "Let him go, Shaka. You can't torture the man."

"I am merely questioning him," she says, her eyes locked on the pire's face. "It will not become torture unless he tries to nod. Who sent you?"

"Apricot flambé. Fling the warbled soup, for jewelry is not penultimate. Gazpacho!"

"Interesting. How about now?" She twists the arrow slightly to the left—I expect him to scream, but he reacts by shuddering and then beginning to sing: "On top of old Smokey, all covered with snow, I lost my poor—"

"No . . ."

She twists the other way, and this time he shrieks. "The smell! Shoe polish! Make it stop, make it *stop*!"

"For God's sake," I say and grab her arm. She ignores me.

"Tell me who sent you, and the smell will go away."

"I can't stand it! *I can't stand it!*"

"Let him go," I say, "Or you'll be the one with something sticking out of your eye."

"You should really let go of my arm. I might accidentally drive the arrow deeper."

About the only alternative I have is to draw my gun and shoot her, or chop her damn hand off. The only reason I don't is because I know she can kill the Lugosi quicker than I can move.

"All right, all right," the Lugosi sobs. "The Shadows sent us. The Crooked Shadows."

"Why?" she demands.

"Revenge. For killing one of them. That's all I know, I swear."

She releases the arrow, and he sags in Charlie's grip. I let go of her arm. Cassius hasn't said a word during this entire exchange, but now he speaks up. "You must have good medical facilities here. If you wouldn't mind showing Charlie the way?"

She studies him for a second, then says, "Of course. Follow me."

She marches off, Charlie carrying the now unconscious pire in his arms. I'm about to follow them, but Cassius puts out a hand and stops me.

"Are you kidding?" I say. "I'm not going to leave a prisoner alone with her—he'll wind up a pile of dust with a few bones sticking out."

"No, he won't. Shaka's methods might seem brutal, but she won't just execute a prisoner. She's learned what she needs to know. Besides, I think Charlie would have his own opinion if she tried."

"Well, how about what the Lugosi said? The Shadows think she killed the Sword of Midnight."

"If she had, do you think she'd interrogate a suspect in front of us to reveal that information?"

He had a point. "So the Lugosis are being played, too."

"They were meant as a distraction to steal the shield, that much is true. They believe the Crooked Shadows hired them, which also fits the facts. But as to who actually took the shield—"

"—That we don't know." I'm already taking out my phone. "We need to get Eisfanger here to process the scene."

He nods. "Maybe we can get something else out of the Lugosi. And pay attention to Shaka—she's the best tracker on the planet. If the thief left any kind of trail at all, she'll find it."

By the time I get to the infirmary, Shaka's gone.

"Said she needed to pick up the trail before it got cold," Charlie tells me. "Thought I should stay with the prisoner."

"Yeah, stay here," I tell him, and sprint back the way I came.

There's nobody at the banyan tree. Either Shaka's already stalking the thief, or she's just taken off. Either way, I have no idea where she's going—

I almost smack myself in the head over my own stupidity. I run back to the security hut, where Cassius—as usual—is one step ahead.

"The Lugosis disabled the system," he says, indicating a bank of dead monitors. "That's why they hit here first, to cover their tracks. Shaka's probably still in the park, but we can't tell where."

"Damn it. How about the security logs?"

"Those are archived; they should be fine."

"That's good—because other than a brain-damaged fanpire, that's about all we have left."

I spend the next couple of hours downloading footage onto my laptop and reviewing it. Cassius organizes whatever details need to be handled between the staff of the park and the cleanup squad that arrives to deal with the aftermath of the attack. Charlie helps me check the security recordings—he's got sharp eyes, and there's a lot of material. We're looking for Shaka's movements before, during, and after any of the murders, especially times when she's not accounted for.

By the time Cassius shows up with Eisfanger, my eyes are starting to blur, my head is beginning to ache, and I could cheerfully go without seeing another zebra for the rest of my life.

"Wow, this place is *cool*," Eisfanger says. He's wearing an honest-to-God pith helmet, even though it's the middle of the night. "I've always wanted to go on a safari but never got around to it."

"Well, here's your chance to play Great White Hunter," I say. "Come with me."

I take him to the excavation by the banyan tree. "Here's where it was buried. Shaka took off in a hurry, so she either picked up a trail or knew where the thief was going."

Eisfanger sets his case down on the ground. "I can do this better if I get hairy," he says, sounding almost apologetic.

"Call of the Wild on line two. Go ahead, pick up."

He shifts. I do my best not to laugh—a werewolf in a pith helmet is just hard to take seriously.

He starts to sniff around the site. I leave him to it—if he finds anything urgent, the security hut isn't far away.

Cassius is still there when I get back. "I've been talking to the people Shaka worked with. She had many friends, but none of them knew her well. I've already had the second best tracker take a look at where the shield was buried—he says that whoever took it got there the same way we did, walking from the path. He couldn't find a trail leading away."

"So the thief either vanished or figured out how to fly the damn thing."

"It looks that way. I've also tried talking to the Lugosi, but he's no longer coherent. It'll take a while for his brain to heal."

Charlie steps out of the hut and joins us. "Just finished up with the security recordings."

"And?" Cassius asks.

"Hard to say. She spends a lot of time in the bush and out of sight. My professional opinion—if she's as good as I've heard, she could've slipped away on any of the nights. Especially if she had air transport."

"I have to agree," I say. "There's nothing proving she was gone, but there's nothing conclusive to give her an alibi, either."

Cassius nods. "Let's hope Eisfanger comes up with something we can use."

"There are no tracks leading out of here," Eisfanger says.

"We already knew that," I say. "The thief must have taken the aerial route."

"Let me finish. Just because there's no tracks doesn't mean there's no trail—there's just no trail on the *ground*."

I frown. "You can track someone through the air?"

"Well, no. But apparently Shaka can."

"How do you know?"

"Because she took to the trees."

Cassius and Charlie are back at the security hut—it's just me and Eisfanger out in the bush. "How do you know? The other tracker didn't find anything like that."

"The other tracker didn't have my equipment. It's one thing to follow a herd of wild buffalo, and another to locate the spoor of the African Queen."

"Spoor?"

"Okay, not spoor, exactly. More like very tiny amounts of spiritual trace." He holds up a feather in a plastic bag. "I used this—it's highly sensitive to etheric vibration. I was able to harmonize it to the fletching on one of her arrows. According to the feather, she went up this tree."

"And then?"

He shrugs. "It's got to be really close to any trace to detect it. She apparently leapt from this tree to another one, and so on. I'm not really trained for that sort of thing."

I consider trying to follow her, and reject it. She's undoubtedly moving fast; going tree-to-tree will be painstakingly slow, and we'll lose the trail more than once. Besides, I know better than to take on the Queen of the Jungle on her own turf. At this point, our best option is to let her go, hope she's actually going after the thief and wish her the best.

"Anything else?" I ask.

He indicates the hole in the ground. "This site was mystically as well protected as the storage locker. It was dug up with a pair of shovels."

"Wait—a pair of shovels? How can you tell?"

"Well, normal forensics wouldn't be able to—dirt is usually too crumbly to hold a good tool mark, and most shovels wouldn't leave anything distinctive anyway. But I found a couple of roots that had been damaged, and they remembered being damaged simultaneously. Two digging implements were being used at the same time."

"So we've got another suspect."

"There's something else. I found footprints, too—big ones. I took casts." He kneels and pries up a large white patch of plaster to one side of the hole. "See?"

"Those have to be at least a size eighteen," I say. "Looks like some kind of work boot. They're deep, too—the guy must weigh over three hundred pounds."

"They go all the way back to the path. There's no security camera where he ducked into the underbrush, but a guy this big has to stand out—plus, he'd be carrying two shovels."

"There's nobody like that in any of the footage," I say. "He would have been as obvious as a nudist at the North Pole. How about his companion?"

"I only found the one set. What do you think it means?"

I sigh. "It's obvious, isn't it? We're looking for the ghost of Bigfoot. And his invisible friend . . ."

Cassius arranges transport for our prisoner, and all of us head back to Seattle. It's a frustrating trip; Cassius insists he knows nothing about invisible giants, and won't put out a BOLO on Shaka due to her delicate diplomatic status. I'm angry at myself for letting her out of my sight, angry at Cassius for loyalty I can't blame him for, and slightly annoyed at Charlie for how well he's taking all this.

We take all the security footage with us—maybe Gretch's team can give us a better analysis, spot something we missed—and I get a pleasant surprise when I walk into the intel division: Gretchen herself is there, maneuvering carefully from desk to desk like the *Queen Elizabeth 2* negotiating a path between islands. She's wearing a billowy black frock that's severe and managerial while using enough fabric for a small tent. She smiles when she notices me and says, "Hello, Jace."

"Hi. You look . . ."

"Enormous?"

"I was going to say great."

"The original meaning of which was 'enormous.'"

"Okay, you got me. I was cleverly trying to hide my insult inside an etymological riddle, but I couldn't find any way to work in the word *zeppelin*. How are you doing?"

"Zeppelin is an apt metaphor. I am generating a great deal of gas, my blood pressure is elevated, and my mood is prone to abrupt explosions. Earlier today I nearly invaded Poland on a whim."

"I'll keep that in mind."

"You shouldn't be working," Cassius says from behind me. "In your condition—"

"Excuse me," she says sweetly, and I get out of her way. Which is good, because a second later she has a knife to Cassius's throat.

The room gets very quiet.

"I'm still fit enough to do this," she says, in an eminently reasonable tone. "Which should lay to rest any fears about my physical capabilities. As to my mental state, I'll let you decide after the meeting."

Cassius gives her a smile with only a little nervousness in it. "The weekly global synopsis? I thought you might have delegated that—"

"I haven't. My office in ten minutes?" The knife vanishes as quickly as it appeared.

"As you wish. But first, Jace has some new information for you."

I give her the recordings on a flash drive and a brief rundown on the situation. She nods, asks a few curt questions, then takes the drive. "I'll have Mahmoud check it. He's particularly good with video work."

"Okay. The other thing I want to talk to you about is Dr. Pete."

"Jace, I told you I can't discuss his past—"

"I know. I just wanted to know if he's all right."

She pauses. "He's fine—still at the safe house. I'm meeting him later; you can come along if you'd like."

I don't know if *like* is the right word, but there are things the Doc and I have to discuss. "Yeah, fine. Let me know when you're leaving."

I make some phone calls. Xandra tells me Galahad has been behaving, and wants to know how many more nights she's going to have to cover for me. I tell her I should be able to get him off her hands tonight, then try Dr. Pete's cell. I get a message saying the number is currently "not available," which could mean the safe house has some kind of jamming station—spooks are fond of them, they're good for disabling remote bombs—or maybe he took off in such a hurry he forgot to pay his phone bill. Doesn't really matter; I'll be seeing him soon anyway, and then he can deal with Galahad. I've got enough problems of my own without worrying about a hyperactive anthrocanine, though I will kind of miss the big lug—his coffee-making abilities in particular.

Charlie's hanging around my office, reading a magazine. He doesn't look up when I come in, but says, "I gotta take off today. Got a thing."

"Yeah? What kind of thing?"

"Recertification. Lems have to do it annually."

I take a closer look at the magazine: *Swingdance Monthly.* "Yeah, I can see you're really boning up for that."

"It's nothing. Couple hours and some paperwork, I'm done for the year."

It makes sense—most cops have to go through something similar when it comes to firearms. Since an enforcement lem is basically a walking, talking gun, I guess they need periodic checkups. "So what's that entail? Have to get your pitching arm realigned?"

"Full physical. Test all my seams, top up the topsoil. Make sure nothing's leaking, cracked, or punctured." He hesitates, then says, "And I gotta take a psych test."

"Yeah, the Bureau did the same kind of thing. Want to know how you're handling job stress, that kind of stuff."

"That's not what it's for."

I lean up against my desk, cross my arms. "What do you mean?"

"Enforcement lems aren't like others. We have a certain . . . failure rate."

"Oh? And what happens when one of you fail? You explode or something? Should I be worried?"

My tone is light, but his face isn't. "No. I'll be fine." He gets to his feet, tosses the magazine on the chair, turns to leave.

"Hey," I say as he opens the door. "What happens if you don't pass?"

"If I fail," he says, "I won't be coming back."

He shuts the door in my astonished face.

FIFTEEN

I rip the door open a second later. *"Now hold on just a goddamn minute!"*

Once again, everybody in earshot goes quiet. Charlie stops in his tracks.

"You think you can drop a bombshell like that on me and just walk away? Get back here, *now!*"

He turns and does so, without a word. As I close the door, I hear someone in the office say, "What's a bombshell?"

"Explain," I say firmly.

"It's very simple. Enforcement lems are animated by predators; that means that although we don't eat, we still have the instinctual drive to hunt and kill. If those instincts ever get out of control, we become a danger to the ones we're supposed to protect. That can't happen."

"What's that mean, 'out of control'? How can they tell?"

"They have tests."

"Tests? So if you see the wrong thing in a Rorschach blot, they *execute* you?"

"It's a reasonable precaution."

"The hell it is! You put your life on the line as a public servant, and they treat you like a piece of faulty equipment?"

"Jace." His voice is firm. "To a certain degree, I *am* a piece of equipment. I was built, not born. I have a natural affinity for killing, and that affinity has to be monitored. I'll be fine. I've gone through this many times, and never had any problems. Honestly, it's the animates based on mammals that tend to go off the rails."

"Really?"

"Sure. Us cold-blooded types are much more level-headed."

I can't tell if he's kidding or not. All I know is that I really don't want him to walk out that door. "If you're putting me on about this," I say, "I will carve a hole in your chest and lock you in a room with a dozen cats and a box of laxative-laced catnip."

"That sounds unpleasant."

I take a deep breath to make my snappy comeback, but nothing comes out. We just look at each other for a moment, and don't say anything.

"Just come back," I finally say.

He nods. This time when he leaves, I let him.

Damn it.

Eisfanger finds me in the bar.

It's a little hole-in-the-wall I found, a few blocks north of the NSA offices. Both thropes and pires drink here, so it's open pretty much all the time. It's lit mainly by neon beer signs and a fluorescent over the pool table, but the bar is long and oak and they keep a decent nonmagicked scotch on hand. I think I'm the only human who drinks here, but the other customers assume I'm a thrope and leave me alone. I picked it mainly because of the jukebox, which is an old-fashioned monstrosity the size of a fridge that plays actual records. It contains exactly two selections that I listen to.

He slides onto the bar stool next to mine, looking around as he does so. "Hey. You, uh, sure about this place?"

I take a sip of my scotch. "No. Right now, quite frankly, I'm not sure about *any* place. Where I come from we can do surveillance from orbit, and this world seems to have almost all the technology we do plus magic. So if we're being bugged by an invisible enchanted flea with a cybernetic uplink, it wouldn't really come as that much of a surprise."

"But—you picked the place."

I sigh. "You wanted a private meeting. Not at the office. This is what I came up with. What's going on?"

"First, the lava sample you gave me is a match to the one found at the storage locker."

About what I'd suspected, and not really that helpful. "What else?"

"Lucy Barbarossa's corpse de-bronzed. Aquitaine's bones reverted yesterday, but I didn't learn anything new from them. Barbarossa, though—that was a different story." He leans toward me, the kind of excitement in his face that only a truly bizarre detail can produce in a professional forensics tech. "Jace, Barbarossa was killed *first*."

I try to figure it out for myself. "Being turned into metal would have stopped any decomp or animal predation, so she could have been there a few days—but what about the brain segments? Did you find signs of a preservative or refrigeration?"

"No, no. I told you, it was the body itself that tipped me off. It was *out of sync* with the neural tissue."

"You've lost me."

"One of the things forensic animism can do very accurately is measure age—even in a corpse—and when I compared the residual energy of the body and the brain, *they weren't the same*."

"Which one was older?"

"The brain. By two days."

I took a second to process that. "So Barbarossa was killed three days ago . . . but her body had been dead for five?"

"That's what you'd think. But I'm not talking about age in terms of how long something's been *alive*—I'm talking about how long something's *existed*."

I take another sip of scotch. "I'm not sure I'm following. You're saying the brain's existed for two days longer than the body. How is that possible?"

He settles back on his seat, looking smug. "Chronistic displacement."

"Chron—oh." I sit up a little straighter. "Time travel. The Midnight Sword."

"Yeah. We don't have any technical specs for what it can do, but one of its abilities is supposedly to affect time. If the killer used it to send her brain back in time two days after he removed it, it would result in the body having existed for two days *less* than the brain. I figure he killed her, turned the body into bronze to preserve it, then took the brain home to do his little dissection and mummification project. When he was finished, he used the sword to tear open a rift in time so he could return the individually wrapped slices to the crime."

"But why?"

He looks at me blankly. "I have *no* idea. Isn't that your department?"

I think for a moment. "There's a number of reasons the killer might have done it that way. Ease of transport, more privacy, lets him control when the body is discovered . . . but the vic was discovered in a fairly secluded place, with an actual submarine parked a few feet away. I don't think privacy or transport was an issue."

"Then what?"

I finish my drink, set the glass down on the bar, and throw some bills down after it. "Only one reason I can think of . . ."

The sun's almost ready to rise as I step out of the bar, pink and orange lighting up the eastern edge of the city. The air is cold and damp, steam rising from a grate on the sidewalk. Eisfanger doesn't follow me—he no doubt thinks he should wait a few minutes so we won't be seen together, though I don't much care either way. For the first time in this case, I feel like I've managed to snag the thread that's going to unravel the whole thing; I don't know what it's connected to or if it'll break if I tug too hard, but I know it's important. By the time I get back to the office, I've got a wide smile on my face—it is, I think, going to be a good day.

Boy, am I wrong.

Gretch is a very interesting woman, and I have no trouble imagining her being involved in any number of unusual situations: tracking Yetis in the Himalayas, yes; conducting espionage in a café in Belgium, yes; parachuting into a war zone an hour before dawn, yes.

Shopping for baby clothes, no.

"Thank you so much for joining us, Jace," Gretch says. She's in the middle, Dr. Pete on her left, me on her right. We're strolling through the one of the many corridors of the Seattle City Underplex, or as I like to call it, the Batmall.

Gretch walks like no pregnant woman I've ever seen. I don't know if it's the accelerated pregnancy, her vampire strength, or sheer determination, but she doesn't waddle; she marches, her posture straight, her head high. You'd think she was smuggling a beach ball instead of a carrying a baby.

And she's remained firmly between Dr. Pete and myself, ever since he arrived to pick us up in his car. I suspect it has more to do with all the maternal hormones surging through her body than her stated commitment to professional privacy, though I could be wrong. In any case, if she thinks hauling me out in public and keeping a swollen belly between me and the Doc will keep my mouth shut, she's wrong—I'm just waiting for the right moment, that's all.

I first stumbled on the Batmall a few weeks ago, when I was looking for a decent shoe store. A few hours later a security guard found me sprawled on an escalator, shoppers stepping over my prone body, moaning, "Natural light . . . natural light . . ."

Okay, it's not that bad, but the place does cater to pires—it's completely underground, laid out in a maze that you'd need echolocation to make sense of. I'm not sure how many levels it goes down, but at least five—and some of it's over a hundred years old.

In 1889 the Great Seattle Fire leveled over thirty city blocks. The city decided to build *over* the ruins as a deterrent to flooding—which they'd also had a problem with—and effectively created a huge urban basement. Now, believe it or not, this is exactly the same thing that happened in my world—only there the place was basically sealed off and forgotten about.

Here, the sun-shy part of the population thought they could definitely do something with that much subterranean real estate. They expanded on it, dug even deeper, turned it into a huge shopping center. I think the reason the Pike Place Market here is so run-down is because it can't compete with this place.

And now here we are, God knows how deep beneath the earth, Gretch keeping up a steady stream of innocuous small talk while Dr. Pete sucks nervously on a Red Julius and won't meet my eyes.

Gretch spots another store, grabs both our arms, and marches us in. "This place looks like it has a nice selection.

What do you think, Jace—bats or leeches?" She holds up a blood-red jumper with little cartoon versions of the latter on it. "I'm not crazy about the color, but I suppose it would hide stains . . . is that a good thing?" Suddenly she sounds a little anxious, and I realize I'm being arrogant in assuming the only reason she's here is to provide a buffer between me and Dr. Pete.

"It's a good thing," I assure her. "And personally, I'd go with the bats."

"I suppose . . ."

I manage to sneak behind her and grab Dr. Pete by the arm. "You and I," I say, "have something to discuss."

"I'm sorry, Jace, I just can't—"

"You need to take Galahad back."

"—uh, yes, of course. I'm sorry I dumped him on you, but—"

"No buts. I'm still not sure if you asked me out of genuine concern for him or because you thought it would slow me down, but it was rude and ill conceived either way."

"You're right."

"I know. Oddly, it's not giving me a great deal of satisfaction."

He digs in his pocket and pulls out a plastic cassette case. "I know this doesn't make up for anything, but here. I found this a while ago—I thought I'd give it to you when you needed a pick-me-up."

I take it, but put it in my pocket without looking at it. "Thanks, I'll pull it out the next time I'm feeling low. Right now, though, I'm feeling *angry*—which makes this feel more like a bribe than an apology."

That shakes him a little. Why is it men think you have to accept an apology, just because one is offered?

"Okay," he says. "You have every right to be angry. I'll make arrangements for Galahad to come and stay at the safe house. Guess I should have done that in the first place."

"Guess so."

Gretchen has remained completely quiet during this, but now she pops between us like a referee at the end of a round and says, "There's nothing here that appeals to me. Let's move on, shall we?"

"Yeah," I say. "That sounds like a good idea."

I'm a fumer. I tend to fume. Not so much when I have an outlet—then I'm more of an exploder—but when I don't, I fume. Right now, striding down a mall corridor while Gretchen tries to get my attention focused on baby booties, I'm giving out enough metaphysical vapor to power a paddle wheeler. Dr. Pete is studiously pretending nothing is wrong while slowly edging away from me, Gretch is trying to be chatty, and me—I'm just steaming away on my own private river and not paying much attention to what's on the banks.

I guess that makes what happens next my fault.

We've just rounded a corner, and the corridor has narrowed considerably. No actual stores down this way, just tiled walls with a fire exit on one end and what seems to be the entrance to a loading dock. We're all halfway down it before any of us even notices where we're going.

When we stop and turn around, they're waiting.

It's the same group of wrappers that threatened me before. Guess their eyes have had time to heal—though this time, they're not taking chances.

"Nice sunglasses," I say. "What, no white canes?"

Anorexic Elvis—the one who nailed me with the Blood Cross—seems to be the one in charge. "You messed up my hand, bitch," he says. "I don't know what kind of damn hardware you using, but you ain't gettin' a chance to use it again."

There are five of them. Dr. Pete's already in mid-transformation, but I have no idea how useful he'll actually be in a fight. And Gretchen?

Honestly, if Gretch weren't as big as a house, I think we could have taken them together. As it is, I'm not going to put her child in danger. "Gretch, run," I say. "Get help—"

That's as far as I get. Did I mention before how fast pires are?

The first one slams into Dr. Pete while he's still sprouting fur. The second one nails me before my gun can clear its holster. The rest—

The rest are coughing their lungs out. There's a little gray canister on the floor between them and us, and it's spinning around and spitting a yellowish mist that's filling up the corridor quickly. I may not have the nose of a thrope, but I know tear gas when I smell it. Tear gas cut with lots and lots of garlic. I should have known Gretch wouldn't go out in public without being prepared . . .

I don't have time to thank her, or even glance in her direction. I'm flat on my back with a pire on top of me, and I guess he's more of a traditionalist than he looks because his fangs are going straight for my throat. He's got a hand clamped on both of my wrists, and the only positive element in the situation is that I've managed to actually get the Ruger free. Well, not free, exactly—it's pointed to the side, and there's no way I'm breaking my opponent's grip.

He stops with the tips of his teeth just barely denting my skin. I feel something cold and wet slide against my neck. "You about to learn about a brand-new world," he rasps, then licks me again.

"And you're about to learn a brand-new word," I say. I squeeze the trigger twice; the Ruger roars and spits fire. Gunsmoke and chipped ceramic tile fill the air as I shoot the wall right next to us—and suddenly there's a dissolving sack of wet, rotting flesh pinning me down instead of a vampire, as one of the bullets finds a vital organ.

"Ricochet," I snarl, and shove what's left of him off me.

Gretch's gone—she must have sprinted for the fire doors at the far end after tossing the tear gas. She's probably already on the phone for reinforcements, so all I have to do is hold these guys off until—

I can't see Dr. Pete.

That's because he's buried under a pile of bodies, bodies that are moving so fast their arms and legs are just a blur. At least four of them have escaped the gas and piled on him, and the beating they're delivering is like—I don't know how to describe it. I see flashes of silver, too, and realize they're using more than just their fists. Clubs, blades, I can't tell—and then I'm firing at anyone I have a clear shot at.

Two go down and don't move. The other two turn on me, and I have time to take one out with a heart shot before the other swats my gun out of my hand with an impact that leaves my whole hand numb. It's Anorexic Elvis, and this time he intends to finish the job.

He doesn't make it. Dr. Pete, now in half-were form, has reached out and snagged him by one ankle. Elvis tries to kick his way free, but Dr. Pete refuses to let go. It's hard to believe he's still conscious; his muzzle is covered in blood, half his fangs have been smashed out and one of his eyes is gone.

Elvis realizes a more direct approach is called for. He twists in Dr. Pete's grip, drops to one knee on his victim's chest, and starts to slam his fist into his face, again and again. I realize that the glint I saw is a pair of solid silver knuckles, a heavy chunk of metal that he's hammering away at the Doc's face with.

"Tair says hello, fool," he growls. Dr. Pete's grip finally loosens and falls away. Elvis turns back to me—but the Doc's bought me enough time to recover the Ruger.

I don't say anything clever. I just shoot him until I hear the click of an empty chamber.

I slump against the wall, shaky and dizzy from adrenaline. The cloud of tear gas moves lazily away from me, propelled by some invisible air vent breeze. *It's over,* I tell myself. *It's over.*

And then I hear the loud, echoing scream from the stairwell, and know I'm wrong.

SIXTEEN

I sprint for the fire door. I find Gretchen just inside it, sprawled on the concrete steps, unconscious. Her water's broken, and it's a lot redder than it should be. That could simply be because she's a vampire, but I don't know.

Phone. Must find phone. I dig it out with shaky fingers, drop it, curse loudly, and nearly drop it again after picking it up. I force myself to calm down, take a few long, slow breaths, and dial 911. After I give them the relevant information, I call Cassius. Then I call Charlie, but he's not picking up—probably in the middle of being tested.

Then I reload my gun, and wait.

Cassius's people get there first—somehow, I'm not surprised. A field medic checks both Dr. Pete and Gretchen coolly, tells me that the Doc is in serious condition but will make it. He hesitates when I ask about Gretch, then says, "We have to get her to the hospital ASAP."

The paramedics show up a minute later, but Gretchen's already gone—the field medic snapped together a collapsible stretcher, and then he and another agent loaded her on it and literally *ran* up the stairs. Let's hear it for supernatural strength and stamina.

I just hope Gretch has her share.

The cops arrive after that. I show them my NSA badge,

and when they start to get snippy I wave over a couple of large thrope agents to explain exactly how much trouble they're going to be in if they don't shut their traps, put away their notebooks, and go find a doughnut shop to have been in for the last half hour. I'd do it myself—it's the kind of thing I normally live for—but I feel like I have exactly one, fraying nerve left. Me blowing a gasket is not going to help anyone.

I wind up carting away the shopping bags full of Gretch's purchases. It seems really important I be able to tell Gretch I took care of it so she won't worry.

I stuff them in the trunk of the car and get on the phone to Cassius. He's already at the hospital, and gives me directions. Gretch has just arrived but he doesn't know how she's doing—all he knows is she's going into labor.

No matter how fast I drive, everything seems slow. The little voice in the back of my head—the one that says the most inappropriate things at the worst times—has moved up to the front and gotten itself a bullhorn.

Wow, what a day. Your partner's on his way to the trash compactor, the guy you have a crush on was beaten half to death, and your best friend will probably die in childbirth right about . . . now.

Shut up shut up shut up. I am not going to lose three of the only people on this godforsaken planet I give a damn about—

Two out of three? Still pretty good—if by good you mean really, really terrible—

Not happening. Not one, not two, not any of them. Dr. Pete will be fine. Gretch will be fine. Charlie will be fine.

Dr. Pete, okay—though, sucky job protecting him, I gotta say. Dating you would be like going out with a national disaster—

One soul-numbing criticism at a time, okay?

You didn't protect Gretch. You didn't protect Charlie. You didn't—

Shut up shut up SHUT UP!

I realize I'm screaming it, pounding on the steering wheel, tears running down my face. I pull over before I have an accident, put on my four-way flashers and just shake for a minute.

I can handle being afraid. I can handle staring evil in the face from a few inches away. I can even handle the possibility of losing someone I care about. What I can't handle is being hit with all three within twenty minutes, and knowing the last one might be my fault.

Two minutes later I'm back on the road. My breathing is steady. My hands do not shake. The voice in my head is still there, but the bullhorn has been switched off and I'm not listening anyway.

Mostly.

"She's in surgery," Cassius tells me.

We're in the waiting area of the maternity ward. This hospital is very different from either of the places I was in before; it's larger, newer, sleeker. It feels more like a place a Beverly Hills pire would go to have a little designer plastic surgery . . . if (a) an immortal being actually aged, and (b) the idea of performing surgery on a vampire wasn't a ludicrous idea.

Except, of course, that's exactly what Gretchen is going through.

"God*damn* it," I spit. "I don't know what any of the *rules* are anymore! I hate this world and I hate *you* for dragging me here!"

Cassius ignores my outburst. "Her advanced pregnancy is causing complications. The child is drawing life force from her faster than she can give it, and that's putting a severe strain on her body. It's basically a race at this point."

"A race?"

"Yes. To see if she can give birth before the baby kills her."

I stare at him. "Gee, don't feel you like you have to sugarcoat it or anything."

"Some people need a cold dose of reality to help them focus."

"You could have just slapped me."

"I considered it. But you hate clichés, and I hate being shot."

"Good point. Plus, this is a hospital. Guns are kind of noisy."

"Are they? I thought it was just a personal statement on your part, like women who wear too much makeup."

Funny, isn't it, how quickly you latch on to the familiar when you feel like you're losing control? I hadn't realized just how comfortable my back-and-forth with Cassius had become until we both slip into it while our friend is near death. Maybe it's just laughing at the shadows, gallows humor, but it feels like something else. Something more.

"She'll be all right," he says. "She's strong. You know that."

"Yeah. Yeah, of course she is."

"Would you like to see Dr. Adams? I understand they brought him in a few minutes ago."

I hesitate, and he says, "I'll call you as soon as I hear anything."

"Sure."

He gives me directions to another floor, and I take the elevator down. I realize on the way what's been bothering me—on a subliminal level—since I got here: It doesn't smell like disinfectant. I guess sterile procedures just aren't as important when you have a supernatural immune system.

I find Dr. Pete in a private room. I half expected him to be hooked up to an IV, oxygen tubes sticking out of his nose, wired to various beeping machines and monitors—but that's overkill for a thrope. His arms and legs are immobilized by splints, though, and he's still in half-were form. Guess he'll heal faster that way.

He looks over when I come in. There's a gauze patch over one of his eyes.

"Hey," I say. "How are you doing?"

He nods, which isn't terribly informative. I look down and see that all of his fingers are in splints, too.

"Looks like you won't be talking for a while. That's okay. I just wanted to let you know that Gretch is—well, she's in labor. Cassius says she'll be all right."

His fingers twitch. His muzzle opens and closes, and I can see that most of his teeth have been shattered. He whines, which rises to a howl.

"Calm down," I say. "I'll keep you updated, I promise—"

A nurse rushes in, a silver-needled hypo in one hand. She ignores me completely and jabs it, smoothly and efficiently, into his neck. His howl immediately drops a few octaves, sputters, then dies down to a groggy snarl.

The nurse, a tall and imposing redheaded pire with arched eyebrows like something out of *Star Trek,* finally acknowledges my presence. "What do you think you're doing?"

"I'm—I was just—"

"This patient is in seclusion for a reason. His bones have to set properly, and that can't happen if he's trying to hold up his end of a conversation."

"But I—"

"He is in a great deal of pain. We couldn't give him any painkillers until we'd x-rayed and splinted the bones, because that might cause him to lose consciousness and possibly revert. The shot I just gave him will help, but he's not going to be very coherent for a while. So anything you have to say to him can wait."

"Okay," I say. I don't have any desire to chew her out, or even argue. "I'll go." I turn around and leave.

Back to the maternity ward waiting room, where there are no pacing fathers, nobody handing out cigars. I realize that the process must be very different for pires; two immortals giving up some of their youth in order to create a new life would make every birth a powerful, singular event. Not that the arrival of a human baby isn't—but imagine that you know this is the only child you'll ever have. Imagine that after spending decades or centuries without aging, you suddenly find yourself getting older. And all this is a relatively new development; pires have only been able to give birth since the end of World War II. For some of them, it's the most transformative thing to affect them since they gave up being human.

Which is why the waiting room is empty—all the parents are together, inside. Except for Gretchen, who's alone.

I ask the nurse behind the counter for news. She's a slender Indian woman with a red dot on her forehead, and she tells me—in an Australian accent, no less—that Cassius has gone in to be present during the birth.

"Is she doing all right? Can I go in?"

The nurse consults her monitor. "Well, we don't normally allow more than the parents to be present. This is a special case, so we've made allowances for Mr. Cassius. But it's a bit tricky right now—I'm afraid you'll have to wait."

Great. I slump into one of the chairs and sulk, which very rapidly yo-yos into fretting, then anger, then worrying. How can Cassius just abandon me like this? How could Dr. Pete get himself so badly hurt I can't even yell at him? Why the hell are the walls painted that absurdly annoying shade of yellow?

I don't bother telling my brain to shut up. At this point, it's about the only company I have.

Finally, the doors push open. A doctor stands there, her gown bloody. She walks straight over to me. "Are you Jace Valchek?"

I feel a little light-headed. "Yes."

She smiles. "Both baby and mother are doing fine. Would you like to come in and see them?"

I blink. I nod. I follow her through the doors and down a hall.

And then I meet someone new.

I'm really not sure what to expect. Some part of my brain is conjuring up images of mad scientist laboratories, crackling Jacob's ladders on the bedposts and hunch-backed interns named Igor. What I get is less medical than most hospital rooms, but still pretty normal. Gretch is in a hospital bed, the back cranked to let her sit up. There's no window, but a tall floor lamp provides soft illumination. Cassius is seated in a comfortable chair beside a table with a vase full of flowers on it. He's leaning forward, talking to Gretch, his voice low and intent; she looks tired but not exhausted, and all her attention seems focused on him. Which is a little odd, considering the small bundle she's holding against her chest.

"—considering the situation in North Africa right now, I think Mahmoud could handle it. And the Libyans are in a holding pattern, so that's not going critical any-time soon."

"I suppose," she says. "But have you taken into consid-eration—"

"A-*hem*," I say. "Are you actually *debriefing* this woman?"

The looks on their faces are identical: kids caught with their hands in the cookie jar. "It's nothing," Cassius says hurriedly, "just a few office details that needed clearing up—"

I come over and perch on the side of the bed. "For God's sake, the woman just gave birth. And how about an introduction, huh?"

Gretch looks down at her new offspring, and *beams*. Her smile shines so bright, I'm half convinced she's going to burst into self-induced flames at any second. "Jace, this is—well, she doesn't have a name, yet. I just call her Love."

"Hello, Love," I say softly. "It's a pleasure to meet you."

The baby looks like—well, a baby. Hard to believe it's a supernatural being, one without a pulse or the need to breathe, but there you go. I reach out to touch one of her tiny hands, and am pleasantly surprised to find she's just as warm and soft as any other baby—but a lot more durable, I guess.

"You're okay? She's okay?" I ask.

"Yes. I understand Dr. Pete is as well, though somewhat worse for wear."

"Yeah, I just went to see him. Pretty banged up, but he'll recover."

She looks up, and the old Gretchen—all business and not someone you want to cross—is back. "I took a chance with the tear gas. It was meant to slow them down and force them back while we retreated—apparently I misjudged their commitment."

"No battle plan survives engagement with the enemy," Cassius says. "It could have worked."

"But it didn't," I say. "Mainly because those wrappers

wanted revenge too badly to give up. Revenge on Dr. Pete—and on me."

Cassius leans back in his chair. "I've been checking on the thrope that's after the doctor—and coming up with nothing. This 'Tair' has no background, no history. He showed up out of nowhere, insinuated himself with local crime elements, and has demonstrated a certain ruthless efficiency in his dealings ever since. I've been unable to discover anything else."

I shake my head. If the head of the National Security Agency can't dig up any facts on someone, I don't know who can. "Look, I know you won't discuss Dr. Pete's past with me, but can you at least tell me if this vendetta Tair has against him is personal or business?"

"I wish I could." Cassius sees the look on my face and adds, "I don't mean that I won't tell you, I mean I don't know. While Dr. Pete definitely made some enemies when he disappeared, this Tair seems unusually focused on his target. My sources tell me that he essentially brokered a deal, offering to deliver Dr. Pete in return for employment. His actions indicate both ambition *and* hatred."

Gretchen nods. "Not the type to give up, then. The loss of his men won't stop him."

"No, he'll just get more," I say. "And go after Dr. Pete again. Is the hospital secure?"

Cassius nods. "I'm having him moved as soon as he stabilizes anyway."

"Good." I stifle a yawn, then look at my watch. "Good Lord, it's late. Or early. Whichever." It's more than that, of course—a post-stress-and-adrenaline crash that I'm all too familiar with. "I really need to lie down and get some sleep before I fall over."

"I'll walk you out," Cassius says, rising from his chair. He gives Gretchen a look I can't interpret: guarded, reluctant. "We'll talk later, all right?"

"Very well." The look she gives him back is almost the same.

We walk back down the hall and to an elevator. "I've made a decision, Jace," he tells me as he presses the button. "I no longer feel that I—or any of the surviving Bravos—are secure, so I'm reassigning my duties as head of the NSA."

It takes a second for me to get my head around what he's just said. "You're stepping down?"

"I've always surrounded myself by capable people. Washington will pick a successor if I'm eliminated, but in the interim I've left instructions for the various department heads to follow. The organization will continue to function while—"

"While what? While you just give up and wait to be assassinated?"

The doors open and he steps forward, me a step behind. "Not what I had in mind at all, actually."

All the anger I had been directing at myself seems to have found a new target. "You can't just quit! There are people who *rely* on you—"

"I'm not quitting, Jace. I'm refocusing. Our target has proven able to get to almost anyone, and he's become exponentially more dangerous with every artifact he's acquired. If he tries a frontal attack—say, on the NSA offices—the casualties will be brutal. I can't allow that. I'm going underground until the threat is neutralized . . . and I fully expect you to be the one to do it."

The sinking sensation in my gut is more than the elevator going down. "That doesn't exactly make sense. The killer has no way of knowing you've left—"

"He's had no trouble pinpointing any of the other Bravos."

I realize what he's really saying. "And you don't think he'll have any trouble locating you, even if you do go to ground. You're setting yourself up as a target."

He shrugs. "Not a very good one, though. He already has the armor—I doubt he'll make a run at me."

"But you're going to give him the chance?"

"Yes."

"That's crazy."

"You're the expert."

The elevator lets us out in the underground parking. There are thrope agents—big, hairy half-weres with elaborate compound bows and body armor—standing on either side of the door. They weren't there when I arrived, but I'll bet they're now at every entrance and exit in the building.

"Okay, I'll play along," I say. "Where are you planning on painting the bull's-eye you'll be sitting in?"

"I thought I'd share yours."

I realize we're walking toward my car, not his, and stop. "Wait. You don't want to endanger a building full of highly trained intelligence ops and killers, but have no problem with doing the same to me."

He stops by the car. "More or less."

I grin. "That's the sweetest thing anyone's said to me all day . . ."

I drive Cassius to my place. If he's going to hang with me, he's going to have to follow my agenda—and since it's just after dark, I have a were dog and a teenager to think about.

Both of whom are gone when I get there. There's a note explaining that Xandra had something terribly important but vague to do, and took Galahad along. They'll both be back by sunrise, unless they aren't, but I shouldn't worry.

"I hope he's cute," I mutter, tossing the note on the kitchen table.

"Excuse me?" Cassius asks. He's seated himself in the

living room on the couch, and his body language is very formal; I can almost see the desk in front of him.

"Nothing. Well, my reason for coming home just vanished, so I guess I'll head back to the office. Which means you can't come, right?"

"Is there a pressing reason you need to go? I can have any information you need sent here."

I study him for a second before answering. "No, I guess not. If Eisfanger had anything new for me he'd call. And Charlie—" I hesitate.

"Yes, where *is* Charlie?"

"Having his annual . . . whatever you call it. Evaluation."

"Ah. You don't have to worry, Jace—it's routine. Charlie shows no signs of going rogue."

I get out some coffee beans and the grinder. "Easy for you to say. Just when I think I'm getting used to this world, I find out my partner can be put down like a rabid dog. I am *not* okay with that."

"I know it's hard to accept, but there are good reasons for the policy, Jace. Lems are driven by powerful predatory instincts—"

"And you're not?"

"Hemovores are subject to bloodlust, it's true. And no one can deny that thropes have their savage side. But both races are more than just the sum of their urges—"

I hit the button on the grinder, drowning out his reply. He looks annoyed, but he stops and waits for me to finish. "But golems aren't, right? They're just animal-powered bags of sand."

"Pires and thropes have their humanity to balance the equation. Lems don't."

I pour a carafe of water into the coffeemaker. "Then where does Charlie's humanity come from? According to you, he should have the personality of a rock—which, granted, an argument could be made for—but a rock doesn't makes jokes, or enjoy swing dancing, or get annoyed when it loses a cuff link."

"Those are all learned behaviors."

"Yeah. So is being human."

I add the ground beans to the hopper and turn on the coffeemaker, then join Cassius on the couch. "I'm just saying, I don't see much of a difference between lems, pires, and thropes—you all seem half human and half something else to me. About the only significant factor—"

I stop myself. I get up, open a cupboard and pretend to be looking for mugs.

"Is what?"

"Never mind. You drink coffee, right? How do you like it?"

"Made with decoagulated mare's blood. Answer the question."

I sigh, pull out a single mug and close the cupboard. "All three races have history with human beings. But pires and thropes are the only ones that preyed on us—golems were originally created to help people. On my world, anyway."

"You don't have lems on your world."

"Not like here. But we have stories, just like we have stories of vampires and werewolves—and in all the stories I ever heard, the golems were the good guys."

"Our golems don't come from stories, Jace. They come from factories. And the ones that are built for enforcement are animated by the souls of carnivores—of animals made killers by millions of years of evolution. Magic can shape those tendencies, but magic—like any system of control—decays over time. If it goes undetected, a lem can become just as dangerous to the ones he's supposed to protect as the ones he's supposed to hunt."

So can any slave, I think, but I don't say it out loud. Lems aren't slaves, not exactly; they have rights, they're not owned. But every lem is created with a debt hanging over his head, the cost of his own manufacturing. He's expected to pay that debt off, and the ones who don't—or won't—can be arrested. Even deactivated, in some countries. And the rules concerning which profession the lem chooses to work his debt off in are always slanted toward whatever animal was used to create him in the first place.

"Whatever," I say. "I just want him to come back."

We sit in silence for a moment, and listen to the coffee brew. I don't know if I've ever been alone in a room with Cassius that wasn't his office or traveling between floors.

"You still think Barbarossa's the key?" he says abruptly. On the drive over we'd discussed what Eisfanger had told me in the bar, and agreed there must have been an important reason for the killer to hide her time of death.

"Yes. She was killed first—*before* Aquitaine. You said you thought she was having an affair while the Bravos were together, but you didn't know with who. She wasn't attracted to pires or women, and lems are sexless. Which leaves who?"

"Everyone else in the world. She didn't have to necessarily be involved with someone on the team."

"No, but the dream I had after visiting Neil implied a secret affair. And there was something about chains—chains stronger than iron . . ."

I put my head in my hands and try to force the memory out, but remembering a dream is like trying to grab smoke. "Someone on the other side, maybe? One of the cult members? Maybe even Wertham himself?"

"No. Not Wertham—Dark."

Something in his voice tells me this isn't a guess. "What? You know that for sure?"

"I don't know it at all. But it makes sense."

"How?"

"The . . . internal politics of the Hexagon. An alliance with Dark could have proven too tempting to resist, at least initially."

"If so, she had second thoughts. Which would make any double cross she had planned a triple cross—definitely enough to inspire decades-long thoughts of revenge."

"But she'd never trust him enough to let him get close," he points out.

"True," I admit. The coffeemaker lets me know it's done its job, and I get up to fill my mug. I'm just about to take the first sip when there's a knock at the door.

My building has a security buzzer at the front door, which means only people who actually live here should be able to just walk up and knock. Except that so far, none of them ever has.

I draw my gun. Cassius is already on his feet. I motion for him to stay where he is, level my gun at the door and call out, "Who is it?"

"Charlie," answers a familiar gravelly voice.

I'm not stupid—one lem sounds a lot like another. "Just a second, I'm stark naked," I say, and yank the door open.

Charlie meets my eyes. Looks me up and down. "If that's true," he says, "you really need a new moisturizer."

Charlie doesn't tell me about the tests, and I don't ask. He knows about the mall attack, though not about Gretchen giving birth. "I take one day off," he says, "and you almost get yourself killed."

"*Almost* being the operative word."

"*Killed* being the operative word. *Almost* is the word *killed* used to beat up in high school."

Damn, I missed him. "How would you know? When I was in school you were being chiseled out of a cliff."

"And yet my vocabulary is still better than yours."

Cassius holds up one hand, his cell phone pressed to his ear. "Excuse me for interrupting," Cassius says, "but the African Queen's been sighted in the city."

"Where?"

"The rail yards just north of Fifteenth Avenue."

I finish my coffee in one last gulp. "That's close to Queen Anne—Sheldon Vincent's neighbourhood."

"There's no hurry," Cassius says calmly. "She's already disappeared. Agents are on their way in case she moves against Vincent."

"Why would she do that?" I ask.

"Maybe she thinks he has her shield."

"Maybe," Charlie says, "he does."

Cassius has closed his phone, but now it rings in his hand. He answers, listens intently, then says, "Yes. I'm sending my team now."

He snaps the phone shut again and says, "I don't think Vincent is her target. Another body's been found."

"Who is it?" I ask, thinking I already know the answer. I'm wrong.

"John Dark."

SEVENTEEN

The crime scene is at the rail yards, in the last boxcar of a string of five sitting on a siding. They've obviously been here a long time; weeds have grown over the tracks that connect the siding to the rest of the yard. The front three cars are being used for storage, with semi-permanent wooden ramps built up to the doors, but the last two seem to have been abandoned. The final car butts up against a chest-high concrete barrier, with a chainlink fence pressed up against that. The fence has a square flap cut into it, a makeshift door bent back and held in place by metal clips. Two wooden planks form a bridge from the top of the concrete barrier to a hole in the rear of the boxcar.

Cassius talks to the security guards who found the scene while Charlie and I examine the site itself. Considering Cassius's newly declared career as a target, I'm a little uneasy letting him out of my sight—but if Cassius is anything, he's a survivor.

"Looks like a giant rathole," Charlie observes.

"One helluva big rat." The opening into the rear of the boxcar is semi-spherical—about three and a half feet tall—and the edges look crumbly, as if they've been eaten away. I duck through the hole in the fence, step onto the planks, and touch the edge for myself. It comes away in flakes.

"Rust. I think this was carved by the Midnight Sword."

"Handy tool for opening locked boxcars. Just age an opening in solid metal."

I pull out my penlight and click it on. Crouching down, I step cautiously inside.

It takes me a second to grasp what I'm seeing, and another to believe it. It's funny in a horrifying, deeply inappropriate way, grotesque in every sense of the word. I'm looking at a giant blender.

It stands almost to the roof of the boxcar, the base made from painted white plywood. The jar is just a transparent tube, sealed at the top with what looks like a thick metal hatch. Within, John Dark's chest and head rest on top of a thick red sludge that fills half the jar.

I hear Charlie come in behind me. "Ouch," he says. "Looks like the punch line to a really tasteless joke."

"This one's different from the others."

"In what way? Other than the obvious splatter factor."

"The look on Dark's face, for starters. Terrified, in pain and shock. Aquitaine and Barbarossa were both killed quickly, their bodies posed postmortem. I think Dark was actually killed by this . . . contraption."

I shine the light on the base. It's fairly detailed, right down to the buttons marked PUREE, CHOP, and LIQUEFY. "The blades must be made of silver. He got Dark in there—probably unconscious—then waited for him to wake up before turning it on."

"Guess Dark wasn't one of his favorite people."

"No, but you'll notice the killer shut it off before the body was completely destroyed. He wanted us to find it this way and know who it is. It's a message." I move around the boxcar carefully, shining my light on the floor, the walls, the ceiling. No tracks; it's been swept recently.

"A message? What's he trying to tell us?"

"I'm not sure. Killing one of the Bravos' surviving enemies seems as if he's saying he's on the Bravos' side."

"Maybe even one of them?"

"Maybe. Seems a little too easy, though—"

And then I see it. Scratched into the metal of the boxcar's wall, behind the oversize kitchen appliance. Though the scratches are deep, the handwriting itself is as delicate as a quill pen on parchment:

> *This nightly creature reached for the sun,*
> *A crime both arrogant and Promethean.*
> *He could not escape from his whirling fate;*
> *He is no longer Dark—he is merely Late.*

"A poem," Charlie says. "A poem and a giant blender. Ring any bells with you?"

"As a matter of fact it does," I murmur. "I may not know comics, but I do watch TV. And this reminds me very, very much of an old superhero TV show from the 1960s . . ."

"They made *Batman* into a television show?" Neil says. "How odd."

I'm asleep and dreaming again. Neil and I are standing on the deck of a massive cruise ship, at the railing. Behind us, it sounds as if they're celebrating the New Year in the ballroom. It's night, the sea illuminated by a blood-red moon. I'm in a cocktail dress, all silver sequins and cleavage; Neil's dressed in the same leather jacket over a tuxedo shirt and pants. There's confetti in his hair.

"It was, actually," I say. "Very campy. It became trendy for famous actors to play the villain of the week, and they were always strange and stylized: the Riddler, Mister Freeze, Catwoman. More like a collection of obsessions and neuroses than criminals."

"Hmm." He stares out to sea, the moon reflecting crimson in his sunglasses. "And this connects to the latest crime scene how?"

"At the end of every episode, the villain captures Batman and his trusty sidekick Robin and puts them in some kind of elaborate death trap. The vic was found in a giant, homemade blender, but he wasn't killed immediately."

"How do you know?"

"We found hand- and footprints on the inside of the glass, opposite to each other."

He thinks about it for a moment. "Ah. So he was holding himself above the blades by pressing against the glass."

"Yeah. He was put into the jar while drugged, but the killer didn't turn on the blades until his victim woke up and understood the situation."

"Out of sadism?"

"I don't think so. I think he was giving him a chance to escape."

Neil nods. "I'm not aware of this TV show, but the conception reminds me of Batman's early creators—artists like Bob Kane and Dick Sprang, writers like Bill Finger. They often used giant props in their stories; the gigantic penny and oversize Joker card in the Batcave are a legacy from that era. A huge blender is exactly the sort of thing they would have come up with . . . but of course, they would have scripted a less messy ending."

"Yeah, Batman always managed to escape. His villains almost seemed to want to fail—some of them were compelled to leave him messages in advance. Riddles, jokes. My guy left a poem."

I recite it from memory. Neil listens intently, raising his eyebrows at the second line. "Interesting. It's neither a riddle nor a joke, though it does contain several puns: *nightly* and *late,* for instance. Some of the other words may have double meanings as well."

"Such as?"

"*Promethean,* for one."

"Yeah, I noticed you react. Why?"

"It's a reference to both Grant Morrison and Alan Moore, two of the writers I mentioned last time. Morrison introduced a villain named Prometheus to fight the Justice League, and Moore created *Promethea,* a comic book series thirty-two issues long—the same number of mystical paths said to exist in the magic system Kabbalah. It concerns a powerful female warrior with both African and Greek roots, a metaphysical being who possesses a female host and can be summoned in a number of ways—one of which is through reading a poem. She is, in fact, a living form of art itself; sometimes a poem, sometimes a song, sometimes a comic strip or story."

"This Moore—he was one of the 'practicing magicians' you talked about, right?"

"Yes. And the plot lines of the *Promethea* series tie in to several of the themes that seem to obsess your killer—the intersection between imagination and reality, ritual magic used in a superheroic context, transformation from one state to another."

"In this case, from solid to liquid. But not metal, like the previous two." I lean against the railing, watching the hypnotic motion of the waves below. I can see something massive and luminescent swimming far beneath them. "Tell me more about *Promethea.*"

"The series is basically a philosophical lecture on the nature of Kabbalah and the ten levels of the Tree of Life, though there are also more traditional story elements to it. One of the major subplots involves a 'celebrity omnipath,' a serial killer called the Painted Doll. He turns out to be a sophisticated robot."

So now we have an artificial man and a half-African

warrior woman involved. "Do any cowboys, pirates, or gladiators show up?"

"I see where you're going. I'd have to double-check, but I don't believe so—though a sun god does put in an appearance."

He's referring to Cassius's role as the Solar Centurion. "I'm starting to think I'm dealing with more than one person. One's a thief, the other's a killer. One stages elaborate postmortem scenes that refer to comic book history, the other locates and steals powerful, hidden magical items."

"You sound like you're trying to convince yourself."

I sigh. "Maybe I am. The one possibility I can't ignore is that the killer is one of the Bravos that conveniently survived. Maybe even both of them."

"Or one of the ones that hasn't been targeted yet?"

"Brother Stone and the Quicksilver Kid. One I can't locate, the other doesn't have anything to steal—not unless you want a few statues for your backyard."

"So—the two lems? The African Queen and the Solar Centurion? Or perhaps some combination thereof . . ."

I don't reply. I'm missing something, I know it. It has to do with the Sword of Midnight, that much I'm sure of—I just don't know what. I stare down at the water, watching that immense, glowing shape glide past in the depths. Wondering how deep it is, and how large. Wondering what I'd do if it abruptly surfaced and decided to ram the ship like some kind of sentient iceberg . . .

"Penny for your thoughts?" Neil says.

"Sure," I say. "Got a giant one handy?"

He chuckles. We go back to staring down at the ocean.

At least nobody showed up naked this time.

I lie in bed for a long time after I wake up. I run through things in my mind, fitting things together. Sometimes, that's all you need; just some quiet time, with no distractions or crises, to do some thinking.

Then I get up, put some coffee up, and prod the vampire who's asleep on my couch.

Cassius snaps awake like a TV turning on. Once second he's an inert lump, the next his eyes are open and he's there, completely alert. "Yes?"

I shake my head, mutter something dire, and shuffle back to the kitchen.

"Excuse me?"

"I said, I think I know who our killer is. Kind of."

"Who?"

"No. Caffeine first, then revelations."

For an immortal, he's surprisingly impatient. I don't drag the coffee-making process out, but he's practically vibrating with frustration by the time I take my first sip. "Ah," I say. "Okay."

He's seated across from me at the kitchen table, me in my bathrobe, him in the same clothes he slept in. He still looks more composed than me.

"Time travel," I say.

He frowns. "Time travel."

"That's what I figure." I take another long sip. "Barbarossa's sword can cause temporal effects. The fact that she was killed first threw me off, but I think I've got it worked out."

"Go ahead."

"I think there were two people involved from the start—Barbarossa and John Dark. And when I say 'involved,' I mean they were seeing each other, way back in the *Seduction of the Innocent* days. That didn't end well, but Dark survived. I think he and Barbarossa cut some kind of deal with the Hexagon, something that gave the Bravos the advantage when they attacked and let Dark disappear afterward."

He studies me, not saying anything. After another sip, I continue.

"Jump to present day. Dark plans his comeback. He enlists Barbarossa—maybe they rekindle their relationship—and she can't resist the ultimate score: stealing the Bravos' weapons.

"She uses the Sword's time-travel abilities to mess with the sequence of events. The first two thefts—the shield and your armor—go well. They plant volcanic rock at the storage locker to implicate Brother Stone, who's already half crazy with survivor's guilt.

"Then something goes wrong. They have a falling-out, probably over methods. The Sword doesn't want to kill any of her old teammates, and Dark's plan hinges on it. He kills her over it—then uses the Sword to make it appear as if she were killed at a different time than she actually was."

"Uh-huh."

"After that, Dark kills Aquitaine. He makes the crime scenes look like the work of someone both insane and obsessed with comic books. And then—this is really bizarre part—gets killed himself, in one of his own staged scenes. *By Barbarossa*."

I lean back, trying—but not too hard—to hide my triumphant grin behind my mug of coffee.

"I see," Cassius says thoughtfully. "Barbarossa, of course, has traveled forward in time to kill her lover, doing so sometime between when they argue and when he actually kills her. Very clever."

"Thank you. I haven't quite worked out the actual sequence of events, but I think—"

"There's only one problem."

"Which is?"

He shakes his head. "Jace, the Midnight Sword only causes temporal *effects*. Actual jumping around in history isn't possible. If it were, don't you think a thief like

Barbarossa would have taken advantage of that a long time ago?"

I blink. I finish my coffee. I get up. "I'm going back to bed. Wake me when I'm as smart as I think I am."

"Jace." Cassius gets up, stops me with a hand on my arm. "Don't be so hard on yourself. You're dealing with a lot of unpredictable elements, from political agendas to unnatural laws."

"I know that. But I'm used to dealing with crazy people, and what goes on inside some of those skulls makes this seem as straightforward as a soup recipe. It's just—damn it, I *know* Barbarossa is the key. I just don't know where the goddamn *lock* is."

"Which is largely my fault." His tone is confessional, not accusing.

"You're just doing your job. I'm sure that if I were in your position I'd be just as protective of my secrets—"

"I'm not so sure. I've lived a long time, and I've made many hard decisions—but that doesn't mean I've always made the right ones."

"Nobody does, Caligula."

He refuses to take the easy, bantering way out. "That doesn't mean you ignore your mistakes. Or stop trying to fix them."

I sit down on the couch and motion for him to sit next to me. He does. "Okay. There something you need to tell me?"

"Yes." His eyes meet mine. "Maybe this is a mistake, but I can't watch you flailing around in the dark anymore. It's time you learned about the Hexagon—and what its real purpose is . . ."

EIGHTEEN

"The Hexagon," Cassius says, "was formed in 700 BC. Its first members were two lycanthropes and two hemovores: Romulus, Nebuchadnezzar, Makeda, and Nefertiti." He pauses. "They were all rulers: of Rome, of Assyria, of Egypt. Makeda was better known as the Queen of Sheba. They came together to establish an alliance between the two supernatural races and originally called themselves the Quadrangle—the name was changed in the sixteenth century when two golems were added to the ruling council.

"Their plans were far reaching. Long lives had shown them that countries rise and fall, but a dynasty—properly tended—could last forever. There were two problems, though: Thropes had many children, which could tear apart a ruling family with internal strife and power struggles; and pires didn't procreate in the natural sense at all, while a bloodline based on turning human victims didn't have the kind of stable continuity a dynasty required. The group established a set of protocols to counter these problems.

"The lycanthropes agreed to a system of arranged marriages—essentially a breeding program. Litters would be limited through sorcery, producing only one or two heirs at a time. These would be groomed as future rulers, their loyalty to the Hexagon ingrained from birth.

"The pires had to use a more complex method: human proxies—usually powerful warriors or rulers—bound to them by magic and manipulated into mating with each other. The child produced would be taken away at birth and raised by pires, and then turned when it came of age."

"By who?" I ask. "The male pire, or the female?"

"Both, actually. The ritual used was the precursor of the one used today to impart life force from pire parents to their offspring. It wasn't nearly as powerful, but it did ensure that certain traits were passed along: qualities like leadership, ambition, intelligence."

I nod. "So the Hexagon are queen and kingmakers. Not so different from royal families marrying off children to produce political alliances—just more focused on long-term results."

"In essence. Magic was also used in other ways—to preserve the genetic legacy of a powerful thrope leader, for instance. Not effective with pires—at least not at the time—but a long-dead thrope could still wind up fathering children centuries later."

"You're talking about artificial insemination. Magic sperm from a dead werewolf."

He smiles. "It doesn't seem as far-fetched when that werewolf has conquered most of the known world."

I take a guess. "Ghenghis Khan?"

"Among others. Not all the Hexagon's children go on to positions of power, but many do. Some even become legends."

"Like the Bravos." It suddenly hit me, a connection so obvious I can't believe I didn't seen it before. "Oh, for— Saladin Aquitaine. It's more than just a memorable name, it's a thumbnail of his heritage."

"Yes. He's a descendant of Saladin, the Egyptian sultan of the twelfth century, and Eleanor of Aquitaine, who was both French and English nobility. Some Hexagon members disguise their names by changing them slightly, but some bear them proudly."

I think about it. "Catharine Shaka. Catherine the Great and Shaka Zulu."

"Yes. John Dark's full name is John Tamerlane D'arc, from the great Turkish conqueror and Joan of Arc. The Sword of Midnight was born Lucille Borgia Barbarossa, after the famed Italian schemers and the pirate known as Redbeard."

Another name was tugging at my memory. "How about Cali Edison? I get the second part, but—"

"Calamity Jane."

"Calamity Jane? Really?"

He shrugs. "We wanted strong genes, aggressive instincts. She was one of the toughest women alive. Combined with Thomas Edison's intellect, you get—"

"A snappy redhead in a jail cell."

"It's not an exact science."

"Guess not. How do lems fit into all this? They don't breed."

He looks away for a moment. "No, they don't. But they're still a large and powerful part of society, one the Hexagon recognized needed to be dealt with. By giving them a say in our affairs, we acquired the loyalty of their own leadership. It's one of the reasons golems acquired rights in the first place—we arranged for it."

Sure. Better to head off the inevitable slave revolt by conceding a few liberties here and there; the most loyal dog is the one you pamper, not the one you beat. "And how about you, Cassius? Who are you descended from?"

He shakes his head. "That's not relevant. I told you earlier that the Hexagon splintered just after World War Two. What you need to know—what may be the most important factor in this entire affair—is what led to that schism."

"You said it had something to do with methodology and direction."

"Yes. Specifically, it was about the hemovore reproductive process."

He pauses. This is a delicate subject, and he knows it. A global spell was cast at the end of the war, one that allowed pires to reproduce the way they do today. The cost of that spell was six million human lives, demanded by the extradimensional fertility god that powered it. It was paid.

"Most of the Hexagon—myself included—wanted to abandon the methods we'd been using for pires up until then. Another faction, headed by John Dark, thought that it was too valuable an asset to give up. The mental coercion used to persuade humans to breed to pire order was more useful when humans still ruled the planet, but it was still a powerful tool. I argued that the human race had sacrificed enough."

"Don't you mean had *been* sacrificed enough?"

He looks back at me, pain in his eyes. "Yes. That's exactly what I meant. It had to be done for my species to survive, but that does not excuse the monstrosity of it. All right?"

"No," I say coldly. "But keep talking."

"Dark formed his own group. He bided his time until he saw an opportunity with Wertham—the rest you know."

I think about it. This puts a whole new slant on things— connections I hadn't made before suddenly seem obvious. Any alliance between Hexagon members was more than just a partnership—it was a potential family. If Lucy Barbarossa was having an affair, it could have led to her switching sides—especially if a child was involved. Which means—

"Gretchen," I say. "How would the Hexagon react to a

nonmember having a child with a member? Or am I wrong, and Gretch's real name is Anastasia Rockefeller?"

"She's not part of the Hexagon. The practice isn't encouraged, but neither is it forbidden—however, a child of such a union would not be groomed for future leadership."

But it might be enough to get the child's father targeted by a homicidal lunatic with a decades-old grudge. Maybe this is about more than revenge or amassing power; maybe it's about a birthright denied. "Cassius, are there records kept of such children? Ones born to Hexagon members, but passed over because of their mixed heritage?"

"Yes, of course—many rise to prominence, anyway. But none of them would have access to the kind of information our killer seems to possess."

"Not officially, no. But maybe Mommy or Daddy spilled the beans . . ."

We don't even have to leave the apartment; Cassius taps into a secure database from my laptop and downloads the files we need. I make coffee and we spend the next few hours poring over the data, trying to find a connection between one of the unsanctioned offspring and our killer.

It's slow going; there are a lot of them, mostly thropes, but no one that jumps out at us. "Maybe we're not looking at this right," I say, leaning back and stifling a yawn. "Maybe it's not someone who didn't have the right mother or father—maybe it's someone who didn't have either one. In any sense of the word."

"A golem? That's unlikely."

"Is it? They're part of the group, but they don't have the same power—no world leadership for them. And you told me yourself that sometimes lems go rogue."

"Yes, but not insane. They essentially revert to their

animal natures, losing their intelligence while becoming more violent and impulsive. It's usually an easy thing to spot, with a very distinctive pattern to it. There's nothing like the kind of complex irrationality we've seen with the staging of the crime scenes."

"So you're saying that lems don't go crazy—they just go wild?"

"Yes. And before you ask—no, the Ghatanothoa effect that's producing mental illness in thropes and pires hasn't affected any lems yet. They seem immune."

So no insane golems. I shake my head, thinking of Brother Stone alone in his self-made crypt, chiseling the forms of the dead. Isn't religion a form of craziness? If so, Stone definitely qualified. Or how about the Quicksilver Kid, hunting down bail jumpers and locking them in the trunk of his car? He hadn't seemed crazy to me, but—like Stone—he was a loner. Maybe he reverted to the persona of the rattlesnakes that powered him when he was alone, spent all his time lying on a rock in the sun.

It was an absurd image, but there was something there. The killer had exhibited two patterns of behavior, leading me to believe there might be multiple suspects—but what if there were just multiple personalities? Could lem personas fracture, dividing their animal essence from their civilized one?

When I suggest the idea to Cassius, he's dubious. "I've never heard of anything like that—but you're the expert in these sorts of matters. If you think it's a possibility, we'll look into it."

I rub my temples with the heels of my palms. "Yeah, that's the problem, isn't it? I don't know what is or isn't possible. Throw me an easy pitch like time travel and I get all discombobulated. Give me a full-fledged schizophrenic any day."

"Well, it's not completely random, is it? There are patterns we can analyze, facts we can study. It's not hope-less."

I shake my head. "No, of course not. I—"

My phone chimes. "Hello?"

"Jace." I recognize Neil's voice. "Sorry to disturb you like this, but I was reading through some back issues and an image caught my eye. It might be nothing, but I thought you'd like to know."

"An image? Of what?"

"Your first victim. I'm looking at a panel depicting a skeletal version of the Flash right now."

Suddenly I don't seem quite so tired. "What's the context?"

"His death. Chronicled in a maxi-series called *Crisis on Infinite Earths*."

"Parallel realities again."

"Very much so. Neither Grant Morrison nor Alan Moore was directly involved in this particular series, but it does chronicle the death of several major characters."

"So this was the last appearance of the Flash?"

He chuckles. "Oh, no. Death in the comic book realm is at best a temporary setback; it's often used to relaunch the character in a different direction, or simply to boost sales. This particular version of the Flash did remain dead for quite a long time, but even he eventually returned—at the hands of Grant Morrison, in fact."

"How did he die?"

"Racing backward through time to avert a catastrophe."

Backward through time. I sigh. "Thanks, Neil. I appreciate the call—I may not be getting any sleep for a while."

"My pleasure, Jace."

After he hangs up, I tell Cassius what I've just learned. "Too bad my time-travel theory sucks," I say.

Cassius looks distracted. "Still, any information might eventually prove useful . . ."

"What's on your mind?"

"Hmm? I'm sorry—I was thinking about Gretchen, actually."

I get up and stretch. "Maybe we should take a break. Go see how she and Dr. Pete are doing."

He frowns. "Jace Valchek, suggesting a social visit over casework? I may have to ask to see your ID."

I'm already heading to the bedroom to put on some street clothes. "Only human, Caligula. Even I need the occasional breather—besides, it's a good way to reset your brain. Let your subconscious chew on the situation for a while, see what it spits out."

We take Galahad with us. He's been asleep in the bedroom since Xandra brought him back, but he's more than happy to go for a walk. I'm kind of getting used to having him around, though with him and Cassius both crashing here it's starting to feel a little crowded. I'm sure Dr. Pete will be happy to see him, anyway.

"Wow," I say. It turns out that a lack of visitors is the least of Dr. Pete's worries.

His room is almost unrecognizable. Tapestries embroidered in arcane symbols hang on the walls, incense burns on a shrine in the corner, and there's a little old lady stirring a large pot of something on a hot plate beside that. Wolf cubs dart out from under the bed, between my legs and out into the hall, where they sniff at Galahad's bare feet curiously. A dozen or so of Pete's family form a circle around his bed, all of them in human form and chatting like they're clustered around a punch bowl instead of an invalid. There's violin music playing, and it's not recorded.

In the midst of all this is the same tall, imposing nurse who read me the Riot Act last time. She looks considerably more frazzled, though not defeated. I wish her well; I've dealt with Pete's family before, and they are formidable.

Except they're not really his family. They're a fiction, created by the NSA to provide him with a cover. Not completely made up, of course—I have no doubt they're actually related to one another, just not to Dr. Pete. I wonder what happened to his actual relatives.

Cassius and I push our way inside, Galahad right behind us. The nurse spots us, gives us a grim look, and says, "Visiting hours will be over in twenty minutes. At that point, I *will* clear the room, if I have to use a flamethrower."

"So noted," I say. "Good luck with that."

She stalks out of the room, clipboard under her arm. I feel sorry for her next patient.

Dr. Pete is looking better—his eye hasn't fully regenerated yet, but his teeth seem to have grown back in. He's still in splints and half-were form, but his one eye is open and focused on me.

"Hi," I say. He nods, weakly. Can't talk, of course, or use sign language yet. That's as far as I get anyway, because now the family has noticed me. I've only been to Dr. Pete's once, but you'd think I was some sort of long-lost relative from the way I'm treated; within a few seconds I'm the one that's surrounded and being inundated with sympathy. Lots of hugging and squeezing of shoulders, arms, hands. "Thank you, I'm fine," I say over and over. "Really. I'm okay. Thanks. That's very sweet."

Leo makes his way over from the opposite side of the bed. He was introduced to me as Pete's father, and he's definitely the head of the Adams pack. He's got two pointy gray tufts of hair that stick up from head, but they always remind me more of Bozo the Clown than anything wolfy.

"Jace," he says, and gives me a big hug. "We need to

talk," he whispers in my ear, then lets go and stands back. "Such a terrible thing that's happened to our boy." His eyes are filled with pain.

"He'll be okay. I, uh—"

"I was wondering if you could pick up some things for him from his office," Leo says. "Let's step outside for a minute, I'll get you a list."

Cassius glances my way as we exit, but doesn't follow.

Leo leads me down the hall and to a waiting area, almost identical to the one outside the maternity ward. He sits, and motions me to do the same.

"So," I say. "What would you like me to bring?"

He studies me for a second before answering. "That was a lie. What I need from you is your understanding."

"About what?"

"Do you know how hard it is to sign with broken fingers? Not to mention painful? But when we came here to see Peter, he insisted. It took him a long time, but he finally got his message across. Do you know what it was?"

"I—no. I have no idea."

"*Tell Jace the truth.* About himself, his past. He wants you to know what he did, for whatever reason."

"That's not necessary. People who think they're about to die will say things they regret later—"

He shakes his head. "No. Peter is a doctor, a good one, and he knows that his body will heal. He wants this done because he's had what thropes call a tearaway experience—an injury so painful it lays bare what is and isn't important to the one that suffers it. This is what's important to him, and I'm going to honor that."

He hesitates, gathering his thoughts before he speaks. "The Adams pack may seem like a close-knit clan, but that is not because of shared blood. It is because of shared pain. We are, in truth, a ragtag bunch of misfits, outcasts from larger and stronger packs—or at least our ancestors were. Mongrels and half-breeds are our heritage, and none of us care. Many of us fled from the purges of the war, and still carry those scars with us.

"We take in those that need it. Your employer, David Cassius, he knows this. He was the one who asked us to take in Peter."

"Did he tell you what Peter did?"

"Yes. We would not have accepted him otherwise. I will not excuse his actions—what he did was terrible. But many of us have done terrible things, Jace." He meets my eyes, unblinking. I don't know about him, but I can't deny the truth of that statement when it comes to myself.

"He has tried to atone for his deeds," Leo continues. "To act, not apologize. The dead, after all, do not care about apologies."

"No," I say. "They don't."

"He respects you a great deal. What you think is important to him. Listen to his story with an open heart, that's all I ask of you."

I keep my voice neutral. "Go ahead."

"The study of human medicine is not a terribly profitable one. And it requires a great deal *more* study—human beings are prone to so many conditions, aren't they? Despite this, Peter persevered. Over the course of several years, he acquired a number of debts. One of these was to a criminal organization called *La Lupo Grigorio*."

"The Gray Wolves." This world's equivalent of the Mafia. "I know who they are."

"Then you know what they are capable of. They required a shaman versed in biothaumaturgy—golem activation. Peter had been moonlighting in that field to make some extra money, and they pressured him to work for them. He was young and broke and most of all naive—after all, he was simply helping to create life, wasn't he? What could be the harm?"

Leo sighs. "I know, I know. He was a fool. He thought he was simply bending the rules, adding laborers that would exist off the books—but still, he reasoned, at least they would exist."

"For a while."

"Yes. He did not learn until later how brief and brutal that existence often was. When he did, he planned to turn himself in."

"Planned?"

"I wish Peter's story was unique, but it is not. The Gray Wolves are old and cunning, and they always need people with Peter's skills. Over time, they have evolved a strategy to ensure the continued cooperation of their employees."

He pauses again, begins to speak, then stops. "They," he says softly, "know about . . . breaking things. Objects, structures. People. I don't know if you truly understand how important a pack is to a lycanthrope, but it is more than family—that is simply flesh and blood. The pack is part of your *soul*."

I don't know what to say to that, so I keep quiet. After a moment he continues.

"You can always turn to your pack when you are in trouble. No matter what kind, no matter what you have done. Peter knew this, as all thropes do. Even more than a thrope's strength or ability to heal, it is this knowledge that gives us the most security. A thrope that belongs to a pack is never alone.

"Unless," he says, his voice bleak, "the pack itself is destroyed."

It takes me a second. "My God. How many?"

"Eleven. Not a large clan, by most standards—it's one of the reasons he was chosen. Slaughtered in their beds in what seemed a botched robbery, with the Gray Wolves ready to accept him as one of their own while he was still in shock. You'd be surprised how many such victims accept, even if they suspect the truth. Even if they know for sure."

I shake my head. "No, I wouldn't. The desire to belong is one of the strongest drives the human psyche has—and primal urges always come to the fore during grief. He wouldn't have been the first victim to identify with his attacker—or the first to grab a dubious lifeline when it was offered."

"That is true—but that is not what he did. He went to the authorities instead. And that is how he came to be with us."

"Witness relocation. I get it."

"I don't think you do." He leans forward, eyes intent under shaggy brows. "He *is* a member, of our family and our pack. He is a decent, honorable man who was the victim of his own bad judgment and has devoted the rest of his life to making amends. I speak to you not as someone who harbors such fugitives professionally—though I certainly do that—but as a man who considers himself Peter's father."

"What do you want from me, Leo?"

"Just give him another chance. Let him heal, then talk to him. He's worth your friendship, I promise you."

I rub my forehead. "All right, I will. But I have a question for you, first."

"Anything."

"Do you know a thrope named Tair?"

No recognition in his eyes, no change in his body language. "No, Jace. I do not." If he's lying, he's too good for me—maybe not in an interrogation room, but right here and now.

"He's the thrope responsible for what happened to Peter," I say. "He could be working for the Gray Wolves, but his motivations seem personal. I haven't been able to find out anything about him, and Peter claims he doesn't know who he is, either."

The look on Leo's face darkens. "Whoever he is," he growls, "he will regret the day he was whelped."

"Yeah," I say. "He will."

Leo returns to the hospital room, but I stay in the waiting area—I suddenly feel drained, just not up to the crush of people and the sight of Dr. Pete all bandaged up.

Sometimes, the worst thing about a case is the sense of loss—not just the loss of a life, but the emotional gravity that the death generates, a swirling pit dragging down everything near it: careers, relationships, hopes. Sal Aquitaine's child would never know her father. Lucy Barbarossa's mysterious lover would never hold her in his arms again. All John Dark's plans and schemes would, in the end, have to rise or fall without him.

It's always the survivors who bear the scars. Catharine Great Shaka, robbed first of her country and now of her legacy. Silverado, AKA the Quicksilver Kid, a loner now even more alone. Brother Stone, toiling endlessly in his self-created tomb, his only companion his guilt. Even Cassius had been diminished by the loss of the Solar Centurion's armor; if nothing else, it was a link to his past, the symbol of a simpler, more romantic heroism that the head of the NSA could no longer afford to indulge in.

But maybe that heroism had always been an illusion. Maybe the Bravo Brigade had never been anything but soldiers doing a job, an extension of the Hexagon's will. Maybe the only one who still thought of them as heroes was my comic-book-obsessed killer—and he was crazy.

"You know, that almost makes sense," a familiar voice says.

Familiar in a very weird and unexpected way; it's Jerry Seinfeld. A television is on in the waiting room, bolted to one corner of the ceiling, and an old rerun is showing. It's the one where Elaine meets a group of friends who are the exact opposite of Jerry, George, and Kramer. This episode is considerably different from the one I've seen, of course; by "opposite," they mean that Jerry's counterpart is a thrope and Kramer's is a pire, as opposed to the other way around. Jerry refers to them as being from "Bizarro-world," where everything is backward from normal reality. Jerry's counterpart even has a little figure of Bizarro in his mirror-image apartment, in the same spot where Jerry keeps a statue of Superman. Bizarro looks exactly like Superman, except the S on his chest is backward and—

It's only on screen for a second, but it's enough to start the cascade of facts that's been building in the back of my brain.

The Flash, running backward through time.

The *Seduction of the Innocent* murders, with their metaphysical reversal of punishing the blameless.

"That's it," I say softly. "That's the pattern I couldn't see. Makes perfect sense, now—perfect non-sense, to be exact."

I meet Cassius halfway down the hall, which is good; I don't have time for awkward socializing. "I think I may have broken the case," I say. "But I'll need Eisfanger's help to be sure."

"What have you learned?"

"That I've been approaching this case from the wrong direction. Literally."

NINETEEN

Cassius arranges for Eisfanger to meet us on the roof of the building in an NSA chopper. I hate talking over the roar of helicopter blades, but I do my best to explain my theory while we're in the air.

"It's all backward," I say. "Saladin Aquitaine's body was the beginning, but the staging of the scene referenced both the beginning *and* the end of the Flash's life. Taken on its own, as a singular image, it doesn't mean anything—but comic books *aren't* singular images; they're panels. Images in sequence. I couldn't see that until I had more than one image to work with, and even then it took me a while to see that the images were reversed."

"I thought we'd established that Barbarossa was the first victim," Eisfanger says.

"I'll get to that. Here's the way your average superhero career goes: It usually starts with the acquisition of an archfoe, someone he battles on a regular basis. If the superhero sticks around long enough, he eventually joins a team of other superheroes. If he lasts a really long time and starts to get stale, he gets a reboot in the ass—usually highlighted by some sort of epic sacrifice, like dying to save the world—before being relaunched in a different direction.

"Which is where our killer started: at the very end, where the hero has been reimagined. That's why Barbarossa was first, and why her death referenced Morrison's *Doom Patrol*. It was a comic that symbolized the reimagining of a Silver Age character—which is exactly what our killer is. After that came Aquitaine, the reverse of a noble sacrifice—it was a selfish act that makes things worse for Gretchen, literally stealing life away from her. Then the Solar Centurion's armor and African Queen's shield were stolen—the team-up aspect, only reversed. Finally, there was John Dark's murder; the acquiring of a superhero's nemesis is turned into the disposal of one."

"All right," Cassius says. "I'll defer to your expertise. But that doesn't explain how you arrived at the identity of our killer."

"Bizarro," I say. "He's an old Superman villain. He does everything backward—including thinking. I didn't know who he was until *Seinfeld* explained it to me for the second time."

"You watch *Seinfeld*?" Eisfanger asks. "Get out!"

I restrain my urge to push him out of the helicopter. "Bizarro has his own special language, where he says the opposite of what he means. He says good-bye when he shows up and hello when he leaves. He tells his friends that he hates them and his enemies that he loves them—it's more reverse logic, but at a personal level. But it's not just a speech impediment—*he acts the same way.*"

I take a deep breath before continuing. "It's not just the sequence of events that our killer has reversed. It's his motives, too. He saw killing Dark as being a benevolent act; he saw robbing the Bravos as helping them."

"Wait—why would he act benevolently toward someone that's supposedly his nemesis?" Cassius asks. "Is that another reversal?"

I sigh. "Yeah, I know, it becomes a maze of mirrors after a while. Reverse a motivation twice and it goes back to being the original reason, right? Remember, Dark was killed by the kind of weirdo death trap that a villain usually locks a hero in; maybe he was supposed to escape the way the hero always does. That part doesn't quite parse . . . but everything else does. See, while Bizarro's costume is a virtual duplicate of Superman's, the character himself resembles a crude statue of chiseled white stone. Sound familiar?"

"Brother Stone," Cassius says. "But Jace—lems aren't subject to insanity."

"No, they're not. *But Brother Stone isn't a lem.*"

Cassius stares at me. "Impossible."

"Not a word I throw around much anymore. Think about it: You've got thropes and pires and golems on your secret council, but no humans. What if one saw an opportunity to join and took it?"

Cassius scowls at me. "I suppose a shapeshifter could do so, though any long-term masquerade as a thrope or a pire would be detected. But a lem?"

"A solitary lem with a mysterious past. He was supposedly brought to life by a group of monks—but when I talked to him, he claimed to be the only member of his order, at least in this reality. We know he can shift his shape—how else can he move when he's made of stone? And I think he can change more than just his form—I think he can change what he's made of, too. From stone to copper to silver, letting him stab thropes with a fingertip or channel lightning—the electrified state of Aquitaine's body was a statement about Transe's decision to direct Wertham's power into the earth instead of the sky, causing a volcanic eruption instead of a storm."

"It's possible," Eisfanger says. "Humans have a natural facility for changeling magic; pires and thropes don't. It could even account for the transformation of Doctor Transe's bones and Barbarossa's body."

"If my theory's correct, it should be easy to verify. That's why you're here, Damon; he may have some kind of magic concealing what he is. If so, I'm counting on you to crack it."

Eisfanger shrugs. "Shouldn't be that hard to do. I'll use Wittgenstein; he's got a keen nose for shifters." Wittgenstein is a rat skull Eisfanger keeps around, one still inhabited by the spirit of its former occupant.

Cassius abruptly digs in his pocket, then presses his cell phone to his ear and says, "Yes?"

The look of alarm on his face sets off all my own. "On our way," he snaps, then signals the pilot. "Turn it around," he says. "Get us back to the hospital. *Now*."

Gretchen.

I should have known, I keep telling myself. *I should have known.*

I thought I was so smart. I figured out all kinds of details on the trip back, mostly to keep myself calm instead of imagining what we might find when we get there. I figure out why there were huge footprints at the game park: Stone was distributing his weight by giving them a broader base, making them look like a giant's instead of just someone very heavy. There hadn't been two people with shovels unearthing the shield, just one who could turn both his hands into spades. I even think I have a pretty good idea why the murders had started with the Sword of Midnight.

So why couldn't I see that Stone would go after Gretchen's baby?

He hadn't wasted time with subtlety, which was a bad sign. He'd simply smashed his way through a window riding the sky-shield, grabbed the infant from the nursery and left the same way. I'm standing in the middle of a room full of squalling babies, broken glass everywhere, Cassius in one corner giving nonstop, terse orders into his phone. Gretchen's standing at the broken window, staring out into the night, her hands clenched into fists, her hospital gown flapping around her like a pale green shroud.

"Jace." Gretch's voice is as hard and cold as a tombstone. She turns around and stares at me. You don't see pires do the transformation thing very much—usually only when they're really, really angry. Their eyes go red as blood and their fangs lengthen, making them look exactly like the supernatural creatures they really are.

That's how Gretchen looks right now.

"Find him," she says. Her voice scares me.

"I will, Gretch. I promise." *Because if you don't,* a little part of my brain suggests, *she will tear your head from your body with her own hands.*

Think. Gotta think. Gotta see this from a deranged, living statue of a monk's point of view. One who thinks he's a superhero.

Okay, he started at the end and is working his way back to the beginning. What comes before facing your nemesis?

Your origin, of course.

Every superhero has one. Spider-Man got bitten by a radioactive spider, Batman saw his parents killed in front of him, Captain America—okay, I don't know Captain America's origin, but that doesn't mean he doesn't have one. Bitten by a radioactive flag or something . . . focus, Jace, focus. He's a shapeshifting golem. What was Bizarro's origin? The Web site I found said he was made from some kind of duplicating ray . . .

But that doesn't matter, because Stone's crazy. The logic he's following is fractured and incoherent, based on a backward structure but still pretty free-form; you don't

chop a woman's brain into sixty-four pieces due to rigor-
ous logic. Speaking conceptually, what was Bizarro's
origin?

The opposite of Superman's. And Superman was—

Oh my God.

"Cassius!" I say. "You guys have rockets, I know you
do—does Boeing still do aerospace contracts?"

"I'll call you back," he says into his cell phone, and
snaps it shut. "Yes. There's a satellite launch research facility in Renton."

"That's where he's headed."

"Why?"

"I'll tell you on the way," I say, headed for the door.

"Jace!" Gretch calls out behind me. Her voice is more
anguished than angry. "For God's sake, why is he taking
my baby to an industrial plant?"

I hesitate, but don't look back. "I'm not sure," I say,
"but I'll get her back, Gretch. I will."

And then Cassius, Charlie, and I run out the door.

"I'm surprised she didn't try to come with us," I say as the
chopper lifts off.

"She did," Cassius says, punching in another number
on his cell phone. "I gave agents orders to restrain and
sedate her. She's too weak to help and I have enough to
worry about." His voice is hard, efficient, and anyone not
in my line of work would probably think that means he
doesn't care. They'd be wrong. Every cop gets that tone
when they're chasing someone who's hurt family—
totally, utterly focused, all the anger channeled down to a
tight little beam like a rage laser. From now until we catch
this guy, we're not individuals. We're a machine. Ego,
history, personal conflicts all fall away; nothing matters
but the target. This must be what a pack feels like when
it's hunting.

"Explain," Cassius says.

"He's going to try to launch the baby into space," I say. "Superman came here from a dying planet in a rocket-ship, as an infant. He's going to reverse the procedure, send her away from a living planet."

"Again—why?"

"Because it completes the sequence. It's the first panel—there isn't anything before that. Oh, and because *he's insane.*"

"It's hard to believe he fooled us for so long," Cassius says. He sounds more as if he's talking to himself than me or Charlie.

"We humans are tricky like that," I say. "I'm guessing the whole 'secret identity' thing both exacerbated his condition and made it easier to conceal his mental insta-bility. He's been leading a double life for decades; when he started losing control, he managed to contain it to just one of them."

Neither Cassius nor I comes out and says it, but we both recognize the deeper implications of Stone being human; namely, that he has to be working for someone else. Some-one not in John Dark's splinter faction.

Someone human.

"Security at Boeing's pretty tight," Charlie says. " 'Course, that probably won't count for much against someone with a flying, force-field-projecting shield, a sword that can cut through time, and magic solar-powered armor."

"He may not be wearing the armor," Cassius says. "It'll impede his shapeshifting ability."

"Don't forget about Transe's magic gem," I say. "It's probably the most powerful item of all."

"And the best encrypted, magically speaking," Cassius says. "He hasn't used it so far, near as I can tell. Pray he doesn't."

The chopper's coming up on Renton now, and I can

see the rectangular, block-long buildings of an industrial park. It's well lit, but there's a jagged scar of light emanating from one of the roofs that doesn't look like it belongs. "Set it down there," I yell at the pilot.

"I can't land on that roof!" he yells back. "I don't know if it's strong enough!"

"Then just get us close enough to jump!"

He does. Cassius leaps out, nimble as a cat, while Charlie makes a landing just as graceful but a lot more solid. I manage not to hurt myself.

The hole in the roof is the size of a Buick. Impenetrable force field plus mass of stone body times velocity equals sudden improvised skylight.

"Stay back," I tell Cassius. "If he is wearing the armor, you can't get anywhere near him."

"I'm aware of that," Cassius says. He doesn't sound happy.

Charlie and I peer inside. What we see is a large industrial space, the floor three stories beneath us. Lots of high-tech equipment around the periphery, but what's got my attention is the large, distinctive shape in the middle of the room.

A rocket.

Guns—except for mine—don't exist here, due to a magically induced blind spot that affects everyone on the planet. Missiles—in the sense of pointy-shaped things that blow up on impact—don't exist, either. But rockets, the kind that put satellites in orbit and men on the moon, that they have no trouble with . . . and it seems I'm looking at some sort of prototype right now.

"What's he doing?" Charlie whispers.

"Fueling up," I say. "Those are tanks of liquid oxygen."

The rocket is on some kind of mobile gantry, currently in a horizontal position. The nose cone is configured like a clamshell, and it's wide open.

And then I hear it. A thin, heartrending wail. Gretchen's baby.

She's lying in the middle of the nose cone, strapped in to some kind of jury-rigged harness. Stone's busy with the hoses feeding the LOX to the rocket's fuel tank.

There are two dead security guards near the door. I wonder if they're the only ones.

The good news is that he isn't wearing the Centurion armor. The bad news is that the sky-shield is parked only a few feet away, a large oval shape hovering about two feet off the floor. From what I understand, anyone traveling on the thing is pretty much invulnerable, plus it's smart enough to let things—like arrows—out, while not allowing any projectiles in. Not sure how it'll affect hand-to-hand combat, but if Stone hops aboard he could probably just ram us to death.

"We have to get the baby to safety *and* keep him away from the shield," I whisper.

Cassius is abruptly next to me. "Correct. Charlie, target Stone. I'll get the child." And with that, he jumps through the hole.

Charlie's fast. He puts one of the silver-coated steel balls he keeps in a spring-loaded holster up his sleeve into the back of Stone's head while Cassius is still in the air. It's enough to take out a thrope, a pire, or even most lems.

But Brother Stone is something else.

The ball bounces off his skull with a *klang!* loud enough to make my ears ring. It gets Stone's attention—his head snaps around just in time to see Cassius, now about fifteen feet off the ground.

Stone points at him, in the most extreme sense of the word—his entire arm lengthens into a silver spike ten feet long, one right beneath Cassius's falling body. Cassius manages to twist his torso enough that the spike misses his heart when it impales him, going in just under his ribs and out right next to his spine. Because Cassius wasn't directly over Stone when he leapt, the spike curves halfway down its length, thickening toward the base where it began life as Stone's right arm. Cassius actually slides halfway down the rod running through him, like an impaled worm at the bottom of a fishhook.

I jump a second later.

I don't have any time to think, I just act. Cassius's body is between Stone and the shield now, and I hope that's enough to keep the monk from doing the same thing to me that he just did to *oh God I forgot he's ambidextrous*.

Luckily for me, so is Charlie.

Who would have thought falling three stories could take so long. I'm almost bored by the time it's over, if by bored you mean so frightened I'm paralyzed and I think I forget how to breathe. I have more than enough time to get extremely annoyed by whoever has decided to start up that jackhammer, though—

That would be Charlie. Raining ball-bearing destruction down on Brother Stone with both arms, metal on metal mayhem as fast as a Gatling gun. If at first you don't succeed, ramp up the firepower and try again.

It keeps Stone off balance long enough for me to complete my trajectory, which ends exactly where I was aiming: on the shield itself. I'm gambling that either the force field will interpret me as some kind of attack and bounce me off—force fields are soft, right?—or it'll think I'm just a rider in a hurry leaping into the saddle like the Lone Ranger with a two-for-one coupon for Tonto chow.

Okay, that came out a little more racist than I intended, but I have *no time* to tell my brain to shut up because now that the shield has caught me like a cradle catching a baby I have a much less metaphorical baby to rescue. One that's too far away unless I can somehow make this damn thing do more than just hover—

Stone makes a motion as if he's flicking a booger off his finger, except his finger is ten feet long and shiny and the booger is Cassius. Surprisingly, this doesn't work, though Cassius does go sliding to the end of the spike—where he stops himself by reaching out and grabbing it, like a confused and suicidal fireman. For a second I think he's actually going to start hauling himself back the way he came, hand-over-hand, but then I realize he's pulled something out of his pocket.

It appears to be a small pump-action bottle of window cleaner. Of course. That spike is looking *awfully* tarnished, not to mention covered in bits I don't want to look too closely at. Cassius gives it a good spraying.

"Giddyup!" I blurt. "Open Sesame! On Cupid! Shazam!"

The shield stubbornly refuses to budge. I abandon the verbal approach, grab an edge with either hand, and *will* it to move toward the nose cone.

It moves.

Unfortunately, it picks the quickest and most obvious route, which is right past Stone. He's kind of busy, though, screaming in agony as whatever Cassius sprayed on him is apparently a little more corrosive than your average cleaning product. His metal skin bubbles and hisses, vapor curling off it, and then Cassius drops to the ground as the chemical eats right through. He's still got a chunk of metal lodged in him, but he's free and Stone's lost some body mass.

I'm past him and to the nose cone, the shield halting when I want it to. I start to fumble with the baby's harness, then draw one of my scythes and snap the blade out. Cut her free and worry about nicks later.

Right about then is when Charlie, now out of ammo, draws his *gladius*—that's a Roman short sword he keeps tucked into a scabbard in the lining of his jacket—and does his own leaping. He manages a much better landing than either of us, planting his knees squarely on his target's shoulders and knocking him to the ground. He drives the blade two-fisted into the back of Stone's neck, no doubt hoping to separate his head from the rest of him.

Good plan, but flawed in execution. I'm chopping away at the straps with the scythe, and I've almost cut the baby free when Charlie comes flying past me. I look back to see Stone, sword still sticking out of his neck but on both feet and looking very upset.

"You will not interfere with the Divine Will of the Multiverse," Stone says. His voice is intense, full of righteous fury. "I'm retconning it all, don't you see? Going backward so we can start *all over* again, and do it *right* this time."

"I never was much for revision," I say. "More of a first-draft girl, myself."

If I can just get the baby free, the shield will protect both of us. Unfortunately, Stone knows that, too—which is why he ignores me and does something to the control panel at the side of the gantry.

The nose cone starts to close. I manage to hack through the last of the straps, spilling the baby onto the floor. She shrieks in pain and fear, though I figure as a pire she isn't actually hurt. I jam my scythe between the closing clamshell doors, keeping them open—and then the rocket itself starts to move. He's raising the gantry, trying to point the thing at the sky. I scrabble for purchase, but I can't grab the scythe because it might pop free, and the surface of the nose cone is too slick to hold on to. The rocket tilts higher and higher, and I slip back and onto the shield.

Down below, Cassius and Charlie are advancing on Brother Stone for round two. Cassius has pulled the spike out of his gut, but he's in bad shape; he's moving slow and has one hand pressed against his stomach. Charlie's out of ammo and has lost his sword.

And if we don't stop him, Stone'll launch this rocket as soon as it's fully upright. It probably won't clear the hole Stone made when he broke in, but I doubt if pointing that out will stop him; he seems to have a very nonstandard take on the whole cause-and-effect thing.

Up, I think, and the shield rises. Think I'm starting to get the hang of this. I'm going to have to circle around to the other side to pull the baby out—can't risk knocking the scythe free—but I can do this.

Cassius and Charlie are out of my line of sight. I make a long arm, reach inside the nose cone and snag the kid. We should be all right now—

That's when something slams into the bottom of the shield, *hard,* and when I discover an interesting fact: While the shield will protect whoever's riding it from harm, its magical mojo doesn't do squat for falling off the damn thing.

I do my best to shelter the baby when we hit. Only from around a dozen or so feet up, but it's a concrete floor and I land on my back. All the air goes out of me with a grunt, and pain rushes in to fill the void.

Got to get up, I think groggily. I took a pretty good whack to the skull, too. *Got to—*

"You're not going to ruin this," Stone says calmly. He grabs the baby away from me with a hand like flows like molten metal, wrapping her in a shiny silver cocoon. "You can't."

I'm on the other side of the gantry now, and so is Stone. No sign of Charlie or Cassius. Very bad. I consider drawing my gun and realize it's probably pointless; I doubt it could do enough damage to stop him.

"I don't understand," I say, very clearly and calmly. You'd be amazed how often that gets them to talk; sometimes the most important thing in a fractured world is finding someone who *does* understand. The real question is, is he desperate enough to try to explain?

"I became a monk for the stillness," he says. Ripples of color and texture are moving in slow sine waves across his face, his body; copper and granite and iron and jade, like some kind of humanoid ultimate lava lamp. "For the quiet contemplation of the universe. But when he approached me, asked me to work for him, I couldn't say no—there was too much at stake. It was too important. And terrible things happened . . ."

"I know. I've seen your shrine."

"I just wanted the voices in my head to stop. I couldn't talk to anyone, not without revealing what I was. So I thought—maybe I could just leave. Go somewhere where this hasn't happened yet."

"Another reality?"

"Yes. And I knew someone, someone who might be able to get me there . . . but he had a price. I had to do things for him. Get things for him. He told me that when he had enough power, he could help me . . . *cross over.* But that doesn't matter anymore."

Uh-oh. "Why not?"

"Because he showed me that I can never *have* stillness. I can never have peace. He showed me *his* world, showed me it with his mind, and the scales fell from my eyes. Clones of men bitten by radioactive spiders who make deals with the devil. Mutant rock stars who can teleport to Dyson spheres in other galaxies. Asgardian thunder god frogs. Transsexual shamans who travel in time, green shapeshifting child actors battling blood cults and the Wrath of God creating a giant duck that gobbles a mobster alive . . . and all of it, always changing, past and present and future, shifting and contradicting itself and never, ever staying the same. It was absurd. It was horrifying. It was beautiful."

Tears run down his face, little mirrored blobs of mercury that explode into a thousand shiny beads when they hit the floor. I wonder if that's why we found traces of quicksilver at one of the murder sites.

"It changed everything, because I saw that everything *is* change. I couldn't go somewhere else, somewhere perfect, because there is no such place. What I had to do was make changes *here*. Make the right changes, and everything will shift. That's what magic *is*."

The gantry stops, locking into place with a loud mechanical *chunk*. It's fully raised now, the nose pointing out the hole in the roof.

"I get it," I say. "You just want to fix things. But you've made a mistake."

"No. I haven't." His body shifts, extending upward into a growing pillar. It's a solid gray color now—granite, I'm guessing. He puts the baby back in the nose cone, then pulls my scythe out. The clamshell whirs the rest of the way shut.

I risk a glance around the gantry. Both Charlie and Cassius are down, a black spill of volcanic sand seeping from a wound in Charlie's chest. I have no idea what that means, how hurt he actually is. Cassius seems to just be out cold.

I draw my gun, then think better of it. Rocket fuel and bullets are not a good combination. I wish I could just T2 his shapeshifting ass with some liquid oxygen, but this isn't a movie—I'd just wind up blowing all of us sky-high.

I'm running out of options here. I can't shoot him, my backup is down, and Captain Rushmore is about to launch Gretchen's firstborn into orbit for reasons so crazy I don't know how to argue with them.

But I've got to try.

"You can't launch this thing without listening to me.

This is the beginning of the story, right? The part where you need to explain the . . . the *premise*. You need to set everything up *properly,* don't you?"

He's shrunk back down to his normal height, his skin looking more like marble now. "Of course. The premise . . . that's where you set up the *rules*. We'll have *new* rules now. Rules that make sense, rules you can live by and that never, ever change . . ."

I'm just stalling now. "Tell me. Tell me *all* the rules."

And now he looks confused, for the first time. "What? I can't do *that*."

"Why not?"

"Because," he says, "I'm not the one making them."

A loud beep from the gantry console gets my attention. I glance over—and see that a single, very long, ductile filament of gray is swaying over the console like an anorexic cobra. A filament that Brother Stone extended from his foot, along the floor, and past me without my ever noticing.

"Launch in one minute and ten seconds," a prerecorded voice announces calmly. "Countdown commencing at mark."

Sneaky bastard. And here I thought he would just go through me.

Okay, down to a very few options. Shoot the console? Try to drag Cassius clear, or Charlie? I don't have time for both and Charlie's probably too damn heavy anyway, but Cassius at least has a chance at surviving ground zero of a rocket launch. I take a step backward, thinking hard, and—

Cassius and Charlie are gone.

Not on their feet, not hiding in the shadows and planning a last-minute attack, just *gone*. I've got a good view of where they lay, and they aren't there anymore.

"You should leave," Brother Stone says. He hands me

my scythe, the gesture formal and almost ritualistic. "The beginning is about to end."

"We'll leave together."

"No. I'm staying here. Fire and thunder have haunted my dreams for fifty years; tonight, I will hear them for the last time." He smiles. "And I will be at peace."

"Thirty seconds to launch," the calm voice reminds me. No more time to argue; I sprint for the blast doors.

TWENTY

I don't know how far away I have to get or how much damage the launch will do; this facility was only designed to build and test rockets, not launch them. Plus, I've noticed that the relative invulnerability of thropes and pires sometimes leads to a shocking lack of industrial safety measures.

The doors are heavy and thick and it takes me long, precious seconds to wrench one open. Through an antechamber, another steel door, a stairwell of reinforced concrete heading down. One flight of steps, two, three. I'm at the entrance to some kind of bunker, and I'm just yanking that door open when I hear the hissing, roaring rumble of the engines igniting. I get inside, slam the door behind me, and clap my hands over my ears.

It gets louder. The temperature starts to climb. The room shakes like an oversize die in a giant's fist. I think I'm screaming but I can't hear my own voice.

It goes on and on, and I wonder if the rocket's actually managed to launch or just hit the roof and exploded—and then the noise dwindles and dies. I take my hands away from my ears cautiously. It must be a hundred degrees in here, and I'm sure it's worse outside.

But I have to get out there. I saw something in the second

before I ran, something that gave me hope for the survival of Gretchen's child.

Charlie and Cassius weren't the only ones who disappeared. The shield was gone, too.

I search the room, which is some kind of safety bunker, and find a gas mask clearly intended for thropes but still able to function on a human-shaped head. I put it on, test the doorknob to make sure it isn't red-hot, and pull the door open.

The corridor outside is filled with hot, thick white smoke. I make my way back up the stairwell, feeling like an entrée taking a tour of an oven.

The blast doors are too hot to touch. I don't even try to open them. Instead, I head the other way down the hall, looking for an exit.

I find Cassius and Charlie sprawled on the floor of the foyer, the shapes of their bodies dim in the smoke. Cassius has an ugly gash on his forehead—caused by a silver fist, no doubt—but the fact that he hasn't imploded into a pile of dust means he'll be fine. I'm more worried about Charlie, so I kneel and check him out. His chest has been punctured in several places, but placing him on his back has stopped any more from leaking. His face seems a little flatter than normal, like a partially deflated balloon. He told me once that his life essence was mixed with the sand he was filled with, and if he lost too much the spell that animates him would pop like a soap bubble. I have no way of knowing if that's already happened.

The entrance door to the building has been torn off its hinges, and the smoke swirls past me and outside, slowly clearing. I can see the night sky, and the climbing star that's the rocket. How long has it been since it's launched? A minute? Two? How long before—

The star flares into sudden brilliance, a new sun. The fireball hangs in the air for a second before shrinking and beginning its relentless, final descent.

"No," I breathe. "No, come on, come *on* . . ."

I stare at that speck of falling brightness, growing fainter and fainter, willing there to be something else, something small and dark and moving fast, so fast I probably can't make it out but I know it's there, it's *got* to be there . . . I find myself outside, the gas mask torn off and thrown aside, searching the sky wildly and shouting, "Where are you? Where *are* you, goddamn it?"

"You're looking the wrong way," a voice says mildly.

I whirl around. Catharine Great Shaka stands on her sky-shield, hovering a foot above the ground. She's got Gretchen's baby nestled in the crook of one arm—a strangely silent baby.

"Oh, no," I say. "No, no . . ."

"She's fine," Shaka says. "Just exhausted. She's asleep."

"I can't believe you pulled that off."

"What, retrieving an infant from a rocket in midair?" She gives me an exaggerated shrug. "The shield did most of the work. Had a little trouble ripping the nose cone open, but I always carry a good knife." She pats a sheath at her side.

"That's not a knife, that's a machete with a gland problem."

"Here." She hands me the infant gently. I can hear sirens in the distance, getting closer. "I should really be gone by the time they get here. Too many questions for somone in my position to answer—and I've got what I came for, anyway."

I nod, too weary to argue. It's not like I could make her stay, even if I wanted to. She crouches—making herself more aerodynamic, I guess—and the shield soars away into the night. In a second she's no more than a dark speck in the sky.

I look down at the sleeping child in my arms. "When you get older," I tell her, "you better believe your aunt Jace is never, ever gonna let you forget this . . ."

"Rrrrrrr," Charlie says.

"Are you clearing your throat?" I ask. "You sound like a motor trying to turn over. Which, I guess, you kind of are."

"What—hey. I ain't dead."

"Nah. Leaky, sure. But I did my best to, uh, remedy the situation."

He tries to sit up, and I put a warning hand on his chest. "Stay where you are, sandman. You've still got a lot of holes in you, and if you start moving around you'll undo all my hard work. The paramedics will be here in a minute."

"Stone? The kid?"

"Kid's fine. Stone's a puddle of molten slag—he decided to watch the launch from underneath the rocket's exhaust."

"I should be dead. Why ain't I dead?"

"Stop sounding so irritated." I told him about the African Queen and her last-minute save. "She'd been stalking him for a while, obviously. She hung back and waited for the right moment, then hauled you and Cassius out of there. Once she had the shield, she used it to rescue the baby."

"Good for her. But I took some serious damage, partner; and I lose enough silica, it's just like a human bleeding out. So how am I—"

"—still here and as annoying as ever? That would be thanks to me."

"How?"

I tried not to sound embarrassed. "Well . . . you lost a

lot of beachfront, Charlie. I followed the trail all the way back to the blast doors. And then I found the room."

"What room?"

"More of a closet, really."

"What kind of closet?"

"A . . . broom closet."

There's a pause.

"So you—"

"Swept you up."

"And then?"

"Found that plug you don't like to talk about."

"And . . . *refilled* me."

"More or less. Had to stuff some of your holes with paper towels—it was all I could find."

"Wait. That shouldn't have worked. I mean, yeah, good thought, I applaud your intent, it's just that I'd already lost enough mass to make me pass out inside—and you couldn't have recovered anything on the other side of the blast doors. So how am I able to—"

"Argue like the obstinate walking boulder you are?" I hear the screech of tires as emergency vehicles pull up outside. About time. "Let's just say I gave you an improvised transfusion, okay? Now shut up and save your strength."

And then the room is full of agents and paramedics and red-and-blue flashing lights. I make sure Charlie's in an ambulance and being taken care of before I let anyone look at me. Cassius is still out cold, but I refuse to be worried; like I said, in his case any injury that doesn't turn him into a pile of dust is one he'll recover from.

When the baby, my partner, and my boss are all in the hands of medical personnel, I finally let a paramedic examine me.

"Those are nasty burns," he says, studying the palms of my hands. "Forget to use your oven mitts?"

"Something like that."

He wants me to come with him, but I have things to do. I let him bandage me up, accept the offer of a handful of painkillers, and then get moving.

I've got a killer to catch.

I shouldn't go in alone. Going in alone is dangerously stupid; I should have thropes in body armor and compound bows, some heavyweight enforcement golems, and maybe a combat magician or two.

I bring Eisfanger.

"Why are we doing this, again?" he asks nervously for like the seventh time. We're parked in my car on the street, half a block away from our target.

"Because you're the only person I trust who isn't in the hospital."

"But I'm really not a field agent—"

"Look, Damon. If I'm right about this—and I am—the person behind this has connections that run deeper than some countries. I can't risk somebody in the Agency tipping them off or, worse, laying a trap. We have to act quickly, before they move on to the next phase of their plan."

"Which is?"

"I don't know."

"But—I'm really confused here. I thought you said Stone was dead."

"He is. Puddle of slag in the middle of a blast crater. But I got him to talk before he went to that great quarry in the sky, and he told me he was working for someone else."

"Who?"

"He didn't specify. I thought it had to be someone human at first, someone who got him to infiltrate the Hexagon, but what he said made me realize it was somebody else—somebody who was already a member."

"And now we're going to—what? Go in and arrest them?"

"Something like that. You ready?"

He swallows, then pats the aluminum case he holds on his knees. "Yeah. Just give me a second."

He shapeshifts into were form, snow-white fur sprouting all over his stocky body. When he's done, we leave the car.

The grounds have a high stone wall around them, and the front gate is locked. I solve this by shooting the lock.

I thought we were sneaking in, Eisfanger signs.

"Plans change," I say. "Maybe he'll think it was a back-fire."

We march straight up to the house. It's as large as I remember, and there don't seem to be any lights on at all.

Nobody home? Eisfanger suggests.

"Lucky I brought my spare key," I say, and shoot this lock, too. The door swings open and I stride on in. Eisfanger darts past me, then pads silently down the hall and out of sight. Hopefully his nose will tell him where to go.

No lights have come on, and if there's an alarm going off it's a silent one. "Vincent!" I shout. "I know you're here! Show yourself!"

Okay, so breaking into an empty house and yelling at the walls might not *seem* like a brilliant plan, but I know he's here. In fact, I'm pretty sure he's got some kind of secret lair in the basement, and that's probably where he is right now. He's collected all his toys—except for the shield, of course—and now he'll want to play with them.

A light comes on upstairs. A warm, buttery light that gets brighter as it gets closer.

He steps into view at the top of the stairs. He's wearing the Solar Centurion armor, but it's not turned up as bright as it was when Cassius wore it. He's got the Midnight

Sword in a scabbard on his belt, and the Quicksilver Kid's throwing knives on a bandolier across his chest. He's holding something in his right fist that I can't see clearly.

"Hello, Agent Valchek," Sheldon Vincent says. "I'm surprised you're here. The climax was the big fight at the rocket facility—epilogues are for books, not comics. They're a more conservative medium when it comes to length."

"Blame it on my nagging need for closure," I say. "The fight was impressive, I'll admit—lots of drama, things blowing up, plenty at stake. Heroism, sacrifice, last-minute saves, and a tragic death for the tormented villain. Bravo."

"Yes. Six of them, in fact. Can I ask what led you to me?"

"Bizarro—an insane golem who had to do everything backward. Once I understood the reference, I found all sorts of links to the character throughout the case. There's only one problem: He was created in 1958, while comics here were banned two years earlier. There's no way he could find his way into a *Seinfeld* episode—not unless the character was imported from my world, by someone both a member of the Four Color Club and a writer. You never mentioned your stint as staff writer on the *Superman* TV show in the 1960s."

"It's not a time I'm proud of. The technology of the era couldn't capture the grandeur of the genre."

"It did a good enough job to make Jerry Seinfeld a lifelong fan. And you even managed to sneak in a tribute to a literary sibling of yours—a very well-known creation of your mother's."

He smiles. "Very astute. Yes, my full name is actually Shelley da Vinci. I assume I don't have to explain the second half."

"So, the result of a union between Mary Shelley and Leonardo—or at least his genetics. Quite the legacy to live up to—I don't blame you for changing your name."

"Legacy? It's a curse." He's not smiling anymore. "My mother was the author of *Frankenstein*—the very first Industrial myth—and my father was one of the most revered scientific and artistic minds in history. Do you have any idea of the expectations that surrounded me? And I very nearly didn't exist at all—the Hexagon was always more focused on politicians and warlords than creators. I was an experiment . . . one many considered a failure."

"But not John Dark. He was one of your champions, wasn't he? And when the time came, you returned the favor. You made sure he survived the attack at Mount Saint Helens. You helped him cut a deal."

"That's what the Hexagon does. Endless maneuvering, alliances and betrayals and political brokering. Everyone owes us favors—even the Crooked Shadows. We make kings, we make queens." His voice is bitter.

"That's not what you wanted to make at all, was it?" I ask. "You wanted to make something else. You wanted to make *art*."

"It's who I am. It's *what* I am. And the comic book form is the greatest medium of them all—it's the only one that combines the visual and the textual, which means it engages both hemispheres of the brain at once. And comic book art is deeply symbolic, not merely representational; it's a language itself. Alan Moore understands that. Grant Morrison understands that. And they understand that language is the basis of all magic, even though they live in a world where access to mystic forces is limited."

Okay, I've got him geared up for a rant. And why not? He's holding enough firepower to incinerate me or change me into a frog, and all my allies are in the intensive care ward. Almost all of them, anyway . . .

"In a way, I have you to thank for all this, Agent Valchek. Or maybe I should refer to you as the Bloodhound? Yes, I know what your co-workers call you. It's no Sword of Midnight, but it'll do . . . and it was your actions, after all, that led to the release of the Ghatanothoa footage on the Web."

I glare at him. Subliminal imagery of an Elder God spliced into the equivalent of a YouTube clip had gone viral, the resulting effect being mental instability in a certain percentage of exposed thropes and pires. NSA projections put their number at around 120,000 worldwide—not so bad, except that until now the supernatural races had been immune to mental illness and had little experience in dealing with it.

"Yes, I was one of the ones who watched it," he says. "And I knew I was watching something extraordinary. The government's pathetic attempts to suppress it—including their claims that viewing it led to madness—only confirmed my suspicions."

He takes a step downward. I fight the urge to back up. "It's just like they said. What we call fiction are actually other universes, real places with real people in them. Every writer, every artist, knows that feeling when the images, the words, just flow; when you feel less like a creator and more like a conduit, when something is being expressed *through* you instead of *by* you. When that happens, you've become a channel for the energy of the multiverse."

"Yeah? Then there must be some crappy alternate worlds out there, because I've read some pretty bad books."

He laughs, low and deep. "But that's the key, Bloodhound. Craftsmanship. See, no matter how inspired the writer, he still has control. He can choose, he can change the direction of the plot. It led me to one inescapable conclusion: that a writer—a truly inspired writer—can not only channel true information, but actually affect events. Transform reality. And isn't that the definition of a god?"

He's halfway down the staircase now. The heat coming

off him is like an open oven. My hands remember what happened less than an hour ago, and pulse in pain.

"So you're a god," I say evenly. My brain is feeding me many, many inappropriate responses, some of which are downright hilarious, but now is not the time to make with the funny. "What does a god need with weapons?"

"It was necessary to the plot," he says, as though that explains everything. "I knew what I had to do when Brother Stone came to me. I'd been thinking about it for a while, studying the rituals that Wertham had done, and I finally figured it out. A spell that would give me the kind of power to change reality here as in the universes of fiction. I just had to *reverse* everything."

He steps off the staircase, now only a yard away from me. "The secrets weren't in Wertham's rituals, though I learned some valuable things from them—how to induce the transformation of flesh and bone to metal, for instance. No, the true insights were in the comics themselves, encoded there for anyone with the right eyes to see. One of Superman's most powerful foes is an imp from another dimension, a being who can manipulate reality with a thought; the only way to defeat him is to make him say his own name, backward. Most writers made him a joke, but Moore demonstrated how powerful—how *significant*—he really was. Morrison wrote a mini-series about a sorceress named Zatanna, who recites all her spells by speaking backward. He knew, too. And now, so do I."

"But Stone didn't," I say. "He wanted you to transport him to another world, but you found out he was human and blackmailed him into helping you steal the Brigade's weapons. You could locate them because you kept blood samples from each of the Bravos when you created the *Brigade* comic book—even a small amount of the Quicksilver Kid's mercury. And you started with the Sword of Midnight, because you knew Brother Stone could get close to her."

"Yes. They used to be lovers. I found out when I established a psychic link to his mind, so we could communicate without being detected; he simply dug a tunnel from the inside of his mausoleum into the forest when he wanted to come and go without being observed. I used the link to coerce him when he hesitated, and he reacted badly. Too much guilt there already."

Yeah. I could see the dynamic. A human half crazy with self-recrimination and a thrope half crazy from exposure to an extradimensional presence. Plant both halves in the fertile imaginative territory of comic books, and watch them bloom into a whole psychotic. Their link probably reinforced every irrational thought they had, bouncing obsessions between their minds like a deranged game of Ping-Pong.

"Whatever you were trying to accomplish," I tell him, "it's over. Gretchen's baby survived. Your . . . *spell* is incomplete, and Stone's dead."

"It doesn't make any difference. It's the sequence of events that matter, not the deaths. Those were incidental."

I shake my head, but don't take my eyes off him. "Incidental?"

"Yes. I told you Stone reacted badly." He stares at me, unblinking, his face lit by the glow of the helmet that surrounds it. "He committed the murders, not me. In my opinion, he was quite mad."

Even though I know he's the crazy one, for a second I doubt myself. It's not his utter assurance that shakes me—I once met a schizophrenic who could explain, in minuscule detail and with complete assurance, how chipmunks ruled the Earth—but the fact that on this world, his explanation almost makes sense. There *are* alternate realities, there *is* magic; both are inescapable parts of my life now. The very fact that an essential element of his craziness is a psychic link with a monk made of living stone illustrates the problem nicely: When the world itself is this nuts, even a raving lunatic could be right on the money.

But da Vinci isn't. Eisfanger didn't find any traces of spell-weaving at any of the murder sites—that part is all in da Vinci's mind.

"If Stone was crazy," I say, "you were the one who pushed him over the edge. He was no killer. He'd been living with his guilt for decades, had found a way to atone for it. See, human beings are used to craziness; we're all a little bit crazy half the time anyway. But you're not. You couldn't handle the sudden instability in your own head—so you pushed it into his."

Okay, he's close enough. I hope this works . . . "I'm going to pull my cell phone out, all right? There's something on it I want to show you."

I put my hand in my coat pocket very slowly, keeping eye contact, trying to radiate sincerity and harmlessness. He doesn't try to stop me, but he probably figures there's not a lot I can do to him. He may be right.

And then I have my gun out and pointed at his face.

"Don't even twitch," I say evenly. "Unlike most of the people in this reality, you know what this is. You know what it can do. It's loaded with silver-tipped bullets and packs enough of a punch to take your head clean off. I know right now your brain is trying to tell you that ridiculous, clunky-looking thing in her hand couldn't possibly hurt a god-like being such as yourself. *Don't listen to it.*"

Being this near to him is like standing too close to a bonfire. Sweat forms on my forehead and rolls into my eyes. "Listen to *me,* instead. You're an intelligent man. You have connections. You know where I'm from, you know what my area of expertise is. You really think Cassius would go to the trouble of bringing me over if I wasn't damn good at what I do?"

"You're an expert in the science of criminal profiling, specializing in psychopathic personalities," he says. "I don't dispute your credentials, Bloodhound."

"Good. Then tell me why I'd risk my life with a powerful opponent I know to be insane *with a weapon that clearly isn't a threat?*"

I watch him think it through. The reason guns never caught on here is entirely artificial, the result of a spell cast centuries ago. As it was explained to me, the spell has three levels: The first level persuades people that the idea of using explosions to power weaponry shouldn't be taken seriously, and the second persuades people that the logic of the first should never be examined too closely. The third level is another problem entirely, and one I hope I won't have to deal with immediately.

Because I'm from another reality, I'm immune to the spell's effects. And the werewitch that told me how the spell worked also told me it was possible to break it, though she hadn't explained exactly how. I thought I knew—you could make it collapse under the weight of its own internal inconsistencies, but only under a very particular set of circumstances. Circumstances that I figure I'm stuck right in the middle of.

"You can't be bluffing," he says. "There's no point. Obviously you believe you can hurt me with that thing—"

There's a very solid-looking door to my right, probably oak. I put a bowling-ball-size hole in it with one quick shot, the sound of the shot startling da Vinci into taking a step backward. I center the barrel back between his eyes. "Still think it's harmless?" I say.

He frowns. "That isn't—it doesn't—"

"It works here just fine. It works here just as well as it does on my world—*just as well as they do in the comics.*"

His eyes widen. No matter how many bulletproof guys there are flying around in spandex, they always seem to run into crooks with guns. People do get shot—innocent bystanders or hostages, usually, but bullets and their victims are still part of the mythology that's so important to da Vinci's worldview. Until now, he's been able to compartmentalize that part as fiction—but fiction and reality have already collided in his mind, the difference between the possible and the impossible blurring. The artificial barrier imposed by the spell is one of the few things separating them, and I've just hit that sucker with a battering ram.

"You must be insane," he whispers. "That thing is *ridiculous*. I don't want to think about this!"

Level two. Gotta keep hammering away. What other comic book characters use guns? "The Lone Ranger used silver bullets, didn't he? Worked just fine for him." I don't even know if the Lone Ranger had his own comic book, but I figure it's a good possibility. "Or how about Dick Tracy? *All* cops carry guns where I come from, Shelley."

A sudden inspiration strikes me. "How about *Batman,* Shelley? How did he get started? What happened to change the trajectory of his life? What event triggered his transformation from spoiled rich kid to vigilante?"

"His . . . his parents were killed. By a criminal." Da Vinci's voice sounds thick, slurred. His eyes aren't tracking properly.

"How? *How* were they killed?"

"They were shot. *Shot.*" He puts a glowing hand to his head, suddenly unsteady on his feet. "Killed by a thief's bullet, shot by a robber as he was running away and Spider-Man could have stopped him but didn't so his Uncle Ben was shot, and you wouldn't think a single piece of metal so small could change so much, but it does, it does and now the guilty must be punished, but Batman doesn't use guns, never guns, heroes don't use them but the Punisher does, lots and lots of guns and bombs and that's all he does, shoot and shoot and shoot, it's crazy, it makes no sense, but the Shadow knows, twin forty-fives and the weed of crime bears bitter fruit—"

He staggers backward, his own insanity hurling itself against the reef of the spell, an irresistible force smashing against an immovable object. I should take the opportunity to just shoot him, but I'm not an executioner.

He raises his right hand, the one clenched in a fist, and now I can see something poking out by his thumb—he's holding on to some kind of elongated crystal, one that does more than just shine with reflected light from the armor; it seems to have its own internal glow, something that shimmers and pulses with different colors before shifting to a steady crimson.

Da Vinci shakes his head once, then fixes me with a look that no longer seems uncertain. "That was impressive," he says. "You might have been able to shut down my mind completely if not for one thing. I have the Balancer."

I see now that the crystal he holds is emitting blue light from one end and red from the other. The Balancer gem, the one Stone took from Doctor Transe. Not entirely clear on what it does, but from its name I guess it's counteracting the chaos I set off in da Vinci's skull.

"Amazing," he continues. "I never even suspected the existence of that spell, but now that it's gone everything seems different."

"Situation hasn't changed," I point out, the Ruger still aimed between his eyes.

"No," he agrees. "But my priorities have."

He throws a gauntleted arm in front of his face at the same second the armor bursts into brilliance. I squeeze off three fast shots as my vision flares into white pain, and hear three distinct ricochets off metal. The Ruger would punch through any ordinary kind of armor, but whatever the Centurion suit is made of isn't ordinary.

I throw myself to the side and snap off two more shots, but it doesn't sound like I hit anything but the wall. Then my wrist goes numb and I hear a heavy thump on the floor next to me.

I can't feel my hand. Why can't I feel my hand?

My vision clears slowly. Da Vinci is standing over me, the Midnight Sword pointed at my heart. I try to aim my gun at him, but I don't have it anymore.

Or my right hand.

My arm just ends. There's no pain, no blood. I bring it closer, trying to blink away the spots in my vision, and see what looks like a perfect transparent cutaway at the stump. I can see blood vessels, muscles, an artery—but I'm not bleeding.

"Get on your feet," Da Vinci says. "Or I'll send your head where your hand went."

I glance down. The Ruger's lying on the floor, but my hand's nowhere to be seen.

I'd applaud, if I could.

He takes me to the basement. Access is through a hidden door in the study, but at least we don't have to slide down Batpoles. I'd have a hard time doing that one-handed.

I'm feeling kind of shocky, which is to say light-headed, flushed, and short of breath. My heart's pounding like I just ran a marathon. "What happened to my hand?" I say, trying to make it sound like a demand rather than a plea.

He motions me into the stairwell with the sword. "I sent it through time. It still exists—in fact, it's still connected to you—but nerve impulses are more complicated than blood flow, so you can't feel it. It'll return in around an hour."

Great. My hand is off having adventures while I'm the prisoner of Dr. Frankenshine. I wonder where the hell Eisfanger is—and then I get my answer.

He's lying sprawled and unconscious in the middle of the large room at the base of the stairs. I know he's unconscious and not dead because he's still in were form. Half a dozen red-feathered darts jut from his back like an abortive attempt to sprout wings. His aluminum case is open, though—maybe he managed to accomplish something before he was brought down.

"I see you didn't come alone after all," da Vinci says. "Unfortunately for your partner, I have an excellent security system. He's lucky he isn't a pire; options for dealing with them are considerably more lethal."

I look around, trying to focus through the shock, looking for options of my own. What I see is—

All the madness that da Vinci's managed to hide.

It's not the Batcave, it's not the Fortress of Solitude. It's a nest. The walls, the floor, the ceiling, everything's been coated in layers of overlapping comic book pages, a crazy quilt of brightly colored images that cover every surface, firmly glued in place. It's not just the walls, either—I can see the outline of a desk, several chairs, a large bookcase, and a globe. The whole room looks like it was attacked by some kind of mutant wallpaper virus, one that's been festering and growing in the dark; the layers are so thick in places that the right angles where the walls meet the floor and ceiling are now gentle curves.

The only things in the room that have escaped the paper are a few pieces of equipment, including a workstation atop the covered desk. That, and the brass cowboy bolted to the far wall.

"Right," I say. "The cavalry is already in custody. Outstanding."

The Quicksilver Kid nods at me, which is about the only part of his body he seems able to move. "Ma'am. Sorry you got dragged into this."

"I'm used to it. Happens so often I'm thinking of getting scuff plates mounted on the backs of my shoes."

"Have a seat, Bloodhound," da Vinci says.

He motions to one of the encrusted chairs, and I reluctantly perch on it. "Boy, this day is just full of firsts. Never thought I'd be sitting on Superman's face—"

He backhands me, almost casually. It knocks me right off the chair and makes my ears ring. I can taste blood in my mouth.

"Do not blaspheme in this place," da Vinci says. "I will not allow it."

I take my seat again, slowly. "Right. Exactly where are you going with all this, Shelley? You've got the Bravos' weapons—well, four out of five, anyway—but your partner's dead and you've completed the sequence you set out to. What's supposed to happen now?"

"I would have thought that was obvious. The characters have gone through their paces, the plot has unfurled. Now it's time for publication . . ."

He takes one of the silver throwing knives from his bandolier, crouches, and stabs it into the floor. It goes in all the way to the hilt without so much as a sound. He moves a few feet and does so again, talking as he works. "This is what gives the ritual *power,* you see. Unlike the first *Bravo Brigade* comic, the one that ended the industry here, this story line will be published on another Earth. *Your* Earth, Bloodhound. I will use the Sword of Midnight, boosted by the energies of the Balancer gem, to cut a hole not just in time but across dimensional boundaries. It will focus on a writer from your reality as a conduit, and my story will be read—not just by a few members of a secret society, but by thousands. And in reading it they will complete an occult circuit, conferring a great deal of occult power to *me.*"

He's rammed five of the knives into the floor in a rough circle, and now he's tying the end of a slender white rope threaded with silver around the haft and hilt of one of the knives. He runs the rope in a line to another of the knives, loops it around the haft, then across to another one. In a minute he's formed a pentagram; he finishes by running the cord around the perimeter to form a circle, then tying it off where he began. Almost immediately, the silver wound through the rope starts to shine with an unearthly light.

"Lie down in the center of the circle, please," he says. "You can do it willingly, or I can beat you into submission first."

Neither choice holds much attraction. I consider attacking him—I still have my scythes—but I could only use one, and he's got the speed, the reach, and the annoying tendency to take away my vision and my limbs. I grudgingly comply.

He adds me to the pattern, tying my ankles and my one wrist. "Looks like you've hit a snag," I say as he pins my stump down with one hand. "You're out of extremities to attach things to."

"Yes," he says, "but I have two more knives."

He drives the blade through my wrist and into the floor. It hurts a lot worse than losing the hand did, and I scream—more out of anger than pain, believe it or not. "I am *through* with having sharp things rammed through my body," I hiss.

"I don't think so," he says, his voice matter-of-fact. "I still have one more knife . . ."

He stands up. "But I was in middle of some rather delicate preparations when you arrived—the Balancer gem must be attached to the hilt of the Midnight Sword, and that requires tools from my studio. I'll be back in a minute. Don't worry, you won't bleed to death; I'm sure I missed the artery."

He turns and heads up the stairs. I hear him lock the door behind him.

"If you've got a plan," the Kid says, "now might be a good time to crank it up."

I try my bonds, and am rewarded with a bolt of unbelievable pain and absolutely no movement. "My partner, snoozing on the floor," I gasp. "Did he say or do anything before the darts got him?"

"Yeah. He tried to pry me off the wall first—that didn't go so well, but he loosened my one arm up some. Then he pulled out a rattle and a pouch of some kinda dust, started shaking them around and muttering. He was over by the computer tapping away when the darts got him—came out of a slot in the wall, over by the bookcase."

"What did he say?"

"Just one thing: Tell Jace they're unlocked."

"You're sure? Unlocked?"

"Maybe not. I wasn't really paying attention, seein' as how the situation didn't seem particularly dire."

I was beginning to think "deadpan sarcasm" was a genetic trait among lems. "Why aren't you dead, anyway?"

"Ain't it plain? He needs someone to pin this all on. Two lems working together won't be hard to sell, not when they're both dead. You're gonna wind up with one of my knives in your heart—prob'ly the same one they'll find in my hand. Don't figure I'll be in any shape to say different."

Unlocked. Did he mean the files on da Vinci's computer? If so, I don't see how that information is going to do me much good. What else could be unlocked—doors, windows? I try to think like Eisfanger, to see the world how he sees it. I'd sent him in to gather information, to find out anything that could give us an edge, and if he said something was unlocked that something has to be important.

And then, I have it.

"Kid. Tell me *everything* your knives can do, and make it fast."

"They cut or penetrate damn near anything. Not time, the way the Midnight Sword does, but spells or magic or anything that's been enchanted. Once they stab into something, they become part of it. Only one that can pull 'em free is me, so you're pretty well stuck—"

"Maybe not. Tell me *how* you get them free."

"Grab and pull, how else—"

"No, no! Tell me what goes on in your head when you're doing that. Don't you concentrate, or think in a certain way?"

"Hmm. 'Spose I do." He's quiet for a second, and I suppress the urge to scream at him to hurry up. "It's sorta like—thinking about opening my hand at the same time I'm actually closing it."

I turn my head, stare intently at my impaled wrist, and try to feel my missing hand. Try to remember what it feels like to squeeze, to feel my fingers gripping something solid. Send that down my arm, to wherever my missing five digits currently reside—and then think about the opposite, relaxing my hold, spreading my fingers wide.

Nothing happens. But when I give an experimental tug, my arm lifts off the floor easily, leaving no hole behind in the papered floor. The knife drops from my forearm as I lift it, sliding from my flesh with no sensation at all and thumping to the floor. My wound immediately begins to seep blood at an alarming rate.

"How the hell did you do that?" the Kid asks.

"All the Brigade's weapons were keyed to their respective owners. In order to use them, da Vinci had to *unlock* them—but that means anyone can use them."

Okay. I've got one bleeding, handless arm free. Way to go. I'll be out of here in no time.

I fumble at the knife with my forearm, and manage to get it closer to me than before. Now what? I can't pick it up with a nonexistent hand.

My hand does exist, though, just not at this moment. It's still connected to me, like a long-lost daughter that's moved to another state and never writes. I just have to find a way to get her to visit . . . and then, in a flash of counterintuition, I see the solution. I fumble with the knife, getting it onto my legs and then wedged between my thighs, blade up. I concentrate on the blade being as sharp as possible—and then I slide my stump past the cutting edge, repeating the motion that severed my hand in the first place.

My hand reappears. It's a little dusty, but otherwise unharmed.

"Good thinking," the Quicksilver Kid says. "You cut through the spell that sent it off in the first place—"

And then we both hear it. The door at the top of the stairs, unlocking.

I grab the knife and cut the rope holding my other wrist. The knife severs the cord like it was made of cheese, but doesn't do so much as nick my skin; it's like the blade knows what to cut and what not to.

The door opens. Golden light spills down the steps.

I lean down and free my feet with one quick slash. In another second he's going to be able to see me. I jump to my feet and dash for the wall the Kid's bolted to, hoping I can free him as quickly as I freed myself.

Footsteps on the stairs. A sharp inhalation of breath. Any second now a blast of concentrated sunlight is going to turn me into ash . . .

But what I hear instead is the solid *whump* of one body slamming into another, followed by the crash of both onto the floor at the foot of the stairs.

Da Vinci is facedown, with an angry thrope on top of

him who's doing his best to claw da Vinci's head off. The armor is protecting him from the worst of it, but he's dropped the Midnight Sword. It juts upright from the comic-paneled floor, the Balancer gem glowing where it's mounted across the hilt.

For a second I think the thrope is half mummy, some kind of were version of a wrapper, but then I realize the bandages are more than just cosmetic.

It's Dr. Pete.

I have no idea what he's doing here or how he found me, and I don't have time to worry about it. The knife shears through the bolts pinning the Kid to the wall as easily as they did my bonds, and in a few seconds I've got the lem down from the wall.

Light and heat flood the room, and suddenly the air is full of the stink of burning fur. Dr. Pete howls in pain, dives to the floor, and rolls to put out the flames. The Kid grabs his knife from my hand.

Dr. Pete has managed to put himself out, but now the floor itself has caught on fire. Da Vinci gets to his feet, looking around for his sword. I can't let him get to it.

No gun, but I still have my scythes. I pull them, snap out the blades, and put myself between him and the sword. I know exactly what he's going to do, so I've got my eyes tightly closed when he triggers the sunburst, the world going bright scarlet behind my eyelids. My scythes are basically *eskrima* batons with knives sticking out of them, and I don't need my vision to turn the area immediately in front of me into a very dangerous place to be.

Unfortunately, da Vinci's a better fighter than I expected. He drops to the ground, staying below the pattern of strikes I'm weaving, and kicks my legs out from under me. I go down hard on one shoulder and lose one of the scythes.

Which is the opportunity the Quicksilver Kid's been

waiting for. With me out of the way, he's got a clear shot. He pitches his one knife straight at da Vinci's heart.

Too bad Dr. Pete picks that moment to lunge. The knife punches into his back, missing his heart and spine but embedding itself in his shoulder blade. He ignores it and swipes at da Vinci's eyes, snarling like a chain saw.

Three on one, and all he's got is the armor. That, and the home-field advantage . . .

Another flare of light, but this one is much more contained; Da Vinci blasts Dr. Pete in the chest with a beam of focused light, one that throws him backward across the room. He slams into the Kid, who's bending down to grab another knife from the floor, and momentum carries both of them into the far wall.

I spring to my feet, but Da Vinci's faster than me. He leaps, grabs the sword, and has its point against my throat before I can counter with the scythe. Time seems to stop.

"Nobody move," da Vinci says. "Bloodhound, drop your weapon." He seems quite calm, not even angry. From the corner of my eye I can see Dr. Pete and the Kid, both crouched in the corner. The Doc looks like he's signing something to the Kid, but the angle's all wrong and I can't read it. Neither can da Vinci—I'm in the way. The flames are starting to spread and the air is getting smoky.

I drop the scythe. "If you're going to skewer me," I say, "Do it now. I'd prefer to go out on my feet."

"No," he says coldly. "I've changed my mind, Bloodhound. You've cost me the shield and caused me a great deal of trouble. I think the best solution to this problem is that you never came to this reality in the first place."

"What?"

He smiles without humor. "The Midnight Sword can cause temporal effects, but with the Balancer gem adding to its power it can do much more. I'm sure you've heard the term *retconning* in your research into comic books? It means 'retroactive continuity'; it refers to changing a character's past, unmaking their history so that a new, more interesting one can replace it. I'm going to sever the cusp that brought you here. You'll wind up back where you belong, with a head full of mixed-up memories of a place you've never been, of relationships you've never had. It'll probably drive you insane . . . but maybe not. You're better equipped than I to judge."

I wonder if he's right, or just crazy himself. I wonder if I can stop him . . . and if I even want to.

"I don't think that's going to happen, myself," a voice says. It's coming from the top of the stairs, and it's a voice I recognize.

The voice is Dr. Pete's. The thrope standing there isn't him.

His hair is longer, shaggier, and black instead of brown. There's a gray streak down the middle that I recognize. He's dressed in black jeans, a black leather jacket over a bare chest, and combat boots. He looks like Dr. Pete's twin brother.

"Hey," Tair says. "Am I interrupting something?"

"Who are you?" da Vinci demands.

"Me? I'm an innocent bystander. Okay, the innocent part is definitely open to interpretation—"

"Explain, or I'll kill her."

"Short and to the point. Okay, let's see: Somebody stole my life. I was doing just fine, business was good, and suddenly everything changed. People didn't know me. The ones that did know me had some crazy ideas about who I was and what I was about. I did some checking around, and guess what? It was *him*." Tair points at Dr. Pete, crouched in the corner and growling. "I don't know how or why, but he's not only stolen my life, he's *twisted* it. *And I want it back*."

He starts to come down the steps, very slowly and deliberately. "I thought maybe I could just scare him into leaving, but that didn't work. Then I thought I'd just kill him—but for some reason, I *can't*. Some kind of magic stops me from even trying, though some friends of mine did make a pretty good effort. And then, tonight, he comes tearing out of the hospital his bosses have him stashed in, and heads out to an industrial plant that's on fire. I follow him, and after sniffing around the fire for a while he comes here."

He's halfway down the stairs now. "Thing is, I know this place. Never been here before, but it feels real familiar. And the closer I got, the more I felt some kind of pull, like I'm supposed to be here. Anyone care to explain that?"

I realize I was wrong about Tair looking like Dr. Pete's twin. He's younger than the Doc, his body language more aggressive.

"Stop where you are or I'll open her throat," da Vinci says.

Tair stops, and his gaze flickers to me. "Yeah? Why should I care—"

And then things happen very quickly.

The Quicksilver Kid bolts to his feet. He's got his hands clasped, with one of Dr. Pete's feet braced in the middle. I've seen lems throw a lot of things, but this is the first time I've seen one toss a thrope. Dr. Pete hurtles through the air like a furry javelin, obviously trying to grab me and get me out of harm's way.

Da Vinci swings the point of the sword away from my throat.

And through Dr. Pete's chest.

TWENTY-ONE

The force of the impact drives it all the way through and out the other side. He hangs there for a second as the sword and his entire body lights up with crackling, scarlet lightning—and then, he vanishes.

The look on Tair's face isn't what I expect. Fear, triumph, even contempt were all options I would have thought possible—but what shows up is realization. Comprehension.

"Well, well, well," Tair says, a smile starting to spread on his face. "Happy birthday to me . . ."

Da Vinci hasn't just murdered Dr. Pete. He's murdered his history, just like he was planning to murder mine.

There's only one thing I can think of to do. I grab the wrist of da Vinci's sword arm and throw my body against his chest. He's a lot stronger than I am, but I have leverage; as long as I can keep his arm extended he can't get all stabby on me.

Which doesn't mean he can't flash-fry me, of course. Agony screams through both my already burned hands as he heats up, and my jacket starts to smolder where it's in contact with the armor.

The Kid has another knife in his hand, but I'm in the way again. "Throw, damn it, throw!" I yell.

Tair is abruptly in front of me. "Hey, bright boy," he says. "You forgot to wear your visor." He jabs da Vinci in the face, his hand a blur.

Da Vinci howls and drops the sword. I let go of his arm and dive to the ground, covering the sword with my body and giving the Kid a clear shot. That must have been one helluva punch.

I hear a meaty *thunk* above me—and then the clatter of armor as da Vinci's body collapses on top of mine, the armor's light and heat turning off like a switch's been thrown instead of a knife. A knife now embedded in da Vinci's forehead.

Tair shoves the body aside, but doesn't help me up. Instead, he reaches down and picks up the sword as I scramble to my feet.

"Nice toy," he says. "I think I'll keep it."

That's when I notice the hand he's holding it with is in were form. One clawed forefinger drips with gore up to the knuckle. I glance at da Vinci and see the ugly wound where his right eye used to be. No wonder he dropped his weapon; whatever magic protected his face from the armor's sunlight obviously didn't extend to enchanted knives or thrope fingernails.

"Ahem," the Quicksilver Kid says. He's got another knife in his hand, and he's staring at Tair pointedly. "This dance over, or are we gonna have another go-round?"

Tair grins at him, then at me. "I'm good. Got me a shiny new toy, a shiny new life . . . hell, maybe even a shiny new girlfriend."

"What?" I manage.

"Oh, come on," he says. "Maybe I don't know you, but I know myself. And no matter what kind of goody-goody I turned into, I doubt my taste in women changed. And no *way* would I risk my skin for a woman I wasn't already involved with."

He holds his hands wide in invitation. Blood runs down the hilt of the blade and drips to the floor. "Well, you lucked out, didn't you? Traded in the old model for the new. Fewer miles, better acceleration . . . and I handle *real* well on the curves."

I glare at him. This . . . imposter isn't Dr. Pete. He's the person Dr. Pete could have been, if he hadn't straightened his life out. He's a collection of bad choices and attitude—but under all his bravado and ruthlessness, he still has the potential to *become* the man I knew.

The man that's now dead.

"We were friends," I say. "Nothing else."

He holds my gaze for a second, and I look away first. He laughs. "Like that, huh? Okay. I like a challenge. Hell, it's what I live for."

And then he leaps for the stairs, wolfing out in midair and making it out the door in two more bounds.

"Maybe I should have put a blade in him," the Quicksilver Kid says.

"No," I say. "No, I'm—it's all right that you didn't. He doesn't deserve that."

"Wasn't talking about killing him. Could have put it in his leg. Slowed him down some." The Kid walks around the room, collecting his knives. When he's got them all, he kneels by da Vinci's body and strips it of the bandolier. I notice for the first time that he's leaking little beads of mercury from where the bolts penetrated his arms and legs.

"You, uh, need those holes looked at?"

He slides each of the knives into its sheath and buckles the bandolier on. "Nah. Got a patch kit in the car, take care of it myself. And I best be going."

"Where?"

"Hunt down that thrope. Figure the bounty should be considerable to get that sword and the fancy jewel back."

He stumps up the stairs without a backward glance.

Behind me, I hear someone whine, and whirl around—but it's only Eisfanger, finally waking up.

He slowly transforms back to human. "Whuz," he says thickly. "Whuz happened?"

I stare down at da Vinci's body. "I guess someone didn't make their deadline."

And that's it, pretty much.

I call an NSA cleanup crew, but not until I've stripped da Vinci's body of the armor and stashed it in an upstairs closet; Cassius will appreciate getting it back. Then I drive Eisfanger and myself to the hospital, where I get my wounds properly bandaged and look in on Charlie.

He's in the lem ward, which looks a lot more like a garage than a medical facility. He's on a raised platform, lying on a hard rubber pad, the only bedding a cylinder-shaped cushion under his head. He's also naked.

"Jeez, Charlie," I say, looking to the side. "You couldn't use a sheet or something?"

"For what?" he says. "As the man once said, there ain't no *there* there. Hard to be embarrassed by what you ain't got."

I know he's right, but somehow his complete lack of genitalia makes it worse. "It's not so much embarrassing as disturbing." I spot his fedora hanging on a coatrack and hand it to him without looking. "Put this somewhere strategic, okay?"

I give him a quick summary of the events at the da Vinci house.

"Sheldon Vincent, huh? And of course, you couldn't wait for me."

"You were out of play, and I didn't know for how long. Da Vinci would have killed someone else—if I hadn't come along, somebody would still have wound up in that pentagram."

"Well, I was banged up pretty bad," he admits grudgingly. "Guy that patched me said I'd lost a dangerous amount of my insides. Said the only thing that saved me was that someone had the presence of mind to insert a big chunk of animist-charged metal into my chest."

"How about that. Those paramedics sure are prepared."

"Thing is, the metal was real hot. Melted the plastic a little going in, but the sand absorbed the heat after that."

He glances down at my bandaged hands. "Looks like you got banged up a little, too."

"This? Nah. Burned myself making toast."

"Uh-huh. Careless of you."

"Guess so."

We look at each other for a moment. "I think I'm gonna get dressed now," he says.

"Yeah. Good idea—Ahh!"

"What?"

"Did you have to start with the hat?"

"It was in my hand."

"And now it's on your head. Which would be fine, except you're *still* not wearing any *pants*."

"I could take it off again."

"No, no, it's fine. Just trouser up, will you?"

I find Cassius standing beside Gretchen's bed, staring down at her sleeping. He looks up when I come in. "Jace. How are you?"

"Second-degree burns on my hands. Wrenched shoulder. Mild concussion. Knife wound to my right wrist, right beside the two punctures already there. How about you?"

"I'm fine. Wish I hadn't been unconscious for the last few hours, but I've been brought up to speed. Feeling somewhat stupid, honestly."

"About Sheldon Vincent—or should I say, Shelley da Vinci?" I shake my head, then wince as a bolt of pain goes through it. "Don't be. He kept himself at a distance from events, using Stone as his proxy. There was no way to connect the two, not in any rational manner."

"But you did."

"Yeah, well, sometimes rationality is a one-trick pony. I think I heard that in a cartoon once."

He hesitates, then says, "I understand that certain items are still missing."

"The Midnight Sword and the Balancer gem are. The Quicksilver Kid's on their trail, though—I have the feeling they won't be missing for long."

"And the armor?"

"Safe. You can pick it up later."

He nods, then looks back at Gretchen. "Her child is fine. I think the African Queen just bought herself a great deal of political support."

"Gretch's still zonked out, huh?"

"Yes. They tell me she broke two of the orderlies' arms when they tried to restrain her, too. Dr. Pete was just arriving to visit her when all the commotion broke out—he disappeared from the hospital right after that."

"Yeah. About that . . ."

I do my best to explain what's happened to Dr. Pete, though I'm a little unclear on the details myself. "He's calling himself Tair now. He was shadowing me for a while—I almost caught him in a supermarket, but he threw me off by shifting to were form and pretending he was after Dr. Pete. Thing is, he *is* Dr. Pete—a Dr. Pete that could have been, anyway."

It takes a lot to make Cassius look worried, but he looks worried now. "That's unfortunate. Peter had a troubled past—if he'd continued on that path, he would have become a very dangerous man. And now, it seems, he has."

"Yeah—in the blink of an eye." I shake my head. "We're not going to just give up on him, are we? I mean, this isn't some criminal that may or may not be worth rehabilitating—this is Dr. Pete. We know that underneath it all he's a good person."

"Of course we won't give up, Jace. But the magic that triggered his change was meant for you—it's not just a powerful spell, it's a powerful spell gone wrong. Reversing it will be difficult, maybe even impossible."

"Then we'll do it the old-fashioned way. Worked the first time, didn't it?"

He smiles. "Yes, it did. And this time, he'll have you on his side from the very beginning. I'm sure that'll make a difference."

Gretchen shifts and mutters something in her sleep. I notice that both her wrists are still in padded metal restraints. "Not taking any chances with Gretch, huh?"

"She'll wake up with her baby beside her. That'll calm her down in a hurry—but I don't want her disabling another orderly before her head clears."

"Yeah, she's got enough to worry about. Single motherhood and getting used to aging again."

"I'm hoping I can alleviate some of that."

I frown, not sure what he means. "Excuse me?"

"It's possible—if you act quickly—to replace a pire father with a surrogate, another donor for the child to draw life force from. I'm going to offer to do so for Gretchen."

For a second, I can't even process it. David Cassius, a vampire who's spent unknown centuries in the body of an eighteen-year-old, is giving up some of his youth. "I—what? Are you serious?"

He gives me a carefully neutral look. "I'm very serious, Jace."

"Don't get me wrong, I think that's wonderful, but—you and Gretch? Really?"

"It's not like that," he says. "She's one of my most valuable operatives. I have the years to spare—even nine of them will leave me relatively untouched. I think it's time I added a little more . . . *stature* to my image, anyway."

"Stature, sure. Maybe you should grow a mustache, too—I understand that really impresses the girls. And helps you get in bars."

"I'll take that under advisement."

"Plus, you can finally move out of your parents' basement and get that cool bachelor pad."

"Are you done?"

"Me? Never. I'm a work in progress." I pause. "And I guess you are, too. Or will be."

"It's not that big a deal, Jace."

"'Course not, Caligula. It's not a big deal at all. And definitely not the sweetest thing I've ever seen one friend do for another."

I lean over and give him an impulsive kiss on the cheek. He looks a little surprised, starts to say something, then stops.

"Well," I say. "I better get going. I've got—you know. Things. Call me when she wakes up, okay?"

I leave him there beside the bed, still looking like he has something to say.

I do some hard thinking on my way home.

Now that the case is over, it's back to hunting Aristotle Stoker. I'm beginning to think that the best way to do that is to have *him* start hunting *me* . . . and in fact, I may have already set that in motion.

My last lead on Stoker had him researching Ahasuerus, the sorceror who created both the golem race and the anti-firearm spell—and the one that brought me across the dimensional divide. If Stoker is looking for Ahasuerus, then the best way to catch him is to bring Ahasuerus to me; and since Ahasuerus is the only one that can send me back, I need to locate him anyway.

Which might just happen on its own. The third level of the no-guns spell is an alarm system. If the spell is ever broken—even in only one person's mind—the alarm is supposed to go off, alerting the spell's caster. Presumably so he can show up in person and eliminate the problem.

I don't know if it'll still work now that da Vinci is dead. Guess I'll have to wait and see—but if and when he does show up, he's in for a surprise.

I pick up the comic book from the seat beside me. It's the one Dr. Pete lent me, the one of the Bravo Brigade that the government printed. The stated reason for its existence was to counter the power of the Kamic cult—but it was printed *after* the attack on Wertham, when the members were already dead and their power drained into the bulk of a volcano.

The government completed the ritual anyway, though. Blood from the Bravos went into the ink, the comic went into the hands of thousands of kids, and then the government used a flimsy excuse to recall and destroy every issue they could get their hands on—except for a select few, no doubt, locked away in a Hexagon or NSA vault for future use.

But they didn't get them all. Which means, if I understand my Animism 101 correctly, that the remaining ones still have all the power of the Bravo Brigade's spell locked up in them. I don't know how to access it—but human beings have a natural affinity for magic that pires and thropes have to work at.

If I concentrate, I can feel the slightest hum of *something* coming from the comic in my hand. Looks like I have some studying to do . . .

Because when Ahasuerus shows up, I'm going to be ready.

"Oh boy," I say. "Home sweet—"

"Jace!" Galahad says, and tackles me like a linebacker.

I hit the floor with a thud, and shove him off me as he attempts to lick my face. "What the hell?" I manage, getting back to my feet.

Xandra looks up from where she's curled up on the couch, reading a magazine. "Hey, Jace. Gally's glad to see you."

"Jace! Jace!"

"So I see. Down, Galahad." He promptly kneels on the floor, which is endearing but a little creepy. At least he's wearing pants. "Xandra, what's he doing here? I thought your family said they'd take care of him until—"

"Uncle Pete's gone missing again. Guess you're back to square one."

And then it hits me. No more Dr. Pete. He won't be coming by to pick up Galahad like he promised, he won't be volunteering at the anthrocanine clinic. Galahad won't have the run of that place anymore—it might even have to shut down.

"Ah, well," I say, and sink onto the couch wearily. "I was kinda getting used to having him around, anyway."

"I thought you'd worked things out with Uncle Pete," Xandra says. "I mean, I know he took off from the hospital— but he's all right, isn't he?" She looks at me quizzically.

Damn. I'm really not ready to have this conversation. I jam my hands in the pockets of my coat, and find something cold and metallic in the right-hand one, something plastic and rectangular in the left. My brain's too exhausted to analyze this, so I just pull both objects out.

In my left is the Blood Cross. Sharp, silver, deadly. It makes my forearm ache just to look at it.

In the right is a cassette tape, the one Dr. Pete gave me. The one he said would cheer me up, the one I was too angry to look at. I realize what it is, and start to laugh.

"Are you all right?" Xandra says as I lurch from the couch and put the cassette in my scavenged tape deck. Please, God, let it be functional.

"I'm fine, sweetie. I've got something to tell you, but we should listen to this, first."

"But you're crying."

I hit PLAY. And then I'm laughing again, laughing and sniffing and rubbing tears out of my eyes, as the sublime, ridiculous tune "How Much Is That Doggy in the Window" warbles out of the speakers.

Good-bye, Dr. Pete. I really hope I see you again.

Read on for an excerpt from DD Barant's next book

KILLING ROCKS

Coming soon from St. Martin's Paperbacks

I have this recurring dream where I've been ordered by a federal judge to join a support group.

"Hi," I say. I'm sitting on a folding chair, part of a circle of people. "My name is Jace, and I am a human being."

"Hi, Jace," everyone choruses.

"I've been a human being for—well, thirty-some odd years. Actually, where I come from, pretty much *every-one's* a human being."

A large woman in a floral-print house dress puts up her hand. "Don't use the people around you to justify your actions," she says primly.

"But it's true," I insist. "No vampires, no lycanthropes, no golems. And then I got shanghaied into this universe by a shaman named Ahaseurus—believe me, when I find that guy, we are going to have *words*—and now I'm trapped here until I catch a Free Human Resistance terrorist named Aristotle Stoker—"

A weasely guy with a ridiculous mustache and a BELA LUGOSI FOR PRESIDENT t-shirt puts up his hand. "So none of this is your fault?"

"No! I'm telling you, I was kidnapped out of my own bedroom—"

"Why you?" he asks in a nasal voice. "Are you trying to say you're different from everyone else?"

"I *am* different. I'm a criminal profiler for the FBI, specializing in hunting down homicidal psychos—a job that doesn't seem to exist here. Pires and thropes and lems don't go crazy—well, they never used to, anyway—so they need me to hunt down Stoker, who's definitely out of his gourd—"

The woman in the flowery dress shakes her head. "I don't know what that means."

"Mentally unstable. Deranged. Squirrely. Nuts. Wacko. Out to lunch—"

Nasally Mustache frowns. "You're no different from anyone else, Jace. You have to accept that before we can help you."

"—insane in the brain. Off his meds. Unable to locate his marbles. Needs to be fitted for a long-sleeved love-me jacket so he can hug himself all day long, bats in the control room, long-term resident of a rubber room, lights are on but so is the vacancy sign—"

The woman sighs. "Sounds to me like you're in denial, Jace." The rest of the group mutter and nod their heads. "Normally we insist that members finish each step in the program before they go on to the next, but in your case I think we'll make an exception. You need to go right to Step Thirteen."

She gets to her feet. So does Nasally, and everybody else.

"Being human doesn't have to be a life sentence," someone says. Coarse grey hair sprouts on the woman's face as it lengthens into a muzzle filled with long, sharp teeth. Nasally's teeth are getting longer too, his eyes turning blood-red.

"Fur or fangs?" he says as they all reach for me.

That's usually when I wake up.

At least they didn't threaten to turn me into a golem.

Much as I care for my partner and official NSA enforcer, Charlie Aleph, I really wouldn't want to go through life as a three-hundred-pound, plastic-skinned mannequin filled with black sand. Not that he's ever been human himself— Charlie's body is animated by the life force of a long-dead T-Rex, distilled through careful animistic magic by this world's shamans. It's something they do here a lot—though they usually use cattle or some other large animal to charge the lems' batteries—because golems make up something like nineteen percent of the planet's population. Of the rest, forty-three percent are lycanthropes, thirty-seven vampires. One percent is all that's left of the human race.

Welcome to my life.

I've discovered that a few universal truths hold firm no matter what alternate world you're in; for instance, Mondays always suck. On a planet loaded with hemovores they tend to suck even more, in both volume and intensity.

"Morning," Charlie says in a deep-voiced rumble as I get on the elevator. He's his usual natty self, wearing a double-breasted dark green suit and matching fedora with a tan snakeskin hatband. His tie is black silk with an emerald stickpin, which complements both the black chrome shininess of his plastic skin and his highly polished shoes.

"It is, isn't it?" I mutter. "A.M. As in Awful and Malignant."

"Rough weekend?"

"No. Angels massaged my feet while I bathed in sunbeams and chocolate."

"Wouldn't that be messy?"

"It sounded better in my head." I take a long slug of coffee from the travel mug in my hand. "Will to live . . . returning," I say. "Damn. Thought I had it beat this time."

"The day's still young."

"Thanks for reminding me."

"Something's up." He glances at me and frowns. "Not

you, obviously. But Cassius wouldn't call us in this early unless it was important."

I give him a withering glare, which has about as much effect as a laser on a mirror. David Cassius is our boss, the head of the National Security Agency, which for some reason is based out of Seattle here. He's a very old, very powerful pire, and he looks like an eighteen-year-old Californian surfer boy—or at least he did, until recently.

The elevator doors slide open and we step out into the NSA offices. It looks pretty much like the offices of any intelligence-gathering agency in my own world—lots of people in lots of cubicles, the murmur of voices and machines, people in suits and ties striding along clutching laptops or file folders or paper cups of hot blood.

Yeah.

See, that's the thing about this place. It does a real good job of seeming normal, at least on the surface—but then some little detail comes along and whacks you between the eyes. Cars look like cars until you notice how many of them have windows tinted so dark you can't see inside, even through the windshield. At Easter, the bunnies aren't made of chocolate—though there's still a hunt and kids still stuff their faces. And during the full moon, every thrope beneath it participates in a massive, three-day party that makes Rio during Carnival look like a Mormon picnic. Okay, that last one isn't all that small, but at least I only have to deal with it once a month.

You can make up your own joke. I mentioned it's Monday, right?

We march through the room to Cassius's office, which has a large, smoked-glass window beside the door. The other side is sometimes blocked by retractable wood paneling, depending on whether he feels like watching his people work. Mostly, just the fact that he might be looking makes them work harder.

Cassius's office looks more like a study—dim lighting, lots of books. He's sitting behind the desk, and of the four chairs in front of it, two are occupied: one by Damon Eisfanger, a forensics shaman, and one by Gretchen Petra, one of our top intel experts.

Cassius is dressed in his usual dark-blue suit, his short blonde hair neatly combed, his hands clasped together on the desk like a high-school student at his first interview.

"Hey, Damon," I say as Charlie and I sit down. "How's the baby, Gretch?"

"Growing at a prodigious rate," Gretch says. Gretch is British, sharper than a room full of razors and just as dangerous. She appears to be in her late thirties, wears her blond hair pulled back into a tight bun, and dresses like a librarian. She's a pire who recently had her first child, Anna—there's a spell here that allows that. As long as the parents are both willing, they age six months for every year the child does. The kid becomes a full-fledged immortal when the spell is cancelled, restopping the clock for the parents, too. That means Gretch is actually older than when we first met, though she doesn't look it—and so is Cassius.

Cassius isn't Anna's father—her father was murdered by a psychopath I helped catch. But he did agree to take on the victim's time-debt, which otherwise would have fallen completely on Gretchen. My surfer-boy boss is growing up, after spending Lord-knows-how-many years with his internal stopwatch stuck at late puberty.

Damon Eisfanger just nods at me. He looks a little nervous, and I wonder why. Damon's a thrope, his bloodline descended from a pack of arctic wolves that gives him his ice-blue eyes and snow-white crewcut. The wide, muscular build he gets from the other side of his family—sometime in the past a wolf-bitten pit-bull chomped one of his ancestors, passing along the lycanthropy curse and adding a few additional canine genes at the same time. Damon's a geek who looks like he lives in a gym, but he's also a friend who's slipped me information that could get him in trouble.

"Jace, Charlie," Cassius says. "Good morning to both of you. Sorry to get you out of bed so early—"

"Oh my God," I say. "You have a zit."

"Excuse me?"

"A zit. On your face. I realize you may not recognize it because the last time you needed skin care products they hadn't been invented yet, but that little yellow thing at the edge of your hairline wasn't there yesterday."

"I wouldn't know, Jace. I don't own a mirror."

"Point taken. Are you a squeezer or a grower? Because I really don't want to have to sit here and watch that thing expand every day—"

"Jace—"

"Hey, is your voice changing?"

Cassius sighs. "Are you done?"

"I've got more material, but not all of it's ready. Let me do a polish and get back to you."

Cassius taps his keyboard and a panel behind his head retracts, revealing a large flatscreen. The face on it drives a stake through the heart of the wisecrack I was about to make.

Aristotle Stoker.

"Do this right," Cassius says, "and you might not get the chance to perform any of it."

It's a shot of him walking down a street dressed in a trenchcoat, sunglasses hiding his eyes. He's a big man, six and a half feet easy, with the build of a linebacker. Good-looking in that craggy, implacable way that speaks to the cave-woman genes—one look tells you this is a guy who'll bring you a sabre-tooth rug and a stack of mastodon steaks on the first date.

Time-stamp on the photo is three days ago. "Where was this taken?" I ask.

"Brussels," says Cassius. "He was spotted coming out of a meeting with a representative of this man." The picture changes to a shot of a man sitting at a sidewalk café, cup raised to his lips. His upturned collar and hat shade most of his face, but what I can see has an odd, shiny cast to it. "Is that a lem?" I ask.

"No," says Gretchen. "He's human. He goes by the name of Silver Blue, and he's an arms dealer. The color of his skin is a self-imposed condition known as argyntia, caused by consuming large amounts of colloidal silver. It makes him immune to lycanthropy, obviously—in fact, no thrope can even touch him without suffering severe burns. Silver, of course, isn't quite as deadly to hemovores—so he also consumes an entire bulb of garlic every day."

"Shiny *and* smelly."

"And dangerous," says Cassius. "Silver Blue supplies black market weapons to anyone who can pay for them. That includes the Free Human Resistance, which is no doubt why Stoker was in touch. It appears that some sort of major deal is under way, and more than just the FHR are involved. Also present at the meeting was this individual."

The picture changes again, now showing me a golem dressed in a pair of cargo pants, steel-toed work boots and nothing else. At first I think the picture's in black and white, but it's not; the golem's gray, not a variation I've seen before. Most lems are a sandy sort of yellow, though enforcers like Charlie are black.

"Tom Omicron," says Charlie. "Founder of the Mantle."

"The Mantle?"

"They're a radical golem rights group," says Gretchen. "Based out of Nevada. Much of the golem production in the country is centered there, due to the soil. The Mantle advocates civil disobedience, workplace sabotage, and criminal negligence as tools for social change. Essentially, they believe in isolationism; golems shouldn't even associate with the other races, let alone work for them. They've tried—unsuccessfully, thus far—to organize several general strikes of all lem workers. Considering how many golems are employed in essential support services, the consequences could have been disastrous."

Sure. Most lems were used as manual labor, but that included everything from forklift operators to construction crews—not to mention soldiers. If they all decided to put down their pallets, shovels, and crossbows at the same time, it would bring the world to a halt.

"There were four people at the meeting," says Cassius. "Silver Blue himself was not present, but he sent his top lieutenant. I'm afraid it's someone we're all familiar with."

The next picture is of Dr. Pete.

Except it's not Dr. Pete, not anymore. It's Tair. He still has Dr. Pete's boyish good looks, but there's a streak of grey dyed into his hair now, and his eyes have a glint of cruelty in them that Dr. Pete's never did.

Dr. Pete was the man who looked after me when I first came here. He treated my RDT—Reality Dislocation Trauma—and saved my life when my heart stopped. He was a kind, gentle man with a large family that cared about him.

And now he's gone. Not dead—erased. In the kind of weird magic whammy that would be impossible on the world of my birth, Dr. Pete had his history rewritten, changing a vital decision in his past from a good choice into a bad one. It sent him down a very different, very dark path . . . and it's not that surprising to see where he's wound up.

"I'm sorry, Jace," says Cassius. "We all cared about him. But this is not the man we knew. He's not just smart, he's ruthless and ambitious. He's become Blue's right-hand man in a very short period of time for a reason."

"The last time we saw Tair," I say, "he'd just stolen two very powerful artifacts."

"The Midnight Sword and the Balancer gem," says Cassius. "The first can cut through time itself, the second is able to manipulate and meld large amounts of magical energy. Sheldon Vincent not only managed to mystically unlock both items—making them usable by anyone—he bonded them together. We believe Tair offered this weapon to Silver Blue in return for employment."

"But that's not all he's done to prove himself," says Gretchen. Her voice is firm. If circumstances had unfolded differently, Dr. Pete would have been the one to deliver her baby. "He's demonstrated both ruthlessness and loyalty. He's killed his own kind, Jace—more than once."

"I guess he'd have to," I say. "Blue doesn't sound like he would trust a thrope or a pire to work for him unless they did." I try to keep my voice as neutral as Gretch's; I am a professional. Two major shocks in as many minutes don't faze me at all, including the fact that someone I once considered a trusted friend is now a murderer.

Then Cassius hits me with shock number three.

I recognize the new face on the flatscreen, too. It's the bony, hawk-nosed profile of the shaman that brought me to this world, a man I've only met in a half-waking dream. I'm not supposed to know who he is, but I've done a little digging on my own.

His name is Ahaseurus. He's a very old, very powerful sorcerer—in fact, he's the one who designed the spell that turned unliving dirt into walking, talking golems, centuries ago.

And he's the only one that can send me home.

Oh, sure, another shaman *could* do it—if I fulfill the

terms of my contract and catch Stoker, that is—but cross-dimensional magic is tricky. Only Ahaseurus can put me back where he took me from, a few minutes or hours from when I disappeared out of my own bed. This whole, alternate-universe experience would become nothing more than a series of fading memories, made real only by the scars I've accumulated since I got here. If anyone else tries, I'll lose decades, both personally and objectively—I'll arrive back home an old woman, in a world that's moved on without me.

"Well, well, well," I say. "You found that shaman you misplaced, huh? Where was he, behind the couch?"

"His name is Asher," says Cassius. "I see you remember him, Jace. He's an Agency asset that's gone rogue—we believe Silver Blue is brokering some sort of deal between him, the Mantle, and Stoker—though exactly what is on the block has not been determined. What we do know is that he doesn't seem to be representing any other organization; whatever his agenda is, it's personal."

Gretchen nods. "That suggests Asher has something to sell, and both Stoker and the Mantle want it." Eisfanger hasn't said anything the entire time, and all he does now is give me a quick, nervous glance. Cassius and Charlie just stare right at me.

"Right," I say. "Three of the four principals have connections to me, and the guy with something for sale is the same one that dragged my sorry ass across the cosmic divide. Gee, what do you think he's offering up for grabs?"

"It's not that simple," says Gretchen. "True, Asher does possess a certain mystic knowledge of you that no one else does—but we're really not sure how that would be valuable to anyone but you."

"Depends on what he can do with it," I say. "Can he use it to eavesdrop on me? Control me? Make my head explode?"

"Uh, no," says Eisfanger. "He can use it to locate you—but I'm going to set you up with a masking spell that'll take care of that."

"And then what?" I ask. "You lock me away somewhere for safekeeping?"

"No," says Cassius. "I'm going to give you exactly what you want, Jace—the chance to go after both Stoker and Asher at the same time. You're going to spearhead the task force we're putting together to take them down."

I blink. I smile. I *grin*.

"Where and when?" I ask.

"The meet is sometime in the next few days," says Cassius. "I've assembled a strike team—you leave within the hour. You'll rendezvous with them on the ground, coordinate a tactical strategy and be in place when your targets congregate. After that—assuming you manage to take Asher alive and either kill or capture Stoker—you'll be going home."

Home. The word sounds strange in my ears. An obvious joke about Auntie Em burbles into my forebrain, but never makes it out into the air. There's this sudden stinging sensation in my eyes.

"Good God Almighty," Charlie says. "You actually made her shut up."

"Screw you, sandman," I say. I take a deep breath through my nose and pretend I don't hear a sniffle in it. "You know you're taking point, right? If I'm outta here, you're expendable anyway. Right?"

"Wouldn't have it any other way," he says. He puts just enough softness in his voice to make me want to punch him.

I can't believe it.

I might actually be going *home*.

Death definitely blows.
And dying sure does bite…

Don't miss the first novel in
THE BLOODHOUND FILES
from DD Barant

DYING BITES

ISBN: 978‑0‑312‑94258‑8

Available from St. Martin's Paperbacks